THE
WILD
BARON

Catherine Coulter

"Open your mouth just a little bit and bite the end of my finger. Not hard, just a little nip."

Her eyes flew open. "Why?"

"No, that's too wide. Just enough so you can get the end of my finger with your teeth. Why, you ask? Well, I doubt you'll find it disgusting, and I would enjoy it." His fingertip was soothing her bottom lip, light, easy, when she closed her eyes again, opened her mouth just a crack and bit him.

It wasn't a nip. On the other hand, he didn't bleed. He laughed. "That was a start. Now, just a bit easier. Don't try to draw blood, all right?"

He laid his finger on her mouth, waiting. Finally, she parted her lips, not far enough, but as he'd told her, it was a start.

MORE PRAISE FOR
CATHERINE COULTER'S
LEGACY Trilogy:

"Lively characters . . . an exuberant adventure."

—*Booklist*

"Old secrets, a pirate's legacy, and a cast of wonderful characters are part of this funny, lively, and occasionally mysterious story." —*Library Journal*

"Full measures of Coulter's trademark blend of wit and Regency romance make for a sparkling final installment of her Legacy trilogy . . . Coulter's fans should be well pleased by this entertaining tale." —*Publishers Weekly*

"Coulter's characters quickly come alive and draw the reader into the story. You root for the good guys and hiss for the bad guys. When you have to put the book down for a while, you can hardly wait to get back and see what's going on." —*The Sunday Oklahoman*

"There is murder, mystery and sex in this engaging story . . . It's hilarious at times and in the usual good writing and intricate plotting style of Ms. Coulter."

—*The Chattanooga Times*

**Turn to the back of this book
for an exciting preview of**

THE MAZE

**Coming soon in hardcover from
G. P. Putnam's Sons**

THE
WILD
BARON

Catherine Coulter

JOVE BOOKS, NEW YORK

THE WILD BARON

A Jove Book / published by arrangement with
the author

PRINTING HISTORY
Jove edition / April 1997

The Putnam Berkley World Wide Web site address is
http://www.berkley.com/berkley

ISBN: 0-515-12044-8

A JOVE BOOK®
Jove Books are published by The Berkley Publishing Group,
200 Madison Avenue, New York, New York 10016.
JOVE and the "J" design are trademarks
belonging to Jove Publications, Inc.

PRINTED IN THE UNITED STATES OF AMERICA

10 9 8 7 6 5 4 3 2 1

To Judy Cochran Ward, the finest chef in Marin.
She makes your taste buds dance.
She's also an excellent friend.

1

ROHAN CARRINGTON, FIFTH BARON MOUNTVALE, BELLOWED
at his brother's portrait, "If you did this, George, and if you
weren't already dead, I'd thrash you within an inch of your
bloody life. You little bounder. Were you even capable of
such a thing?"

Even as he yelled, Rohan felt a knot swell in his throat.
George had been dead nearly a year. No, George couldn't
have done this. George was studious, a scholar with no interest in matters of the flesh. Rohan remembered once, a long
time ago, their father had taken him and George to Madame
Trillah's on Cliver Street. At the sight of a very voluptuous
redhead with magnificent breasts, George had blanched and
then run half the way back to Mountvale Townhouse.

After that, their father had left George alone. George had
stuck to his maps and his studies. At least so Rohan had
always believed.

"No," Rohan said, his voice low and deep now, his eyes
still on his brother's portrait, painted when George was eighteen. "I don't believe this damned letter. It was another young
blood using your name, wasn't it? Did you really manage

to bring yourself to the sticking point and ravish a young lady? Hell, did you even know what 'ravish' meant?

"What does this man who calls himself her father want from me? Stupid question. Money, of course. Damn you, George—or rather damn the man who did this in your name."

George didn't answer.

The last Carrington to ruin a young lady and find himself shackled as a result had been Rohan's great-grandfather, the fabulous Luther Morran Carrington. Old Luther would shake his head, according to Rohan's grandfather, and mutter that he'd only tossed up Cora's skirts one miserable time and he'd nailed her but good. He'd continued to nail Cora fourteen more times, eight of his children surviving into adulthood.

Rohan pulled the bell cord behind the immaculate mahogany desk. His secretary, Pulver, must have been standing just outside the door, his face pressed against the wood, for he was in the library in but a moment, not a bit out of breath. He looked pale, gaunt, and put-upon, all three of which he deserved, because, as his friend David Plummy had told him, "It serves you right, slaving like you do for the Wild Baron. Just look at all those uncivilized hours he keeps, and he works you harder than a dog in all the hours in-between. What's more, he beds more women than you and I will ever even speak to in our lives and everybody loves him for it, just like they love his mother and his father. He's a philanderer. It isn't fair, damn him. As for you, Pulver, you deserve to look like you're on your last legs."

Pulver would shake his head mournfully, but the truth of it was that Pulver enjoyed himself immensely. Working for Baron Mountvale gave him a certain cachet. He'd even been set upon by several ladies trying to bribe him to get them into the baron's bedchamber.

Pulver came to a halt in front of the baron, who looked bilious and whose fair hair was standing on end. He was curious to know what news had sent his master over the edge. It wasn't every day that the baron talked to himself.

"Pulver, get my solicitor Simington over here. No, wait." The baron broke off, staring at the portrait of his mother that hung beside George's above the mantel. It had been painted when she was twenty-five—nearly his age now. She'd been glorious when she was young, and she was still incredibly beautiful at forty-five. In her younger years she had been wilder than a storm-tossed night, and he'd been told from his earliest memories that he was just like her, and like his proud papa, of course. They'd told him that he'd been blessed with their wild blood and tempestuous natures.

"No," he said, bringing himself back to the problem at hand, "I will see to this myself. It's strange and I don't believe a word of it. Besides, if there's no bastard, how can one prove ruination? And there's no mention at all of a bastard. Surely there would be mention in the bloody letter if there was a bastard, don't you think?

"No, I must do it myself. I don't want to, but I must, dammit. I will be gone for three days, no more."

"But, my lord," Pulver said, near desperation in his voice, "you must need me to do something. You are agitated. There is even a wrinkle in your sleeve. Your cravat is crooked. Your fair locks need a brushing. Your valet would not approve. Perhaps you are not thinking too clearly."

Rohan waved the letter in Pulver's face. "I am thinking clearly enough to know that I will probably put a bullet through this bleater's brain. The man's a damned liar—that, or someone else is."

"Ah," Pulver said. A woman has managed to get hold of him. Was she a former mistress he didn't want to see anymore? She wanted money?

"I am a very good negotiator," Pulver said with a modesty he did not possess, not budging from in front of the baron. "I can deal with almost any bleater in London. Give me a bleater from outside London and I'll mash him."

Rohan became aware that his secretary was bearing down on him. "Negotiator?" he repeated, distracted. "Oh, you must be thinking about Melinda Corruthers. She was a tough little bit of leather, wasn't she? That was well done of you, Pulver. You convinced her that she was swimming up the wrong creek since I had truly never heard of her before. Well, this isn't the same. I will handle it myself, I owe it to my brother. Turn down all invitations for the next week.'' He paused, frowning, looking into his secretary's gaunt face. ''Eat something, man. You look skinnier than you did just yesterday. People already believe I pay you so little that you can't even afford a turnip for your dinner. Even my mother thinks I torture you.''

Pulver was left standing where he was, watching the baron leave the library, that piece of foolscap wadded in his hand. It had to do with a woman. A woman and his brother? Surely that was beyond strange. Which brother? Neither of the baron's brothers was the least like him. It was a start. Pulver mentally arranged the few facts already in his possession. Not much, but he was patient. He could begin to imagine the look of envy on David Plummy's face when he heard about this new exploit.

Rohan strode into his bedchamber and paced, muttering about a straight-as-a-stick younger brother who must have had wicked friends who had used his name. His valet, Tinker, who didn't hear the baron's muttering, even though he tried, packed a valise for him. Tinker wondered why his lordship wasn't in a better humor. Surely this trip must involve a female. Nearly all the baron's trips did. Everyone knew that. The baron was famous for his trips to his little hideaways. But more than lust and passion seemed involved here. What could it be? Tinker was patient. He would find out soon enough. He wondered if Pulver knew more than he did.

Rohan didn't think of Lily until he was tooling down the Reading road at a fine clip, some fifteen miles out of London. He sighed. He'd forgotten to send a message to her to tell her he wouldn't see her this evening. Ah, there was so much to be done. Well, he wouldn't be gone more than three days.

Who the hell was this Joseph Hawlworth of Mulberry House, Moreton-in-Marsh, a town that wasn't far at all from Oxford, where George had lived and pursued his solitary education?

Susannah raised her face to the sun. It felt wonderful. It had rained continuously for two days, making everyone testy, but today the sun was shining as if God himself had sent it blazing down just for her. She gently patted the rich, black dirt around the base of the rosebush. She moved on to a patch of candytuft, her pride, sent to her by her cousin who had spoken to one of the gardeners in Chelsea Gardens and learned that the flowers had come from Persia to England just a few years before. John had managed to spirit a cutting out of Chelsea Gardens to her the previous fall. Now as she lovingly traced her fingertips over the dark evergreen leaves to the shower of white flowers atop the stem, she remembered his note, telling her that the name "candy" had come from Candia, the ancient name of Crete. She wondered if she could ever work that bit into a conversation with her father. Probably not. She wondered if she would ever be able to work that bit into any conversation, with anyone in the environs. Probably not.

She jerked out a particularly nasty weed, made certain that the soil was well drained and moist, and prayed the sun would continue shining, for the candytuft thrived with sun.

She turned on her heel at the sound of a curricle drawing up in front of the cottage. Her father was supposedly in Scotland, so he'd told her, but she knew he was very likely gambling away his shirt with his cronies down in Blaystock. She sighed and rose. A tradesman? No, it couldn't be. She had made very certain that all the tradesmen had been paid before she allowed her father to leave Mulberry House, complaining bitterly under his breath about what a shrew she had become.

Who would come in a curricle? She rounded the side of the house to see a magnificent gray snorting and prancing to a stop. The man driving the curricle was speaking to the horse, a spirited conversation that drew an occasional snort from the massive animal, who stood at least seventeen hands high. When the horse quieted, the man looked about, probably for a stable lad.

Susannah called out, "Just a moment and I'll fetch Jamie. He'll take care of your horse."

"Thank you," the man called back.

When she returned with Jamie, who had been napping in a mound of fresh hay at the back of the small barn behind the house, the man was patting the horse's nose, still speaking to him.

"Oh, aye," Jamie said, sprinting forward now. "Yicks, jest ley yer peepers on that purty boy. I'll feed him good, Guv, don't ye worry. Wot's the name of this beauty?"

"Gulliver."

"Odd name fer sech a manly beast and that's what ye be—manly—despite they cut off yer conkers. Gulliver, aye, the name niver come to me ears afore, but who cares? I'll take 'im now, Guv. All gray ye be, and that lovely white star in the middle of yer forehead. Come with me, ye purty boy."

Rohan had never heard such an odd rendering of the English language. It was both illiterate and intriguing and very nearly sung in a deep baritone. He watched the stable lad lead Gulliver and his curricle toward the back of the house. Gulliver was prancing beside him, shaking his mighty head at the lad's words, just as he did with Rohan, only it seemed to Rohan that his horse was showing more enthusiasm with the stable lad, a damned stranger, than he normally did with his true master, the one who paid for his oats.

And Susannah watched him watch his horse. When Jamie and Gulliver were gone around the side of the house, she was left standing in the drive looking at the man in a very elegant greatcoat with at least six capes. He took off his hat and ran his fingers through his pale blondish-brown hair. He was young, not above twenty-five or twenty-six, and very handsome. Too handsome, and probably very well aware of it. She frowned. He looked familiar, but she couldn't place him, not at first.

It took her ten more seconds. She sucked in her breath and took a step back. She said, "You're George's brother. You're the Wild Baron. Goodness, I didn't realize how alike you looked."

She was so pale he thought she would fall over in a dead faint.

"Oh? You're entirely wrong. George had black hair and dark brown eyes. We looked nothing alike."

"I don't understand," she said slowly. "Why are you saying that? George had eyes nearly as green as yours—he said his were the same color as his father's—and his hair was just a bit darker blond than yours."

Well, damn. His ruse hadn't paid off.

"Very well," Rohan said. "It was George, then. You did know him." Perhaps it also meant that she wasn't part of this plan to skinny down his coffers. At least he now knew one thing for certain. It had been George, as fantastic as it seemed to Rohan.

"So," Rohan said, not bowing, not offering to take her hand, not doing anything except standing there, looking at the run-down house, bricks missing from one of the chimneys, and the beautiful gardens that surrounded it. "Since you guessed who I am, since you described George nearly to his eyebrows, then you must be the girl my brother supposedly ruined?"

She stared at him. The black smudges of dirt on her face stood out starkly against her pallor. She had become mute.

"You're not, then. Very well. You're a maid, and a dirty one at that. You simply saw George when he visited here? You work at this house? For that paltry bugger who wrote me that impertinent letter? If you do work here, you don't appear to do a very good job. The place looks like it's ready to fall down and crumble."

She got hold of herself. "That's true enough, but I ask you, how could a maid be responsible for how the house looks on the outside?'' That stymied him and she smiled to herself. She realized, of course, that most self-respecting maids would turn up their noses at her. Her hands were dirty, there was black dirt on her muslin gown and under her fingernails, her hair was straggling about her face.

She let him wriggle free from that one finally, saying, ''I not only work here, I also live here.''

''Then you are not a maid?''

''No, I'm not a maid.'' She didn't say anything more. She watched him draw a piece of foolscap from his greatcoat pocket. He waved it at her. ''If you live here, then perhaps you can tell me why this man named Joseph Hawlworth wrote me this insolent letter telling me that George had ruined you? It is you who are ruined, is it not?''

2

HE WAS SILENT FOR A LONGER TIME THAN IT USUALLY took his valet to arrange Rohan's cravat. Rohan wasn't a patient man, but he managed to hold himself quiet. He fairly bubbled with questions, but he would be patient now. He would wait her out. Finally, spreading her dirty hands in front of her, she said, "I'm not ruined. I was never ruined."

"Did you really know my brother George? I realize you know what he looked like, but were you really close to him?"

"Yes, I was, but he didn't ruin me. May I read the letter my father wrote to you?"

He handed it to her. She had to smooth out the creases. Those creases bespoke a fine anger. Well, good, her father deserved it. She read: "*My Lord Mountvale, Your brother, George Carrington, ruined my daughter. You are the head of the Carrington family. It is now your obligation . . .*"

She sucked in her breath. Her father's intent was painfully clear. Very slowly, very carefully, she folded the paper and handed it back to him. She said, "My father made a grave mistake." She just looked at him. "George did not ruin me," she said again, her litany. She hated this. Of course now she knew why her father couldn't wait to leave Mulberry House. He'd written this damnable letter to George's brother, then hied himself out of the line of fire, leaving her to deal with his blackmail scheme. Her father had no idea that George's brother was a debauched satyr whose appetites, according to George, brought new meaning to the word. But then George had grinned and rubbed his hands together and said his brother was the very best in the world. She hadn't understood that, particularly when George had told her that she was to avoid his brother until George had the chance to arrange everything just right, to explain her to his brother. He said earnestly that if his older brother viewed her as a threat to him—George—he would destroy her without a second thought, despite what George could say or do. It had all been very confusing.

Now she was facing George's older brother. There was no George to aid her. She had never planned to see the baron at all, to meet him or speak to him. She had certainly never wanted him to know about her.

Rohan slipped the folded letter back into the pocket of his greatcoat. "I was more surprised than I can say when I received this impudent letter. So this Hawlworth fellow is your father?"

"Yes, he's my father. He isn't here."

"And he is the master of this magnificent house?" He was staring right at the chimney stack that had lost a load of bricks.

"He is the master. I'm the daughter, but George didn't ruin me. I've already told you that. I mean it. You may leave with a clear conscience. I neither want nor need anything from you. I'm sorry my father did this. You may be certain that I will burn his ears for his attempt to do you harm."

This was unexpected. Rohan didn't like unexpected situations. And this one had been nothing but unexpected from the beginning. What stunned him still was that it had been George the scholar, the budding cartographer, the studious young man, who hadn't ever appeared to grasp the reality that there was a fair sex. George had managed to rouse enough lust to make love to this lovely young lady? And she was a lady, dirt and all. It was in her bearing, in the way she spoke so clearly and precisely. "Why are you so dirty?"

She raised her head and smiled, a lovely smile really, not that he cared. "Look around you. I am the gardener here. I am very good. Flowers and plants love me. Shall I show you my lilies and iris and candytuft? My roses are the most beautiful in the area."

A gardener, was she? Now that was something, but he wasn't about to let her sidetrack him. "What do you mean, George didn't ruin you?"

"Just what I said. You may leave now, sir. Let me go fetch Jamie for you. I'm sorry I had him take away your horse and curricle in the first place."

"No, wait." He lightly grasped her sleeve. "Listen, you're not what I expected—at least at first glance you're not. I want to talk to you. My brother has been dead nearly a year now. If you knew him, then I want to hear you talk about him. It appears that George had interests I wasn't aware of, namely you."

She said very quietly, "George had many interests in the time I knew him."

"Then why didn't you come to his funeral? Why didn't he come to me and tell me about you?"

"He was trying to find the perfect moment, he told me several times. I guess he didn't ever find even close to a perfect moment." She shrugged. "Then it was too late. As for his funeral, I couldn't come."

"Why?"

"I was needed here. I couldn't leave."

There was more here than met the eye. So George had been trying to find the perfect moment to tell him? Tell him what, exactly? That he wanted to marry this girl whose face was smudged with dirt and was really quite fine-looking and was a gardener? "Look, can we go inside? I'm hot and thirsty."

"If you are so hot, then remove that greatcoat."

He frowned down at her. He wasn't used to a woman

carping at him—well, a bit of carping, and that was usually amusing. His mother did it brilliantly, always following it with a smile to curl a man's toes. He shrugged off the great-coat. "I'm still hot and thirsty. Are my britches to be next?"

She didn't look remotely interested or remotely shocked at his improper words. Actually, she didn't want to take him inside, but she probably had no choice. She couldn't see him leaving until he was satisfied, until, in short, he was good and ready. But she had to get rid of him. She wasn't about to take any chances.

She stilled a moment and listened very carefully. She heard nothing. Finally she shrugged and said, "Very well. I will be glad to give you something to drink, perhaps even a small cake, but then you must leave."

"You don't want money from me?"

"No. Come inside," she said, her hands fisted at her sides. Of course that was what he expected. She probably would have expected the same thing if she'd been in his boots. She shuddered at what her father had written. She didn't know yet what she would say to him once he returned to Mulberry House, but it wouldn't be at all filial.

He followed her into the dim entry hall of Mulberry House. It was very cool inside, simply because the windows in the hallway were covered, not letting the sunlight in. He followed her into a nearby smallish room that was nonethe-less filled with light, no draperies on these windows, and very little furniture. There was a single sofa covered with an ancient yellow brocade and set on fairly new Egyptian feet, two chairs that looked vastly uncomfortable, and a single carpet that was clean and looked quite cheap. The oak floor was well waxed, and there was no dust that he could see in the corners.

This place could certainly use some money. He looked around him and curled his lip. Why the devil didn't she want any of his groats? What was going on here?

She pointed to a chair and walked out of the room without a word or a backward glance.

He remained alone for a good ten minutes. He had stared at those Egyptian feet for at least eight minutes of the ten. Then she returned carrying a tray. "I have brought some tea and lemon cakes. They're only a day old and still fresh enough."

"You're also the cook?"

"Usually Mrs. Timmons comes in from Upper Slaughter, but this week her daughter had twins and she has to see to the rest of the children."

"Oh." He eyed her as he picked up a lemon cake. He took a bite. It was sour and dry. He swallowed, barely. It actually tasted no worse than the near-moldy slices of bread served at Almack's.

"My father doesn't like my cooking either. He says that I look at a loin of pork and it turns into a boot, fit only for Lolah the goat. As for these poor cakes, I've never been able to figure out just how much lemon juice to squeeze into the mixture. Also, I was very low on sugar and the cakes surely need more of it."

"I cannot help you."

"No, I imagine that you have never done anything for yourself in your life."

That was a low shot a man couldn't tolerate. "If I tried to make the lemon cakes, I wouldn't muck it up. That is because I can read a recipe, I have a brain, and I know how to use measures. This is drier than the wheels on my curricle. It's stuck in my throat."

"If it's stuck in that throat of yours, then how are you able to talk so much?"

He grunted at that and drank some tea, expecting warm swamp water. Instead, it was delicious, India tea, his favorite. He nodded. "Now," he said, sitting back on the old yellow brocade, "tell me how you came to know George and how he didn't ruin you, or did ruin you, according to your father."

"No," she said. "The only reason you're here is because of my father's accusation. You will not hear again from him, I swear it. Thus there is nothing you need to know. You may leave in good conscience." She rose. "Good day, my lord. Have a safe journey back to London."

He waved his hand at her, a finely shaped hand with clean, buffed nails, a strong hand. "You claim you knew my brother well. Tell me how you met him."

She sighed, as if much put upon. "I really wish you would just leave and go back to London."

"How do you know I'm going back to London?"

"You're the Wild Baron, are you not? Surely that is where most gentlemen of your ilk reside?"

He was occasionally called the Wild Baron, a sobriquet that usually amused him and that certainly pleased his proud mama, but from this young lady's mouth it sounded like a rank insult. He drew up stiffer than the fireplace poker that stood at an odd angle in the corner. "I am not notorious. And I wish to God that whoever pinned that silly nickname on me would fall off the face of the earth. Did George tell you that?"

"Whenever he called you the Wild Baron, it was with much affection. He said it was in the blood, tainted blood evidently. He said that his other brother, Tibolt, was a very serious, very holy young man, a vicar, who hadn't inherited the tainted blood. George said your parents were renowned for their lechery, beloved for their vices. Any antic they pulled was eulogized. George said that your father rubbed his hands together whenever he heard of one of your exploits and said you were as wicked as the devil himself, that you were his proud first fruit."

"Don't forget my mother's blood in this rhapsody of yours." Damn, he hadn't meant to say that. He sat forward, his hands clasped between his knees. "Listen, I have no knowledge that my father ever said such things. He died two years ago. My mother, however, is still very capable of carrying on her own wild escapades. She is herself, nothing more.

Still, you're just parroting foolish tales. It is no more than gossip.''

"I do occasionally read the *London Times* and the *Gazette*. You appear with great regularity in both papers. You indulge in exploits that appear to titillate everyone in society. You must be a very busy man, since I have read that you have enjoyed liaisons with most ladies in London, that you have made outrageous wagers with the Prince Regent and have won, that you have been known to fill a lady's bathing tub with champagne and, well, what followed is better left unsaid.''

"It wasn't all that expensive a champagne. As to the ladies, you actually believe all that drivel? I do not cozy up to married ladies. Scarcely do I get all that close to them, despite what they wish. No, what you've read is preposterous, gross overstatements—well, most of it must be.''

He stopped cold. He sounded ridiculous and he wanted to kick himself. Why was he trying to convince her that he wasn't a satyr? He was quite pleased, all in all, with his reputation. He would have to think about this. She'd made him say things he would never normally say. She had raised a smooth brow and was giving him the look of a tolerant mother superior to an errant novice.

"It's none of your business,'' he said, set the teacup in its saucer with a snap, and rose. "Your father wrote specifically that George had ruined you. What did he mean? Did George seduce you? Relieve you of your precious virginity? Did he leave you in a ditch? What exactly did the poor boy do to you? You are not exactly a toothsome young maiden of seventeen.'' Irritated, he slashed his hand through the air, then said, "At least you're cleaner than you were when I first saw you. But there is still some dirt beneath your fingernails.''

"I know. I couldn't find my gloves. I thought you wanted to know how I came to be acquainted with your brother. Well, no matter. We met and that was that. George didn't do anything that I didn't want him to. My father is mistaken. You may leave now, my lord."

He said abruptly, "How old are you, Miss Hawlworth?"

"I am nearly twenty-one."

"George was twenty-three when he died. I had thought you would be much older, an experienced woman to take advantage of a green young man."

"George, green? Yes, I suppose he was. He was very shy, quiet, and he loved to read maps, any maps." She paused a moment, frowning down at the lemon cake.

Rohan said, sitting forward on the settee, "It wasn't that George was a prig, but he was a rather solitary young man, loved his studies, particularly maps, and I would have wagered that he was a virgin when he died even though I knew he wasn't."

"No, George was no prig. Nor was he a virgin. At least he told me he wasn't. There is no way I would be able to tell is there?"

"No. Now, how old were you when you met George?"

"I don't recall exactly."

"You are being evasive. Tell me the bloody truth."

"There is little enough to tell. And it makes no difference to anything." She had the gall to shrug.

He was furious, but he wasn't about to show her how very angry he really was. She believed that bedding more women than resided in an English village was his mission in life? A Carrington family tradition? In his damned blood? Damnation, it was supposed to be and at this moment, he hated it. He wanted to pick up the sofa with its ridiculous Egyptian feet and hurl it through the windows, except it wouldn't fit. He drew a nice deep breath. "Then tell me more about George."

"He was too handsome for his own good, just as you are," she said in a matter-of-fact voice that robbed her words of any compliment "He was smart. But he sometimes seemed lost to me, as if he wanted to do something or be someone different from what he was, and he just didn't know where to go or what to do. That sounds strange, I know, but it was often the impression he gave me. He was loyal, in his way."

This was the George he knew. Quiet, studious George. "Loyal in his own way? What do you mean by that?"

"He did not abandon those whom he had taken in affection, those to whom he had made commitments."

"Of course he wouldn't. Would you care to be more specific?"

"No. I will also tell you that he drank too much. It worried me a great deal."

"I never saw George take a drink of anything in his entire life. The George you described is my George, all right, except for this drinking. Are you certain it was George and not someone who used his name, someone who just happened to have looked a bit like him, a bit like me?"

She rose quickly. "Just a moment. I cannot believe that I actually understand what you mean."

She left the drawing room. He heard her light footsteps on the stairs. When she returned just a few moments later, she was carrying a sketch pad. She rifled through the pages, then handed the pad to him. He saw a startling likeness of George. She was an excellent artist. The figure in the drawing looked shy and wistful, yet there was something yearning in that expression she'd captured. What was it? It was puzzling, but perhaps it was just that the artist had rendered that yearning look he didn't recognize. He handed her back the sketch pad before he realized he wanted to look through the rest of the drawings.

"That is George."

"Of course it is."

"You do know how he died?"

"I know that he drowned. The *Gazette* gave no details. There was no way for me to find out more."

"Of course there was. All you had to do was to write to me, but you didn't. Very well, you've pursed your lips together so tightly your mouth has nearly disappeared. He and some of his friends were in small yachts, racing from Ventnor to Lucy Point. None of them knew that a freak storm was blowing up. It hit them hard, driving George's yacht into the cliff just above Lucy Point. The boat splintered. The young man with George survived. George didn't. His body was never recovered. If he had been drunk at the time I would have killed him if he hadn't died. But of course he wasn't drunk. George didn't drink, I told you that.''

"Yes, you did," she said, and nothing more. She didn't cry, but she was remarkably pale. He held his peace and sipped more of his tea. Finally, after she'd eaten the last bite of a lemon cake, she said, "You're right, they do taste quite sour. I must work on that recipe."

"Ask Mrs. Timmons to teach you."

"Yes, perhaps I will. Now, surely you have to leave, my lord."

He shrugged. Why not? There was nothing for him here. Perhaps a bit of George he hadn't known, but George was dead, and what did it matter now? The chit wasn't going to say anything more about George and he couldn't very well force her to. But the father—he really wanted to know what her damned father had to say. "Where is your father?"

She stiffened straight as an oak sapling. "He is not here."

"I can see that he is not. Where can I find him? He's hiding from me, isn't he? He left you here to face me."

He was so close to the truth that it rattled her for a moment. How could he possibly know that? Then she managed to say, "I won't tell you. You might challenge him to a duel. You might knock out some of his teeth. He needs all the teeth he has. He can't afford to lose any more."

"I won't knock out any of his bloody teeth, even though he likely deserves it. Where is he?"

She shook her head. Her lips were a thin line again. She had felt pain at George's death; he didn't doubt that now. He saw a smudge of dirt at her hairline that she had missed when she'd washed her face. It blended right in with the dark brown of her hair. A warm, dark brown that looked rich and soft. Ah, but her eyes were cold and distant. Those eyes of hers, they were a bright blue gray—not dark and mysterious, but rather light and mysterious, like the oddly faceted sapphire he'd bought some three years ago and kept. His mother had selected it from Rundle and Bridge. She didn't know he hadn't given it to a mistress.

He said nothing more. He merely picked up his greatcoat and strode out of the house, with her dogging his heels. Why? Did she believe he wasn't going to leave? Did she think he was going to steal that settee with the ridiculous Egyptian feet? Did she think he was going to hide in the stable? The curricle was standing there in the front drive, but there was no Gulliver. When he rounded the side of the house he saw Jamie brushing Gulliver, singing at the top of his lungs to the huge gray gelding. It was not an edifying song, but it was catchy.

> "There was a young fellow from Lyme
> Who lived with three wives at a time.
> When asked, 'Why the third?'
> He said, 'One's absurd!
> And bigamy, sir, is a crime.' "

Rohan boomed out laughter. The stable lad had used the best King's English and had sung the limerick in a rich baritone fit for a lady's musical soiree.

"Jamie," Susannah said, coming up alongside the baron, "is the local master of the limerick. He does accents. He's really quite excellent."

"Yes, he is." He watched Jamie lead a rather reluctant Gulliver out from behind Mulberry House. His own horse didn't want to come to him? Rohan yelled, "Come on, you miserable devil, you faithless sod. Oh, all right. If you like, I'll learn some limericks and sing them to you."

Gulliver whinnied and pawed the ground with his front hoof. He perked his ears first toward Jamie, then toward Rohan.

She was again dogging his heels. He took the reins from

Jamie's hands, nodded the boy away, then backed Gulliver into his traces.

She watched him fasten Gulliver into the straps, readying the horse to pull the curricle. He was quick and efficient. He looked up once to see a frown on her face. She kept looking up at the second floor.

"Did you lie to me? Is your father hiding upstairs?"

"Certainly not. Aren't you done yet? You should have asked Jamie to do it. He's had more practice than you. He's faster."

"I am perfectly capable of rigging Gulliver in," he said, his voice cold and stiff. Did she believe him to be a total wastrel? A completely useless sod? Well, he supposed most people believed that and loved him all the more for it. Strange world.

"There, you did it again, looked up at the second floor. What is up there? Who is up there? A mad uncle? Look at you. You even have your hands crossed over your chest like an Italian soprano. What is the matter?"

At that moment, a child wailed.

3

"THAT," ROHAN SAID THOUGHTFULLY, NOT LOOKING UP at the window, but rather at her set face, "wasn't your father."

The child let loose with another furious wail, louder this time.

She left him at a dead run.

Rohan yelled, "Jamie!"

He gave Gulliver's reins over to the stable lad, saying even as he was striding back into the house, "Sing him another limerick. Then write it down so I can sing it to him later."

He saw the hem of her skirt disappear at the top of the stairs. He stopped cold.

Child?

What was he supposed to do? He turned quickly toward the open front door. He would leave. That was exactly what he should do. Yes, leave right this moment. Now. This child had nothing at all to do with him. It was just her little brother or little sister. No, the child didn't have a thing to do with him.

He heard Jamie singing in a light falsetto voice,

"There was an old man from Blackheath,
Who sat on his set of false teeth.
Said he with a start,
'Oh, Lord, bless my heart!
I've bitten myself underneath!' "

He heard Gulliver whinny loudly. Traitorous horse.

Rohan turned slowly on the bottom stairs and looked up-ward. There was no child crying out now. There was com-plete silence. He didn't want to, it was none of his business, but he started up the stairs, climbed every one of those nar-row, steep steps until he was at the top. He turned right and walked down the narrow corridor. He passed two closed doors. He paused outside the third, just inched open. He didn't want to, he shouldn't have, but he did. Quietly, he pushed the door open a bit further.

She was sitting there in a rocking chair, rocking slowly back and forth, a girl-child in her arms. She was singing softly to the little girl, rubbing her back in soothing, wide circles. She was looking down at the child, a finger of her left hand lightly stroking her cheek. The child heaved with sobs, then slowly she calmed, stretching out all boneless in her arms. She was speaking softly now, and rocking, back and forth, back and forth. "It's all right, lovey, quite all right. You just had a bad dream. It's all right, all right."

He must have made a sound. He didn't think he had, but he must have made some noise because she looked up. She stared at him, her face as white as the lace on her collar. The child, sensing her distress, stiffened and pushed away from her.

"Shush, shush," she whispered, hugging the child against her. "No, lovey, it's all right. Just lie against Mama. It's all right."

Mama? She was this child's mother? No, impossible. Surely it was a little sister. Mama? But she'd sworn that George hadn't ruined her.

He turned and walked down the corridor, walked slowly down the stairs. He wanted to walk right out that front door, climb into his curricle, and let Gulliver run like the wind, as far away from this place as he could go in as short a time as possible.

Instead, he went back into the sparsely furnished drawing room. He poured himself some more tea. He eyed another lemon cake but couldn't bring himself to take it.

He sat there for a long time.

Then she was standing in the open doorway, silent and still, unmoving, just looking at him, no expression at all on her face.

He said, "You told the child you were her mama. Is this true?"

"No. Hearing that simply soothes her."

He rose slowly. "How old is the little girl?"

He saw that her face was awash with a lie and added quickly, "I saw her. I'm not a complete fool. Don't begin to believe you could ever deceive me."

"Very well. She is three years and five months old."

"Then she cannot be George's child. She cannot be your child. You told me you were twenty-one. If she is three, then you birthed her when you were eighteen, which means you were impregnated when you were seventeen. George would have been only nineteen. It can't be George's child. He would have told me, for God's sake. It isn't as if you became pregnant and then he was killed. No, this isn't a baby we're talking about here, it's a child, a little girl. She isn't his child, is she?"

"No," she said. "Of course not. She's my little sister."

"Very well." He walked out of the drawing room.

She was on his heels in an instant. "Where do you think you're going?"

He was striding back up the stairs, down that narrow corridor, this time quietly opening every door.

"Stop it, damn you, just stop. Leave, please, just leave."

He turned to face her. She was out of breath.

"Where is the child?"

"Won't you just go away? You know you want to."

"That's true. However, I can't." He knew he could leave

if he really put his mind to it, if he just forced himself to turn about and march back down those steep stairs, outside to the singing stable lad and Gulliver. George's child. George's bastard. He couldn't believe it. He wouldn't believe it.

He kept walking.

Her shoulders slumped. "All right, this way."

The little girl was asleep on a narrow bed, on her stomach, one arm wrapped around a doll that had very little hair left on its head. A light blanket was tucked around her.

Her face was turned away from them. The small head was covered with blond hair.

"What is her name?"

"Marianne."

His heart began to pound, slow, dull thuds. Marianne, the tiny daughter of Squire Bethony who had died coughing blood when she was only five years old. The little girl had been George's best friend. George hadn't spoken for nearly eight months after she died.

"Does she have a second name?"

"Yes. Lindsay. Her name is Marianne Lindsay. It's my mother's name."

The pain was sharp and hard to his heart. Slowly, he turned to face her. "You know where her first name comes from, don't you?"

"Yes, I know."

The child stirred, sucking her middle fingers.

"Do you still insist that the child is your sister?"

"I suppose it wouldn't do much good now."

"None at all. Please awaken her. I want to see George's child. I want to see my niece."

She leaned over and gently began rubbing the little girl's back. The sucking sounds speeded up. "Wake up, Marianne. Come on, lovely, wake up. There's a fine gentlemen who wants to meet you. Come, love." She picked the little girl up, wrapping the blanket around her, kissed her small ear, then turned her to face him. The child's eyes slowly opened. Rohan stared into his own eyes, into George's eyes—a bright, soft green, the color of nearly all the Carrington males' eyes for the past three generations.

He swallowed. Slowly, he touched his fingertip gently to the little girl's face. She drew back, frowning.

"It's all right, lovey."

"Yes," he said, his voice very low and as gentle as a soft spring rain, "I'm your uncle."

The little girl took her fingers out of her mouth. She stared at him, those green eyes of hers intent and deep as a vein of emeralds, "What's an uncle?"

"I'm your papa's brother."

A small hand with two wet fingers touched the cleft in his chin. "You have a hole in your chin just like Papa did."

"Yes," he said, and swallowed.

"I don't have one. Mama told me God doesn't give them out to everyone."

"That's right. But God did give them to most of the Carrington male children."

"Mama told me that Papa would yell when he shaved himself because he always cut himself in that hole."

"It is difficult." Rohan couldn't remember seeing George shave himself. He'd had little to shave. But he had evidently stayed in this house, had bathed in this house, had shaved in this house.

"I wish God would give me one. Did you know that my papa went to heaven?" All this was said matter-of-factly. Marianne then stuck her fingers back into her mouth and began to suck vigorously.

"I have no likeness of George, except that charcoal sketch I made of him two years ago. Marianne will forget what he looked like soon."

"That isn't true. The sketch is fine. She won't forget."

She shrugged. "I am but an amateur. It isn't good enough. There's no hope for it. She will forget."

"No, she won't." The words were there, spoken, out of his mouth, hanging there stark in the air between them.

She said calmly, with a good deal of composure even as

she lightly bounced the little girl up and down in her arms, "There is nothing for you here, my lord. Very well, it's true that she is George's daughter. You already guessed that. Her likeness to him is very pronounced, but surely that means little or nothing to you. She isn't a boy. She can't be important to you in any way."

"When will she be four?"

"In November, the fourth of November."

"You didn't tell me why you didn't come to George's funeral, just said some nonsense about how you couldn't. You could have come. No one would have known who you were."

So he wanted the truth. So be it. "There wasn't enough money for me to come. Don't give me that supercilious sneer. I'm not pleading or begging or trying to make you feel sorry for us. We go on wonderfully well. It is only my father who occasionally loses his sense and thus his money. He is a gambler, and that is probably what he is doing right now. Gambling. It was just that at that particular time there just wasn't enough money. The vicar—he was good enough to come and we prayed for George here." She stopped speaking then, just held the little girl tightly against her, her head bowed.

Gently, he lifted her chin with his fingers. Tears were streaming down her face.

"At least George knew his daughter for more than two years."

"Yes."

"Didn't George know his daughter?"

"Of course, but he couldn't be here often. He was studying so very hard at Oxford."

But wouldn't George have been just as content studying his maps and his Latin and his history books here? Evidently not. Why hadn't George told him about her and his daughter? It made no sense.

And then, of course, he understood.

"What last name does she carry?"

The tears dried up and the back stiffened. The little girl stirred, aware of her mother's distress.

He watched her soothe the child, lifting her over her shoulder and lightly patting her back. She sobbed twice, three times, then heaved a deep sigh. He smiled, unable not to.

Finally, she laid the little girl back onto her bed, covered her, waited a few more minutes to make sure she slept, then motioned him away.

At the head of the stairs, he said again, "What last name does she carry?"

"Her last name is Carrington," she said, and walked ahead of him down the stairs.

She turned at the bottom of the stairs. "George and I were married in October of 1806, at Oxford. My father gave his permission, since I was only seventeen."

"George didn't have my permission. No one would have allowed him to wed without my permission. I don't blame you for maintaining this lie. You must deal with the local folk. The little girl is George's bastard, but I will see that she doesn't suffer for it. I will do my best to—"

They were facing each other in the dim entryway. She drew back her hand and slapped him hard.

"How dare you? No, I don't mind that you have insulted me, but to believe your brother guilty of such infamy?" She raised her hand again. This time, he managed to catch her wrist. His head was still spinning from her first blow.

"You're very strong," he said finally, but he didn't let go of her wrist.

She was panting, furious, trying to jerk free of him but unable to. "George told me again and again that you would merely laugh if he told you about us, if he told you about Marianne. He said you would send him to Australia and take Marianne away from me. He said you'd probably sell me as a bond servant in the Colonies."

Rohan just stared at her. George had said that? No, it wasn't possible, it just wasn't.

"Then he'd laugh and say that you were the best of brothers, despite all your secrets and your philandering. I never knew what he meant by that.

"But you don't know anything, my lord. Also, since it's obvious you don't believe me, I will show you our papers. Not because I care what you think of me or Marianne, but because I care what you think of George. Then I want you to leave. You have never been a part of our lives. I decided long ago that George was never going to allow you to be part of our lives. I certainly don't want you to be now."

He was utterly baffled. None of this made any sense.

He had a niece named Marianne. He didn't even know the mother's name.

When she returned to the entryway where she'd left him waiting, she handed him an envelope. Inside was a parchment that looked very official. Sure enough, it was the marriage certificate. He recognized his brother's signature. He read the preacher's signature. Bligh McNally. There was no need for him to read more.

Very slowly he handed it back to her.

"Your father wrote me that letter because he wanted money. It's obvious there isn't much of that here at Mulberry House. You haven't asked me for money, so either you don't want any, or if you do, you're playing the game with a strategy I have never before witnessed."

"I don't want your money. I never wanted your money. George expected to inherit some of his father's money when he became twenty-five. Unfortunately, he didn't make it."

He looked off into the distance for just a moment, then smiled. He took the plunge. He said, "Ah, but you're wrong. Didn't he tell you? No, of course he didn't. Aunt Mariam died after George did. He had no idea that she would leave him money, some twenty thousand pounds. That money came to me, since George was dead." He drew a deep breath, aware that he was very possibly wading deeper into the River Styx. "It should now go to George's daughter."

Money, she thought, staring at the baron. George had actually left her money, all unknowingly. Well, no, actually the baron was offering her the money and he didn't have to. Not just a shilling or two. No, real money—twenty thousand pounds. It was a vast sum. She doubted she'd ever seen more than twenty pounds at any one time in her entire twenty-one and a half years.

It was more than enough to live on very comfortably, forever. The good Lord knew she had ample experience living on a frayed string. Twenty thousand pounds—no frayed string anymore. She and Marianne would be safe. Toby too. All three of them would be safe.

She looked him straight in the eye. "That would support Marianne and me forever. Will you truly give us George's inheritance?"

"There's only one problem," he said slowly, wondering how the devil these damnable words were seeping out of his own mouth, feeling himself sink deeper. Then he saw the little girl's face, that small smile of hers, identical to George's, and his heart contracted. George's child. He couldn't leave her here. He wouldn't.

Now the ax would fall, she thought, watching him. Did he want to bed her? George had panted after her—no other way to put it—but she'd loved him and wanted him to marry her, and thus he'd had no choice if he wanted to bed her. He'd married her all right and proper and then almost immediately impregnated her.

She hadn't blamed him overly when he'd left her once the morning illness had begun. Watching someone vomit wasn't an elevating sight. And she'd been so tired and tiresome. She was glad when he left. She'd felt wretched and guilty, the two emotions nearly dragging her into the dirt. But then he'd come back. He always returned to her.

Still, the baron remained silent, just looking intently at her. "You want me to go to bed with you," she said dully and looked past him out the open front door to where Jamie was still singing to Gulliver, the huge gray nodding his head. She wondered if his hooves were tapping a beat in the ground. "That is your only condition."

"Oh, no," he said. "Surely not that. You're not sufficient for me. You're too thin, you have dirt beneath your fingernails, and I doubt your conversation goes much beyond what a three-year-old wants to hear. No, I think not. Don't get me wrong, it's not that you're ugly or even plain. You're just not in my style. No, that's not the problem." He accepted what he was doing and why he was doing it. It was just that he'd never done anything like this before in his life. It would certainly confound his dear mama. On the other hand, he knew her face would be as radiant as a star when she met George's daughter.

"What is the problem, then?" He'd insulted her from here to the garden and back. Wasn't he a satyr? Didn't he want every woman he saw? Even one with dirt under her fingernails? And she wasn't all that thin.

He studied his own fingernails. They were well buffed and clean. He said without looking at her, "To inherit George's money, you must come onto the stage, so to speak. You cannot remain here at Mulberry House. You must take your place as the widow of the late George Carrington. In short, you must come to my home and live the life you would have had if George had lived."

He was mad, utterly and undeniably mad. No doubt about it, but he couldn't, he wouldn't, leave the little girl here to live with a grandfather who was probably also a drunk besides being a gambler. He would like to take just Marianne, but he knew her mother would never allow it.

"London?"

"I have a house there. You make it sound like one big fleshpot. It's not, you know."

She was shaking her head. "No, no, truly, everything is just as I like it. I wish to stay here. It's true my father is in one of his rather low periods and I am never certain how long it will last. All I want is protection for Marianne. Please—"

"You will not beg again. It doesn't suit you. Marianne is my niece. She is flesh. She will live as a Carrington. If not London, then we will go to my estate in Sussex until you accustom yourself. She will not remain here."

"You make Mulberry House sound like a pigsty. It isn't. It's just that Papa is on one of his lower swings and—"

"Papa can swing in any direction he pleases. My niece will not live well or hand-to-mouth according to his luck. Do you want her to grow up knowing her dear grandpapa tried to blackmail her uncle?"

That did revolt the senses, she thought, but things were moving too quickly. "Where do you live in Sussex?"

"Near Eastbourne. It's but two miles from the coast. It's beautiful country, all hilly, with ancient rocks that poke up here and there and quite take you by surprise. It's near where the Battle of Hastings was fought. When you walk over that ground, you can practically hear the Normans and the Saxons axing away at each other. The weather is pleasant as it can be anywhere in England."

"My father?"

Rohan just shrugged. He still wanted to pound the man into the dirt, but, after all, he had through his daughter given him a niece—George's daughter—so he didn't feel as violent as he had before. "There should be no problem. Your father can visit you. On rare occasion. Make that very rare. I will make him an allowance so that he can continue living here at Mulberry House."

She didn't know what to do. She didn't know this man. But she knew of him. He was a womanizer, a man famed for his debauchery, just as his father had been, just as his mother still was. She couldn't imagine having a debauched mother, a debauched mother-in-law. According to George, the Baron and Baroness Mountvale had long been adored by Society. The more wicked they were, the more adored they became. Apparently the same perverse equation was true for the current baron, the Wild Baron. She splayed her hand. "Why are you offering to do this?"

He looked down at her, but he really saw his brother's
face the last time he had been with him, only two days before
he'd died. George had been flushed because of something
he'd come across by accident. He refused to tell Rohan about
it, just said it wouldn't interest him.

Rohan wondered now if George had ever intended to tell
him about— "I don't know your name," he said.

4

SHE SMILED UP AT THE UTTERLY BAFFLED EXPRESSION ON his face. She wanted to laugh, but didn't. "My name is Susannah. It was my mother's name."

"You will come with me to Mountvale House?"

Susannah thought of the small serving of beef that was left in the kitchen. She had a total of six pounds to her name, money she'd hoarded for the past year and a half, a shilling at a time. She'd already mended Marianne's dresses so many times they wouldn't last much longer. But what swayed her was the thought that Marianne would grow up thinking her grandfather was the way a man should be, that this was the way a family should be. She looked at the baron, searching his face for perfidy. She realized he was also offering her escape. He didn't know it, but he was. But would she be safe with him?

He knew what she was thinking, but he said nothing, just let her search and search and finally come to a decision.

"It is very kind of you to offer, sir. But it isn't simply a matter of just Marianne and me."

"If you're referring to your father, no, he won't live at Mountvale. I value my silver too much for that."

"My father is not a thief."

"If this letter he wrote me is any indication, he isn't all that far removed."

"He was simply concerned. His judgment clouded for a brief time, that's all. He's half Irish, you know. He's very good with horses."

"His judgment can cloud until it rains, but it won't be at Mountvale."

"It's not my father I was speaking about."

"What's the matter now? You want Jamie with you? Fine, I'll hire him. Besides, I doubt Gulliver will willingly let him out of his sight now. He's the first person to seduce my horse besides me."

"No, it's not Jamie. It's Toby."

"Who the devil is Toby? Your favorite cat? If Toby's a good mouser, I don't mind carting him with us."

"Toby is my little brother."

Rohan just stared at her. "Your little brother," he repeated slowly, trying to gather his wits. "You have a child and a little brother?"

"Yes. Tobias Hawlworth. He's eight years old, and I'm really more his mother than his sister. His mother—our mother—died birthing him." Ah, the pain of that. Susannah had been terrified that she would die as well when she became pregnant with Marianne. But the birth had been relatively easy, thank God.

"But your father wouldn't allow him to leave. This Toby is his heir, surely—"

"I understand, sir," she said, and there was acceptance in her calm voice. "But I could no more leave Toby than I could leave Marianne. Thank you for coming. I'm pleased that you got to meet your niece. Good-bye."

She was trying to shove him out the door. When that didn't work, she walked outside herself, waving for him to follow her. Gulliver looked in her direction and neighed. Jamie patted the white star on his nose.

"Good-bye," she called again.

"Susannah! Where are you? Susannah?"

A boy came dashing around the side of the house. He was tall and skinny as a post, and his hair was as black as a sinner's dreams. He skidded to a stop in front of her. With a big grin, he shoved a notebook into her hands. "Here, just look at this, Susannah. It's my Latin translations and Vicar Horkle said they were the best he'd ever seen. See, he even wrote "excellent" on the first page. What do you think of that?"

She was silent until she'd opened the notebook, read what the vicar had written. Then she smiled at the boy, grabbed him, and kissed his ear. "You're a marvel, Master Toby, just a marvel. Ah, but look at that rip in your shirt. Look at your shoes, all scuffed and dirty. What did you do? Oh no, Toby, you fought with that Finley boy again, didn't you?"

Rohan saw more evidence of fisticuffs than his sister did. Toby's knuckles were bloody, the knee of one pants leg was ripped, a bruise was coming into its colors on his cheek. He cleared his throat. "Did you win?" he asked.

The boy beamed. "Yes, sir. I knocked him right off his pins, lifted him clean in the air, and tossed him over a log. Of course, he got in a couple of wallops, but I held him down and stuffed leaves in his mouth. I think he swallowed one with a caterpillar on it."

It was an image that brought back a score of memories. Rohan smiled, unable not to. Then he laughed, something of a rusty sound since he was a reprobate of some repute and no reprobate of any distinction at all laughed all that much.

As for Susannah, she froze tighter than a spigot in January. Slowly, ever so slowly, she said, "Toby, this is Lord Mountvale. He is Marianne's uncle and just come for a brief visit. Say your hellos and good-byes, for he is on his way now."

"Hello, sir," Toby said, and bowed. There was a deep, loud, rending sound. The boy gasped, backed away, and then turned and ran.

"Oh, dear," Susannah said, "It would seem he ripped his pants. Please go now, sir. I must see to my brother."

"No," Rohan said. "Let me do it."

"He's hiding in the far eastern end of the stable, my lord," Jamie called out, and Gulliver neighed.

She grabbed his sleeve. "But you're a stranger and I'm his sister. It's up to me to take care of him, it's—"

"Don't move. I'll be right back."

It wasn't until Rohan was standing in the doorway of the dim stable that he wondered what he was doing. He didn't know this boy. What did he care that the little nit was embarrassed because he'd ripped his britches?

He heard himself call out, "Toby? Don't run, it's just me, Rohan, er, Lord Mountvale."

He heard the movement of hay and walked to the end of the stable. The boy was crouched down against the wall, trying to press himself through the wood, really, his face in his hands.

Rohan said, "My horse is skittish. I don't like to leave him waiting. It oversets his nerves. If Jamie runs out of limericks to sing to him, I have no idea what will happen. He could even bolt. And then I would have to walk to the nearest town and likely get very testy in the process."

Toby nearly jumped out of his skin. He stared at the gentleman, who was, in truth, the most handsome, polished-looking gentleman he'd ever seen in his life. The gentleman looked somehow familiar, but how could that be possible?

Toby wanted to sink through the hay and bury himself at the bottom, but he scrambled to his feet.

Rohan said, "Are you bare-assed or is it just a little tear?"

"I'm bare-assed, sir. Leastways, my right part is."

"You're lucky I'm here and wearing a coat." He shrugged out of his riding jacket and handed it to the boy. "Once when I was bare-assed on both parts, I had to walk all the way home and through my parents' house before I could cover myself. That amounted to three maiden aunts, countless maids, and my mother's abigail, who screamed her head off at the sight. As I recall, my older sister trailed me up the stairs, giggling all the way and pointing. I wanted to pound her, but she was too much bigger than I was."

"How old were you, sir?"

"About eight or nine."

"I'm eight. My sister's older than I am too."

"Ah, just the right age, then. Turn around. Yes, the coat covers all shortages. I don't think your sister would giggle at you."

"No, she'd carry on like a mother. She'd twitter and moan and try to hug me until she'd cracked my ribs. She'd look at my knuckles and moan some more and sigh deeply. She'd try to act brave that I was brawling and got hurt, only I'm not really hurt at all, just a little bit."

"Yes, you're right. Just like a mother. Perhaps giggles would be better. I daresay that since you're wearing my coat, she won't be hot off the mark to hug you for fear of wrinkling my clothes."

The boy walked next to him out of the stable. "You're really Marianne's uncle?"

"Yes. I'm taking you, Marianne, and your sister back to Mountvale House. That's my home in Sussex. It's close to the English Channel. Do you like to fish?"

The boy's eyes shone. "Fish? And swim? Maybe I could learn how to sail?"

"Yes, all those things."

"Oh, sir, that would be grand." His face fell. "But Pa, sir. What would Susannah and I do with Pa?"

"Pa will remain here at Mulberry House. We will find a nice woman to come and look after him. You may visit him whenever you wish."

Rohan feared the boy's face would crack from the huge grin that split his mouth wide. The bruise on his left cheek was flying shades of yellow and green. Rohan's coat flapped around his knees, and some blood off the boy's knuckles had gotten on the cuff. Rohan pictured Tinker's fat cheeks turning red when he saw those cuffs. He wondered if he had a secret way of removing a bloodstain.

● ● ●

Susannah sighed, much beset. "It appears you've given me no choice at all. Very well. I suppose there's no hope for it. I will come to Mountvale House."

"Your enthusiasm overwhelms me. Do you need assistance packing up yourself and the children?"

"No, it will be no problem."

"Then I will be on my way. I cannot remain here. There is no chaperon. Is there an inn somewhere close?"

"On the coach road, just as you ride into Moreton-in-Marsh. The Gourd and the Raisin. I have heard that the sheets are clean and Mrs. Dooley serves a fine dinner. You must have a glass of her cider. She is very proud of it."

"Shall I ask her for the recipe so that you can try to bungle it?"

"It is a secret. She won't tell a soul until she's nearly dead. Then, she claims, she will tell only her eldest daughter, Maude."

"A pity. Very well, I will see all of you tomorrow, then. Ah, don't worry about the blood on the cuff. My valet can have the pleasure of fretting over it. He will doubtless claim it gave him apoplexy." He gave her a brief wave, climbed into his curricle, and took the reins from Jamie.

Already, she thought, as she watched him speak to Jamie, for a rather long time, really—already he was taking over. She watched him give Jamie a coin that made him do a gawky little jig in the drive, then he was away.

She looked after him until he was gone from her sight.

She walked upstairs to her bedchamber to pen her father a letter. He had succeeded beyond his wildest dreams, but for his children and his granddaughter, not himself. Well, yes, for he would no longer have to put up with Susannah nagging at him, preaching at him, being a worse shrew than his wife had been. At least that's what he mumbled in an aggrieved voice.

She smiled as she pictured the woman she would pay to see to him. Mrs. Heron was a terror. She was also very lucky. Susannah knew her to win every wager she'd ever made, including the one just last month with the vicar. He had never figured out how Mrs. Heron had known that Rob Longman would put two pounds in the collection plate that one particular Sunday when he'd never put in more than a shilling before. She also played cards like a shark. Susannah's father didn't have a chance. She smiled as she heard Toby singing at the top of his lungs.

What had Lord Mountvale said to him to make him ready to fall onto the ground and kiss that gentleman's boots?

When Rohan arrived the following morning just after seven o'clock, Susannah was nearly out of her mind. Marianne was shrieking because Toby had stepped on her doll, Gwen, and the left arm had ripped off. Toby was standing in the middle of the small kitchen holding Gwen, trying to figure out how to re-attach the arm, Marianne was pounding the wooden floor with her fists, and Susannah was spilling warm milk on her gown.

Rohan walked into the kitchen, took in the pandemonium, and walked out again. His ears were ringing. He wasn't used to children, and this child's lungs were formidable.

"Sir!"

Damnation, what was a man who'd obviously disintegrated into an idiot the previous afternoon to do? There was Toby, standing there holding that damned doll in one hand and the severed arm in the other.

"Sir, do you know how to fix Gwen?"

"Gwen?" Hadn't Charles II had a mistress named Gwen? He shook his head at himself. "Oh, the doll." He hadn't the foggiest idea. Susannah appeared, Marianne on her hip, still crying, trying to pull away from her mother and leap on Toby.

"Well," Rohan said.

"Here, take Marianne. I'll fix Gwen. Toby, you get our valises and put them in the curricle. Yes, go now. Everything will be fine."

Rohan found himself, for the first time in his life, in sole possession of a child, a very small child who was wriggling and pushing against him and crying "Gwen" at the top of her lungs.

He held her firmly and followed Susannah back into the kitchen, where she fetched a basket and sat down. She threaded a needle and began to sew Gwen's arm back on.

"Don't hurt her, Mommy, don't hurt her."

Susannah said without looking up, "Please give her a cup of the warm milk. I didn't spill all of it."

Rohan held the squirming little girl against his side as he poured the pan of milk into the waiting cup. He knew it was a bad idea, he knew it, but nonetheless he lifted the cup to Marianne's mouth. She shrieked and slapped his hand away. The milk went flying—on him and on the floor.

He held Marianne under her arms and away from him. He looked her right in the eye. "You will be quiet this instant, Marianne."

The voice was one she'd never heard before—stern, low, and mean. To the amazement of the two adults, she shut her mouth.

Susannah looked up at the sudden utter silence. She smiled at him. "Nearly done."

When she handed Gwen back to Marianne, the child took her doll, tugged several times on the arm, then sighed deeply, put her fingers in her mouth, and collapsed against Rohan's shoulder.

"She's easy," he said. "Very easy."

"Sometimes. Upon rare occasions. After she gets what she wants. You'll see."

He watched Susannah clean up the milk mess. She handed him the cloth to wipe himself off. Then he followed her from the kitchen and watched her pull on her bonnet and pelisse and, finally, straighten Toby's jacket. She took Marianne from him and said to her little brother, "I have left Papa a note, Toby, so you're not to worry. Mrs. Heron will come and take care of him. She told me last night."

"Mrs. Heron." The boy choked. Then he grinned, that

blazing grin that showed a mouthful of straight white teeth, a grin that quite simply lit up the dim entryway. He said to Rohan, "She can outwager Papa. She always wins. And she gloats. I feel sorry for him."

"Perhaps she can make him change his ways," Rohan said. "A good woman, and all that rot."

"Oh, no," Susannah said as she walked out the front door, Marianne now hiccuping, her head on Susannah's shoulder, "I imagine that she will fleece him and he will owe her more money that he can ever pay her."

Rohan stared at the curricle. There were four of them. The curricle held two comfortably. "All right," he said slowly. "Toby, you will be my tiger, all right?"

"A tiger? What's that, sir?"

"You will ride standing on the back and shoot any bandits that attack us. If we are on any toll roads, you will jump off and pay the toll."

Toby was so excited, he stammered his gratitude.

"He'll lose most of his enthusiasm by the time he's been standing there for two hours," Rohan said. "It's safe enough. Don't fret. Now, you hold tightly to Marianne."

Jamie suddenly appeared around the side of Mulberry House, riding a swaybacked mare that looked to be on her last hocks.

"Yes, Jamie's now in my employ. He said that only Hera here was in the stable and she's your horse. He'll ride her, then take turns with Toby as my tiger."

She said slowly even as she settled herself on the rather narrow padded bench beside him in the curricle, "You have quite taken over my life."

Actually, he thought, she and all the denizens of Mulberry House had quite taken over his. He said, giving her a crooked grin, "Well, someone had to. If I hadn't come along, your father would have landed all of you in debtor's prison. That wretched roof would have fallen in on your heads. Marianne would have become a gambler. No, no, don't say it again. I know. The poor man is merely suffering some small, insignificant reverses."

"More or less," she said and pulled her shawl over Marianne.

"We will take our time. It will take us three days to reach Mountvale House. When we get to Oxford, I will hire a carriage. It won't be long."

"I know" was all she said. She took only one long look back at Mulberry House. She didn't see anyone. Then she settled back and enjoyed the wind pulling at the ribbons on her bonnet. He drove well.

Rohan slowed Gulliver an hour later on a sharp turn in the road. She was leaning on his arm, sound asleep, Marianne equally asleep in her arms.

He could only shake his head at himself.

Yesterday he had been a man without any ties, no particular burdens piling up in front of him. Of course, a man in his position had responsibilities, duties, but he'd been bred to them all his life. And they were duties a man could get his teeth into, duties a man could understand. Surely no man could be bred to understand this.

Jamie was whistling in the wind beside them. Toby was yelling at the top of his lungs from his tiger position, "I don't see any bandits, sir!"

No, Rohan didn't see any either. What he saw was a multitude of dark clouds suddenly appear on the horizon.

When a raindrop hit Marianne's nose, she jerked awake, jumped when another raindrop hit her cheek, turned to Rohan, and howled.

"Oh, dear," Susannah said, coming awake with the bouncing little girl on her lap. She stared blankly up at the sky, then said, "I hadn't planned on this. It's raining. Oh, dear."

Rohan sighed. What was he to do now?

A raindrop hit him square in the eye. It did not, he thought, portend good things for his future.

5

BARON MOUNTVALE'S PARTY OF FIVE ARRIVED SODDEN IN
Oxford some thirty minutes later. As Rohan pulled Gulliver
to a halt in the inn yard of the Purple Goose, just off High
Street, the rain suddenly stopped and a brilliant sun appeared
overhead. From one instant to the next, the pesky storm was
over.

Rohan was an Englishman. He should be used to the
weather, but this storm had taken him by surprise. He looked
up, cursed, and shook his fist at that wretched sun.

To his surprise, when Susannah came out from beneath
his coat, her bonnet feather straggling over her cheek and
ropes of wet hair hanging down her back, she looked at him
and laughed. "Wouldn't you just know it," she said, patting
Marianne's damp cheek. "Just look, lovey, it's a glorious
day again." Marianne nodded slowly, looked over at Rohan,
who appeared to be more drowned than not, and laughed
along with Susannah. Soon Toby joined them, then Jamie.
Gulliver, the bugger, whinnied, with Hera quick to answer.

Rohan didn't laugh. His bones felt sodden. He could practically feel the exquisite Spanish leather boots crumbling at
his abuse. The ostler came out of the inn at a dead run,
having quickly recognized the baron's curricle. If he wondered what his lordship was doing with a woman, two chil-

dren, and a stable lad, he had the good sense to keep it behind his tongue.

Within ten minutes, Susannah had stripped both herself and Marianne. She prayed that Rohan would do the same for Toby.

Surely he would.

And he was, at least he was trying. The boy was modest. He didn't want to take off his wet clothes in front of Rohan nor did he want any help. Rohan stood there perplexed for a moment, then suddenly remembered his own modesty when he'd been a boy of Toby's age. And George's. Oddly enough, Tibolt, the vicar, hadn't had a modest bone in his body, ever.

He said easily, "I'll have tubs of hot water fetched for us, Toby. When you get those wet clothes off, you wrap yourself in my dressing gown, the blue one over there on the bed. I'll be back in five minutes. Keep yourself warm."

That should give the boy enough time.

He also ordered hot water for Susannah and Marianne.

Since Toby wasn't about to bathe with him in there, Rohan took himself off to see to Jamie and the horses. Jamie was in the stable, already in dry clothes, singing to Gulliver while he brushed him. Even Hera looked interested as she chewed on a carrot.

> "When her daughter got married in Whister
> Her mother remarked as she kissed her,
> 'That fellow you've won
> Is sure to be fun—
> Since tea he's kissed me and your sisters.' "

Jamie was singing in a high falsetto. Over and over he sang the limerick until Rohan imagined that Gulliver would begin at any moment to tap his huge hooves against the straw. As for Hera, she nickered, but Rohan didn't know if it was a nicker for Gulliver or for the limerick.

"I must write these down," Rohan said as he clapped Jamie on his shoulder.

"I'll give 'em ye, milord," Jamie said easily, descending immediately into that god-awful English that was nonetheless very charming to the ear.

"In about an hour, you will come to the parlor in the inn for your dinner."

This Jamie took exception to, being just a stable lad, but Rohan had no intention of letting the boy out of his sight. If Jamie became ill from that blasted rain, they would all be in dire straits.

Thank the good Lord, no one became ill. As for Jamie, Rohan finally gave in and let him eat in the kitchen. Dinner was more peaceful than not because Marianne fell asleep in the middle of her soup. Toby was so fascinated with the barmaid who served them, all he could talk about was the expanse of her that showed.

"A gentleman," Susannah said finally, after frowning at him for several minutes—a ploy that didn't work—"does not speak of matters of that nature."

Rohan choked on the turtle soup. The barmaid's breasts were beyond big, they were vast. If he were Toby's age again, he would also be staring until his eyes fell into the soup.

"But, Susannah, how does she keep all that stuff inside her gown?"

"Gowns are designed to keep everything where it belongs. Believe me on this. Now, you will eat your soup, Toby, and when she returns with the beef, you will keep your head down or, if you must look at her in order to tell her what you want, you can look at her left ear."

Toby didn't ever give the barmaid's left ear a glance, but on the other hand, he wasn't so stupid as to remark out loud on her endowments again.

"You contained yourself well," Rohan told Toby when they were once again in their chamber.

"I just didn't know anything like that existed," Toby said in awe.

Rohan didn't say a word. Later, he turned his back until Toby was tucked into the truckle bed beside his bed. He was damned if he'd share a bed with a boy who probably flailed his way through the night.

"Oh, yes," Rohan said as he blew out the single candle. "There's a lot that you will learn exists. We will ease you into it gradually. Then when we're in London, I'll show you marvels that will leave you blank-brained. Why, we'll even go to Astley's."

He couldn't believe he'd made that offer. He scorned people who went to that vulgar place. But children adored the animal performances, and there were oranges to eat and candied almonds, and scantily clad girls who rode on the backs of horses. Ah, so much.

He could always send Pulver with the children. Yes, that was an excellent idea. That would serve gaunt-faced Pulver right for trying to stick his nose in the baron's business.

"Sleep well, my lord," Toby said.

Rohan grunted.

Thank the gods, no one sickened during the night, and they were on their way the following morning.

The weather held until they reached the Pilsney Hills, the highest of which overlooked Mountvale House. Rohan jumped down from the carriage seat and opened the door. "Everyone out. I want you to see my home. It's really quite lovely, what with the Channel beyond and the smell of the sea in the air."

It *was* lovely, Susannah thought, easing Marianne to the ground so she could walk with Toby to the peak of the hill.

Mountvale House sat atop a gentle flat-topped hill a mile in the distance. It was surrounded by maple and oak trees. Only one road wound its way to the house from the west, and it was thickly lined with trees and bushes. She knew that in the summer the trees would meet over the road to make a canopy. It would be incredibly beautiful. As for the house itself, it wasn't a vast mansion, tall and imposing, standing in the middle of nothing in a huge, grassy park. No, it was old, perhaps three hundred years or so, and its worn peach bricks were covered with thick green ivy. There was only a narrow front lawn lined with yew bushes. On all other sides there were gardens filled with more flowers than Susannah had ever seen in one place in her life. The gardens weren't flat and separated by hedges either. No, each of them was terraced until it nearly reached the edge of the forest. There were fences there, to keep out deer and other animals who would consume many of the plants in an instant. On the fences was jasmine that draped over and around, with small white and pink flowers. There were roses aplenty, blooming wildly, yellow daffodils, tulips as red as a stormy sunset, lilacs from the lightest lavender to the darkest purple, and so many other flowers and shrubs that it took Susannah's breath away.

"It's so beautiful," she said, ignoring the house, gazing fixedly at the terraced gardens. "In the middle of summer, it must be breathtaking."

"I'm glad you think so," Rohan said, completely indifferent. "Actually, there are few flowers at my house in London. Here, though, I have an army of gardeners. My mother wishes to have the house surrounded by greenery and color." He added as he flicked a nonexistent piece of lint from his jacket, "If you like you can give them advice, since my mother is abroad. You can direct them. If you want, you can even grovel in the dirt alongside them. I had the gardens terraced some four years ago. My mother wished it so."

"Do you ever grovel alongside the gardeners?"

He arched an elegant brow at her. "Hardly. I am not a gardener."

"Even though you did it for your mother, your selection of plants, the building of the gardens—it's all superb. I imagine that in July and August the house disappears. All the eye can see is bright and vivid color." She turned to look up at him, a quite lovely smile on her mouth. "Someday perhaps your mother will design a garden for me."

"You can ask that of my mother when you meet her," he said slowly. He looked down again at his sleeve, saying, "Old Cupability Brown gave her a good deal of fodder for designs. As I said, I did her bidding and carried everything out."

"His name is Capability, isn't it?"

He just grinned down at her.

Her face was radiant. She clutched at his sleeve. "Oh, thank you. To work in those beautiful gardens—I should like that above all things. But isn't that a rather tame sort of activity for a man of your nature?"

Actually, he thought, cursing himself, he didn't know any gentleman of his reputed nature to be even remotely interested in gardens, regardless of whether or not his mama had inspired the idea. He said easily, "A man should have many parts, I've always believed. Now what do you mean, 'my nature'?"

She had the grace to flush just a bit and shrugged, "It's nothing, really."

"Ah, you were being impertinent?"

"Well, you are well known for wildness, aren't you? Just as were your parents?"

"You told me that George said this."

"Yes, and—Marianne! No! Toby, catch her!"

She was off at a dead run, Jamie chasing behind her. Gulliver, curse the bugger, was running after Jamie.

Rohan raised his face to the sky. "My life was perfect just four days ago. Why, Lord?"

Then he sprinted after his horse.

He heard Hera neigh behind him and knew she'd be passing him any minute. Jamie had been riding Gulliver and leading old Hera. Now there she was, her mane streaming, dashing after Gulliver like a colt. Or was it Jamie? Even the two nags pulling the carriage were prancing about; he wondered if they too would be on the run any minute.

Marianne didn't tumble off the peak of the hill, but it was close. Toby was stuttering with fear and wanted to throttle her for scaring him so badly.

Rohan watched Susannah pick up the little girl, give her a good shake, then hug her so tightly that she yelled.

Blessed silence. It was satisfying to be able to actually hear his spoon move through the thick lobster soup. He tapped the spoon against the side of the exquisite golden bowl. It made a fine, tinny sound.

He looked down the expanse of the dining table to see Susannah gazing around her, not with awe but with a critical eye. He frowned. What the devil did she have to be critical about? Mulberry House was a slum compared to Mountvale.

"You don't care for Mrs. Horsely's lobster soup?"

"It's quite good, as I can see by your empty bowl. No, I was just thinking about how I'd forgotten how silence didn't make any noise at all."

He didn't like that observation. He didn't want to be echoing her thoughts or hearing her echo his. It was unnerving.

He said abruptly, "I must find you a chaperon. Mrs. Beete, while a maiden lady of a goodly number of years, is the housekeeper, not a companion. Let me think. There must be some unattached lady hereabouts who could still any tongues that exhalt in wagging."

"It seems rather silly, doesn't it? I'm a grown woman, a widow, and yet Society still deems it improper for me to stay in the same house with a gentleman. Not, of course, that you are necessarily a gentleman in all circumstances."

"Are you being impertinent again, ma'am?"

"Oh, no. It's just that I was nourished for five years on tales about you. George never tired of recounting your adventures."

Adventures? What bloody adventures?

She was smiling at him—no, it was closer to a smirk. He said easily, "Truth be told, I have only begun my adventures. I am not yet turned twenty-six. Surely I shall fill a dozen weighty tomes with scores of adventures by the time I finally shuck off my mortal coil. Ah . . . what sorts of adventures did George recount?''

She said nothing more until a footman in bright crimson and white had removed the soup. The butler, Mr. Fitz, directed two other footmen to bring another half-dozen silver dishes, all covered with silver domes.

"There seems to be quite a lot of food here," she said, her voice just a bit awed, finally. He didn't tell her that he'd asked Mrs. Horsely to outdo herself for his guest. Why he'd done that, he had no idea. As Fitz lifted off the silver domes, abundant rich odors rose, mingled, and wafted. Rohan's stomach growled.

Susannah was indeed awed now. There were lamb cutlets and asparagus peas, veal, curried lobster, and even a plate filled with oyster patties. There were bowls of peas, potatoes, stewed mushrooms, and more plates that she couldn't see because they'd been set too close to the baron.

He remarked in a bland voice, "Ah, yes, I specifically requested Charlotte à la Parisienne. Don't you think it looks delicious?''

Susannah had no idea what this Charlotte done in the Parisian way even was. Ah, but that look he was giving her. "No," she said as she spooned a bit of boiled tongue and broccoli onto her plate. "I don't think it looks all that tasty. Perhaps it has been cooked a bit too long? Perhaps the Charlotte was a bit long in the tooth before she went into the pot?''

He laughed, then stopped abruptly. He had to stop doing this. It wasn't what he, Rohan Carrington, Baron Mountvale, was supposed to do. He was supposed to sneer and seduce. He had a reputation to maintain. He had countless more adventures to launch, and laughing immoderately at a silly something a lady said simply wasn't appropriate. Not for him.

His fond mama would be aghast.

"The ratafia ice pudding is very good," she said after he

hadn't opened his mouth for a good ten minutes, except to shovel in food. He'd laughed at her jest about the Charlotte, yet he'd instantly shut it off, just like a spigot. It was odd. Didn't he like to laugh? Did he not laugh until after a certain hour? She was coming to like him, but she didn't understand him.

He merely nodded now. He tried to look bored, but he was eating Mrs. Horsely's sea-kale, and it was so good that all he could do was look blissful.

When Toby burst into the dining room with two footmen at his heels and Mr. Fitz following more sedately, his white hair standing on end, Rohan bounded out of his chair.

"Oh, my goodness," Toby gasped, panting hard. "Sir, hurry! Susannah, you, too."

Rohan didn't have a chance to ask what the devil was the matter. Toby was already out of the room. He could hear his pounding footsteps going back up the stairs.

"My lord," Mr. Fitz said, then abruptly stopped, for what was there to say? "I will come along," he said and motioned to the footmen to follow him.

Susannah nearly passed Rohan on the stairs. At the landing, they heard a shriek.

"Oh, God." Susannah grabbed her skirts up to her knees and ran as fast as she could toward her bedchamber, where she'd put Marianne down for the night some three hours before.

Toby was standing in the doorway, dancing up and down, waving, calling out, "Hurry, hurry!"

Rohan simply picked the boy up and moved him behind him. He ran into the room—only to draw up. At first he didn't see anything. Then he saw the open window. Then he saw Marianne crouched outside on the narrow balcony, humming, waving her hands.

It was a drop of a good thirty feet to the ground.

Susannah lightly placed her fingers on his sleeve. She called out quietly, "Marianne? Lovey, what are you doing out there?"

The little girl looked back at her mother. "The man opened the window. He said I'd have fun out here."

What man? But Rohan didn't say it out loud. He saw the panic in Susannah's eyes, and ignored it for the moment. "Marianne," he said very quietly, "Your papa used to sit on that ledge when he was a little boy. It is fun. However, it's late now. It's dark. A sharp wind might blow up and whisk you right over the Channel to France. You don't want to go to France without your mama, do you?"

"Maybe," Marianne said after a moment of thought.

"Lovey," Susannah said quietly as she began walking toward the open window. "I don't want you to move. I don't want you to whisk away to France without me. When you whisk anywhere it will be with me. Now, don't you move. I'm going to bring you back inside."

"I'll get her," Rohan said.

But Susannah was already at the open window. It was set high off the floor and she frowned at that. She managed to pull herself up onto the window ledge. "Don't move, Marianne." Susannah crawled out onto the balcony, slowly, very slowly, speaking quietly to Marianne all the while.

Toby stood beside Rohan, the two of them stiff as boards, not speaking. Mr. Fitz and the footmen stood silent as the dead just inside the nursery door.

"That's it, lovey, that's it. Now, turn around and come to Mama. Don't look toward France. I don't want you to whisk off. That's right, crawl to Mama. Good girl, that's it."

"Oh, my," Toby breathed out when Susannah had Marianne pressed against her. "Oh, my."

"Indeed," Rohan said. He stepped forward, took Marianne from Susannah, and tucked her under one arm. He gave Susannah his other hand and hauled her back through the window.

Rohan sat down in the elegant rocking chair in the corner of the room. "Light more candles," he told Fitz. Then he began rocking Marianne. After a while, he said, very quietly, "What man was here, Marianne?"

6

SHE REARED BACK IN HIS ARMS. SHE RAISED ONE DAMP
finger that she'd been sucking to touch the cleft in his chin.

"Come, Marianne, what man?"

Still staring at that cleft, she said, "A nice man. He said
he'd let me sit on the ledge if I would stop yelling. He said
he had to find something. He said it was all right for him to
be here because he knew you."

"He opened the window for you?"

Marianne nodded.

"He set you on the window ledge?"

"No. He put a chair next to the window. I got up all by
myself."

Good Lord. "Did you stop yelling?"

She grinned at him. Naturally she'd stopped. What a forbidden treat the man had offered to her.

"Marianne, can you tell me what the man looked like?"

"You," she said, pressing her middle finger against the
cleft in his chin. "He looked like you." Tired. She collapsed
against his chest. Sucking was the only sound in Susannah's
bedchamber. Rohan said quietly, "Do you think she'll sleep
through the night now?"

Susannah could only nod. She stood there, stiff with
shock, nearly as frightened as she'd been for those endless

hours she'd spent with her mother in labor. There'd been nothing she could do then. But now, she was the mother. Marianne was her responsibility. And she could have died.

"Susannah? Just stop it. Marianne is fine. Can't you hear her slurping on her fingers? Get hold of yourself. That's better. Now take her and put her down. I will have one of the maids stay with her until you come to bed. I'll have two maids come if you would like."

"Two maids," Susannah said.

"At least," Toby said, so white in the face Rohan thought he would be ill. "Make one of them a man. With a gun."

By nine o'clock that evening the house had been thoroughly searched, all the doors and windows secured, and footmen set to patrol the house throughout the night.

The baron, Susannah, and Toby sat in the Mountvale drawing room, a lovely room that smelled of fine old silk, rich oak, and lemon wax.

Toby was saying, "You told me, sir, just to look in on Marianne before I went to bed. Well, I just walked in, sir, and there she was, sitting out there, singing and talking to herself until she saw me. Then she wanted me to come out and play with her. I told her no, told her to come in this minute, but she wouldn't. I tried to get her in, but the little nit just scooted closer to the edge. It nearly flipped my heart over. I'm sorry, sir."

"Don't be silly, Toby. You did precisely the right thing. My own heart was in my throat when I saw her. You did well."

"Do you have any other brothers, my lord, except Vicar Tibolt?" Susannah said. She was seated so quietly, her eyes never leaving Marianne, who was all tucked up on a settee in the shadows of the corner of the drawing room, the maid on one side of her and the footman on the other.

Rohan slowly nodded. "No, just Tibolt. But he wouldn't harm any of God's varmints, as he calls children. He's got humor about him, although our parents never admitted to it, and he positively reeks of goodwill. No, Tibolt isn't the man who opened that window and put the chair next to it for Marianne to climb out on the balcony.''

"Tibolt?"

"Yes, Toby. My father gave the naming of one boy to my mother and he named the other. My mother was the one who selected the name George. My father likes the unusual, the extraordinary even. I believe Tibolt was a bishop in ancient Constantinople. Perhaps George told you that our father was renowned for his, ah, benign wickedness. He thought it a great joke. Naturally, he wanted Tibolt to be just as wicked as he was. My father hoped the irony of it would amuse him until he stuck his spoon in the wall.''

"Goodness," Toby said, "I'm glad Papa didn't do anything like that to me.''

"It appears that there ended up being no irony at all,'' Susannah said.

"Indeed.''

Toby gave a loud yawn.

"It's time for you to go to bed, Toby,'' Susannah said.

Toby stood up immediately, but he didn't move. He looked down at his toes.

"What's the matter, love?'' Susannah asked.

Toby blurted out, "Could I sleep in your bedchamber, sir? It's not that I'm scared, but, well—''

"I was going to suggest it, Toby. I think it might make me feel a good deal better if you were to sleep in my bedchamber,'' Rohan said. He sighed. An eight-year-old boy sleeping in his chamber? Well, they'd done it for the past three nights. The boy didn't snore. If Rohan did, Toby hadn't said anything. Rohan rose. "I'll tell Fitz to fetch a bed to my room.''

"I don't like what happened, sir.''

"Neither do I. On the morrow, I will see if I can't figure out who visited Marianne. It certainly wasn't my brother Tibolt.'' It couldn't have been Tibolt. Marianne was just a little girl. She was wrong about the man looking like him.

He looked over at Susannah as he spoke. Again, he saw

the stab of panic in her eyes. And something else. Fear? What the hell was going on here? He didn't say anything until Toby had left the room. "Now, perhaps you'd like to tell me what this man was looking for?"

His voice was soft and soothing, just the sort of voice to make one spill one's deepest secrets without hesitation. She shook her head, shaking that damned voice away. She didn't know what to do. She picked up the sleeping Marianne and settled her over her shoulder. Then she left the drawing room, Rohan behind her.

She said finally, her voice quiet so as not to disturb Marianne, "There is something, but I can't believe it would have anything to do with this."

"Will you allow me to be the judge of that?"

"I think I'm being silly."

"Tell me."

"You sound, my lord, like a judge, all stiff and mean," she said as they walked side by side up the front staircase.

"*My lord?*" He cocked a thick brow at her. "Surely after watching you climb through a window and out onto a balcony—your ankles all bare, your stockings showing to your knees—shouldn't you give it up and call me Rohan again?"

She wouldn't look at him. They stopped at her bedchamber door. She laid Marianne down on her own bed, and the child began sucking on her fingers.

"Tell me. Let me decide if it's silly or not."

There was no hope for it. Actually, she realized she wanted to tell him everything. She didn't want to keep this to herself any longer. She said baldly, "The first break-in at Mulberry House was just before last Christmas. We were all out visiting neighbors. When we returned, we found papers scattered everywhere, furniture tipped over, several of my mother's Dresden shepherdesses thrown to the floor and broken. Nothing seemed to be missing. Then, two months later, the same thing happened again. Only this time, Toby came home earlier than expected. He was struck over the head. And just three weeks ago there was another robbery."

"Only nothing was taken."

"No, but whoever did it made a horrible mess all three times. I guess that was another reason I didn't argue so much about coming with you. I was terrified that one of us would be in the house if and when the robber came again. Toby wasn't badly hurt, but it scared me to death."

"You have no idea who the robber was?"

"No idea at all."

"You have no idea what the robber was after?"

"No."

"Well, since he returned to Mulberry House three times, he obviously didn't find what he was looking for. It seems doubtful he found it the third time either. And you're wondering if the man followed you here to Mountvale?"

She leaned against the wall next to the closed door of her bedchamber. They could see candlelight from beneath the door. "Do you think it's possible?"

"Yes, of course. All we have to do is figure out what it is this man wants."

"I've thought and thought. We have so little, nothing of any interest to anyone. No, I have no idea at all."

"Perhaps you could have given me a bit of warning?"

His voice was low and gentle, but she wasn't fooled. She saw the pounding of the pulse in his neck. He was very angry. "I'm sorry. I honestly believed that no one saw us leave. I thought everything would change when we left Mulberry House and came with you. I never wanted to place you in danger. Oh, God, Marianne could have fallen off that ledge."

"Stop it. Marianne is fine. You can hear her sucking her fingers. Very well, now that I know what is happening, I can take steps. You are tired, Susannah. Why don't you put yourself next to Marianne on the bed?" He gently touched his hand to Marianne's soft hair. "Don't worry. We'll speak more about this tomorrow. I'm not blaming you, at least not too much. Good night, Susannah."

"Good night, my lord."

He grunted at that, turned on his heel, and took himself to his imposing bedchamber. He shaded the candle with his cupped hand to keep the light out of the boy's eyes, the boy who was sleeping not three feet from him on a truckle bed. He looked too pale lying there, a shock of black hair falling over his forehead. A handsome boy certainly, but more important, Toby was a good lad, intelligent, and he deserved better than what his damned father would provide for him, which would be almost nothing, curse his blackmailing heart.

He shook his head at himself. Good God, was he now to play the role of the boy's father? Rohan sighed. He was only twenty-five. A man of his reputation wasn't supposed to even recognize the existence of children.

Life had become very complicated. Seducing a woman was surely boy's play compared to this. He rather thought he would like to retire to Tibolt's vicarage for a week or two, to relieve the strain on his nerves. Before he fell asleep he wondered why Toby hadn't said anything about the break-ins at Mulberry House. Because his sister had asked him not to. He had a lot to think about.

That night Toby snored.

All the servants were standing in a line in the entrance hall the following morning, obviously waiting for him.

He eyed them as he walked down the stairs. He said to his butler, in that easy way of his, "It looks to be a blowy day, Fitz."

"Yes, my lord, it does. Perhaps my lord would like a cup of coffee whilst Ben here tells you what he found near to the stables? And whilst you eat your scrambled eggs, Mrs. Beete can tell you what she heard in the middle of the night? You can chew thoughtfully on your toast whilst Elsie tells you what she knows, that is, if she knows anything at all. Indeed, I do not believe that I will allow her in the breakfast parlor. I will pass along her story."

Fitz's hair was standing a bit on end, and that was a shock. The Carrington butler of twenty-five years, who had himself set Rohan on his first pony, didn't look at all content. As for Mrs. Beete, the Carrington housekeeper for longer than twenty-five years, who had come to the house when his mother had married his father, she looked at him like a vicar would look at a sinner who refused to renounce his wicked ways. It was odd, though, for she looked at Tibolt just the same way, and the good Lord knew that everyone believed him to be holy.

Rohan nodded. "Very well. Mrs. Beete, when Mrs. Carrington comes down, please see that she has all she needs for the little girl."

"Just imagine, my lord," Mrs. Beete said in her lilting soft country accent, "Master George being secretly married all these years. Such a timid, scholarly boy he always was. It still fairly noodles my brain."

"It noodles mine as well."

Fitz said in a very quiet voice, "I would have doubted it, my lord, but the little lass is the image of Master George. So wonderful it is to have something of Master George live on. Actually she's also the image of your mother and you as well, my lord."

"Yes, I know. Now, as for Toby—"

"I'm here, sir."

"Ah, so you are. You were still snoring when I left you. Did you wash?"

The boy looked down at his toes. "Well, not exactly."

"Go back upstairs with Rory. He will help you. He wants to become a valet. He can practice on you. Now, Fitz, Mrs. Beete, let's go to the breakfast room and you can recount all the happenings of the night."

Ben had found a swatch of dark blue wool snagged on a low tree branch near the stables. "So you believe that a man was riding too close to the tree and ripped this material off his coat?"

Ben nodded. "It looked that way, my lord."

"It also looks fresh," Rohan said, turning the wool over in his hand. It was finely woven. No common scoundrel had worn this. This was a gentleman's quality wool. He slipped the piece of fabric into his pocket.

"Now, Mrs. Beete, what did you hear?"

"As you know, my lord, my suite of rooms is at the far end of the house. I woke up toward the middle of the night. I realized that I must have heard something. I went to my window and looked down. There was a man there, my lord, tucked away in the shadows just beyond the second garden terrace."

"Why didn't you raise the house?"

"Well, my lord, I couldn't believe my eyes at first, not after all the excitement, and so I shook my head a minute before I looked again. When I looked the second time, the man was no longer there. It's possible that I imagined him, what with all those flowers of your lordship's weaving about in even a slight breeze and the shadows cast by the forest trees."

"And Elsie?"

"Oh, that silly girl," Mrs. Beete said. "She is new to Mountvale, my lord, and doesn't yet realize that she cannot indulge in Drama. She is known in Braisley as a flighty girl given to exaggeration and tomfoolery. She enjoys attention, my lord."

"She's very young," Rohan said, remembering the skinny little redheaded girl peeking at him from behind a god-awful statue in the corridor on the second floor. "Let her be a bit flighty, Mrs. Beete."

"Yes, my lord. That was my intention. Actually, my lord, I thought your mama would enjoy the girl, and that is why I have overlooked her lapses."

"That is kind of you, Mrs. Beete. Now, Fitz, what did Elsie say about all this?"

Fitz cleared his throat. He looked plainly embarrassed. "She said, my lord, that she saw a man in the gardens. This man wasn't alone. There was a female with him, a female with abundant yellow hair. They appeared to be in the throes of intimacy, my lord."

"Ah. And what else did they do to arouse Elsie's suspicions?"

"Well, it appears that Elsie decided to confront them. She wanted to know who they were, but when she got to the gardens, they were gone. That is her story, my lord."

"So we have some amorous neighbors or servants."

Fitz looked clearly shocked.

Mrs. Beete turned red. "Nonsense, my lord. Our neighbors or servants are never amorous, particularly in your lordship's gardens."

Rohan wondered what his fond mama would have to say to that. He would have to remember to tell her when she returned from Italy. He hoped she would come to Mountvale. She preferred London, truth be told, although she occasionally yielded to the call of a handsome country footman. Rohan looked at the footmen in their crimson and ivory uniforms. Ah, that man—Augustus, from Wales—he just might bring his mama on a visit to Mountvale. He was dark as a sinner, his eyes a wicked dark brown. He looked strong, muscular, and was certainly not over thirty. Rohan could only shake his head. No blaming her. He was her son, as she had reminded him often enough, giving him one of her brilliant smiles. His papa had reminded him often enough too, slapping him on the back from the time he'd been only fourteen years old and nearly sending him into the wainscoting.

Rohan needed Pulver. He also needed his valet. He penned a quick letter to his secretary and sent Augustus off to London to fetch both of them. He was chewing on the nib of his quill pen when he remembered his Aunt Miranda, who lived in Brighton. An answer to prayer. Of course she would be delighted to come to Mountvale and play chaperon. After all, he supported her. He only hoped she was still alive.

She was leaning over a plot of primroses, red, pink, blue, gold, and white flowers all spilling over each other. He saw her lightly touch one of the crinkly light green leaves. He himself was particularly fond of primroses, not of course that

he had ever remarked on it when with his friends in London.
But, truth be told, their vivid colors warmed him to his toes.

On either side of her were two of his gardeners, Ozzie and
Tom Harker, brothers who had been in his family's service
for more years than Rohan had been on the earth. They were
both very tall, very thin, and nearly bald. All three of them
were talking with a good deal of animation. If he wasn't
mistaken, Ozzie looked rather pained. As for Tom, he was
grinning from ear to ear. He wondered what was going on.

"Good morning," Rohan called out.

The men straightened, but she didn't. He heard her begin
to whistle. He nodded to Ozzie and Tom and watched them
take their rakes and trowels off to a distant plot of stocks.

"Did you know," Rohan said not one foot from her ear,
"that fairies take shelter under primrose leaves during rain-
storms?"

"Oh, yes," she said, not turning to look at him. "Did you
know that when Saint Peter dropped the keys to heaven they
became primroses wherever they landed on earth?"

"Ah, but I can top that one, Susannah. Did you know that
the primrose is a symbol for wantonness?"

She did turn to face him then. She didn't look at all
shocked or offended. Instead she was grinning. "I should
have expected you to know that. Indeed, that's the only reason you know anything about primroses at all, am I not
right?"

He said, his eyes clear and calm, "Did you love George?"

"You think to take me off balance? To make me spill out
my innards without thinking?"

"I am accounted to be rather good at it. I would appreciate
it if you would begin to spill."

"I will tell you the truth, my lord. There is no reason not
to. In the beginning, yes, of course I loved George. Later,
well, he made it difficult. He came rarely to Mulberry
House."

"You will tell me about how difficult he made things for
you later. I've been thinking about our adventure last night.

Let's say that the fellow who searched Mulberry House three times managed to follow us here to Mountvale. Let's say he somehow discovered which room you were in, managed to slither his way into the house without a soul observing him, cajoled Marianne so that she'd be quiet. Then, I fear, Toby must have come into your bedchamber. He didn't see the man. He must have been hiding behind the door. Toby runs out to get us. The man again manages to slither out of the house with no one observing him, but he does rip his coat on a tree limb near the stables.'' Rohan pulled the swatch of dark blue wool out of his coat pocket and handed it to her. "Ben, one of the stable lads, found this early this morning. I don't suppose you recognize it?''

"No, I don't. It appears he didn't have time to do anything. There was no mess, no ripped up valises, no papers tossed to the floor. Oh, God, what if he had hurt Toby?''

"He didn't. Forget it.''

She looked at him. It was odd, but she really looked at him for the first time. She was still so afraid that her brain was barely working, but yet she was staring at him, recognizing that he was beautiful. He was tall, but he wasn't massively built. Rather he was lean, well formed, she could see that clearly what with him wearing tight buckskin breeches. His face was well sculpted, almost too perfect a face for its own good. And those eyes of his—Susannah imagined that if he turned those eyes on a woman, she would have little resistance. They were a dark green, as cold as a winter sky if he was displeased or as hot as the roiling sea if he was laughing. Or doing other things. Interesting other things. With her, perhaps. She shook herself. This was ridiculous. He was a womanizer. It was his stock-in-trade.

"Would you care to tell me why you're staring at me?''

She shook her head.

"Ah, then perhaps you'd care to tell me what you're thinking?''

Why not? "I was thinking it's a good thing you're beautiful. Surely a man who was also a womanizer wouldn't be all that successful at it if he looked like a toad."

"Beautiful? Me?" He began to laugh. He laughed louder.
Mrs. Beete called down from an open upstairs window, "My
lord! Are you feeling just the thing? Perhaps cook's breakfast
kidneys made you a bit liverish?"

He'd laughed again. He'd even laughed loudly. No wonder
Mrs. Beete thought he was sick. He called up to her, "I am
liverish. There is no other explanation."

"Why," Susannah said, "does Mrs. Beete think you're
ill? You look perfectly fit to me. You're grinning, not at-
tending at all. Very well, then. Did you know that the Harker
brothers want to give me a racing kitten? They say they will
teach me how to train it, but the training process must be
kept secret. I have never heard of racing cats before, but
perhaps it could prove interesting. What do you think?"

And he laughed again. Then, quite suddenly, he was quite
serious. "A racing kitten? No, surely you have misunderstood them."

"No, that is what they're giving me."

"It isn't fair," he said, kicking a rock with the toe of his
boot. "They never offered me a racing kitten. Why did they
offer you one? They only just met you. How can they possibly know that you can deal with one of their racing kittens?
You could bungle the whole thing."

"I will let you train the kitten with me, if you like."

It was half a bone. He took it, but he didn't like it. "Very
well," he said finally, his voice all grudging, "but I still
wanted my very own. Curse them."

7

ROHAN SAT BACK IN HIS VERY COMFORTABLE LEATHER chair behind the huge mahogany desk in the library. He'd done all he could for the moment. There was a quiet knock on the door.

"Come," he called out.

It was Fitz, standing taller than he had in at least five years. He looked as arrogant as a peer of the realm on his worst days, but today he could be the king. He said with grave formality, "I've got all the men together, my lord. They await you on the east lawn."

There were men from Mountvale village, many tenant farmers on the estate, and all his people as well. Even Mrs. Beete was standing beneath an apple tree, her arms folded over her massive bosom. Ozzie Harker was holding one of Rohan's best mousers in his arms, rubbing its chin. The brindle cat looked blissful. The brindle cat was also supposedly half wild.

At least seventy-five men and a sprinkling of women stood there. He saw Susannah standing near the back, holding Marianne in her arms, Toby beside her.

They all looked grim.

"Thank you for coming," Rohan began. "You all know by now that a man broke into the house last night. He tried to search Mrs. Carrington's bedchamber, but Toby chased him off. How he managed to get in, how he knew which bedchamber belonged to Mrs. Carrington, I don't know. Ben found a piece of wool on a tree branch near the stables this morning.'' Rohan motioned for the men to pass it around. ''I want you to keep your eyes open. If you see any stranger, anyone wearing clothing of this blue, immediately inform Mr. Fitz.''

He offered a reward, which was well received, then offered all the men Mrs. Horsely's famous cider, but only a single glass. More than one glass and the drinker would take off his clothes and dance while singing a bawdy song.

To no one's surprise, the men cheered the cider louder than they did the reward.

Later, Rohan handed Fitz the sealed letter. ''Post it, please, Fitz. It's very important.''

''London, I see, my lord.''

''Yes, to a gentleman I can trust. Phillip Mercerault, Viscount Derencourt.''

''We have not had this much excitement since your dear mama fell from that pear tree into Raymond's arms, not that this is the kind of excitement that leads to a serene and settled state of mind. You remember the footman, Raymond, don't you, my lord? A very nice young man, of good character and pleasant humor. I will never forget how fortunate it was that he was standing at that particular moment beneath the pear tree.''

Was Fitz indulging in irony? It seemed more than likely.

''No, this is far more exciting. You didn't see Marianne sitting on the edge of the balcony. Actually, I long for some boredom. This could be dangerous, Fitz.''

''I understand this same man broke into Mrs. Carrington's house three times?''

How had he known that? Rohan blinked away the question and just raised a brow. Fitz knew everything.

''It appears to be the same man. And that is why I have written to a gentleman I trust in London. Is breakfast ready?''

"Yes, my lord. Miss Marianne is in the nursery with Betty. Master Toby is in the village acquainting himself with the vicar, as you suggested he do."

"Yes. Mr. Byam gives lessons, as you know. I wish Toby to determine if he would like to tutor with him. I trust Mrs. Carrington isn't yet occupied training her racing kitten."

"No, my lord. The racing kitten doesn't arrive until next week. Mr. Harker doesn't like to hurry these things. He believes it's bad for the feline's mental works. Mrs. Carrington awaits you in the breakfast parlor."

She chewed on the slice of ham, the slice so thin she could nearly see through it. It was the most delicious ham she'd eaten in her life.

"I have written both to my mother to tell her of her grand-motherhood and to my aunt Miranda, who, if she's still walking on terra firma rather than lying in it, can come to live here."

She stopped chewing. She had changed her gown. This one was muslin, a green faded from too many washings, that was banded with a dark strip of green beneath her breasts. The sleeves were short and puffed, the neck high with lace trimming. Her shining brown hair was tied back with a black ribbon and hung halfway down her back.

"You are going to a lot of trouble, my lord. Are you certain that you wish to—"

"Yes. Also, you have very nice hair," he said, realizing in the same instant that he wanted to slide that thick hair through his fingers, something he hadn't realized just the day before. He pulled his thoughts up short and helped himself to scrambled eggs. He wanted to pull a curtain of her hair to his face and smell her scent and feel her hair on his cheek. He had to get a hold on himself. This wasn't at all like him. He cleared his throat, but what came out of his mouth as a prelude wasn't what he planned. "Your eyes are a nice shade of gray blue. However, your gowns—at least the ones I've seen—aren't worthy enough. They look like you've worn them for a decade. They are on the edge. I have decided to have a dressmaker from Eastbourne come to see to things.''

Her fork clattered to her plate. Her face was no longer serene. It was suddenly splotched with color. "My lord, you will not. All you have to do is give me George's money. I will see to myself, Marianne, and Toby. Truly, you are very kind, but I do not wish you to spend your own money on me, and I do not wish to be indebted to you.''

"I can't give you the twenty thousand pounds.''

Baldly said, but there it was.

"But you told me—''

"I told you that you had to live as one of the Carringtons, which you are. You are also to be the responsibility of the head of the family, in this particular case, it is I. Aunt Mariam's will specifies that.''

"But then where does the twenty thousand pounds come in? If I continue to live here, can I not have it?''

"Oh, no, you're to have an allowance. The inheritance is paid out in small increments each quarter, until you're a very old lady.''

"That is a very strange bequest. Also, I am a widow, George's widow. Surely she can't have meant to foist a widow off on the Carrington family? Surely a widow shouldn't have to deal with an allowance?''

He shrugged, slowly chewed another bite of bacon—crispy, as he liked it. The ground seemed a bit shaky beneath his feet, but he persevered. "Sorry,'' he said. "There's no way around it. You're a Carrington. The will states that you are my responsibility. However, you don't have to live here. If you would prefer to live with Tibolt at the vicarage, it's about twenty miles east of here in Edgeton-on-Hough. But it is very small. I doubt Toby would fit in. Besides, Tibolt will have to marry in the near future. Surely you wouldn't want to intrude on newly married persons?''

"You are saying you are the only Carrington?''

"The only *available* Carrington. No, there is also my mother. She enjoys traveling a great deal and doesn't spend all that much time in England. But when she comes for a visit, perhaps she will look at her granddaughter, sigh with grandmotherly delight, and decide to sink roots.'' He frowned over that. ''However, I wouldn't count on that happening. In fact, I have a very difficult time picturing such a thing. My mother is fancy-free, you know.''

She laughed at that, throwing up her hands. ''Your mother, sir, sounds like an original.''

''Oh, she is. I am quite fond of her. Now, about some new gowns for you—''

''No, I don't believe so. When will you give me my allowance? I plan to save it.''

How the devil could a will forbid saving the wretched inheritance? All Rohan knew was that he wasn't about to let her leave Mountvale. Why? Common sense didn't matter in this case. She wasn't leaving.

''You could save a bit, I suppose. But you know, I plan to do a bit of entertaining. You will act as my hostess. You cannot be a Carrington hostess in any of the gowns I've seen.''

She concentrated on the small pile of eggs at the edge of her plate. ''I will think about it,'' she said finally, not looking at him.

It was a dark, stormy night, the kind of night that made Rohan itchy and restless. He was pacing his library. He stopped and drank the tea in the bottom of his cup. It was cold.

''My lord.''

He nearly tripped, he turned about so quickly at the sound of her voice. Susannah was standing in the doorway, her rich hair long and loose down her back, wearing a faded light blue nightgown and a dark blue dressing gown, both suitable for a maiden lady of indeterminate years. It had probably belonged to her mother, or to her grandmother. It didn't matter. She looked altogether delicious. He hadn't thought she looked delicious at all yesterday or the day before, but he did now. It made no sense. He wouldn't put up with this. She was a mother, for God's sake. She was also delicious— no, that was absurd.

He meant his voice to sound unfeeling, and it did. "It is after midnight. What do you want?"

"I remembered something that perhaps could be helpful to us. I saw the candlelight from beneath the door and thought to tell you."

He pointed to a chair. As she walked in front of the fire-place toward him, the embers suddenly spurted into flame. He saw clearly through the dressing gown, through the night-gown.

He swallowed. He needed to go to London. He needed distance from her. Just a bit of distance and she would return to normal and so would he. Why hadn't he doused the embers in the fireplace?

He swallowed again. "Sit down," he said, this time louder. If she didn't move out of that blasted light, he would find himself in the situation of having to sit quickly behind his desk. Surely she would realize what that meant, partic- ularly if his eyes were glazed over at the same time, he was staring at her breasts, and he had difficulty speaking plainly and clearly.

She moved to stand behind a wing chair, leaning slightly forward. It brought more hair over her shoulder to cascade over her left breast. It was a very seductive pose. Didn't she realize that? Was she doing this on purpose?

"What did you think might be important?"

She cocked her head at him. His voice was harsh and he wasn't smiling. "You are in a strange mood tonight, my lord."

"I am not in any kind of mood and I forbid you to speak of it."

She grinned at him, unable not to. He was being perverse and, oddly, it was quite charming. He looked harassed. Her smile fell away. It was because she'd brought all this trouble to his door. It was all because of her father's letter. She prayed that Mrs. Heron was skinning her father at cards, winning every groat he got his hands on. At least if he had nothing to bet with, he would have to remain at Mulberry House. Even now the baron must be cursing both her and her father for the predicament he was in. She looked down at her clasped hands and sighed.

"I'm sorry I have brought you all this misery. It's all my fault, I well realize it."

"But you knew the thief just might come here along with you, did you not?"

"Yes, but not really. Well, I hoped he would give up once he saw where we were coming. After all, this is a real house, not like Mulberry House." She looked down at the soft brocade on the chair and began to pet it as though it were a cat. The material was soft and warm, and he suddenly imagined her hands on him, petting him. He snarled. He would shortly be a candidate for Bedlam. He heard her say, her voice filled with even more misery, even more apology, "It was possible and I knew it. I suppose that means, despite any excuses, that I'm not a very good person."

"Yes, that is what it would mean."

The hurt was unexpected. She looked up then. "It's the children. I couldn't leave the children in danger."

"It appears they are still in danger."

He was right and she felt flattened by his words. She tried to straighten her shoulders, but it was difficult. She said very quietly, "Is this quarterly allowance enough for me to afford a small cottage near Mountvale, since I must be your responsibility and must stay near you? I will take the children and leave. Your life can become again what it was."

He gave her a mean look. "Just what do you mean by that? 'Your life can become again what it was.' " He mimicked the condemnation in her voice, the sarcasm.

Her chin went up. She hadn't really meant that, even though it was true. He was looking at her as if he'd like to throw her out the library window. They were large windows—she'd remarked upon them earlier. He could do it.

"You are an unmarried man," she said, trying to be conciliatory. "You have the reputation of a gentleman who lives life for his own pleasure, for his own gratification, and at his whim, for—"

"That is quite enough." He plowed his fingers through his already disordered hair. He had very nice hair, she thought, even though it was standing on end. "Listen, it was my idea that you come and live here. This cottage notion of yours is ridiculous. The thief would have you at his mercy just like he did at Mulberry House. At least here at Mountvale you are somewhat more secure, the children as well. Now, all of this is nonsense. Why did you come in here? What is this miraculous information you have to impart?"

She accepted his dismissal and said, "When I was with George in Oxford some two years ago, some of his friends came into the inn where we were lunching. He introduced them to me."

It was out of his mouth before he could stop it. "How did they treat you?"

"It's strange that you ask." Good God, her innocence was frightening. At least he knew for certain that she had no idea of her real status.

She thought about it a moment, then continued. "They treated me well enough, I suppose, but they seemed to me to have too many high spirits, a lot of backslapping— George's back—and jests I didn't understand. After they left, George seemed a bit embarrassed. His face was red. He wanted to take me home, and he did. He never took me to Oxford again."

"What were the friends' names?"

"I remember only one name for certain and only because it struck me as odd. Theodore Micah. The other man's name—and this is just a wild guess—was, I think, Lambert. I don't recall his last name or whether that is his last name or not."

"Were they as young as George?"

"No, they were older, perhaps six or seven years older.

When I asked George about them, he said they were tutors. They didn't look or act like tutors. They didn't look like they belonged at Oxford. They looked—loud, if you will, their clothes too flamboyant. That's why I thought I should tell you about them. I have wondered, you see, if they had anything to do with breaking into Mulberry House. They weren't students. They weren't gentlemen.''

Rohan didn't want to know any of this, he really didn't. He wanted everything to remain the same in his memory. He wanted to think about George without feeling he'd been betrayed. Who the devil had these men been? They'd certainly known the lay of the land, curse George.

"Thank you," he said, his voice as cold as his heart had been when he was told of George's death. "It's unlikely that they had anything to do with the break-ins at Mulberry House or here. They were probably just a bit of low company. Most young men consort with low company at least once. But I will think about it. It's late. Marianne will be bouncing on you at six o'clock. Go to bed.''

But he didn't want her framed by that light again. He turned around and walked to the sideboard. He didn't pick up the brandy decanter, though a man of his reputation should probably swizzle down brandy like it was eau-de-vie.

"Good night, my lord.''

He said nothing. He didn't turn to look at her. He couldn't. It would have been too painful.

He strode to the stable just after dawn. It was blessedly quiet, the birds still battened down in their nests. The air was chill, but there was only a slight breeze. He didn't pay much attention to the gardens—or to anything else, for that matter.

Ah, the blessed silence. He saw his best mouser, Galahad, the one Tom Harker had been holding and petting, marching along the side of the drive, his tail high. He looked extremely well fed. Even the cat was quiet. Yes, silence. Until he neared the stable door. Then he heard Jamie singing in the sweetest voice he'd heard from him yet.

"There was a pert lass from Madras
Who had a remarkable ass—
Not rounded and pink,
As you probably think,
It was gray, had long ears, and ate grass."

Then, as if on cue, he heard Gulliver neigh in pleasure.
Then another horse followed with a low whinny that went
on and on, and Susannah's mare, Hera, joined in with a lilting snort.

He went into the dimly lit stable to see Jamie brushing
Gulliver while three other stable lads had paused in their
duties and were eyeing him with near reverence. Then they
all yelled out their approval, begging for another one, but
Rohan saw Jamie shake his head. "Sorry, lads, but I can't
spoil me big sweethearts 'ere, 'twould get them all atwitter,
more than one tune a day."

Then the lads noticed the baron standing in the open doorway. There was general consternation, then absolute silence.

Rohan said easily, "Jamie, we do have an ass. His name
is Puck and he roams the north pasture. Do occasionally sing
him that limerick."

"The last ass I sung it to, milord, turned around to show
me this face what sunk a thousand boats."

Gulliver neighed loudly. Did the damned horse even understand Jamie's jests? "That was quite good," Rohan said.
"Doom, saddle Gulliver for me. Quickly, the day is too fine
to waste."

Doom was a thin, slack-jawed boy of fourteen who had
never smiled, as far as anyone knew, in his entire life. No
horse had ever even tried to kick him or bite him. All the
staff believed it was because the horses felt sorry for him.
He'd been called Doom since he was a nit of five.

Jamie walked over to Rohan while he waited.

"This Doom boy, milord, I'll wager ye I'll git a grin outta
'im afore the end of the week. By Friday, aye, no longer
than that."

"A pound," Rohan said. They shook hands.

"I've already got 'im looking at me somethin' fierce whenever I spout me tunes. By Friday, milord. It's strange though, 'e's not beat by 'is pa nor anything like that. 'E's jest long in the face, like."

Rohan rode until noon. He was sweaty, hot, and feeling exhilarated when he arrived back at Mountvale House. He came to a dumbfounded halt at the sight of a large carriage pulled by four brilliant white horses standing in front of the deep-set steps of the house. There were three outriders, all wearing billowing black cloaks. The coachman was wearing pale silver and black livery. The wide front doors of Mountvale were thrown open wide. There was a flurry of bright color. There was a pumping up of lungs, he could feel it.

"My dearest! I'm home!"

CHARLOTTE DULCINA CARRINGTON, LADY MOUNTVALE, accepted a crystal glass of very cold champagne from her son. "... Well, dearest, you see, I was in Paris when I got this *feeling*. Now, Rohan, don't look at me like I've got turnip seeds in my brain. It was indeed a feeling, a bona fide feeling, a very *strange* feeling. I saw this girl—a woman really, but very young—and she looked absolutely terrified. And there you were, standing beside her, looking utterly helpless. What was a poor mother to do? I realized I was *needed*. Naturally I did not hesitate to come to you." She squared her beautiful white shoulders, which in turn thrust out her lovely bosom, and announced in a heroine's voice, "I have come here to arrange things, my son. Whatever is wrong, I will fix it."

"Thank you, Mother," Rohan said. He clicked his glass against hers and forced himself to take a sip. He hated champagne. Nasty stuff. Actually, he drank little if anything, but no one could know that. Actually no one would believe it, particularly about a man of his debauched reputation.

She looked glorious, as usual, in a charming gown of moss green, cut low, naturally, but not low in a vulgar way. His mother was never vulgar.

"You look fit, Mother."

"Yes, dearest, I know. It is nice of you to notice, but then, naturally you would, being of an excessively amorous nature just like your dear papa. Now, who is this young lady who is terrified?"

There were fast footsteps and a loud panting breath nearing the open doorway. "Is that you, Toby? Come in and meet Lady Mountvale, my mother."

Toby took two steps into the room, then stopped and stared. Standing before him was surely the most exquisite creature he had ever imagined. Her hair was a rich blond, thick, piled and plaited atop her head, but parts of it on her shoulders, and there was even some of it falling in lazy curls down her neck, and surely those were diamond pins in her hair that sparkled and gleamed. Her eyes were just the blue of the sky in the middle of the summer when it was hot and there was no rain. Her nose was perfect, narrow and straight, just like Rohan's. Her lips were a light red color, like she'd just eaten strawberries. He managed to tear his eyes away from the Vision. He stared at the baron, shaking his head even as he said, "Are you jesting, Rohan?"

"About what?"

Toby stole another look at the Goddess. "She can't be your mother. She's young and beautiful, but she does have the look of you. But her eyes are blue, not green. Yes, that's it. She must be your sister. Is she your older sister or your younger sister?"

"I don't have a sister, Toby. Stop staring at her. You are only eight years old. She is my mother, I promise you."

Lady Mountvale, who had been regarding the boy with some bemusement, nodded now, determining him to be blessed with a discerning eye backed with very high intelligence. She said with a charming smile, "My boy, it is obvious that you are already well on the path to a future that would render a hedonist proud. I am amazed and gratified.

"Who is this handsome boy, dearest? You haven't pulled a bastard out of your hat and just slipped him in? You would have sired him when you were but fifteen or sixteen. Well done, Rohan. Well done. Your beloved father would have been so very pleased. A pity he never knew. Why didn't you tell him of this delightful boy? It would have gladdened his final days.''

Toby was startled out of his worship. He puffed up like a little cock. ''I am not a bastard, my lady. I am Toby Hawlworth. Even though Rohan thinks my father is a bastard, I am legal, truly.''

''His father is a bastard, dearest? I didn't see him in my dream. This is all very odd.''

''He's a bastard in character'' Rohan said, ''not in the question of his antecedents.''

''Did the father send you this lovely boy so you could tutor him in the ways of the world?''

''No, actually Toby is the brother of that terrified young lady you saw in your vision. Toby, go fetch Susannah. If Marianne is awake, and not in a snit, then have Susannah bring her as well. Ah, tell your sister that she's in for a treat.''

''Yes, sir,'' Toby said, cast one final look at the incredibly beautiful woman who couldn't be Rohan's mother, and backed out of the drawing room.

''Comb your hair, Susannah.''

''What is wrong with my hair, Toby? I just combed it this morning. What is the matter with you?''

''You don't have *her* hair, Susannah. Please, you must do something or else you will feel like a scullery maid.''

Susannah, her hands on her hips, looked straight at her brother. ''You come in here and tell me to hurry. Then you tell me to comb my hair. What is going on? Are there visitors?''

''There is a visitor. Rohan said it was his mother, but he was jesting. She can't be.''

''Whyever not?''

''She's beyond beautiful, Susannah. Please comb your hair. Do you have any shiny pins to fasten in your hair?''

"No, I don't." Nevertheless, she went to the dressing table and began to straighten her hair. She had only brushed it back and tied it with a bow at the nape of her neck. She smiled at Toby in the mirror, then pulled several tendrils to cluster around her ears. "There, is that better?"

He eyed her. "A bit. What about your gown, Susannah? Don't you have anything that would make you look, maybe, er, whiter in the flesh, and perhaps more, er, soft and—"

He didn't know the words, bless his eight-year-old heart. But she now realized that there must be a beautiful woman downstairs with Rohan. But surely not his mother. His mother was a grown man's mother and not a young girl. Wasn't his mother on the Continent, hadn't he told her that? Was it a neighbor? A mistress? Even a man who was as debauched as he was reputed to be still wouldn't bring a mistress to his house, would he? Surely Toby was wrong. Surely the woman wasn't Rohan's mother.

"You want me to be more appetizing, perhaps?"

"I suppose," Toby said with a frown. "But even after I found out what 'appetizing' meant, I still always thought of food. I still do."

She grinned at him and ruffled his hair. "Here," she said, pinching her cheeks, "is that just a little bit better?"

"Her mouth looks like she's been eating strawberries."

Oh, dear.

She had never worn cosmetics. No mother wore cosmetics, at least no mother she'd ever seen. Who was the woman?

"Rohan said you were also to bring Marianne, if she's not in a temper."

"All right. Let's fetch her. Toby, could this woman possibly be his mother?"

He shook his head vigorously. "No, that's impossible. Rohan was jesting with me. She's far too young, Susannah. You'll see. She looks like his sister, but didn't his sister die a long time ago?"

"I believe so."

Could it be his mother, that famous beauty that her husband had adored and Society still adored, who supposedly had more lovers than most ladies had gowns?

Ten minutes later, the three of them stood in the drawing room doorway, Marianne between Susannah and Toby. Since Susannah wasn't eight years old, she didn't stand and stare at the lady. But she well understood why Toby had. The lady was beautiful. No wonder Rohan was so handsome. George as well. She wondered briefly about Tibolt the vicar. If he looked like his mother and his brothers, the young ladies in his flock must be vying with each other to attach him.

Susannah gave a tug to her old and well-worn pale blue wool gown, not that it helped.

"Ah, here you are. Do come in and meet my mother, Lady Mountvale. Mother, is this the young lady you saw in your vision? The one who was terrified?"

"Yes," Lady Mountvale said without hesitation. "This is she. How odd, son, that you would have looked helpless."

Susannah blinked at Rohan's mother, then at him. "I don't understand. What is this?"

"We will speak of it later," Rohan said.

"And who is this little sweetheart?" Charlotte said suddenly, staring down at Marianne.

"That," Rohan said with great relish, utter wickedness in his green eyes, "is your granddaughter, Mother. She is George's daughter. This is Susannah Carrington, George's widow. Toby is her brother."

To Rohan's surprise, his mother went down on her knees in front of Marianne. She made no move to take the little girl into her arms. She just looked into Marianne's face. Marianne stared back.

"She is the image of George," Charlotte said. "She is the image of you and me as well. Ah, but she's got your dear father's eyes." She rose, turned to face Rohan, and burst into tears.

"Mother!"

He held her against him, patting her slender back. "Now, Mother, she isn't that old, just a little girl. She's very young, really. No one would ever believe that you could be a grand-mother.''

Toby said, ''Please, ma'am, Rohan's right. No one would ever believe you were Marianne's grandmother. You look like her mother, except I've never seen a mother as beautiful as you are.'' Toby looked suddenly inspired. ''I think you look like her older sister, ma'am. Just barely her older sister. Why, Susannah looks like an older mother than you do.''

Lady Mountvale raised her head. She even cried beauti-fully, Rohan thought. Tears sparkled like diamonds on her thick lashes. What was this? She was laughing through her tears. ''Oh, dearest, this is the most wonderful thing. Don't you see? This means that George wasn't entirely an aesthete. He did have some hot blood pumping in his veins. Your father and I had lost all hope, for he never paid a bit of attention to any of the young ladies we brought to meet him.

''But George actually begat a child. How I marvel at that! He even brought himself to the sticking point. He married this lovely girl. Ah, it is glorious. And Rohan, don't you agree that Marianne is the image of him? I am so happy I believe I will have Fitz bring more champagne. Does Toby yet drink champagne?''

''The girl is presentable,'' Lady Mountvale said to Rohan, when the two of them were seated companionably in the library late that same evening. ''Indeed, if properly dressed, she would be quite taking. I will see to it tomorrow. Ah, must you drink that nasty tea, dearest? What would everyone say were they to see you?''

He'd forgotten. He tended to forget when he was out of London, but he said quickly, ''It's only a temporary aber-ration, Mother.''

She was still frowning at him. ''I trust so. Now, about George's widow. What will we do with her?''

''She lives here now. I have written to Aunt Miranda. If she's still alive, perhaps she'll consent to living here as well, acting as chaperon.''

"Even old battle-ax Miranda isn't enough of a chaperon for you, Rohan. The last I heard, she was nearing her final reward, or maybe she'd already traveled on to the hereafter. I forget. She never liked me, you know. Odd, but there it is. But I suppose you will need someone, since you have such a grand reputation for seduction and debauchery. It will come out and everyone will believe that Marianne is your bastard." She paused a moment, sipped on her brandy, then brightened. "That is quite acceptable. You don't have any bastards. It's about time you got the proper credit for presenting one to Society and to your fond mama."

"I think that Susannah would prefer that her child wasn't a bastard, Mama."

"I suppose you are right. A legitimate Carrington. How very excellent, indeed." She drank another sip of champagne.

"Now, Mama, would you like to tell me about this wondrous vision of yours? You said that Susannah is the young lady you saw?"

"Yes, and you were standing behind her looking helpless—not something I like, Rohan."

"I don't either. You have no other context?"

His mother scrunched up her face in thought, the result being more adorable than beautiful. "I remember feeling that both of you were in some sort of cave. It was very dim and shadowy. It was an old place, and it looked as if no one had been there in nearly forever. There were other people about, but their faces were vague and blurred. Just your face and dear Susannah's were clear to me. That's all. Sorry, dearest, I remember nothing else."

He didn't know what to think. His mother had had this vision? "What do you think of Marianne?"

"My granddaughter," she said slowly, as if savoring the word. "What a daunting thought for any lady. She is truly the image of George and of you as well. Your father sighed whenever I pointed out that all our boys looked like their mama, except for the Carrington green eyes. He allowed that since I had done most of the difficult part, perhaps it was only fair. I only wish that George had told us he had married, but I suppose that since he was so young at the time he believed we would have forbidden it.''

"Perhaps," Rohan said, wondering how he could turn her from this particular topic.

"I wish George had told us when Susannah was with child. I should have adored seeing to her. I would have given her advice, you know. I could have told her how to deal with that awful birthing pain. It was you, dearest, who brought me the most awful pain, but I have very nearly forgotten it.''

"Thank you, Mother."

"I never blamed you, dearest, but I did scream a good deal at your dear father. As I recall, I called him many names that rarely if ever fit him. Poor man, he was so distraught each time I was in mortal agony bearing a child that he couldn't bear to remain with me. No, he would flee to one of his mistresses and she would soothe him. He felt such guilt for bringing me that awful pain. We went to Italy after you arrived, Rohan. How I adored Venice and all the masked balls and those handsome Italian men. They—well, that's not all that important now.'' She touched her slender white fingers to the brilliant diamond necklace at her throat. "This lovely bauble was for birthing Tibolt.''

"What did Papa give you for birthing George?''

"George came so quickly that your dear papa didn't even have time to leave the house. He had only one foot out the door when George came squalling into the world. I believe he gave me a pair of earrings. As for my poor Clarissa, since she was our only daughter, your papa promised me he would dower her handsomely. That was, of course, all well and good, but I told him that I wanted my reward now. He gave me a mare. You remember Josephine, don't you? She had those beautiful, soulful eyes and that long, sweet face?''

He nodded.

"I will expect you to be as generous to your wife, Rohan.

And you must take a wife, dearest. I am sorry, but it is the done thing. You must have an heir.''

He sighed, plowing his fingers through his hair. "I know, Mama. I have been looking, sort of." He saw Susannah clear in his mind. He quickly shook his head. He was having visions of her, just like his mother had.

"You haven't found anyone yet to please you?"

"No, not yet."

Suddenly he realized that something was amiss. He looked more closely at his exquisite mother. There were actually two spots of color on her high cheekbones, and the color wasn't from the artfully applied cosmetics. He said slowly, "What have you done, Mama?"

She finished off her champagne. "I shall have to ring for Fitz."

"I will ring for Fitz once you tell me what you've done. You have done something that isn't going to please me overly, is it?"

"Her name is Daphne. I know, it's a dreadful name—so terribly Greek, or something—but she is glorious, Rohan. Her bloodline is worthy of ours, and she would do very well as your wife. Her father is Viscount Bracken. I once gave him consideration but decided he wasn't quite to my liking. But this Daphne, she is truly quite beautiful and brings a big dowry. Never would I consider saddling you with a donkey."

He groaned, then rose and began to pace. The thick Axminster carpet beneath his booted feet silenced the sound. Fitz came and this time left the champagne. His mother said nothing more, merely watched him.

Finally he said, "I'm only twenty-five. I won't be twenty-six anytime soon. Not for three more months. I'm not old enough. I will marry, I know that I must, but not this soon, Mama. Daphne? Please, not a Daphne. Tell me she lives in Italy somewhere."

"No, she lives right here in England, actually in Kent. But she understands your nature and your reputation perfectly.

Your life won't have to change, dearest, not really. You can continue with your dissipations and your myriad other excesses. Daphne will provide you an heir and then she can begin her own pleasures.''

"Mama, I appreciate your concern, but I am too young to yet consider taking a wife. I particularly don't want a wife named Daphne.''

His fond mama eyed him for a long time, then finally nodded. "Very well. I will write to Lord Bracken and inform him that you are ill-disposed toward matrimony. It is rather a horrid name, isn't it? Ah, but she is a glorious creature. Perhaps we could convince her to change her name. Would you prefer Jane? Victoria?''

"Let's just forget the glorious young lady, all right?'' He grinned and raised his champagne glass to her.

"Speaking of glorious, what is that new footman's name, Rohan? You know, the one with the deliciously wicked dark eyes? I do believe he has a Welsh look about him.''

"His name is Augustus. I rather thought you would find him to your liking.''

"You are a good son,'' Charlotte said, rose, kissed him, and walked to the door. She said over her exquisite white shoulder, "What do you plan to do with Susannah? I don't mean next week, I mean in the future.''

He looked down at his highly polished boots. He looked back at his mother. "I don't know. But I'd best tell you about Aunt Mariam's bequest to George.''

"I am gaining somewhat in years, dearest, but surely I would know about an Aunt Mariam if there were one in the family. Perhaps she's one of your father's early mistresses and she has the name 'aunt' because he considered her nearly one of the family?''

"No, there's no Aunt Mariam that I know of, but that's surely not a fact that Susannah need ever discover. I think you should come back, Mother, and let me tell you what I've done.''

9

SURELY SHE WAS MISTAKEN. SURELY THAT COULDN'T BE
Baron Mountvale. No, impossible. Susannah drew closer. It
was. He was on his knees planting a marigold with deep-
golden flowers. She heard him humming.

The womanizing, utterly debauched baron was planting
marigolds? And he was treating them tenderly, gently clean-
ing off the roots.

Susannah didn't know what to think. He'd told her that he
had designed the garden for his mother. He'd told her also
that he had no interest in mucking about, and he'd arched a
supercilious eyebrow when he said it. He most certainly
wasn't mucking about now, he was planting marigolds carefully and humming.

Then she realized that she wasn't supposed to be here. Her
mother-in-law had taken her, over her protests, in the carriage to Eastbourne to a seamstress whom she herself approved. The woman had taken ill, however, and they'd
returned long before they were supposed to.

And here was Rohan planting marigolds in his garden. She
quietly walked away. He'd given her food for thought. A lot
of food.

When Rohan came into the drawing room before luncheon
it was to see his lovely mama seated on the floor with Mar-

ianne, pouring her a cup of tea. Susannah was sitting in a chair in the corner of the large room. Sunlight poured in through the deep windows, making his mother's hair look like spun silk. He wondered what the manly Augustus thought of Lady Mountvale. He was probably drooling.

Susannah found herself looking at the baron's fingernails. No, they were very clean and well buffed. No dirt beneath them. He had very nice hands, she saw, then frowned a bit at herself.

"Ro-han!"

Marianne scrambled to her feet and ran to Rohan, her arms raised. He leaned down and picked her up, only to whirl her over his head in the next moment.

"Have you poured tea on your grandmama?"

She studiously traced the cleft in his chin with her finger, then smiled at him. "I want to look like Charlotte when I grow up."

"Charlotte? You call your grandmama Charlotte?"

"Yes, dearest," his mama said from the floor. "One must accept certain things that cannot be changed. However, there is no reason to rub salt in the wound, is there?"

"Absolutely no reason at all. So what have you been doing, little pumpkin, other than serving tea to Charlotte?"

"She told me about my grandpapa. He would have given me sweetmeats."

"Yes, he would have," Rohan said, and for the first time, he wished he had George in front of him. He would have slammed his fist into his jaw.

"Ro-han, you're nearly as pretty as Charlotte."

He pulled her fingers out of her mouth and bit one. "Men are not pretty. We are handsome. That is better than pretty."

"Is Mama handsome or pretty?"

"Your mama is a girl. She has to be pretty. She has no choice."

He turned his head at Susannah's laugh. "Weren't you invited to the tea party?"

"No, dearest, I did not invite her. Susannah is not cooperating with me. I have offered her the use of several of my gowns until we can go again to Eastbourne, but she refuses. She is proud, too proud. Therefore, she must suffer."

"No, it isn't that at all," Rohan said. "She refuses because she knows she cannot fill out your gowns, Mama. She does not want to be humiliated. She is simply protecting herself."

"I could fill it," Marianne said.

"We will discuss that in another fifteen years," Rohan said. "Now, Susannah, isn't this true?"

Susannah sighed. "It was difficult, Rohan. We walked along the street in Eastbourne and all the men swooned when they saw your mother. I'm sure they took me for her maid."

"That is true only because you refused to borrow one of my gowns," Charlotte said with great reasonableness. "Well, not entirely. But nonetheless, don't complain about it now. It is your own fault. Now, this is something you don't know, Susannah. I have spoken of this to Rohan and have told him that he didn't entirely understand his late aunt Mariam's will. There was an initial sum of five hundred pounds to be given to George—and thus now to you. Then the quarterly allowances begin. Isn't that splendid?"

Susannah wanted to cry. Five hundred pounds! Goodness, what she could do with such a sum! She could refurbish Mulberry House, she could have the roof replaced, and—

"Don't even think it," Rohan said as he set Marianne on her feet.

"But if it is my money, what can you possibly have to say about what I do with it? Indeed, sir, how could you possibly know what I was thinking?"

"Your face is a very clean window to your thoughts, Susannah. At least to me. You will not put a farthing into Mulberry House. You will not place a single sou in your father's palm. You will use the money to refurbish yourself, not that derelict house or your equally derelict father. Also, Toby and Marianne are in need of clothes. Perhaps you could even buy Toby a pony. He needs to learn to ride."

Susannah looked at her mother-in-law. She rose from her chair. "I am keeping my temper, ma'am, only because he is your son and I do not wish to discomfit you."

"You are a daughter-in-law of great fortitude," Charlotte said. "However, my dear, if you do not occasionally yell to remove blockages in your liver, you will doubtless become bilious, not a very savory condition."

"Very well." Susannah drew herself up and yelled, "How dare you try to give me orders when it is my five hundred pounds? You are a high-handed bas—well, baron!"

"What did you really wish to call me? I wonder. Are you certain about the will, Mother? She really gets five hundred pounds now? Are there no stipulations attached?"

Charlotte looked down at the magnificent emerald ring on the third finger of her left hand. "I am sorry, dearest, but there are no stipulations."

He knew then, of course, that if she could have, she would have quickly added some, but it would have sounded like a sham, which it was. Oh, well. He gave Susannah a look of considerable dislike. "You will spend the money as I have instructed you to. I am the master of this household, the head of the Carrington family. You will obey me."

"This is not your fiefdom and I am not a serf. Besides, now that your mother is here, that excuse of yours that you need a hostess no longer holds."

"I don't like having you look like a wench from the poorhouse. It will make my neighbors think I keep you on a stingy string. Everyone will talk about it behind their hands. I will be snubbed the next time I am in Mountvale village."

"This gown was my mother's."

There was a bit of shaking in her voice and he should have been warned, but he had jumped on his horse and had dug in his heels to ride it. "Your mother never would have intended her daughter to look pathetic. I can even see your ankles. A lady doesn't walk around with her ankles hanging out. What's more, your stockings are bagging. It is distasteful, ma'am. Use the money to fix yourself."

"I'm truly sorry, ma'am," Susannah said, "but I can't help myself." She ran at Rohan and punched him as hard as she could in his belly.

He grunted, doubling over. "That was quite ably executed," he said when he could speak again. "I am glad you didn't hit me any lower. A man can't speak as soon after a blow to his—" He saw Marianne looking at them with great green eyes. "Never mind. You will go to your room, Susannah. You may be certain that I will deal with you later."

"Mama, why did you hit Rohan?"

Oh, dear. She'd been foolish. Before she could find an excuse, Rohan said, "I have been teaching her how to defend herself, Marianne. You heard me tell her that her hit was very good. It was. I will teach her more." He was certain he heard Susannah growl.

"Before you go, Susannah," Charlotte said calmly, as if nothing at all had occurred to overset anyone or anything, "my son was telling me about your troubles. Someone breaking into your house and then into Mountvale. It disturbs me. We must put our heads together and figure out what the man wanted. If we discover what the thief was after, then it only makes sense that we'll also have the motive."

Susannah could only stare at the glorious creature who was looking limpidly up at her from her position on the carpet. "I agree with everything you said, ma'am. But didn't you hear him? Didn't you hear the way he spoke to me? *He ordered me.* Surely you didn't approve of that?"

Charlotte curled a blond curl around her finger even as she gently removed Marianne's fingers from her mouth. She shrugged even as she eased Marianne onto her lap and leaned back against the settee. "My dear, he is my son, my eldest son. He never gave me a moment's worry growing up. He accepted all his dear papa's teachings and all of mine. He pleased both of us from his earliest years. He has gained a reputation that is formidable for one of such a young age. He has made me very proud. What is the mother of such a son to do?"

Susannah blinked once, twice, then drew a deep breath, but still it didn't work and her mouth opened. "But, ma'am, he is a lecher, a—"

"I am not a damned lecher!"

"Yes, dearest, you are." Charlotte paused and pursed her lips. "But I would never call you that. It is too blunt a word, too harsh. 'Lecher.' Goodness, it makes the wearer sound very unamiable, and all know that Baron Mountvale is the most charming of gentlemen. He is in demand. He is beloved. The ladies search him out. If there are excesses—which I pray there most assuredly are—it is the ladies who force them upon him. But not all of the time, I trust. Rohan?"

"No, Mother, not all of the time." There was, he saw, nothing for it. He threw up his hands and said, "Susannah, we are having a small soiree on Friday night. There will be at least a dozen of our neighbors. I would appreciate it if you would gown yourself appropriately—as George's widow, not as my hostess. Now, I'm taking Toby riding. He should have returned from his lessons with Vicar Byam."

"I thought you wanted me to buy him a pony out of my five hundred pounds."

"You will. But I have decided that Toby is too old for a pony. It is Marianne who needs the pony. Toby will have a horse. I will even select the horse. Branderleigh Farm is not far from Mountvale. We will go there. Right now, though, I have several horses that will suit him."

"Gentlemen," he heard his mother say before he was out the door, "do not like to be contradicted to their faces, Susannah. You were married to George, surely you learned that."

"No, ma'am. George wasn't often at Mulberry House. I learned little or nothing."

"Oh," said Charlotte, wondering if George had lost his hot blood immediately upon begetting Marianne. It sounded, depressingly, as if he had. "I'm sorry, my dear."

"So was I, ma'am." Not entirely, Susannah thought as

she carried Marianne upstairs for her nap. The last several years, she had rarely seen him. She doubted he would have known his own daughter if he'd stumbled over her in the street. But he had supported them until he had died.

Five hundred pounds. When she gained her bedchamber, she immediately sat down at the small writing desk, drew a piece of foolscap from a delicate drawer, and began to make a list.

She wanted to kick herself when she realized later upon review, that she'd written "clothing" at the very top.

The baron was a lecher who planted marigolds, with great care. It was all very strange. "Lecher." Charlotte was right, it was an intolerable word. It didn't suit him at all, which had to be odd as well, since he was a renowned womanizer.

Susannah was deeply asleep, alone for the first time. Marianne was sleeping in the Mountvale nursery with her new nursemaid, Lottie. Betty had left to tend to her ill mother. Susannah was dreaming about a man—a stranger to her— who was digging about in flower beds. He kept saying over his shoulder that he didn't like bulbs, that they always rotted and he'd be damned if he'd plant any more of them.

He pulled out a grayish bulb, whirled about, and held it up to her nose. "Smell it," he said.

She didn't want to, but she breathed in deeply. She began to choke. The smell was sickly sweet. Then it was in her throat and it burned and she was choking.

She began to struggle. Suddenly she was awake and there was a man standing over her, holding a damp cloth over her nose and mouth.

She tried to rear up, to jerk away from that cloth, but his hand was on the back of her head, forcing her face into the cloth. She held her breath, striking out with her fists, but not for long. He hit her squarely between the shoulder blades, and her breath whooshed out.

She felt light-headed and dizzy, then she felt nothing at all.

• • •

"My lord, Mrs. Carrington is gone!"

It was Fitz, his face as white as his spiffy collar, panting in the open doorway of the baron's bedchamber.

"What do you mean, gone?" Rohan shook his head to clear away the remnants of the strange dream he'd had. "It's only seven o'clock in the morning, Fitz. Maybe she's gone for an early-morning ride, perhaps she's gone to play with Marianne, you know that little imp—"

"She's gone, my lord. Gone! Elsie just happened to look in on her as she passed her room. Her bed was empty, the sheets tumbled and jerked about. Her bedchamber has also been ransacked."

"Ransacked? You're certain? You said that Elsie is flighty, loves drama. Have you checked this yourself?" But Rohan had already thrown back the covers. He was naked, and the wooden floor beneath his bare feet was colder than a patch of ice.

"Your dressing gown, my lord. That's better. You can be seen now, although the maids would perhaps prefer you in a natural state. Yes, I verified that Elsie hadn't been indulging in playacting. Mrs. Carrington is gone, my lord. Her bedchamber is a mess. Someone took her."

Rohan cursed deeply and fluently. "All the doors were locked, we had men patrolling the grounds. What about the footmen guarding the doors?"

"I don't know." Fitz turned even whiter. "Oh, my goodness, I don't know." The old man nearly ran out of the room, the baron at his heels.

None of the footmen had been hurt. None of the footmen had seen anything.

Charlotte tenderly and thoroughly examined Augustus to ensure that he had suffered no injury.

"You neither heard nor saw anything?"

The four footmen shook their heads. Augustus said, "No, my lord. We kept awake since we took over from the others at midnight. There was nothing to disturb us."

Augustus spoke very well. His mother doubtless appreciated that. The baron shook his head. Who gave a damn if Augustus spoke like a country yeoman?

The thief had taken her, but how?

"My lord, I'm sorry, but Marianne wants Mrs. Carrington. She's yelling her head off and Lottie is beside herself. She's new and Marianne doesn't quite trust her yet."

"I'm coming," Rohan said. He and the men had been searching for the past six hours for any sign of Susannah. Nothing, they'd found nothing. He was very worried now, but he didn't know what to do. He wanted a bit of luncheon, then he would go out again. His mother, garbed in men's britches, jacket, and a jaunty hat, had just left to join another search.

Lottie was trying to comfort a squealing Marianne, who was also squirming madly in her arms. Rohan walked to her and said, "Marianne! Stop that racket, you're making my head hurt."

Marianne, taken by surprise, stuck her fingers in her mouth and began sucking hard.

"That's better."

Marianne suddenly launched herself at him. Lottie missed, but Rohan managed to grab her out of the air.

He held her close, his heart pounding. She was gasping, giving small hiccups. "What is this, little pumpkin? Your mama isn't here right now, but she soon will be."

"Mama always kisses me good morning."

That sounded nice. Dear heavens, he was losing what little brain he had remaining.

"I woke up without my mama's kiss."

He kissed her cheek. "There, that's a baron's kiss."

Her fingers went back into her mouth.

"Did you eat, Marianne?"

Marianne just sucked harder on her fingers.

Lottie shook her head. "She wouldn't accept a single bite, my lord."

"Very well, then. I'll take her downstairs. We'll both have our lunch."

Lottie could only stare at the master of Mountvale Hall, the man who was known far and wide for his amorous exploits, his wild dissipations. He was willingly holding a little girl? He was willingly taking her downstairs to feed her? She couldn't wait to go home to begin spreading the news that the baron wasn't acting as he should. Goodness, he even seemed to be quite fond of the child.

Mrs. Horsely came into the breakfast parlor with a plate that had on it small piles of everything a very young person could possibly desire to eat.

Rohan carried Marianne over from the window. Toby was already seated. He looked terrified, drawn and ill.

"Stop it, Toby, we'll find her," Rohan said in a powerful and firm voice, wondering if that commanding voice would convince a flea.

"Yes, sir," Toby said. "I can't eat, sir, else I know I'd puke."

"Then please don't. Have you ever fed Marianne?"

Toby shook his head.

"Then I suppose it's my job. Well, little pumpkin, will you take a bite of these very yellow eggs?"

Marianne stared at the eggs, then looked at him. Tears spilled out of those enormous eyes of hers and fell down her cheeks.

"I want Mama. I don't want yellow eggs."

"I wouldn't either. It's luncheon, after all. Here, take a bite of this nutty bun." He took the first bite, then broke off a small piece and put it to her mouth. She ate it.

He felt as though the heavens had anointed him. He was a natural.

But the euphoria didn't last long. Within ten minutes, Rohan wanted to throw Marianne out the window. She was alternately crying, spitting food onto his waistcoat, mashing eggs with her fingers, and screaming.

"Sir, perhaps I could help."

"You, Toby? You're a brave lad, but this is a battle you can't win. Neither of us can." He sighed and walked out of the breakfast room with Marianne draped over his shoulder. She was finally so exhausted from yelling and fighting that all she did now was slurp on her fingers.

Rohan took her to the estate room, sat down in his father's cracked and worn chair, and rearranged the child in his arms. Soon he would rejoin the search.

Who had taken Susannah and why? It had to be the same man who had broken into Mountvale House the first night they'd arrived. It wasn't Tibolt. He would never believe that.

The how of it was driving him mad. The thought of her in danger bowed him in on himself.

It was Charlotte who found him sleeping, with Marianne pressed against his chest.

She blinked at the unexpected sight.

"Dearest."

He opened his eyes to see the Vision standing in front of him. He shook his head. It was his mother. "Please tell me you have found Susannah?"

"No, we've found nothing at all."

Rohan cursed, but very softly so as not to risk awakening Marianne.

His mother thought him tender and altogether wonderful. Of course, his father had adored all his children, although Tibolt and George had severely disappointed him with their prudish and proper ways, but that had been later, once they were out of short coats. Such a pity he never knew that George had perhaps not disappointed him all that much.

As for Rohan, it hadn't occurred to him that he sounded tender. He just knew he couldn't bear Marianne screeching in his ear again. He rose. "I must go search for Susannah. She must be all right, Mother, she must."

"You will find her," Charlotte said, studying his beloved face. She laid her hand lightly on his shoulder. "You will find her."

10

SUSANNAH MOANED, CLUTCHED HER STOMACH AND VOM-
ited into the moldy straw beside her. She vomited until there
was nothing left in her belly. She fell back against the straw,
panting with exertion.

"You're awake. Finally."

A man's voice, beside her. She felt so weak it was difficult
to turn her head to see him. But she did. He was wearing a
cravat tied over his nose and mouth and an old felt hat low
over his forehead.

"What do you want?" Her mouth felt parched, her tongue
swollen. "Why did you take me from Mountvale? How did
you even get in?"

The man laughed, a laugh muffled through the cravat.
"Ah, now that's a decent question, isn't it?"

As the foul belly cramps eased, fear came surging in. Her
hands were tied in front of her and her feet tied as well, with
just a little give between them. She was wearing only her
nightgown. Her hair fell long and tangled down her back.
"May I have some water, please?"

He grunted. "Yes. But first let's get you out of here. I
can't bear the stench." He leaned down and picked her up.
He carried her out of the small room and down a short corridor into another room. Everything smelled old and rotting.

Boards hung swinging from their nails off walls. She saw no windows. Where was she?

He laid her down on more moldy straw, then rose, saying, "Don't move or I'll hurt you."

She tested the ropes around her wrists. They weren't terribly tight, but they wouldn't give either. She began quickly to untie the knots at her ankles.

She straightened quickly when he returned with a mug. "Drink."

She drank, then spat the first mouthful of water into the straw beside her. The rest she downed eagerly. She lay back, panting, on the straw.

He came down to sit beside her. He seemed tall, well muscled, and young. He was also strong, for he'd carried her as if she'd weighed no more than Marianne. She must remember everything she could, but the fear pounded at her, numbing her mind. She closed her eyes against it.

She saw the baron. He was giving her one of his wicked smiles. Then she saw a marigold held in his large brown hand, heard him humming. She said, "Where are we?"

"Tucked away someplace where no one will find you. I will not toy with you, ma'am. You will tell me where George hid the map and you will tell me right now."

Map? What map? George had never spoken of a map, he had never shown her a map.

"I know nothing of a map," she said as she opened her eyes. She saw his dark eyes gleam with anger, and she added quickly, "I swear it. You robbed Mulberry House three times. You found nothing. You managed to get into my bedchamber here at Mountvale, but you found nothing. That's because there is nothing to find. There is no map."

The man leaned over, grabbed her nightgown in two big fists, and ripped.

Susannah screamed and tried to roll away from him.

"There," he said, holding her down easily. "Now you will tell me everything or I will shortly have you completely naked. If you still refuse, then I will take you. George said you weren't much in bed, but I'll force myself.''

"Please, there is no map.''

He pulled the nightgown open, laying the two jagged edges flat. She lurched up, gasping. He pushed her back down, his hands on her shoulders. He leaned back then. ''Don't move again. Beautiful breasts. I wondered. George said you weren't much of anything, but he was lying. Perhaps he was afraid to tell us of your beauty, afraid we'd come after you and you would welcome us.'' He reached out a gloved hand and cupped her left breast. ''No marks on them from childbearing. Are there marks on your belly?''

Her heart was near to bursting with fear, gut-wrenching fear that made her want to vomit again, only there was nothing to vomit. ''Please,'' she whispered.

''Please what?'' His gloved hand still cupped her breast. His fingers squeezed.

''No, please stop. Listen to me. I don't know about any map. Indeed, I have very few items that belonged to George. I will give them to you.''

He frowned at that and sat back, wrapping his arms around his knees. ''What items?''

''There are several books—George was a great scholar. I know he loved maps of all sorts, but there weren't any.'' She pictured the small locket he had once given her that she had kept. No, it was too small to hold anything, much too small, and she didn't want to give it up. It was the only gift he had ever given her. As for her wedding ring, it had been but three small rubies set in gold. She had sold it some six months before, when it had been low ebb with her father.

''What else?''

He was looking at her breasts. She tried to hold perfectly still, but it was difficult. ''There are a few letters. No maps there. And a waistcoat he left at Mulberry House. There is nothing else.''

He said very slowly, his eyes still on her breasts, ''I don't know if I believe you. No, I rather believe that I don't, at least for the moment.'' He came forward on his knees above

her. He ripped the nightgown to its hem and pulled it open.
She froze with shock.

"No marks on your belly. Aren't I the lucky lad?"

She began to fight. She raised her legs and kicked him,
catching him in his arm and hurling him sideways. Then she
rolled away from him, coming up on her knees. She needed
a weapon, please, God, something, anything.

She saw the hay rake leaning against the wall. She staggered to her feet and grabbed it between her bound wrists.
She had only time to turn before he was on her.

"You damned bitch!" He was panting, he was so angry.
He grabbed at her, but she wrenched free. Her nightgown
ripped under her arm, hanging off her now. She turned on
him, rage filling her, overflowing, and she rammed the handle end of the rake into his chest.

He yelled, falling back, flailing the air until he lost his
balance and, groaning, fell onto his back in the straw. She
had but a moment. She could take only short, mincing steps.
She made the door and flung it open. She wanted to yell her
relief. She slammed the door shut and turned the key in the
lock just as his fists struck hard against the wooden door.
Then his booted foot kicked the door and it shuddered in its
frame. She knew it wouldn't hold long.

She whirled about. She had to escape. She would untie
her ankles after she'd escaped him. There was no time now.

She heard a splintering sound. Oh, God, he would be on
her in a moment.

Rohan and three neighbors, all on horseback, were fanning
through the east meadow. He reined in Gulliver for a moment
at the top of a rise and looked at the sprawl of land beyond.
Suddenly there was a flicker of a memory. Over to the west,
in the maple forest, hadn't there been a small shack in a
clearing that had been abandoned years before? He'd been
only a boy when the gypsies had camped there, using the
shack not for themselves but for their horses. He remembered
how strange he had thought that was. They had piles of hay

in the shack. No, surely it had crumbled to the ground and been consumed by the forest by now. There had been no gypsies in years.

Still, he parted from his neighbors and rode Gulliver hard to the maple forest.

Susannah realized then that she'd been prisoner in a dilapidated cabin that was falling down on itself. But the two doors to those small rooms, they'd been new. So had the locks. What had this place been? Why had there been moldy straw in those two rooms?

Why was she thinking about that moldy straw? She was losing her mind. She had to escape. She was out the front door that was hanging loose on its hinges, nearly ready to crash to the ground. She was in a very small clearing. All around her were maple trees.

She heard him yell, heard the door crash open.

She ran with tiny steps into the forest and barely made it to the cover of the trees before she heard the man shout, pain and rage filling his voice. "Damn you, you silly bitch! I don't want to kill you, I just want what is mine! Come back here or I will hurt you when I find you! Where do you think you will go?"

Oh, God. She could make a foot at a time, not more. She felt the ropes digging into her ankles, deeper and deeper as she strained to pull. He would be on her quickly enough. Was the ground damp? Could he see her pitiful little steps?

There was no hope for it. She couldn't wait. She dropped to the ground and began untying the ropes at her ankles. It was slow going.

She heard him shouting, cursing her, threatening her. She kept working the knots. Finally they came free.

She heard him crashing through the forest. To her right, not far, but not yet upon her.

She jumped to her feet and ran directly into a root, tripped and went hurtling forward. She didn't bring her tied wrists up in time to protect her face, and so she swallowed dirt and leaves.

She felt pain spreading through her and lay there a moment, panting. Where was he? She spat out the dirt, the damp leaves. Her face hurt. She raised her bound hands and felt the scratches. Her fingers came away red with blood.

Then she felt the earth shuddering beneath her. He was closer. In just a few moments he would see her. What was left of her ripped nightgown was hanging off her, but it was white. He would see white in a flash.

She began crawling, keeping as close to the ground as she could. When his voice faded, she stood and ran again. She ran until a stitch in her side brought her to a gasping halt. She leaned against a tree, trying to slow her breathing.

"Well, at last I've got you."

Rohan knew the shack was near. He kept picturing it in his boy's mind. He had to keep Gulliver to a walk, for the trees twisted all around him, the thick branches were weapons, making even a canter impossible.

Then his blood curdled.

He heard a woman's scream. And then a yell. "No, damn you, no!"

He pulled the pistol from his belt. He aimed it into the air. But he didn't fire, even though he knew the blast would echo through the thick forest and alert the man who'd taken her that help was near. He didn't fire because he realized the man would probably escape and he wanted that man very badly.

More than anything, Rohan wanted that man.

He heard the man yelling, cursing.

Then he was on them. The man was on top of her. Damnation, was he raping her? Her nightgown was in shreds, hanging off her, the man was between her legs, heaving over her. Jesus, he was choking her.

Then the man looked up to see Gulliver nearly upon him. For an instant he froze, undecided what to do.

Then he struck her, leapt to his feet, and took off running. Rohan calmly raised his pistol and fired. The impact lifted the man off his feet and slammed him into a tree.

Susannah came slowly up to her knees. Her head hurt ferociously where the man had just struck her. She saw Rohan fire, saw him leap off Gulliver's broad back and run toward her. She turned slowly and saw the man lying some ten yards away at the base of a tree. Was he dead? She hoped not. She wanted to kill him herself.

"Rohan," she said, her voice barely above a whisper. "You came. Bless you."

"My God," he said, grabbing her arms and lifting her up. "Are you all right?" He stared at the dirty face, the tangled hair. He refused to look at her body. On the other hand, he was a man, with a reputation to maintain. So he looked, but only for a moment.

"You came," she said again. "I prayed you would. I'm all right, just sore."

He didn't think, just pulled her against him. She felt his steady heartbeat next to hers. She tucked her face against his neck. "You came," she said again, and yet again. "I was so frightened."

"It looks like you very nearly escaped him. How did he catch you?"

"I had to untie my ankles. It gave him time to catch up to me."

"It's over now." He took off his coat and helped her into it. She pulled it closed over her breasts. It came to the top of her thighs, which was at least something.

"Stay here. I didn't kill him, only hit him in the arm. Let me see what condition he's in."

The bullet had gone exactly where Rohan had aimed it, straight through the man's upper arm. However, his head must have struck the tree when he fell. He was unconscious. Rohan took off the old felt hat and pulled down the man's cravat. The man hadn't wanted her to see him, which meant he hadn't wanted to kill her. That was something. He studied the man's face. He had never seen him before. "Well, hell," Rohan said. He walked back to Susannah, who was standing exactly where he'd left her, staring at him, then at the man.

He untied her wrists. He walked back to the man and tied his wrists behind him. "Now," he said, "let's go home. Everyone has been searching for you, including my mother."

He lifted her in his arms and with more grace than anyone could expect, he got them both on Gulliver's back.

He guided his horse slowly through the twist of trees. He said, not looking down at her, for her white legs were quite bare and his right hand was touching the outside of her right thigh, "Tell me what happened."

It helped to steady her. She spoke slowly, but shock was clouding her mind, and her head pounded, and he had difficulty understanding. But he was determined to keep her mind focused. He asked question after question until he thought he had learned everything.

He said finally, hugging her against him, "You did well, Susannah. I'm very proud of you."

They came out of the maple forest. "Now, turn against me and hold on."

She clutched him against her and felt Gulliver eat up the ground. The wind was cold on her bare legs. The air was cold on her bare belly. Oh, no. She tried to sit up, to somehow cover herself, but Rohan held her tightly.

When they came onto the wide, graveled drive and to the front of Mountvale Hall, there were, unfortunately, at least a dozen men milling about, servants, and several carriages, and doubtless within those carriages several of the neighboring wives.

Rohan cursed. He would go around to the stables, he would—

They'd been spotted. A yell went up.

He slowed Gulliver, looked down at her bare legs and belly, and quickly eased her up so he could fit his coat more closely around her. It didn't work. He couldn't take her to the steps. Every man there would see her.

He guided Gulliver off the drive, then lifted her off the horse's back and set her on the ground. "Hold still." He was stripping off his shirt even as he dismounted. "Here, put this on, my coat over it."

She was weaving where she stood, shuddering. There was no hope for it. He put the shirt on her. Thankfully, it came to her knees. She was trembling so badly that he had to help her fasten the shirt over her breasts.

Beautiful breasts.

He put his coat on her over his shirt.

It wasn't until he pulled Gulliver up before the deep, indented steps of Mountvale House that he realized he was naked to the waist.

There wasn't a thing he could do about it.

Before anyone could speak, Rohan shouted, "I have found her! She is all right. I left the man unconscious in the maple forest near the abandoned shack. Ozzie Harker, you know where that shack is, the one where the gypsies used to camp. Go fetch him."

They were all staring at him, staring at her, in his arms.

Suddenly Charlotte came running lightly down the steps. The men parted to make way. She called out, "Dearest, bring the poor child in immediately. Fitz, have the doctor fetched." She then thanked all their dear friends. But their attention, for the first time ever, wasn't completely focused on the exquisite Lady Mountvale. No, every man's eyes were on Mrs. Carrington's naked white legs. Every woman's eyes were on the baron's naked chest.

Still, he thought his mother's word "child" was a good try.

Rohan cursed as he carried her through the open front doors. Fitz didn't stare. He had too much dignity.

Then Rohan heard cheering. He blinked, not understanding, then realized that as a man with his reputation, he had doubtless just gained another considerable elevation to his status. He looked down at Susannah's white legs, then into her face and saw the bruises on her cheek.

"He struck you?"

"Yes. It rather hurts."

He cursed. He carried her up the stairs, two at a time, yelling over his shoulder, "Fitz, fetch the doctor, quickly. Don't dawdle, man."

Fitz turned to Charlotte even as he waved to Augustus. He said in a very worried voice, "It is normally very quiet when his lordship is in residence here at Mountvale."

Charlotte frowned after her son. "It shouldn't be, Fitz. A man of his appetites and reputation should be surrounded with excitement and action. It would be a travesty otherwise. Poor Susannah. We're in for a problem now, but perhaps it won't look so bad. Just think of the romance of it all. Did his lordship not look dashing carrying her in his arms? And so very manly with his chest naked?" There was more than a good deal of satisfaction in her voice. There was ringing pride. Then she frowned. "But she is his brother's widow. Nothing can come from it, no matter what happens."

Fitz sighed and gave Augustus his orders again, twice, because Augustus was having a difficult time tearing his attention away from the incredibly beautiful Vision, still garbed in boys' clothing.

He looked up the wide staircase. The baron had looked distraught. He'd never seen the baron look distraught before. But the baron's mother was right. A man couldn't marry his brother's widow, whether or not she was wearing his shirt and coat.

11

SUSANNAH MOANED. THE PAIN IN HER HEAD HAD BROUGHT her low. She hated it, but it consumed her. She knew she was crying, but she couldn't hold the tears back.

Rohan wrung the cool water out of the soft linen cloth and laid it on her forehead. "It should be better in a moment. I'm sorry. I can't give you laudanum yet. The man hit you in the head. We can't take the chance. Just listen to me, Susannah, try to concentrate on my voice and my words. Breathe very lightly, that's right."

He began to talk slowly to her, nonsense really, all about his first pony, Dobbs, named after the astronomer Jacko Dobbs, whom he had admired as a boy. "... I was six years old when I taught Dobbs how to jump. I thought he would jump to the stars, a little jest my tutor appreciated. Even my father was astounded at how high Dobbs could jump, except, of course, that Dobbs had just jumped this rather high bush when my father first saw him, and my father wasn't alone. He was enjoying a tryst with a lady from a neighboring estate. But my father stopped what he was doing and clapped me on the back for my excellent training before he sent me on my way. As I recall, the lady also applauded my efforts. She said something about with practice and good fortune I might someday be just like my father. As I recall also, my father didn't have a stitch of clothing on. As for the lady, I think she had pulled my father's shirt in front of her.''

She stared at him wide-eyed, then giggled. ''That's good. That's really very funny, yet you recount it like it could be any story in any little boy's life.''

''It almost could. Well, all right, say the part of the father carrying on a tryst with a neighboring lady.''

She giggled again. He loved the sound of that giggle. ''Don't make me laugh. It hurts. Now, sir, a man of your reputation—I suppose you have taken many ladies to that place where your father was. I'll wager it's a very romantic spot.''

''Very romantic. You're right, of course. A man of my reputation would use his private flora and fauna for assignations. Should you like to visit the spot with me, Susannah?''

She moaned.

Where, he wondered, had that bit of nonsense come from? But it wasn't nonsense. He very much wanted to take her anywhere she wanted to go. He very much wanted her. ''A bit of a backward step, but you're doing fine. Just keep breathing lightly.''

''You're still naked.''

''Just my upperparts. You've seen naked upperparts. You were married. Ah, at last here's Dr. Foxdale.'' He shook the man's hand, saying, ''She was hit on the left side of her face and her head hurts pretty badly. Other than that, I believe she's fine. Except, of course, for these scratches on her face.''

Dr. Foxdale eased himself down beside young Mr. George's widow. He just looked at her for a good long time, noting her coloring, her eyes, her rate of breathing. Then he lightly touched his fingertips to the side of her head and began a slow exploration. She sucked in her breath.

''That was a good blow the villain gave her,'' he said, not to her but over his shoulder to the baron. ''Now, ma'am, how many fingers am I holding up?''

"Three."

"Excellent. And now?"

She counted his long thin fingers until he was satisfied that her wits weren't wandering. He had the darkest eyes she'd ever seen. "You'll do," he said, then turned immediately to the baron. "She has a hard head. To be honest, most of my female patients do. I've often wondered why this is true. Now, I'll bathe the scratches on her face, but there's really nothing more. You can give her laudanum, my lord. Let her sleep the rest of the day, it'll do her good. There will be a good deal of bruising. There's not a thing I can do about that."

He rose after he'd bathed her face, then smiled down at her. "There, not too bad. Good day, Mrs. Carrington."

Never once did he remark on the baron's bare chest, nor, for that matter, did he ever appear discomfited. She heard Rohan say as he walked Dr. Foxdale to the bedchamber door, "They should be bringing back the man who kidnapped Mrs. Carrington. I shot him in the arm. However, the impact knocked him backward into a tree and he knocked himself out."

"I'll stay then, my lord."

The two men shook hands, each apparently well pleased with the other. And the baron was naked to the waist. She wondered if the doctor would have said anything even if the baron had appeared without his britches. Could he do whatever he chose without anyone caring? With, indeed, everyone appearing to admire him, surely to immoderate excess?

He returned in a few minutes, a glass of water in his hand. She watched him measure out several drops of laudanum into the glass. She watched the play of muscles over his belly as he bent over to put the bottle of laudanum back on the tabletop. She had never before seen a man who looked like he did. George had looked well enough, she supposed, but then again, when she'd married George, a man could have had three of anything and she wouldn't have known the difference. Now she knew a little bit more. No man should be beautiful, but the baron was. Blondish-brown hair was soft on his chest, slimming down to a straight line of darker hair that disappeared beneath his britches.

She was suffering from a head wound. Even though she had a hard head, she was still ill. All this was an aberration. A woman didn't overly admire a brother-in-law, no matter what his attributes. This woman didn't. Well, at least this woman would try very hard not to.

She sighed deeply—wishing he would put a shirt on, wishing he would not—and looked at her blanket-covered toes.

"You will feel better in just a moment." He held up her head and slowly fed her the water. She felt the warmth of him against her cheek.

"Thank you," she said, her voice soft and vague. She would not look at him, not ever again. She concentrated on the cherubs that festooned the corners of the ceiling moldings. She felt the pain pulling back, slowly deadening, and releasing her. Her thoughts were blurry, without focus. She heard someone, someone with a soft, woman's voice that sounded suspiciously like her voice, say, "You look very nice all bare. I never thought a man could look like you do. It makes me feel strangely even though I really don't feel very good." From one instant to the next, she was asleep.

He sat beside her, picked up her limp hand, and looked at the slender white fingers. He realized he had forgotten to ask her exactly what had happened. So he looked very nice, did he? He made her feel strangely? He imagined if he told her how he felt, she'd run screaming. Well, maybe not. He smiled, then frowned. He gently laid her hand down and stood. He was a gentleman.

It was dark when Susannah opened her eyes. Only a branch of candles burned atop her small writing desk in the corner of her bedchamber. Shadows twisted and curved about the furniture and the walls, fading into darkness in the corners of the room. But the room was familiar, comforting.

Her head ached only dully now. She felt the swelling on

her face. She didn't want to see herself in the mirror. She got up, relieved herself, then made her way to the window. She pulled back the thick dark-yellow draperies. A quarter of moon shone high in the sky, and a few errant stars peered through the roving clouds.

It would rain before morning.

"What the devil are you doing out of bed?"

She turned slowly at the sound of his voice. "You're not naked anymore." He was wearing a gold brocade dressing gown, rich and thick, but the elbows were nearly worn through. A favorite dressing gown, one enjoyed for many years. But he didn't have all that many years. She supposed, though, that a man of his reputation spent a good deal of time in a dressing gown. And out of it.

Did he detect a note of disappointment in her voice? Yes, it was definitely disappointment. He loved it. He grinned at her, he couldn't help it. "No, I'm not. Sorry, but it seemed civilized to retrieve my shirt from you."

"Surely it was soiled."

"Yes, but I did retrieve it. I didn't put it back on."

She took a step toward him, then stopped. "You didn't retrieve it from me yourself, did you?"

"No. My mother and Mrs. Beete saw to you. Also, my mother's maid, Sabine. Have you yet met Sabine? No? You will. She is quite a treat. Why don't you come back to bed? You're still looking a bit shaky on your bare toes. Does your head still hurt?"

She shook her head, and nearly gasped with the sharp pain. She held herself perfectly still. The pain faded quickly. "It's not bad at all now." She turned to face him fully.

He sucked in his breath, his hands fisting at his sides. "Your face—Jesus, I'll kill that bastard."

She touched her fingertips to her sore cheek. It felt very swollen. She could only begin to picture how dreadful she looked. But she still didn't want to know just how bad it was.

"My God, I hadn't thought the scratches were so bad. But

look at them. You're a mess. Surely he couldn't have done all that to you. What did you do?"

There was utter outrage in his voice. He was also not more than two feet from her now. His eyes were greener than the well-scythed grass on the east lawn. "When I was running from the shack, I fell on my face. It's just scratches. What bothered me more was swallowing dirt and leaves." She tried a smile, but it didn't work.

He reached out his hand and lightly traced his fingertips over her cheek.

"Is that man alive?"

"Yes, but he's still unconscious. Dr. Foxdale doesn't know if he'll ever wake up. He said head wounds are tricky. We'll just have to wait and see."

"He wants a map."

Rohan said nothing, merely took her arm and led her back to her bed.

"Please, not yet. I was growing mold lying in that bed. How are Marianne and Toby?"

"Marianne carried on until I wanted to throw her out of the breakfast parlor window, but I knew you would be distressed if I did. Luckily for me and my poor ears, she managed to exhaust herself in time and fell asleep on me, madly sucking her two fingers."

She could only stare up at him. "You tried to feed her? You didn't leave her with Lottie?"

"Don't sound so astonished, so incredulous. There was no one else to take her. Well, actually it didn't occur to me to ask anyone else. Next time I will. If I see Jamie I will beg him to come sing her a limerick. It certainly works with the horses—why not the little pumpkin? Toby did volunteer—brave lad—but I knew he didn't stand a chance with Marianne. She would have had him lying toes cocked up, pleading for the hereafter. She's fine now, sound asleep. I had no idea so much noise could come out of such a little mouth. I promised her she would see you early tomorrow morning, so prepare yourself. I wouldn't be surprised if she escaped Lottie and came in here at the crack of dawn.''

She was gaping at him. He'd done all that, yet he was jesting about it. But still, it was unbelievable. There was no belief at all in her voice when she asked, ''You are saying that you put Marianne to bed?''

''I didn't give her a bath, or put her in her nightgown, but I must confess that I did tuck her up, pull her fingers out of her mouth, and tell her not to snore. I also gave her a baron kiss since she couldn't have a mama kiss. She really likes the cleft in my chin. Now come with me before you fall over.''

There were two chairs in front of the fireplace, two elegant ladies' chairs, covered with a flower brocade. He led her there. When she was seated, he brought a blanket and covered her legs. Then he himself sat down. The chair groaned a bit, but held, thank God. She was still staring at him. He, a man, had taken care of a little three-year-old girl? It froze the mind. It made her head hurt when it hadn't before.

There was a knock. Rohan just looked toward the door, resignation clear on his face. It opened and Charlotte came in. She was carrying a tray and smiling, a beautiful smile, one that could light up the darkest of rooms.

''Good, my dear, you're awake. You will have a bit to eat, then we will talk.''

At that moment Susannah's stomach growled. Rohan grinned, then laughed at the flush on her swollen cheek. It added a fourth color.

''You see,'' Charlotte said easily, ''it's time. You're hungry, aren't you? Oh, your poor little face. My dear, is the pain dreadful?''

''No, ma'am. Truly, it's not bad. I would appreciate it if you wouldn't tell me how bad I look. I don't want to be cast into severe melancholy. But the food, goodness, I could eat a boot, I think, if it were well boiled, with perhaps a dash of salt for flavoring.''

''Here you are,'' Charlotte said as she placed the tray on

Susannah's lap. "Now, you are to call me Lady Mountvale or Charlotte. My preference is for Charlotte. 'Ma'am' makes me feel dreadfully frail. 'Ma'am' makes my teeth feel loose."

"Yes, Charlotte."

Rohan gave his mother a brooding look. She looked exquisite, her thick blond hair hanging free down her back, tied loosely with a pale blue satin ribbon that matched the outrageously frothy confection she undoubtedly called a dressing gown. She looked delicious. She did not look like his mother. Of course, she had never looked like his mother—anybody's mother, for that matter. She had birthed four babes, yet it hadn't made any difference. He sighed. He wished she would go away, but he knew she wouldn't. There was no hope for it. He rose and fetched another chair.

He said without preamble, as he watched Susannah take a spoonful of chicken broth, "Susannah said the man is after a map. Presumably it is the same man who broke into Mulberry House three times and once before here at Mountvale House. All this effort, for a map?"

"A map?" Charlotte repeated, as she examined her perfect fingernails. "Now surely that is odd. You're absolutely right, dearest, to be incredulous. Why all this bother for a map?"

Susannah said nothing, merely spooned the chicken broth into her mouth. Rohan said, "It's not really all that strange. George has loved maps of all sorts since he was a boy, you know that, Mother. As I recall, when he was only nine years old you gave him a map that was supposedly a sultan's harem quarters with secret passages. You prayed at the time that it would prove beneficial."

"Yes, but it didn't, more's the pity. Well, perhaps it did, given Susannah and Marianne. But, dearest, no one ever tried to steal one before. It must be a very special map. Do you think it could be a treasure map? Now, wouldn't that be exciting. Could George, my darling staid and proper and boring George—who just might not be all that staid and proper—possibly have come across a treasure map?"

Susannah choked on her broth. "Oh, that would be ever so exciting, but I don't think so, Charlotte. If it were some sort of treasure map, then surely George would have said something to me about it. Well, maybe not. I swore to the man that I had only a few of George's belongings and that I had looked. I told him honestly that there was no map."

"Naturally he didn't believe you," Rohan said. He was standing in front of the fireplace, leaning easily against the mantelpiece. "What things of George's do you have?"

The door burst open and Fitz nearly fell through. He managed to straighten. "My lord! Quickly!"

"Oh, dear, what now?" Charlotte said and bounded after the two of them.

"Wait! I will not be left out," Susannah yelled and staggered after them, dizziness nearly sending her to her knees. Rohan turned back, saw her weaving toward them, cursed loudly and fluently, ran back, picked her up in his arms, then raced after Fitz.

"You deserve any headache you get from this," he said. "I will not wring out a damp cloth and lay it across your sweaty brow."

"I never asked you to do that in the first place. Surely it is my right to see what is happening."

They came to an abrupt halt at the top of the wide staircase. At the bottom stood the man, a thick white bandage around his head, his arm in a sling. He was waving a gun wildly and screaming, "Go away, all of you mealy little bastards, go away!" He waved the gun toward two of the footmen who were trying to sneak up on him. They backed off.

"I want the bloody map. It's mine!" He looked up to see the baron holding the woman in his arms, George's woman, the damned woman who was beautiful, the damned woman who had lied to him, who had slammed a hay fork into his gut. He wanted to shoot her, but it wouldn't gain him much at all.

"Damn you!" he yelled. "Give me the damned map! Tell

me where it is or I will begin shooting all these mangy little bastards.''

Carefully, Rohan eased her to the floor. He leaned her against Fitz so she wouldn't fall. Then he began to walk slowly down the stairs.

''What map do you want?'' he called out, all calm and conversational. ''You must be specific or I can't get it for you. She has told me everything. She is confused. But I'm not confused. I can help you. Is this map you want the one George had of that craggy cave in the northern part of Cornwall, near to St. Agnes?''

''No, the one in Scot—no, no, you won't make me spill my innards! You bloody sod! I don't need you, just her!'' He pointed the gun at Rohan and fired. Susannah tried to jerk free of Fitz, but he held her tight. She watched all of it in horror. An eternity passed, but it must have been only the tiniest of moments. Even as the man aimed the gun, Rohan crouched down and lurched sideways. The bullet struck a portrait of a sixteenth-century Carrington, a very handsome gentleman with a wicked look in his dark green eyes, like every other Carrington in the history of the family. The portrait hung there, swinging back and forth, banging heavily against the white wall, until its weight brought it crashing down. But the heavy gold frame didn't crack and break. Instead it hit the stairs and bounced downward until it skidded across the Italian marble tile entrance hall. The man stared at it as it came sliding toward him, as if it were alive, as if it were coming for him. He shot at it, but there had been only one bullet in the gun.

He screamed, trying to run away, but two footmen grabbed him.

Rohan walked to the man, now being held between his two men. The man looked dreadful—wild-eyed and white as death. His mouth worked, but no sound came out. The baron said very gently, ''What is your name? If you will but tell me, perhaps I can help you.''

The man spit on him full in the face.

Slowly Rohan wiped the spittle on his sleeve. "Perhaps I can guess your name. Are you Theodore Micah?"

The man's face turned even whiter, if that was possible. "How do you know of him?" His eyes—cold gray eyes—rolled in his head. There was an odd gurgling sound. Without warning, he slumped to the floor, catching the footmen off guard.

Rohan leaned down and pressed his fingers against the pulse in his neck. It was slow and thready.

He looked over at the portrait, lying face up, his sixteenth-century ancestor looking smug. No, this was silly. It was just a stupid portrait. He frowned. The man had simply collapsed, for no good reason. "Well, our fellow here is still alive. Have Dr. Foxdale fetched again, Fitz. Mrs. Beete, have one of the maids bring some blankets. I don't think we should move him."

"Gullet him is what I'd like to do," Mrs. Beete said, shaking a fist at the unconscious man.

"My lord," Fitz said, his face whiter than that of the man at their feet, "did you see the portrait attack him? It was your great uncle Fester Carrington. Oh, my." Now everyone was staring at the painting, which lay harmlessly not a foot from the fallen man.

Rohan picked up the portrait and handed it to Fitz, whose face spasmed as he took it. Then he looked from one footman to another. "How did this happen? How the devil did he get out of his room and have a gun?"

It was Augustus who stepped forward, shoulders back, chin high. "It is I who am responsible, my lord. I looked at him every half hour or so, since he was still unconscious. I guess I finally dozed off. It is entirely my fault."

Rohan gave him a very long look, then said, "I will speak to you in the morning, Augustus."

12

IT WAS NEARLY MIDNIGHT.

"You should go to bed now, Susannah."

"Not yet. I would have nightmares. How could he have just collapsed like that, Rohan? It happened so quickly. You didn't even hit him. Nobody touched him."

"Probably that head wound did him in. At least Dr. Foxdale believed that to be the case when he examined him just a while ago. Don't worry, we'll find out what's behind all this even if the fellow doesn't wake up again."

"He's not Theodore Micah."

"No, but he knows who that is. You were right to tell me about those two men with George. I had rather hoped they were involved, since we needed names, but I really didn't credit it until tonight. Yes, they are involved, up to their hairlines."

"I hope he wakes up. I'd like to help Mrs. Beete gullet him!"

"I would rather like to see that. Now, if you don't want to go to bed yet, then keep eating the broth that Mrs. Horsely heated for you and tell me the rest of it."

There was a light knock on the door.

Rohan rose, saying over his shoulder to Susannah, "I expected her sooner, truth be told. I suppose she was comforting poor Augustus for his guarding lapse. It wouldn't surprise me a bit.''

"He is handsome," Susannah said. "Those snapping black eyes of his—they simply make me shiver.''

Rohan grunted and she giggled. She thought she heard him snarl, "Women.''

Charlotte was subdued. She took the chair beside Susannah's. "Have you told Rohan anything yet, my dear?''

"We were just beginning, Mother. Now, Susannah, before we were interrupted you were telling me what belongings you have that belonged to George.''

"A vest, some books. I didn't tell him about the locket. It's very small, there couldn't be a map in it.''

"Where are the books and the vest?''

"I left them at Mulberry House. But I had already searched them, Rohan. I'm not entirely without wits, you know, and I decided it must have something to do with George, so I thoroughly examined the three books and tore the lining out of the vest. There was no map there. He had left nothing else at Mulberry House.''

"All right, then, where is the locket?''

"But—''

"Bring us the locket, Susannah.''

"I'm wearing it.'' She lifted her hair to let Charlotte unfasten the clasp.

Charlotte gently undid the clasp. She was on the point of opening the locket when she paused, looked at her son, who had his hand out, sighed, and handed the locket to him, the thin gold chain hanging down between her fingers.

"I know that was difficult for you, Mother, but thank you for the consideration.''

Charlotte sighed. "It is most depressing to have to give you the locket, particularly since I wanted to find the treasure map.'' She looked at Susannah. "One must compromise when one is a woman.''

"Surely this is the first time you've ever been required to do anything remotely resembling compromise,'' said her son as he toyed with the locket. "Father did always say, though, that compromise was the very devil." The locket was shaped like a heart, not at all original but the quality was acceptable.

"If you two would cease your recriminations, I could show you how to open it. You'll see it's much too small to hide anything."

It took her only a moment. "There's this small catch at the bottom, here. There, see, there is a miniature of George on one side and one of Marianne on the other."

Why not of Susannah? Rohan wondered, taking the locket back from her. Very carefully, he removed Marianne's portrait, smaller than his thumbnail. He held the locket close to the candle and gently pressed against the gold, but there was nothing there. It was perfectly flat. Then he pulled out George's small portrait. George couldn't have been more than twenty when it was painted. He was smiling. His shirt had very high points. His hair seemed just a bit longer. He looked stiff, uncomfortable. Rohan shook his head. His memory had simply rearranged itself. George was George, and he'd died, damn him. And he'd left a mess behind. What else had he done?

He laid the small portrait on the table and held the locket close to the light. He felt the gold back. It wasn't flat, as was the other side.

"Well, well," he said slowly, "what have we here?"

Charlotte nearly tripped over her chair to get to him.

Susannah dropped her soup bowl and yelped when the soup splattered on her bare feet. "Goodness, what have you found? Tell us! Don't just stare at it as if it were a snake to bite you. I'll bite you."

Rohan merely toyed with the barest hint of a gold ridge at the edge of the locket. Then, quite suddenly, without his knowing what he had done, it snapped open. He handed the locket to Susannah. "Pull out the paper. It's too small for me to grasp. Be careful, Susannah."

Charlotte sighed and crowded closer.

Susannah managed to press the small square of paper hard enough against her finger pad so that it stuck. Slowly she pulled it away. The paper fell to the tabletop. On top of it landed a very small golden key. Rohan picked up the key. "How could something so tiny fit a lock?"

Charlotte took it from him and laid it flat on her palm. "I believe there's some writing on it, dearest. But that can wait. Is that a map?"

"Unfold it," said Rohan.

Flattened, the paper was only about half the size of Susannah's palm. It was indeed a map—a map that was blurred and faded and very hard to make out. Rohan said slowly, "When I tricked the man, he started to spit out 'Scotland.' Do you remember?"

"I remember, dearest. It was very well done of you. Not only are you delightfully profligate and wicked to a fault, you are of a brilliance that rivals the sun itself."

"I shall surely be ill," Susannah remarked to no one in particular.

Charlotte ignored her. "Your dear father sometimes agreed that you had my brains. I think that you've now proved it conclusively. Bravo, dearest."

"I think I will be ill again," Susannah said. She looked at Rohan, who was paying no attention to either of them. "If you know so much, Rohan, since you are so terribly clever, just where in Scotland? And what does this key belong to?"

"I haven't the foggiest idea," he said, clearly distracted, "on either count, at least not yet. Now, be quiet, both of you. Mother, have one of the footmen—Augustus, if you like—fetch my magnifying glass from the estate room. It should be in the top left drawer of my desk."

His mother raised a perfect blond eyebrow at him, saying, "I am amazed that you would know the location of such a mundane sort of article, dearest. Surely a man of your reputation wouldn't retain memory of something like that. It is something a good servant would know, but not you, not the master, the baron, the . . ."

"Please, Mother, we need the magnifying glass."

Seven minutes later, Rohan was closely studying the small yellowed piece of paper. "It is a map," he said, more to himself than to the two women. "But unfortunately it's only half a map. Now I can see the clean cut along this side. I can make out a body of water by these squiggly lines, and they continue off the paper. See these lines here? They must be paths branching away from the water. Perhaps these blocks are meant to represent houses. And yes, here are words, tiny words, but I can make them out."

He couldn't, however, make them out with his mother and Susannah crowding in on him.

"Susannah, sit down. Mother, your perfume palsies my man's senses. Please move away. Good, now let's see what we've got."

"Rohan, you've been staring at it for an hour," Susannah said, crowding close again. "Come, what do you see? What does it say?"

Slowly he straightened. "It says, 'Seek the room below the tide.' Which makes no sense at all except it might mean it's near the sea. What sea? East coast or west coast? There is another word that has only two letters remaining after the map was cut into two. 'DU'."

"What room?" Susannah said. "One of those little blocks?"

Now that was a kicker. Susannah frowned down at the small scrap of paper, then up at Rohan. "The squiggly lines are a river. Which one, I wonder?"

"I have no idea."

"What's 'DU'?" Charlotte said. "The beginning of a town name? A shop? This is depressing. I had hoped for a better map, even though it is only half a map. It is of no use at all."

"I think perhaps these tiny blocks do represent houses and that they also represent a specific street in some town in Scotland, one that has a river running through it," Rohan said.

"How do you know that?" Charlotte asked, her smooth white forehead puckering in a frown. Rohan traced his fingertip along the blocks. "Yes, I see. That's really quite clever of you, dearest."

"Yes, Mother."

"Excuse me," Susannah said, "but I can see that they represent a line of buildings myself. I am just as clever as Rohan."

Charlotte looked at her thoughtfully. "I don't know you well enough yet to judge that, Susannah. Now, why did George have this map? Why did he hide it in the locket? And this key—"

"Yes," Rohan said, "the key." He laid it flat on his palm close to the candlelight and brought the magnifying glass over it. He grimaced. He tilted the glass first one way and then the other. He became aware that Susannah and his mother were crowding in again. "I can't make out what someone carved on it," he said finally.

Susannah took the magnifying glass and studied the marks on the tiny key. "I believe it's Latin," she said at last. "Yes, it appears to be a name, but it is so worn into the gold I can't make it out."

"Nor can I," Rohan said after a few minutes. "Are you sure it's Latin, Susannah? How do you know it's Latin? You're a woman. Couldn't it just as well be German or Greek?"

"Now, dearest, that sort of remark isn't going to bring you a pleasant rejoinder. I did agree that it is too soon to judge Susannah's degree of cleverness, but I do not believe that she is utterly ignorant."

"Thank you, Charlotte. I think. Yes, it's Latin as well."

There was a knock on the door. Rohan arched an eyebrow.

"Oh, who now?" Susannah said, throwing up her hands and staggering to the door.

"Damnation, you're still too weak to do that. Susannah, stop." She did. He clasped her around her waist and held her against him, saying, "Come."

It was Toby, in his nightshirt. "I couldn't stand it," he said, rushing into speech. "Please, what's happening? Did you find anything?"

Rohan picked Susannah up and carried her to the bed. "You will stay here and you will not complain." He tucked her in, then turned to her brother. "We found a half of a map inside the locket George gave your sister. Written on it is 'Seek the room below the tide.' And two letters of what is perhaps a town name. Your sister here believes there's a Latin word on this small key we found with it. I don't suppose you can make out what's carved into the gold?"

"Yes," Charlotte said, coming closer to Toby, "can you make it out?"

Toby looked at Charlotte, at the lovely clothes she was wearing, and stammered, "I'll try." Toby studied the word, then inked the quill and wrote it out. He looked at Rohan. "It is Latin. I believe it's a name. 'Leo' with roman numerals after it. An *I* and an *X*."

"Leo," Rohan repeated. "Yes, you're right. It's 'Leo IX.' A pope. Well, this could prove interesting. Toby, come with me to the library. We have a bit of looking up to do. No, Mother, please stay with Susannah, otherwise she will come after us and likely fall down the stairs and break her neck."

Charlotte didn't look happy. She saw that Susannah was swinging her legs over the side of her bed, and so she said quickly, "Very well, I'll stay here. But you will hurry, won't you?"

"Yes."

They returned to Susannah's bedchamber in twenty minutes. Rohan was smiling and rubbing his hands together. Toby was looking thoroughly confused. "What is it?" Susannah said, trying to sit up, only to have Rohan gently push her back down. "What did you find?"

"Leo IX was a pope in the eleventh century, specifically from 1049 to 1054."

The women stared at him blankly.

"Why do we have a key that belonged to Leo IX? How-

ever," Rohan continued after a moment, "we checked on
something else too. The map refers to something in Scotland.
What would Leo IX have to do with Scotland? It was a
dangerous, violent time. No pope visited Scotland, but just
maybe a Scot did journey to Rome to see the pope. Toby
and I looked up the king of Scotland during Leo IX's reign.
There was only one. Macbeth. He was murdered by Malcolm
in 1057, who usurped the throne. This happened after the
pope was already dead."

"Usurped the throne?" Charlotte said. "But Shakespeare
made Macbeth the usurper."

"That was all politics," Rohan said, looking down at the
key. "When Shakespeare wrote the play, James VI of Scotland had just come to take Elizabeth's throne, in 1603, thus
becoming James I of England. No, the real Macbeth was a
fine ruler. He was so popular, peace prevailed so thoroughly
throughout his reign, that he was able—" He stopped and
smiled hugely at the two women. Then he began to whistle.

"If you don't tell us, I will flatten you," Susannah said.
"Now spit it out. What did you find?"

"Macbeth was so secure on his throne that he was able to
make a pilgrimage to see the pope."

"Leo IX?"

"Yes, Susannah, it's very possible. Just perhaps the pope
gave him something and Macbeth brought this something
back to Scotland with him. Toby will do more research tomorrow. Of course we could be wrong about the Macbeth
connection, but it seems the best place to begin."

"I wonder where the other half of the map is?" Susannah
said. "I wonder what the pope gave to Macbeth?"

"I don't know," Rohan said slowly. "But one thing is
likely. I think the only place we're going to find answers is
in Oxford. That is, after all, where George got half of the
map, where our prisoner came from. Yes, I'm leaving tomorrow."

"Oh, yes, sir," Toby said, bouncing on his heels in excitement. "That's exactly what we must do. That's where

George lived. He must have known something. We can find out about these other men as well. May I come with you?''

He saw the excitement in Toby's dark blue eyes, remembered his own boundless excitement when he had been Toby's age, and said slowly, "I will think about it. First, we must wait to see if our villain awakens. I'm still hoping that he will tell us something useful.''

"What did the pope give to Macbeth?" Susannah said again, more to herself than to them. "It must have been something he prized, a treasure of some sort. But why?''

"Macbeth was a good man," Rohan said. "Evidently a man to trust. Perhaps the pope had to give whatever it was over to Macbeth. Perhaps he had no choice in the matter." Rohan threw up his hands. "It's all supposition. But it is a start.''

"There is another thing, dearest. Did you forget our dinner and ball on Friday night? Everyone has been invited and everyone has, naturally, accepted.''

"Look at Susannah's face, Mother. Also, she might still be staggering about on Friday.''

"No, I will be perfectly fine," Susannah said. "But he's right, Charlotte—my face is a mess.''

"Two days from now. Hmmm." Charlotte lightly traced her fingertips of the bruises. "They should be light enough by Friday so that some judiciously placed cosmetics will do the trick. Sabine is really quite good. I will have her attend you.''

"She shouldn't wear cosmetics.''

Charlotte straightened, looked at her son, and raised a perfect blond eyebrow. "Goodness, dearest, why ever not?''

He had no answer except, "She doesn't need it. She would look foolish. She would look like an opera girl.''

"He should know," Charlotte said with a good deal of satisfaction. "About opera girls, that is.''

"You cannot cancel the party," Susannah said. "If I look too awful, then I won't come.''

"Very well," Rohan said, seeing no hope for it. "Wear any bloody cosmetics Mother believes you still need."

Charlotte nodded, then said calmly, "I will have no arguments from you, Susannah. You will wear one of my gowns. I doubt Rohan will let you out of bed long enough tomorrow to be measured for a new one."

Rohan felt an intense bolt of lust. She was ill; she was in bed. But it didn't seem to matter. "I'm going to bed. Toby? Are you coming?"

By Friday Susannah wasn't staggering about at all. The bruises on her face had faded considerably. Rohan knew that his mother would powder her all up, but he supposed he couldn't say anything.

As for their villain, the man had finally awakened, but he refused to say a word. He just turned his head to the wall whenever anyone came into the room.

"I wish I had some thumbscrews," Rohan said, loud enough for the man to hear. "I believe I will go to the village and see what the blacksmith has lying about."

There was no getting a thing out of him.

Marianne wouldn't permit her mother out of her sight, letting loose a howl anytime Susannah attempted to excuse herself, if only for a moment. Rohan imagined that the child held Susannah's hand even when she relieved herself.

Toby and Vicar Byam were reading everything they could find about Macbeth, king of the Scots, and his reign.

Rohan and Toby planned to leave Saturday morning for Oxford.

He'd said to Susannah, "You know you can't come. Marianne won't let you go anywhere, and I refuse to relive our first trip through Oxford. It was a nightmare. Besides, this could prove dangerous."

"Then I don't want Toby to go."

He'd nailed himself to the floor with that one. An excellent representative of his gender, he said, "I will think about it."

They were expecting thirty neighbors that warm moonlit

evening. Rohan was pacing the entryway, looking alternately up the stairs for Susannah and gazing at his mother, who was turned out beautifully, her glorious blond hair piled atop her head with long curls down her neck and a pale peach silk gown slithering over her body. One of the footmen was so taken when he saw her that he dropped the dreadfully ugly epergne that had sat for years in the center of the huge dining table.

Where was Susannah? Then he heard someone clear his throat, loudly. It was Toby, standing at the top of the stairs. "Rohan? Milady? Are you ready?"

There was a squeak behind Toby and a wail. "Oh, Toby, how could you?"

"A fanfare," Rohan said loudly. "Commence." He laughed, waiting. Then she appeared beside Toby. Rohan didn't move. Actually, he didn't think he could have in any case. He could only stare at her. "Susannah?" His voice sounded low and rusty. He continued to stare at her, at each step she took, bringing her closer and closer to him.

She walked down the stairs so carefully and slowly that he wondered if she was wearing new slippers and they pinched her feet. She'd sworn to him that she was no longer sore or dizzy.

"I am pleased," Charlotte said. "I shall compliment Sabine myself, although she knows she is a genius."

"Oh, my God," Rohan said, though he hadn't meant to say anything of the kind. He'd seen dozens of women more beautiful than Susannah, but for the life of him they had just disappeared without a trace from his mind.

She stopped dead in her tracks, looking him in the face for the first time. She ran her tongue over her bottom lip. "I look all right? It's your mother's gown, but she assured me that the color suited me. I have never worn anything of this shade of blue. Is it too light? Too dark? It is a wonderful gown. I've never had anything so very lovely. Sabine arranged my hair for me. Is it all right? Do you like all the braids and twists and things?"

He got a hold on himself. "I like that shade of blue and the matching ribbon in your hair. You look acceptable. Yes, fine. Are you ready? I believe I hear our first guests arriving. Mother, come here and give everyone a sweet smile and tell poor Susannah that she won't scare our guests away."

"Yes, dearest. You have not shamed me, Susannah."

"Thank you, Charlotte."

"Where is Marianne? She finally let you go?"

Susannah smiled then, although she was so nervous she wanted to faint. "I promised her cook's apple tarts if she would let go of my ankle."

Toby, garbed entirely in black, just like Rohan, laughed, shaking his head. "Marianne's a little pig. I asked her if she wanted Susannah or an apple tart and she shouted, 'Tart,' at the top of her lungs."

"That sounds interesting," Charlotte said.

Lord and Lady Dauntry were the first to arrive. Rohan liked Lord Dauntry, a man who tended his lands well and treated his tenants fairly. He was lucky in his offspring, but his wife was another matter. She controlled her husband, her four daughters, her two sons, and even the pretentious Mrs. Gibbs, a local matron who could trace her roots to the Conqueror. Rohan was also of the belief that Lady Dauntry could very probably fillet a fish with her tongue without stopping her conversation.

He didn't realize how much of another matter Lady Dauntry was until nearly midway through the evening. Dinner had gone quite nicely, and the dancing had begun.

Rohan danced a cotillion with Susannah, then danced a country reel with his mother. Everyone had treated Susannah with a good deal of curiosity. He picked up some talk about the kidnapping and how he had ridden up to Mountvale House with her naked and sitting on his lap. He'd expected that kind of exaggeration. On the whole, he was rather proud of his neighbors. At least most of their talk was behind their hands. They were polite to Susannah when they weren't talking about her.

He watched her dancing with Amos Mortimer, a rather desiccated older gentleman who raised pigs, not for market but as pets. She danced beautifully. As for Mr. Mortimer, though his thin legs looked barely capable of holding him upright, he could dance and he did it well.

It was nearly midnight when Toby caught him at the end of a country reel. "Hurry! Hurry, Rohan! They've got Susannah and I think they're going to bury her. She looks ready to spit. She also looks ready to fall over. Most of the powder's off her face and you can see the bruises. Hurry, you've got to stop it. You're the only one who can stop it."

"Who? Stop what? What are you talking about, Toby?" But Toby was already running out of the ballroom and up the stairs, Rohan on his heels. Had the man escaped? Had he captured Susannah?

Toby skidded to a halt in front of the open door of the ladies' withdrawing room. He waved to Rohan, his finger pressed against his lips.

"I AM TRULY MUCH BETTER NOW, MA'AM," SUSANNAH said easily enough to Mrs. Hackles, but to Rohan's ears she sounded ready to scream. "You are so kind to inquire about my health. I admit that I was a bit shaky for a little while."

Lady Dauntry had sent in her troops to soften up the enemy. Now she was primed to advance, her cannon all lined up and ready to fire. She gave Susannah a sweet and quite deadly look. "I see that dear Charlotte managed to cover the bruises on your face."

"Yes."

The three ladies were circled around her, between her and the door. This was odd. What did they want? Lady Dauntry continued, "As for the rest of it, I believe you were perhaps dancing a bit on the fast side with young Peter Briar, the poor boy. He really isn't quite up to snuff—your sort of snuff, that is."

What was Lady Dauntry talking about? Susannah said only, "Yes, I had to catch my breath when the dance stopped. Why is Peter Briar a poor boy?"

"As I said, you were on the fast side."

Susannah knew when a double entendre had hit her in the nose. She wanted to leave now, but the two other ladies were effectively blocking the door.

Mrs. Hackles, obviously a crony of Lady Dauntry's, seemed intent on pushing the point in case it had been lost on Susannah: "But this wasn't the first time you were too fast, was it? No, there you were, naked in the baron's arms. His hand was against your naked leg. All of us saw you. Mrs. Goodgame was quite distressed, as were Lady Dauntry and I. Yes, the dear baron was carrying you—in his arms. He had dressed you in his shirt and coat. He had obviously seen you naked."

"But I had been kidnapped," Susannah said, raising her hands in protest, perhaps even to ward them off, then dropping her hands again because she realized it would be useless. "Truly I was kidnapped. The man who kidnapped me is just down the hall. Ask any of the footmen. Ask Charlotte. Ask the baron."

"It isn't that, dear," said Mrs. Goodgame, obviously another fine markswoman. "It's that the baron even brought you up here and put you in your bed. How do we know that? We know everything. He probably even reclaimed his shirt and jacket; it would be in his nature to do so. He has known you, my poor Mrs. Carrington. *Known you.*"

"Yes," said Lady Dauntry, her slick politeness long gone. "We all know that a young woman newly widowed is not all that careful with her reputation."

"But I have been widowed for a year."

"A year is nothing to a woman of your stamp. Indeed, in the presence of your very dashing brother-in-law, you have lost any morals you might have laid claim to. Have you seduced the poor baron? It doesn't matter, you know."

"No," said Mrs. Hackles, the first of Lady Dauntry's Greek chorus, "you cannot trick him into marrying you as you probably did poor George Carrington, who had never looked at a girl in his young life—such a pity for his parents. No, a brother cannot marry his brother's wife. That is the law. You obviously didn't know that, but now you do. It is best that you take your child and leave the poor baron and his sweet mother alone. You have intruded, and it is vulgar."

Susannah could only gawk at them. Her head, which hadn't ached in two days, had begun to throb with a vengeance. Her eyes hurt just from looking at the three women who were marshaling themselves around her, eyeing her with the enthusiasm of a hanging judge facing a room full of thieves. She wanted out of here, but she knew she would have to knock them down to get to the door.

She would try reason. She looked at each of them, splaying her hands. "But what did I do?"

"You took off your clothes and tried to seduce the poor baron, pretending that the man had hurt you," said Lady Dauntry—no hesitation at all. "We have all discussed it. You are not welcome here. Indeed, we wonder if you were even married to poor, stuffy George. The dear baron will find out all about you and then he will kick you out, the little boy and that little bastard with you."

Susannah was ready to crash herself into all three ladies. She hoped she would break an arm, a leg, mayhap even a head. How dare they call Marianne a bastard! She was an instant away from attack when she heard a man's voice.

"Ladies, I hope I'm not disturbing you." It was Rohan, gracefully skirting her attackers, coming into the ladies' withdrawing room, a room no gentleman was supposed to acknowledge even existed. Susannah drew up short, staring at him. How long had he been there? How much had he heard? Oh, dear, what would he do?

He continued in that easy voice of his, "It is pleasant to have such caring neighbors, isn't it, Susannah? You're looking just a bit peaked. I tried to keep you in bed, but you couldn't bear lying there, growing mold, you told me. Now look what's happened. I will have my mother come see to you shortly.

"Ladies, I'm glad you are all here, for if Susannah had become faint, then you would have seen to her. I thank you all for your concern, your generosity."

"My lord," said Lady Dauntry, "surely Mrs. Carrington

is still too unwell to be dancing with such verve. We have already told her that.''

"Yes, I believe I heard you say that," said Rohan. "You know, after listening to you, I have begun to wonder. Do you suppose that since her face still looks like a battlefield, she planned for it to look like that? Do you believe it is cosmetics that make her look so awful? I ask myself, is all this a ruse?''

Mrs. Hackles said, in a very loud, carrying voice that could have deafened a horse at fifty feet, "We will assume that you are jesting, my lord. There is too much sarcasm in it to be an excellent jest, but we will accept it as an attempt at a jest nonetheless. She was quite naked just three days ago—''

"And you were carrying her," Lady Dauntry said. "My dearest husband remarked that your hand was on her leg— the top of her leg. Her naked leg. He was naturally upset.''

"Jealous, was he?"

"My lord!"

"You are purposely avoiding the point," said Lady Dauntry.

All three of the ladies were well prepared to explore that exact point ad infinitum. It was at that moment that Rohan realized it wouldn't end. Susannah would be ostracized. He'd been dreaming when he'd thought that everything would be all right, that his neighbors would fall into line. He supposed he should just give her the twenty thousand pounds and send her on her way. Yes, that would be the right thing to do. It was the only honorable thing to do. She deserved it, no matter what George had done. It would free him of her presence, it would solve all the attendant problems that she carried with her. Yes, that was what he would do.

He said, "Actually, ladies, you are perfectly right. I heard you questioning whether or not she was even married to my brother George, questioning whether her child is a bastard. Let me be frank with you all, for you have known me since I was just a lad and have always had my best interests at heart.'' He drew a deep breath and spit it out, not looking back. ''You are perfectly correct. Mrs. Carrington was never married to my brother George.''

Susannah had been watching Rohan with the admiration that she would feel for a great orator who was demolishing other pretenders. But not now. She couldn't have heard him right. She could only stare at him, as were those three wretched besoms. Her head was pounding now, nausea roiling in her stomach. She managed to ease down onto a chair. She closed her eyes. Perhaps if she kept them closed, all of this would disappear.

''It's all right, my love,'' Rohan said, smiling at her, his voice sweet and soothing. She managed to cock her eye open at that. *His love?* What was he up to? Oh, God, she knew she wasn't going to like it, whatever it was.

''Yes. You see, my dear ladies, it was never George she was married to. I am the Carrington she married. Susannah has been my wife for four and a half years. Yes, indeed. Marianne is our legitimate child.''

The three ladies looked as if they'd just swallowed raw herring.

''That is absurd!''

''That makes no sense at all!''

''You continue with your god-awful jests, my boy!''

Rohan spread his hands in front of him. He actually looked embarrassed, he was a bit flushed with chagrin. ''Well, actually, let me be totally honest here. You deserve it. You see, I was trying to bring my mother around to accepting her,'' the baron said. ''My dear mother didn't want me to marry so young, and indeed, I was the greenest young man when I met and married Susannah. But you see, I fell violently in love with her. I knew I could not take her for a mistress. She is a lady. On the other hand, dear ladies, I didn't want to break my parents' hearts. They wanted me so much to become a sensualist that Society could admire and they knew that it would require years of continual practice and refining of skills. Also, I didn't want to make my father believe that

I had no control over my, er, 'lustful young man' instincts. My father, as you know, believed that a man should be controlled so that he could always give of his best to the ladies.''

"That is true about your dear parents, baron," Mrs. Goodgame said, "but you married this chit? When you were only twenty-one years old? It makes no sense."

"And not tell your parents?" Mrs. Hackles said, an impossibly thick eyebrow inching up. "Surely they would come about if indeed you were married to the girl. You say she's a lady? Just look at her—that loose gown, those cosmetics on her face."

"That is my mother's gown and my mother also applied the cosmetics to hide the bruises."

"Well, it is a different matter when dear Charlotte wears a gown like that. She would look like an angel in that gown, not a loose chit like this girl looks."

Susannah could only stare at Lady Dauntry. She wanted to scream at all of them that she was a lady, that her poor gambling father was half Irish but her mother had been a knight's daughter who was unceremoniously drummed out of the family when she'd married beneath herself. She knew if she opened her mouth, she would yell and then she would be sick. But what to do? What was Rohan doing, claiming that he was married to her? Perhaps she had heard him wrong. Perhaps this was all a game to him.

He leaned closer to the three ladies, who were regarding him as if he had just escaped from Bedlam.

"You all have my best interests at heart, I can see that. You want to protect me. But it isn't a matter of protection. Perhaps you can help me convince my dear mother that I love my wife and my daughter and it is time for me to bring them out of the cellar, so to speak.

"It was I who made up this tale about Susannah's being married to George. Just look at that pathetic little face of hers, ladies. Even without cosmetics covering the bruises, she would look on the pathetic side. I ask you, could that face launch even one ship? No, not even a raft—that is what you're thinking. But she is sweet and she is the mother of my child. She is my responsibility. I cannot very well kick her out.

"Yes, ladies, if my mother still doesn't wish to accept Susannah, may I count on you to assist me to make my dearest Susannah accepted?"

Lady Dauntry was in the biggest quandary of her life. Her tongue was all sharpened, but what was she to fillet?

Mrs. Hackles readily agreed that the girl looked pathetic. What else could she say?

Mrs. Goodgame sighed, her heart touched despite herself. It was an affecting story. Rohan Carrington had disappointed all of them, truth be told, but he had married this girl and she had borne him a child. What to do? She sighed again. She saw clearly that her dear friend Lady Dauntry, their undisputed leader, was looking as if she'd been shot in both feet. She would deal with this, then. She said, "Almeria, Elsa, listen to me. We cannot let our dear boy down. If need be, we must help dear Charlotte understand that she simply must accept this girl here. But, my dear boy, a question. Why did you create this fiction involving George?"

"So I could bring Susannah here to my home. So I could prepare Mother for the treat. Marianne is her granddaughter. I could not bear to keep denying her the flesh of her flesh."

"This would not necessarily be a treat, my lord," Lady Dauntry said, "to our dear Charlotte."

Rohan looked genuinely downcast. It was a very effective pose.

"Very well," Lady Dauntry said at last. "We do not wish you to be hurt over this fiasco. If dear Charlotte cannot bring herself to accept this, then we will speak to her. For you, dear boy, for you."

Rohan gave them a boyish smile that held such relief and gratitude, Susannah was certain he could rival Edmund Kean.

She decided to wait until the ladies left before she killed him.

Lady Dauntry eyed her, seeing that she looked very pale,

despite the nasty cosmetics that made her look very pathetic, just as the dear baron had said, poor boy. "You look sickly, my lady. Don't stare like a half-wit. Since you are the baron's wife, you must be accorded the title."

My lady? Oh, dear, oh, dear.

"Yes," Lady Dauntry continued, in control again now, "it must be accepted that a husband could dress his own wife in his shirt and jacket. It must be accepted that he could carry her, his hand on her naked leg—the top of her naked leg—to her bedchamber. Yes, we will accept this and we will make our husbands stop looking at you as if you were a hussy. We will even accept that you were kidnapped and that our dear boy here saved you." She paused, looking pointedly at Mrs. Hackles.

"Yes," said Mrs. Hackles, jumping in with both feet now that she knew which direction to jump. "We will even overlook this strange tale the dear boy tells. If my own son had done such a thing, why, I'm sure that I would like to meet my grandchild, but I don't know about Charlotte."

Rohan said easily, "She has accepted Marianne, thank the good Lord. It's just that she still believes that Marianne is George's daughter, not mine."

"That is something," said Mrs. Goodgame. "It is just that dear Charlotte isn't expecting this. Surely she believed you would marry a lady of her choosing, one who would be just like her or a milksop who wouldn't say a word when her husband left her to be with his score of mistresses. There would be no other sort of wife for you, in Charlotte's mind."

Lady Dauntry bent a fierce eye on Susannah. "Are you like dear Charlotte?"

"In what way?" Susannah felt as though she were a minor actress in a play, only she didn't know her lines. Nor did she know the ending of the play. Perhaps all the actors would suddenly stop speaking their lines and burst into insane laughter.

"I suppose you've only just met your mother-in-law," Mrs. Goodgame said. "Charlotte, very simply, isn't like any other lady in the land. She is herself. She is so beautiful she is entitled to do anything she wishes, with anyone she wishes. It is a paradox. Her dear husband—the baron's dear father—adored her. Fortunately, he shared the same inclinations. All worked out well until our dear boy here slipped and took a mighty fall. You're only twenty-five, Rohan, and you have a child. Not a mere little babe, but a child. You have a wife. It flabbergasts the mind. It renders one speechless.''

Nothing had ever rendered any of these ladies speechless, Rohan thought.

''Perhaps,'' Mrs. Hackles said, leaning toward Susannah and lightly thumping her fan on Susannah's knuckles, ''you are a milksop. That will do just as well. There is no possible way that you could ever be like Charlotte even if you tried. You're not pretty enough. You haven't a word to say for yourself. You are doubtless lacking in wits. You are perhaps boring. Further, you don't have her sweetness, her divine sense of the wicked and the clever. Yes, you must be a milksop. It is the only thing you can be to make all of this work out properly.''

Susannah jerked out of her chair, her head pounding and her stomach roiling and vomited short of the basin in the corner behind the screen.

''Yes,'' she heard Lady Dauntry say with some satisfaction, ''she is a milksop, so you are saved, my dear boy. Surely a woman like Charlotte—indeed, a woman with any spirit at all—would not have been content to live in the middle of nowhere with little or nothing were she married to you. Had she any spirit at all, she would have arrived on your doorstep, her child in her arms, and demanded to take her place in your home. But she didn't do any of this. No, she stayed where you put her. You will do well with a milksop. You will continue to be true to your nature—as you have, even though you married her. Just look at all you've accomplished in the past four years. You are growing into your dear parents' beliefs and habits and endearing ways. Perhaps we shan't despair."

Rohan heard the sound of dry heaves. He prayed Susannah would continue vomiting. It would keep her mouth shut, so to speak. He prayed that Toby would remain in the corridor, his own mouth firmly seamed together.

He clasped Lady Dauntry's hands in his. "Your consideration and devotion touch me, ladies." He gave each of them a tender smile. A man of his reputation could produce a tender smile for the sourest of old biddies. "Now, perhaps you would consent to see my dear mother tomorrow. You will all convince her that Susannah is a fit wife for me—in short, a milksop wife. You will ensure that she is well on her way to accepting my marriage. I thank you."

He actually bowed, Susannah saw, poking her head around the screen. He was incredible. The ladies then walked out, and she heard scattered words about who would speak about what to dear Charlotte.

She rose to her feet, hanging on to the screen, which wobbled, and said, "I am not pathetic. I could launch a raft. I am going to kill you now."

Not a moment later, Toby came into the room. His eyes looked glazed. He said, "Don't kill him until he can tell me why he told those ladies that you and he were married."

Both of them were staring hard at him. Rohan saw that Susannah's hands were two quite efficient-looking fists. She was still pale; the powder was off and he could see the green and yellow of the bruises on her cheek. Her beautiful gown was askew.

He said gently, "Would you like to clean out your mouth, Susannah?"

"No, not yet. Tell us now, Rohan. I don't want to have cramps in my fists."

He looked at the pitiful girl in front of him, then at Toby, who looked as shocked as a vicar in a brothel, and smiled. "I haven't the foggiest idea why I did it."

14

THEY SAT OPPOSITE EACH OTHER, DRINKING TEA LIKE A companionable married couple after a long evening.

"You asked me why I did something so incredibly unexpected," Rohan said at last, wishing she had said something first, but she hadn't. "I have told you I don't know why I did it, but dammit, Susannah, it is done. It cannot now be undone. Another thing: I don't think it was stupid. I believe this will solve every problem. I'm not sorry I did it." And to his own astonishment, it was true. He didn't regret it at all. The truth was, he wanted to marry her. No wonder he was so comfortable with his lie. However, having told it, he didn't think marrying Susannah would be any easier to execute for having claimed her as his wife.

Susannah was striving for patience. "Rohan, in olden times, you would have been the perfect gentle knight. But what you told those three old witches was a lie, a bold-faced lie. A quite silly lie, really, since anyone can so easily find out that it is a lie. I was married to George. You have just added to my problems. If you and I were married, we would be breaking the law."

"No, we wouldn't."

She just shook her head at him, clearly distracted, thinking, speaking again. "Just send me away. I will never bother you again. I am not your responsibility. I did quite well until you came along."

He saluted her with his teacup. "Now there's a lie that doesn't bear scrutiny."

"Very well, but for the most part I was managing. George did send money—I told you that—up until the time he died."

"How much did he send you?"

She looked down into her teacup. The tea leaves were spread in a strange pattern in the bottom of the cup. She was thankful there were no gypsies about. She would have dreaded to hear what they made of those leaves.

"It is really none of your business, but I will tell you anyway. George didn't have much money, but you know that. He was at Oxford, on an allowance from you."

"Oh? I can't seem to remember how much I gave him per quarter."

"You gave him twenty pounds per quarter. George sent us ten."

He felt the rage boiling up in him. If George had been in the room, Rohan would have smashed him into the wainscoting. He would have yelled at him first, then hit him. "Ten pounds," he repeated, "all of ten pounds per quarter. Yes, Susannah, you must have done very well indeed with all that largesse. Why don't you want to be my wife?"

"You are purposely being obtuse." She sighed. "Listen, Rohan. I cannot be your wife. It would be a sham, a lie. How many times must I repeat it? Wait. Just a while ago you said we wouldn't be breaking the law. What did you mean? Do you know something I don't know? Were those wicked old ladies wrong?"

"Well, yes, I do know something you don't know, and no, they weren't wrong." He drank down the rest of his tea. He carefully set the cup onto the saucer, then with even more care set the saucer on the marquetry table between them. There was hurt coming and he hated it, but there was simply no choice.

Susannah couldn't stand it another minute. The damned man was toying with her. It wasn't fair. She hurled her own cup and saucer at the fireplace, yelling, "This is just nonsense! Will you stop stringing it out? Say what you have to say and be done with it." She sank back down in her chair, her hands covering her face.

"Sir."

Rohan sighed. He should have known Toby wouldn't simply take himself off to bed and accept Rohan's word that everything was under control.

"Yes, Toby. Do come in. Your sister is momentarily in an unsteady state of mind. She will regain her balance in just a minute."

"But, sir, she has never before hurled anything against the fireplace. It was a very lovely cup. Probably very valuable. Mrs. Beete won't like it."

"Ah, but that's one of the benefits to being Lady Mountvale. She can break every cup in the place if she wishes."

Susannah raised her face. "Toby, see that large, ugly vase over there on top of that pedestal? Please bring it to me. I am going to crack it over his lordship's obstinate head."

"Sir, she has never before threatened to strike someone, not like this."

"Don't bring her the vase just yet, Toby. My mother is quite attached to it. No, let us wait a moment. Surely her mental tumult will soon ease."

"My tumult is building, not easing. Toby, you heard what he said, did you not?"

Toby nodded. He was standing very straight, closer to his sister than to the baron.

"Well, do you believe he is quite mad?"

"I believe he is trying to protect you, Susannah. Those old ladies were burying you beneath the carpet. They would have ruined your reputation. Isn't that right, sir?"

"Yes. All three of them were in transports of malicious delight. I saved her, but she isn't thanking me, Toby. There isn't a shred of gratitude in her posture."

"Toby, please hand me that statue of the man holding the world on his knee. It looks heavy, so be careful."

Rohan raised his hand. "Yes, Toby, I know. Her bile has never been this elevated for such a lengthy period of time. Listen to me, both of you. I am being honest—"

"Like you were being with those three ladies?"

"That was different. I saw what I had to accomplish and I did it."

"But, sir, why do you want us? Susannah's right. We're not your responsibility. You don't even know us, at least not all that well yet. It's true that you're Susannah's brother-in-law, but if you will just give her George's twenty thousand pounds, then you will be free of us. I know that a man of your reputation doesn't want children hanging on his sleeve, much less a wife. This is all very confusing, sir, particularly when you couldn't even marry Susannah if you wanted to."

"That's right, Rohan. You'll be free. You can simply tell your neighbors that it was all a jest and that you indeed kicked us out."

He bounded to his feet, knocking his chair over, and yelled, "Damnation! Shut up!"

Brother and sister stared at the baron. He was flushed. The pulse was pounding hard in his neck. He did not at the moment look calm or sleek or aloof. He did not look amused.

"Oh, dear," Susannah said, much calmer now. "All right, Rohan, I won't throw anything at you. You are now taking your turn at agitation. But you must agree with us. For goodness' sake, you don't know me. Why could you ever think that you would want me for a wife? For a wife you couldn't have legally? None of it makes any sense at all."

Rohan looked first at Toby, then at Susannah. "I could marry you and it would be quite legal."

She was shaking her head.

His voice gentled and lowered. He was shaking his own head as he said, "I'm sorry, Susannah, but you were never married to George. The ladies were right—Marianne is a bastard."

She was shaking violently now, whispering, "No, no, it can't be. No, Rohan, I showed you my marriage lines. It was a lovely ceremony, private, of course, but the vicar was kind and—"

"I'm sorry. Listen, the man should have been kind, for George paid him a goodly sum to pretend to marry you. I realized it immediately when you showed me the license back at Mulberry House. I know the man. His name is Bligh McNally. He is infamous in Oxford for doing this exact thing. He makes quite a good living at it. Many young girls have been taken in over the years. George didn't really marry you. I'm sorry, Susannah. It was all a lie."

Toby looked whiter than a fish's belly.

Susannah held herself stiff as a broom handle.

Finally, she said, barely above a whisper, "If you did know it was all a sham, then why didn't you say anything when I showed you the license?"

Rohan looked her straight in the eye. "At first I couldn't credit it even though the truth was staring me right in the face. I had always believed George to be so serious, so studious, such a scholar, what with his love for maps. He told me it was his dream to go on expeditions and become a famous cartographer. I always believed him good-hearted, gentle, and kindness itself. But then he did this to you. It was reprehensible. I couldn't believe it, yet he had done it.

"I couldn't bring myself to turn your life into a shambles before I even knew you or Marianne. Regardless of what George had done, Marianne was still my niece, of my blood. I decided to buy myself some time. That's why I brought you all here. That's why I went along with the lie until tonight."

"You also made up the inheritance, didn't you?"

"He didn't have to, Susannah," Toby said quietly. "Since you weren't ever married to George, if there was an inheritance it wouldn't come to you."

"I made it up." The moment the words were out of his mouth, he knew he'd blighted her to the dirt. She had nothing now, not even the illusion of a choice. She had just been shoved into a very deep well.

"I see," Susannah said slowly. She was staring into the fireplace, at the orange embers that had nearly burned themselves out. "And now you feel so guilty about what George did that you are willing to offer yourself as a sacrifice? You are willing to marry me and claim Marianne as your own child?"

He looked a bit astonished at himself, but his voice was steady as a rock. "Yes, that's about the size of it."

"But, sir, Susannah's right. We're strangers to you. If my father hadn't tried to squeeze money out of you, you would have never even known about us."

"But he did and thus, now I do know you. Listen to me, Susannah, surely it isn't such a rotten plan? I would be a tolerant husband. I would be a good father to Marianne. I will even try to bear with Toby, though he gives me hives and sends me to the brandy bottle with all his wild antics."

"Sir, I've never done any wild antics!"

"I know and that's the point, isn't it? You would be my brother-in-law and that's nice, since I'm fond of you. I am fond of all of you. Stay here. Stay with me. Become my family. I will protect you and in doing so, I will also protect George's memory. I don't want people to know what he did to you. I don't want my mother to know. You see, no matter the wicked indulgences of my parents, there was always a solid core of honor, of fair play. They indulged themselves endlessly, but they would have never hurt an innocent person, never. There is only my mother now, but I don't want her hurt. You must realize that I am very concerned with what I will find out in Oxford. I imagine that you are concerned as well."

Susannah rose and shook out her skirts—Charlotte's skirts. Such a beautiful gown, and now it was wrinkled. She said very clearly, very precisely, "None of this makes sense. You are a womanizer, a man who changes mistresses as often as he changes his cravats, indeed, a man who loves women.

Toby, if you wouldn't mind—please cover your ears."

"Oh, Susannah, don't be silly. Everyone speaks with the highest regard of his lordship's prowess and vigor. Everyone is proud of him."

"That is excessively odd, but no matter for the moment. Rohan, I must be honest about this. I am not a milksop, nor will I ever be like Charlotte."

"You make excellent points there." He rubbed his knuckles over his chin. "However, I quite understand what you are not. In the coming years, perhaps I will learn what it is you are, exactly."

Coming years. It was enough. Indeed, it was too much. She couldn't bear any more of it. She'd believed herself married, but she wasn't. She was naught but a woman with an illegitimate child because she had been a credulous fool, because she had trusted a young man who had seemed so very perfect for her—quiet, gentle, trustworthy. Ah, what a jest on her. What had George been? Why had he done it?

It didn't matter. None of this was real. What it was, she didn't know. She said, "Toby, we will leave Mountvale House tomorrow. We will return to Mulberry House."

"You don't have any money, Susannah," Rohan said, his voice very gentle, yet implacable. "You won't get far. You can't very well walk back to Mulberry House, not with Marianne."

She couldn't find any more words. Just looking at Rohan would always tell her how very stupid she had been. No, she couldn't bear any more. She turned on her heel and walked out of the library.

"Toby, stay here, I'll be back. Then you and I can discuss what can be done."

"I don't think Susannah feels very good about things right now, Rohan."

"I wouldn't either, if I'd just found out what she has." Jesus, it was crippling, this knowledge he'd had to dish out to her.

He would leave her be tonight, but tomorrow—he would not allow her to leave Mountvale House.

She was met on the upper landing by Lottie, looking to be at the end of her tether, holding a yelling Marianne.

"I gave her just two apple tarts, Mrs. Carrington—er, my lady. Just two, like you told me. But her stomach hurts now and I don't know what to do."

From the absurd to the mundane. Susannah took her daughter, soothing her as best she could. "These things happen, Lottie. It's not your fault. I will see if Mrs. Beete has something to make her feel better."

At least she hadn't yelled at Lottie that she wasn't a 'my lady.' "I will see to it," Rohan said, coming up behind her. He looked at the sobbing Marianne, who was draped over her mother's shoulder, her fist stuffed in her mouth. "In a moment, little one, you will feel just fine again."

"Ro-han!"

"I'll be back soon, Marianne." And he was gone. Susannah walked the floor, trying to calm her daughter. Suddenly he was back, carrying a glass. Marianne looked at it and whimpered.

He lifted Marianne's chin with his fingers. "Listen to me, little pumpkin, you will drink this down. Mrs. Beete gave it to me when I was a little boy. It works and it doesn't taste bad. In but a moment of time, you will want to dance a Scottish reel with me."

Marianne hiccuped. "I don't know how."

"I will teach you, but first you must make your belly happy again."

To Susannah's astonishment, Rohan tipped the little girl's head back and began feeding her the liquid. Marianne, who was a great fighter, docilely drank until the glass was empty.

"Excellent. Now I'm going to carry you downstairs. When you feel like dancing again, then we will be close to the piano so I can teach you."

Marianne went to him. With no hesitation at all, she went to him. She was still sobbing, hiccuping. She trusted him.

Rohan said nothing at all to Susannah or to Lottie, merely walked away, Marianne sprawled over his shoulder, her fingers in her mouth. Susannah could hear her sucking those fingers from thirty feet away.

"Well," she said, turning back to Lottie. "I must pack. We will all be leaving in the morning."

"You are traveling to Oxford with his lordship?"

Doubtless Lottie knew very well every word, every expression, every snippet of speculation about the story the baron had told the three old battle-axes. By now everyone did. Soon, all the south of England would know.

"Perhaps," she said, not up to any explanations. She went to her bedchamber, only to find Charlotte waiting for her, exquisite in an utterly outrageous confection of cream silk and feathers. Her blond hair was long on her back, smooth and deliciously soft.

"This is quite an occasion," she announced when Susannah came into the room. "More excitement than I've experienced in at least a fortnight. Ah, but that was a very different kind of excitement from this. One must continually adapt.

"My dear son told me only the barest bones of it, but now you are here and you will tell me every small detail. I know only the very barest bones because he wanted to speak to you, to make certain you were all right. Don't overlook any of those pesky details, Susannah. I don't believe I've ever been so diverted in my life.

"But, you know, it is something of a disappointment. My dearest boy was right about that. I had such hopes for him."

"Lady Dauntry believed you wanted him to marry either someone just like you or a milksop so he could continue his profligate ways with no wifely interference."

"How perceptive of dear Regina. Even after all these years, she can still surprise me. Not often, you understand, but very occasionally. Isn't 'Regina' a charming name? Pity she doesn't live up to it.

"Now, Regina 'buried you beneath the carpet'—I believe

that was the image dear Toby used. Not only Regina but
Almeria and Elsa as well. The three of them together are a
veritable set of Fates, with Regina urging them on and giving
them the proper direction. And here was Rohan, claiming
that you were his bride all along. Let me tell you, married
five years, you are far from being a bride. I have been wondering whether or not to believe him. Is it true that you never
even met poor George?''

Susannah just looked at her helplessly. She was mute.

"You are looking perfectly fagged, Susannah. Come, sit
down. That's right, just sit down. Rohan will take care of
Marianne. Isn't that odd? I saw him take her as if he'd done
it for years. But he has, hasn't he? Was Rohan with you
when Marianne was born?''

"No, he wasn't. There was no time. She came a bit early.''

"What I don't understand is why Rohan brought you here
claiming to be George's widow. Why not simply arrive as
Rohan's wife, if indeed that is who you are?''

She was sinking fast. Soon her nose would be well under
the quicksand. What to do? Tell Charlotte the truth? Tell her
that her beloved, prudish George had lied to her, Susannah,
and betrayed her, all to get her into his bed? What kind of
a man would do that?

A very young man who had no scruples at all. Somehow
she knew that Rohan would never do such a despicable thing.
She shook her head.

"You are thinking of lies that might suit me, Susannah?''

"No, ma'am, not really. It's just that I beg you to speak
to your son about all of this.''

"Ah, so you're afraid you won't tell me the same things
in the same way?''

Susannah could only give her another helpless look. She
was getting rather proficient at it.

Charlotte rose, smoothing her slender fingers over the
feathers at her wrist. "I had thought to enjoy Augustus for
a time, then journey back to Italy. I have always adored
Venice. Actually, I was dallying with the idea of taking Au-

gustus with me. But now there is this—this confusion. I will speak to Rohan. Then we will see, Susannah. Sleep well, my dear.''

At least Charlotte hadn't cursed at her or shot her. She sat back in the chair, closing her eyes for a moment, just for a moment. Then she would pack.

When she jerked awake, it was the middle of the night and she was shivering with cold. She felt about for candles but couldn't find any. She couldn't very well pack in pitch-blackness.

She managed to remove her clothes, smoothing Charlotte's glorious gown over the back of a chair, and sink beneath the blankets.

Just as she was at the edge of falling asleep again, she realized that Rohan surely had given George much more than a mere twenty-pound allowance per quarter.

George hadn't even cared that his daughter have enough. She felt the tears, hot and burning, well out of her eyes and drip down her cheeks. She had lived nothing but a lie. Her stupidity had been boundless. No wonder George hadn't wanted to introduce her to his family. What would he have said? ''Here is my mistress and my little bastard?''

She'd never doubted his word that his father, then his eldest brother, would disown him and her and Marianne. He had to have time, he'd told her again and again. Soon, he'd promised her over and over. Soon they would be together, a family, and everyone would know. No wonder George had visited Mulberry House only rarely those past several years. He'd known that sooner or later he would be found out. Then again, perhaps he hadn't cared. He'd grown bored. He'd not wanted to hear her asking him if he'd yet spoken to his older brother. He no longer wanted them. He no longer wanted his own daughter.

She would have killed him if he weren't already dead.

She had deceived herself for nearly five years, and now she thought she'd die of it. She cursed herself more than she cursed George. She'd always believed she was so smart, saw people so very clearly. She cried until her throat ached, until there were no more tears, but still the pain was deep and hard inside her. George had lied to her because she had so little value, so little worth, that she had merited only a sham marriage.

"AND THAT, MOTHER—EVERY GORY DETAIL OF IT—IS what George did to her." He felt bowed with fury and anger at George, who was gone from them, who would never have to face up to what he had done.

He'd had no intention of ever telling his mother the truth, but like the excellent, cunning mother she was, she'd awakened him from a deep sleep and gotten the truth out of him at a fine clip before he'd cocked half an eye open. He wanted to kick himself. But it was done and now couldn't be undone. She'd gotten him, but good.

He was fully awake now, cursing himself for being such a deep sleeper. His mother wasn't looking at him but rather was standing by the window looking down at the beautiful terraced gardens. He said, "I'm sorry, Mother. I hadn't wanted you to know, there was no need. But you're as shrewd as a mother superior. You got me at my lowest ebb."

She turned slowly to face him. "Yes, dearest, your wits are never fully knitted together when you are first awakened." Charlotte then fell silent. She began to pace Rohan's bedchamber. He was still in bed, of course. Unlike her son, Charlotte had always been an early riser. She was always at her most cunning early in the morning. And, pity for her son, it was only six o'clock.

Rohan still regretted none of his actions from the evening before. He hadn't changed his mind about anything, particularly about marrying Susannah.

He loved her name. It danced on the tongue. He imagined that even in a rage, yelling her name would be a treat.

"You know, dearest, as much as it pleases me that you wished to protect my ears from George's infamy, I would have known that you would never have married a young girl and kept her hidden away. You would have paraded her out and spoiled her rotten, just as you're planning to do now with both her and Marianne."

There was sudden determination in her voice. "Now, no more protecting George. It is Susannah and Marianne who must be protected."

She began her pacing again. "For nearly five years," she said finally, more to herself and the fireplace than to him. She turned then to face her son, who looked delightful balanced upon his elbows in his bed, his hair tousled, whiskers on his chin, at least two whiskers in that cleft of his. But her look was only cursory. "What was George?" she said finally, unable to leave it alone. "This young man I don't recognize?"

"I don't know. I plan to go to Oxford and find out. There is no doubt that he knew the man who kidnapped Susannah for the map. I'm sorry, Mother."

"I know. So am I. When will you go to Oxford?"

"I must go once I have Susannah's agreement to wed me in private. No one else—none of our friends, neighbors, not even Fitz—must ever know the true state of affairs, Mother. As for what I learn, I will try to keep it private."

"Yes, that would be best. I believe you should marry Susannah before you leave for Oxford. She is very proud. George betrayed her, made a fool of her, and she is doubtless tottering from the weight of it. She very probably feels perfectly useless, unwanted, worth less than nothing. Yes, you need to marry her because I fear she just might try to leave Mountvale, thinking to spare you this noble sacrifice. A very quiet wedding. You will obtain a special license?''

"Yes, as soon as I can."

"You will adopt Marianne?"

"Of course." He scratched his chest, realized his mother was looking at him, and quickly pulled the covers to his chin. Then he realized that she'd been looking through him, not at him. Well, she was his mother, after all.

"At least neither of us will have to worry about her once she's your wife. She understands the way of things. She can remain here at Mountvale House, all snug and cozy, while you are in London, doing what you do so very well."

"Why would I want to be alone in London? Really, Mother, when I travel to London, she and Marianne and Toby will be with me."

She didn't say another word, just stared at him. "But she is not like me nor is she a milksop. She told me that herself last night. But nothing else, as you know. Yes, Susannah would be miserable. It would not be just because of you. Think of your mistresses, dearest, all your parties, the Four Horse Club, White's, the opera, the—''

"I daresay that Susannah might enjoy the opera and—'' His voice fell like a rock off a cliff. He just realized how he was speaking to her, his mother. He looked down at his toes, wiggling them beneath the blankets. He cleared his throat. "That is, naturally when I wish to indulge my appetites, I will see to it that she is properly entertained. Surely you know that I would do that well."

The doubt fell from her beautiful face. It wasn't yet seven o'clock in the morning, she wasn't wearing any cosmetics, the sun was flooding through the east window, and she was one of the most beautiful women he'd ever seen in his life. "That is what your dear father always did. Naturally, I did the same for your father whenever I wished to indulge myself. It is what makes a marriage successful. Both husband and wife must be attentive to each other's needs and inclinations. I will never forget when dear Lord Westminster died in that hunting accident. I was devastated, really quite undone. Your dear father didn't leave my side until well after the funeral.'' Suddenly her expression became austere. ''You know, of course, dearest, that you must breed an heir before Susannah will be free to indulge herself. You will explain this to her, will you not?''

''Mother, I don't believe it will be effective. Susannah, I fear, is going to be an interfering wife.'' He raised his hand quickly to hold her off. The last thing he wanted was for his mother to give Susannah instructions on the care and maintenance of a womanizer. But she was obviously appalled. ''I shall bring her around, Mother, you will see. There is no need for you to say anything to her. I will deal with it. All right?''

''I suppose so, dearest. A man of your reputation should be able to bring any woman around to his way of thinking, wife or no wife.''

''Yes, you are right, of course. Now, I will get myself out of bed and make sure that Susannah hasn't fled Mountvale House. Promise me you won't speak to her.''

''Very well. How is Marianne's bellyache?''

''She fell asleep in my arms downstairs in the library. She never realized there wasn't a piano in sight. I suppose I shall have to teach her to dance a Scottish reel today. I think it was the reel. Yes, she would enjoy jumping and hopping about, sucking her fingers all the while Fitz pounded the tune on the piano.''

His mother arched a perfect eyebrow at the image of her son, a man of sterling reprobate character, dancing with a little girl.

Rohan, half an hour later, was whistling as he walked to Susannah's bedchamber.

Sabine, his mother's maid, was straightening the hairbrushes on Susannah's dressing table. For the past three years, Sabine had been trying to get Rohan into her bed. He stopped the instant he saw her and very quietly began to back out the open door.

''My lord! Ah, you are here. To see madame? A waste,

that one. No, it is a female of more interesting habits who would pleasure you, more—''

''Sabine, where is Lady Mountvale?''

''You mean your wife?''

How could he have possibly imagined that every servant within fifty miles wouldn't know every detail? ''Yes, my wife,'' he said. ''Where is she?''

''She was muttering to herself, my lord, about what, I'm not sure. She asked me where her valise was, but when I asked her why she wanted it, she wouldn't tell me. No, she just looked—how you say it—ah, yes, she looked struck and left the room.''

Rohan paused in the doorway, gave Sabine a fat smile, and said, ''I am married now, Sabine.''

She clasped her hands beneath her breasts, heaving them upward, and said, ''So?''

He threw up his hands and left. Where the devil was she? ''Ah, Toby? Where are you off to?''

''I'm trying to find Susannah, sir.''

''Tell you what, you try the nursery, and I'll ask Fitz.''

Neither of them found her.

''Perhaps,'' Fitz said, all new dignity now that Susannah was the mistress of Mountvale House, ''her ladyship is with the Harker brothers learning more about racing cats. Ozzy told me the kitten is very nearly up to racing snuff for her ladyship.''

Her ladyship. If Fitz recognized Susannah as such, it was done. No one—not even the Earl of Northcliffe at his most imperious—would ever disagree with Fitz. It was amusing that Fitz hadn't yet decided if racing cats were beneath a ladyship's dignity.

Rohan said, ''No, she is more likely planning ways to do away with me.''

''I might consider it an option as well, my lord, had you married me and kept me hidden for over four years.''

''Now that is an appalling thought.''

As was his habit, Rohan visited their villain each morning,

to see if he was ready to talk. This morning the door was open, the footman Rory on guard.

Susannah was inside, standing over the man. He still looked very pale, and the bandage was still around his head.

Rohan said quietly, "Stand outside, Rory." He went in quietly and closed the door behind him.

"Why won't you tell me the truth?" she was saying. Obviously this wasn't the first time she'd asked him.

"Go take yourself off," the man said shortly and spit, missing Susannah's skirts by only an inch. It was a nasty habit.

"You and George were friends, weren't you? I remember that you were one of the men I met that day in the inn dining room. Your name is Lambert, isn't it?"

"You were George's little lightskirt. Aye, I knew it was you. Here you thought you was his wife. How we all laughed about that. And it only cost him ten pounds a quarter. Cheapest mistress a man could ever have." The man laughed, a rough, leering laugh, but still Susannah stood her ground.

"I don't believe you. You're lying about a man who's dead and can't defend himself. Please, tell me the truth about George. I need to know about him. Are you Lambert or are you Theodore Micah?"

He turned his face to the wall.

"You're Lambert, aren't you?"

This time the man flinched. Slowly he turned back to face her. "You give me that wretched map and I'll tell you all about George."

"There is no map. If there is, I don't know where it is. I told you that. It's the truth."

"Then that means George did something else with it. I wonder."

"Keep wondering, Lambert," Rohan said, approaching from the corner. "Now that we know who you are, we will soon discover what this is all about."

"Mangy bastard. George said you'd have a bone to pick with this if you ever found out about it. He told us he was real careful around you. He said you acted all indolent and good-natured, but there were depths in you he didn't want to plumb. Looks like George wasn't careful enough, was he? You just go looking, you'll not find out a damned thing. Without the map, you don't have a bloody clue."

He turned his face once more to the wall.

Rohan said slowly, "I think it's time you went to gaol, Mr. Lambert." But there was a problem. The man knew about George's sham marriage. What if he announced it to the world? It was an appropriate time, Rohan thought, to become ruthless.

Lambert didn't go to gaol. Instead, that afternoon, after Dr. Foxdale had pronounced him fit enough, two footmen escorted him to Eastbourne, where he was turned over to Captain Muldoon, along with a long letter from Lord Mountvale. He would be in His Majesty's Navy for six years or until he died, whichever came first.

There was nothing more that Rohan could think of doing. He found Susannah this time with Ozzy Harker, in deep discussion. ". . . Aye, yer ladyship, there be many methods we see at the cat racing course. There's old Mr. Bittle wot stands over 'is poor gray tabby and claps 'is mitts together real loud, right in the kitter's ears. Scares the poor kitter out o' 'er wits. She do run, fur all stiff, tail blossomed out, but most the time, she runs unner the skirts o' the nearest lady."

She smiled, for it was amusing, but she was thinking: I have to stop this. Everyone is calling me my lady. It is a horrible mistake. I must leave.

"Thank you, Ozzy. I have something important I must see to now."

She walked away from him, her head down, and Rohan knew exactly what she was thinking. He followed her to, of all places, his estate room. He blinked when he saw her very quietly, very slowly, open his desk drawers, one after the other. He watched her pull out his strongbox. Unfortunately for her, it was locked.

"Don't you think it would be easier to marry me than be

hauled in front of the magistrate? Stealing money is frowned upon, you know.''

Susannah sighed deeply. She rattled the strongbox once again, then put it back in the bottom drawer of the desk. ''I would have paid you back,'' she said, her voice as dull as the consommé she made for her father whenever his innards rebelled against too much whiskey.

''How?''

That hit its mark. She stood straight and tall, like a veritable Diana. All she needed was a bow and arrows. Her chin went up. ''Why, I think I just might go to Oxford and find myself a protector who will pay me more than ten pounds a quarter.''

''You know, Susannah, George's problem was that he didn't know how to prevent you conceiving a child. And it never even occurred to you. If Marianne had never been born, then he could have continued enjoying you without worrying about offspring. You told me he didn't come around much the past two years. That was because he was terrified of getting you pregnant again.''

She hadn't thought of that; she had only felt the pain of rejection. ''A man of your reputation—why, how could you possibly know what George thought or planned? Maybe it wasn't at all like that horrible man Lambert said. Maybe he was just talking to me like that because he wanted to hurt me. I did escape him and you did shoot him.''

''That's possible, but not at all to the point. Why don't we just put an end to all this? Marry me, Susannah. I will fetch us a special license on the morrow. The local vicar, Mr. Byam, is a lifelong friend of the Carrington family. He would never betray us. He can marry us the next day. Then you won't have to worry about stealing money from me.''

''No, that's true. I would just have to worry about which one of your women you were with when you weren't with me.''

''I know. That's an insurmountable problem, isn't it? A man of my reputation has much to live up to, doesn't he?

Perhaps we could just forget about all my women.'' He waved his hands in front of him like a magician, and snapped his fingers. "There! The problem's gone. What do you say?''

"George betrayed me. I couldn't bear to marry another man who wouldn't even pretend he wasn't betraying me.''

"Perhaps," he said very slowly, very carefully, "perhaps you and I could consider never betraying each other. There would be just the two of us. We would provide all of the entertainment for each other. I believe I could make that vow. Could you?''

She looked like she wanted to punch him in the nose. "Don't be ridiculous! I don't ever want to have a horrible man touch me again. I hated it. It was sweaty and embarrassing and humiliating. All that dreadful grunting and heaving, why—'' She looked as if she had just blasphemed an angel to his face. She slapped her hand over her mouth. Her face turned red to her hairline. "Forget I said that,'' she said between her fingers. "I didn't say it, did I? No, surely I have sufficient breeding not to have spewed that out, don't I?''

"Yes, you did say it. Sorry.''

"No, you must have misunderstood me. Please, Rohan, let me steal some money. All of us will leave and you'll never have to worry about anything again.''

He studied his fingernail. It was short and buffed. He wanted to ease that finger inside her, he wanted . . . "You know, Susannah, physical love between a man and a woman doesn't have to be horrible and embarrassing. I have no understanding at all of humiliation in lovemaking. What could be humiliating? Sweaty, probably so, but that's not so bad when you're enjoying yourself.''

She stared at him as if he had just grown another ear. Her chin went up again. "Since I didn't say anything, I have no idea of what you're talking about.''

He walked to her then. He took her hand and pulled her out from behind his desk. He pulled her against him. She tried to push away, her palms flat against his chest, but he was stronger and he was determined. "Say yes, Susannah.''

Her eyes were on his neck. She shook her head.

He began to stroke his hands up and down her back, easy, gentle strokes. "Everything will be all right if you will just say yes."

Finally, she raised her eyes to the cleft in his chin. "You are a very kind man, despite your reputation. I would be a miserable woman were I to accept you. I would have no honor. Your brother didn't believe I was worth anything other than what he got from me in his bed, which couldn't have been very much. He didn't think I was worth any more than ten pounds a quarter. Surely you aren't willing to sacrifice yourself just because of George's indiscretion?"

16

"I THINK I WOULD MAKE A SPLENDID SACRIFICE."

"This isn't a jest, Rohan. George obviously didn't want me or his daughter. We simply weren't important enough to him. Why would you want something that had no value at all to your brother?"

"What George did was despicable. It has nothing to do with us. Listen to me, Susannah. I will not allow you to say that you have no value—"

"It's true. I have less worth than any decent mistress. It's been proven. Only ten pounds a quarter for the likes of me. Tell me, what does one of your mistresses cost you per quarter? Or has one mistress ever been lucky enough to survive a full quarter?"

He grabbed her shoulders and shook her. He put his face right into hers. He said very slowly, "I will not let you goad me. I will say it again. You have great worth. Don't you dare look down at your damned slippers. Look at me! It gives me pleasure just to look at you. It gives me great pleasure to hear Marianne sucking on her fingers. It gives me great pleasure to have Toby tell me he's never indulged in a wild antic. You are an intelligent, caring woman. I want you for my wife. Let's grow old together and have a dozen children."

"A man of your reputation wouldn't want a dozen children,'' she said slowly, looking at him straightly. Then she paused, frowning. "Oh, I understand now. If I was pregnant all the time then I wouldn't be in London to interfere in your outside pleasures.''

He held his anger. After all, a man of his reputation had to accept certain judgments about his character. The good Lord knew he'd worked hard enough to make sure that people had made those certain judgments. He drew a deep breath, saying calmly, with dead certainty, "Actually, I wouldn't go to London at all. I would walk about patting your belly, telling stories to my child. I would probably wear a perpetual idiotic smile on my face.''

"I don't understand you,'' she said very slowly, still looking at him straightly, everything she felt so clearly writ on her expressive features. "You are reputed to be a great womanizer, a man of a satyr's appetites. Everyone admires you for it, as they do your mother. As they did your father. You are renowned as a connoisseur of women. George said no man had a more splendidly lascivious reputation than you. Then he'd laugh and rub his hands. Naturally, now I understand why he laughed. He was trying to emulate you. I wonder if I was his first?

"No, enough of that. Why in heaven's name would you want to marry me and have a dozen children?''

"Would you believe me if I were to tell you that none of that is true?''

"No.''

"But you haven't seen me hieing myself off to have a woman since you met me?''

"It's only been a bit over a week.''

"Yes, but a man of my reputation must have a woman at least twice a day. Maybe not even the same woman. You know, a woman in the morning and a different woman in the evening. Isn't that what you've heard?''

She gulped. This was plain speaking indeed. "So you're exercising some control. I appreciate it.'' Then her eyes widened. "But wait—you're jesting, aren't you? *Twice* a day?

That's unimaginable, outlandish. Why, it must be sinful. Surely the biggest womanizer of all time didn't have a different woman in for his pleasures *twice* a day?''

He was tempted to laugh, but he didn't. ''Would you consent to believe me were I to tell you that I have sown all the wild oats for a dozen men and am ready to settle down with one woman and that woman is you?''

She couldn't quite say no so quickly to that. She could only stare up at him helplessly. ''But why me? I am nothing, less than nothing. I am worth only ten pounds a quarter. I already have a child by your younger brother. Why me? Wouldn't you want a young virgin of splendid birth and fortune? I have heard it said that rakes prefer virgins, that they—''

''Where did you hear all this about rakes?''

She flushed, a very charming shade of red, really, and he wanted to kiss her. He wanted to do a whole lot more to her, but he was willing to begin with a kiss—or perhaps half a dozen kisses. ''Er, perhaps it was from Mrs. Bingly, who was the local seamstress. She spent her youth as a lady's maid in London.''

''Well, perhaps that is what a *common* rake would prefer,'' he said, lifting her out of the hole she had dug so deep she would fall to China if she kept talking. ''I am not common. I am at least three cuts above common. Thus, what I would prefer must be different. I want you. I want Marianne. I want Toby. However, I will be blunt with you. I do not want your cursed father.''

She persevered, he had to say that for her. She got the rope between her teeth and pulled and pulled. Her hands were kneading his shoulders now. It pleased him that she had no idea she was doing it. ''You wouldn't have looked at me for a second if it weren't for this wretched situation. You wouldn't have looked at me at all even if I'd paraded in front of you without my clothes on.''

His eyes nearly crossed, but he wasn't a green boy. His father had always said that a man without control over his sexual urges wasn't worth spit. "I wouldn't count on that. Did I ever tell you I like your nose? Nice and thin and turned up just exactly right at the end."

He kissed the tip of her nose. "I would have looked at you at least three times. If you were naked and parading in front of me, I would have thanked God for his beneficence and bounty and put a stop to your parading immediately. You are really quite beautiful, but not in the common way. Thus you deserve a man who is also not in the common way. Marry me, Susannah. I will teach you about enjoyment. Together we can learn about what's important to us and what isn't. We will take on life together, you and I. I won't embarrass you in our lovemaking. I won't humiliate you. I swear to you that at least half the groans between us will be yours.

"Let's sweat together, Susannah."

His damned voice was shaking her to the core. His words—no, surely he was smooth in his delivery, and his words sounded perfectly serious—but she'd already been taken in once, and not by a master, like the baron. She'd been taken in by a very young man. Taken in very easily. She'd been the greatest fool alive. Yes, it was madness to believe him. She couldn't listen, couldn't trust him. He still held her loosely, his hands splayed across her back.

Rohan was ready to throttle her for her damned tenacity as she said, aware that even to her own ears, she was floundering, "You must listen to me. You would come to detest me. I told you that I hated all those things men do to women. To me it is disgusting, repellent. It makes me ill just to think about it—having to take off your clothes not just in front of anybody, but in front of a man who has the legal right to do anything he pleases to you—it is horrid and I won't do it again. There, I have told you the truth. I know sex is important to men—surely not as much as twice a day, at least to a reasonable man—but if that is so, then how long would it be before you went back to London to enjoy yourself with a woman who wanted to be with you in that way? For that many separate, er, occasions?''

She actually shuddered. The resulting difficulties of having a reputation as a womanizer had certainly come home to roost.

''I will make you a promise. A vow.''

He kissed her fleetingly on her mouth.

His lips were warm. She blinked and tried to pull away from him, but he didn't let her go.

''What promise? What vow? I don't like sweat. You can't promise not to sweat on me.''

He laughed, he couldn't help himself. ''We'll see about that. My vow is this: First you must marry me. If you decide you can't bear me or my man's body and my demands on you, if you don't like our simply living together, then I will let you go. You will have the protection of my name and you will have ample funds for all your wants and needs for the rest of your life. Marianne will also have the protection of my name and her proper place in Society when the time comes. She will never want for anything. She will make a fine marriage. I will see to that. I will ensure that Toby has a proper education. He will go to Eton, then to Cambridge. Not to Oxford. I make you that promise, that vow.''

Goodness, he was offering her the world. Why? No, there was a huge problem here. ''But you must have an heir.''

''Yes, it's true that it would be nice to have a son to go with my daughter. Yes, Marianne will be my daughter. She will call me Papa. If, however—'' he swallowed hard on this one ''—you can't bear me, then I wouldn't ever get my heir. But again, our line wouldn't die out, since I do have a younger brother, Tibolt. Upon my death, he would take the title.''

''That isn't fair. I would be a wretched human being to consent to that, so I will not. Besides, what if I gave you an heir and then I wanted to leave? I wouldn't be able to take my son with me.''

How the devil was she able to come up with so many

arguments? The woman was a damned well that just didn't run dry. And this argument took the prize. How confident was he? No, the better question was how could he even begin to doubt himself at this point? A man of his reputation had, perforce, the highest order of confidence.

"If you gave me an heir and then wanted to leave me, then you would keep our son until he went to school. However, I would always be active in his life. Do you agree?"

"It is too cruel. No, I can't agree. I am not a monster. No, forget that part of it."

So she was doing herself in with all her own arguments. This would have been fascinating to behold if he hadn't had such a deep stake in the outcome. But she was bringing him the outcome herself. He drew in closer for the kill. "Then what do you suggest? No, we're talking marriage only here. Nothing else. Forget leaving me and running off with Marianne and Toby. That won't happen. I won't let it. Forget leaving me with my heir."

She chewed her bottom lip over that. He had her, he knew it, but still, he hated the questions, the doubts, in her eyes. Finally, she said exactly what he'd expected her to, "You're saying, basically, that I have no choice at all in this?"

"Yes, that's about it."

"Then there is no reason for me to be reasonable, is there? I will agree to your promise. What length of time?"

"Fifty years."

She grabbed him about his throat and squeezed. She tried to shake him. "You make light of everything. You don't take anything I say seriously." She looked into his eyes. They were beautiful eyes, green as the thick grass at the edge of the Mountvale gardens.

But what were eyes in the master scheme of things? "You won't even recognize that my reasons for not marrying you are quite valid?"

"They're not. Can you think of a valid reason?"

She dropped her hands to his shoulders. She stared at his cravat. It looked soft, yet perfect, just like he was, only he was a womanizer. Oh, dear. She swallowed. "At least I thought I loved George."

He felt an intense bolt of rage, but it was gone quickly enough, for George was gone, and life had shifted, dishing out new possibilities. Nothing was the same, thank God. He struck the pose of the reasonable male, which he knew he was. "Susannah, I know you don't love me, yet. You've known me for a week. I don't love you either. How could either of us have garnered deep emotions for each other within a week?"

"Then this would be a marriage of convenience, all the convenience being for me?"

"No, it would also be immensely convenient for my family. We would be protecting George's reputation, and thus the Carrington name. Don't doubt that anyone with even the slightest suspicion would find out quickly enough that your marriage to George was a fraud. This fake preacher, Bligh McNally, is really very well known. No, this is the only solution. I protect George and thus the Carrington family reputation. And you become a real Carrington. Everything will be neat and tidy."

He gave her a blazing smile. "And I get a daughter and a son, if you're willing to oblige me, maybe even a half dozen of each."

"Would you let me go?"

For a moment he thought she was referring to fifty years from now. But no. She was speaking of right now, of today, just walking out of his life. He released her, but didn't move away from her. "No."

She began to pace, just like his mother, her stride long and sure, her brow furrowed in concentration. She didn't have the immense beauty of his mother, but whatever quality she had, it was deep and mysterious and intense. What she was, was unique. What she was, was precious, at least to him. And who else mattered, for God's sake? He wanted her, it was that simple. He thought a few fanciful thoughts of fate, then shook his head. Whatever she was, she fit with him. She was the woman God had fashioned for him and him alone.

He watched her, content for the moment. She continued to pace, pausing every few steps, obviously caught up in very profound thought, then shaking her head, clearing it, and pacing again. Good, it meant she was discarding arguments. All the better for him. He sat down, leaning back in his chair. He rested his head back against his folded arms. He watched her walk, move. She was very graceful. She would sweat nicely.

Suddenly she whirled about to face him. "I saw that. You are smiling. Why?"

"If I told you, you just might attack me. You might run into the library, grab that ugly Chinese vase, and throw it at my head."

"It is probably a loathsome man-thought that made you smile."

"Indeed."

She sat down and arranged her skirts around her. He hadn't noticed before, but he did now. She was wearing one of her three ugly gowns, this one a pale gray, nearly white from so many washings. The damned thing nearly touched her chin. It wasn't cut properly either. It just went straight down from her breasts, not cupping in at all, no band to define her figure. She was wringing her hands. He raised an eyebrow at that.

"Talk to me, Susannah."

"I am still thinking about this heir business. I would have to let you do those things to me—how many times?—in order to become with child."

"It's called making love, at least it would be called that between us. It's a pity that you don't believe that. But you will believe it. Trust me."

Her voice was tart and quite cold. "Making love? Surely that is an invention of some man a very long time ago to draw women in."

"No, actually I don't believe so. But I am not an expert

on the Egyptians, so my opinion isn't altogether learned."

If she'd had the Chinese vase nearby, she would have thrown it at his head. "And there would be no guarantee it would be a boy. I perhaps would have to submit to this for years before you got your heir."

"All true." His eyes nearly crossed again. "I rather like the thought of five girls before we make our boy. Don't be melancholy, Susannah, it won't take all that long, if you don't wish it to. Not more than twenty years."

She actually shuddered. What the devil had George done to her? But he knew, of course. Many men didn't have any knowledge at all about women's bodies. Many men did have knowledge, but they didn't care. He personally thought that all men should have rigorous training in how to make love properly to a woman. His father had certainly seen to it that he'd gotten proper training.

He'd been fourteen when his sire had rubbed his hands together, slapped him on the back, and turned him over to his most skilled mistress, Mary Claire, a lass from Wexford, Ireland, who gave Rohan three lessons a week for six months. Actually, she'd confided to him some years later, he hadn't needed any more lessons after three weeks, but she enjoyed him, and besides, she'd laughed then, his father had paid her handsomely for bringing his boy into proper shape. He tried now to remember if he'd ever felt embarrassment with Mary Claire. He didn't think so.

He still occasionally saw Mary Claire. She was an excellent friend. She had been so distraught after his father's death that his mother had gone to console her. In fact, the two women had been close ever since then.

As for George and Tibolt, they'd also had appropriate training. There'd been no reason for George to be a clod. He'd not been tutored by Mary Claire, but surely his father wouldn't have had him placed with an inept woman. But he had proved himself a clod, obviously. Why? He must have been one of those men who didn't give a good damn about a woman's pleasure. Rohan couldn't imagine such a thing.

Susannah was saying, "My mother was the daughter of a knight. He evidently did something in the Colonies to please George III and was thus rewarded. As for my father, he was a second son, half Irish, with not a sou to his name. Her father disowned her. So you see, my antecedents are on the very edge of acceptable."

"Ah, so your family can't trace itself back to the Conqueror?"

She frowned at that. "I haven't the foggiest idea. I should know that, shouldn't I? I could write to my grandfather. I've never met him, but perhaps he doesn't wish to keep me disowned now that my mother has been dead so many years. My mother used to say that he wore the starchiest cravats of any gentleman she knew. She said he could scarce move his head. Thus it was impossible for him to look down and see his daughter. She said she doubted if he ever saw her except at a distance."

"This sounds highly eccentric. Perhaps there are bats in your ancestral belfry." He raised his hands at her. "No, don't think about throwing that vase at me again. Very well, here is what I will do so you will not feel guilty for your less-than-adequate birth. I will simply lower your quarterly allowance to compensate myself for your lacks."

"I will write to my grandfather," she said firmly. "Surely there must be something of note in the family tree, something salutary to make you commend my ancestors." Then, to his absolute delight, she lowered her head, whispering, "I don't want you to be ashamed of me."

So she was coming around. More than that, she was very nearly there. Excellent. "Who is your grandfather?"

"Sir Francis Barrett, from Coddington, in Yorkshire."

"He sounds up to the mark. We'll see. Have you come up with anything else to torture yourself or me with?"

"I don't suppose that you will tell your mama all of the truth?"

"I already did. Mother is a force to be reckoned with. She woke me up before six o'clock this morning and squeezed me dry before six-thirty." Rohan just realized what a marvelous weapon she'd just handed him, the final nail. He looked for a moment at his fingernails. Then he smiled at her. "Mother believes we should marry as soon as possible, in fact, immediately. She is naturally upset about what George did, but she wants you and Marianne to be protected and she agrees that marriage with me is the only thing to do." He paused, for just the exact small moment, then added, "You know, Susannah, my mother has an incredible sense not only of what is proper but also of when it is just the right time to execute the needful in order to gain the proper."

She sighed deeply.

"Our marriage is the needful."

She sighed again, even more deeply.

He had her.

17

THE VERY SMALL WEDDING WAS PERFORMED BY MR.
Byam, a vicar with a beautiful head of white hair and a deep
resonant voice, who held his living from the Carrington family. He was the soul of discretion, had never been a hell-
thumper, and ignored the array of gossip that came his way.
He quite liked the present Baron Mountvale, despite his reputation. His drawing room was small, but finely appointed,
thanks to Charlotte Carrington. He understood the need for
secrecy, even with respect to the Carrington servants. Thus
the wedding was held in the evening, a Sunday evening,
when every family thereabouts was snug at home, secure in
the knowledge that they had already performed their religious duties sufficiently.

Mr. Byam gave Toby a pat on his shoulder, whispering as
he passed him, "Your sister is lovely. This is a wonderful
day for the Carringtons. Just imagine, our baron is getting
himself married."

"Yes, indeed I am," said Rohan. "Do you approve, sir?"

"Yes, I do, my lord. I had feared you would wed yourself
at Hanover Square and I wouldn't have the opportunity of
seeing it, but now, this is beyond what I could have envi-
sioned. None will ever learn of this. I do believe, my boy,
that your dear father, once he got over his shock, would have

applauded you. You are a good and generous man. Now, my lord, let us get you married before your bride bolts.''

She did look ready to hike up her skirts and run. Rohan moved quickly to stand beside her, taking her hand in a firm grip. It was a cold and damp hand.

Susannah, thanks to his mother, was gowned in a pale yellow silk with an even paler yellow lace lining the bodice and the banding beneath her breasts. It fell straight to the floor, with another narrow band of lace at the hem. The sleeves were long, and sewn with lace. Pale yellow ribbon was threaded through the fat braids atop her head. She looked exquisite.

Rohan swallowed. She was also very pale.

He smiled down at her, saw the strain, the wariness, and now found himself praying that she would go through with it. It was her second marriage to a Carrington. At least this one was real. His mother had sensed that Susannah was still more than uncertain about the union and had kept her so busy she hadn't had time to draw breath, much less fidget and question herself more about what she had committed to.

It seemed to Rohan that the only thing Mr. Byam said was to ask Susannah if she would accept Baron Mountvale as her husband. In this Mr. Byam was a very shrewd man. A long service just might have left the bride in a dead faint or running from the vicarage. By placing the exchange of vows at the start of the service, Byam effectively forestalled either development. Nevertheless, both he and Rohan sighed with immense relief as Susannah responded with no hesitation at all: "I do." Then they heard her swallow hard.

It was done in five minutes, if that. Mr. Byam beamed at them, saying, "This has given me great pleasure, my lord, my lady. Dear Lady Charlotte has provided us some champagne. But first, my lord, you may kiss your lovely bride."

She was married, Susannah thought, staring down at the emerald and diamond ring, a very old ring that had been in the Carrington family since the seventeenth century, Rohan had told her. Married the second time, only this time the ceremony was real and her husband—her true husband—was very kind, she knew that was true. But he also had a reputation as one of the most lascivious men in England. Lovemaking twice a day! It was an unimaginable thought. Surely he wouldn't expect that of her—no, certainly not. She was his wife, not his mistress. Men didn't do that to their wives once they got them pregnant. George hadn't forced himself on her after Marianne had been conceived. Indeed, he hadn't forced himself upon her after Marianne had been born. Susannah hoped that mistresses made a great deal of money. Perhaps they even charged by the time. She knew that was what prostitutes did, so why not mistresses? Or perhaps a mistress negotiated at the beginning, taking into consideration the number of times per day or per week a man would want to do those things to her. Yes, that sounded the more reasonable.

"Whatever are you thinking? Your eyes are dilated. Your breathing has quickened. You looked ready to fly out of here, if you only had a broom."

"You truly don't want to know."

"Later, yes I do, but I want more to kiss you at this moment." Just as Rohan prepared to kiss her, Susannah drew back and said, "You said anyone who was at all suspicious could find out very quickly that my marriage to George was a fraud. Anyone who is suspicious also need only ask Mr. Byam to find out how recently we've wed. I hadn't thought of this before. Goodness, it won't work, Rohan, it—"

"It's done," he said and kissed her. He said quietly against her mouth, "Mr. Byam assures me that he could have his fingernails drawn out and he wouldn't say a word. You're mine now, Susannah. It's legal. And our secret is safe."

His. Her eyes closed as he kissed her. A soft kiss, not at all demanding, just a strange sort of recognition. She didn't try to draw away. She knew it would embarrass both of them if she did. She stood very still, letting him kiss her, feeling his hands resting lightly on her arms.

It wasn't unpleasant. Indeed, she felt something rather

stimulating begin to warm her belly. It was an odd sort of stimulation, gone immediately when he raised his mouth from hers.

He smiled down at her and tweaked her nose with his finger. "You did well. Your 'I do' was a bit on the terrified side, but you did get it out quickly. I didn't have time to chew my fingernails. I'm proud of you. Now, Lady Mountvale, would you like some champagne?"

She nodded. Lady Mountvale. Now it was real. She saw Mr. Byam smiling at something Charlotte was saying. She saw Toby playing with Mr. Byam's old lame terrier, Bushy. She slowly backed away from him. From her husband.

Not even two weeks before, she had been weeding her garden, her hands as black as the sweet earth she'd been digging, worrying about money, worrying about her candytuft, worrying about her father, always worrying about something, it seemed, but still, she had been her own mistress, she had been in charge of her own life. She had been the one responsible for both Toby and Marianne. Truth be told, she'd also been responsible for her father. And she had slept alone.

But now she was a ladyship with no more money worries at all. All she'd had to do was vow herself over to a man she scarcely knew. He now owned her and all the responsibilities as well. It seemed to her that Rohan had gotten the worst end of this bargain, yet he was smiling. He seemed quite pleased about the whole thing. Why? Not only had she brought him endless responsibilities, she'd also brought him danger. Was he mad to look so pleased with himself?

She wasn't so naive as to believe he truly admired her. Perhaps he found her on the palatable side, but surely not more than that. He'd been surrounded by beautiful women his entire life. No, he had done this to save his family honor. Everything else he'd said to her . . . no, she couldn't afford to believe any of it.

He handed her a glass of champagne, then turned and said

aloud, "Here's to my beautiful bride, Susannah Carrington, who makes me very happy."

"Hear, hear!"

That was from Toby, who was drinking two sips of champagne, slipped to him by his goddess, Charlotte.

They left the vicarage soon thereafter. They watched Mr. Byam snuff out the candles, plunging the vicarage into darkness. The candlelight had been lovely as well as practical. Rohan didn't want anyone who happened to see them wondering what they were doing there. "It's done," he said to the carriage at large. "Well, Mother, what did you think?"

"I thought, dearest, that you have carried this off quite nicely. A splendid job, worthy of your dear father. He would have come around to being pleased, once he had gotten to know Susannah and Toby. Not to mention the little pumpkin."

"Marianne the pumpkin," Toby said and yawned. "I like that."

"Yes, I did carry this off well. We must just remember that all we did was accept Mr. Byam's invitation to dine with him at the vicarage. It was a dandy dinner. We all agree on that. Now, it is a bit on the unusual side. But not so unusual that Fitz gave me that *I know you're up to something* look of his when I informed him, thank God. Susannah, you must stop jumping when one of our people calls you 'my lady.' It is what you are now. No more playacting. It's quite real. All right?"

She shrugged, not wanting to even think about what had just happened, about what she was now. And what she wasn't. She said instead, clearing her throat, "Ozzy promised to bring me my racing kitten tomorrow."

"I believe the monthly race is next Saturday. We might not be here for it."

We. He was going to let her come with him to Oxford?

Her eyes flew to his face. He was giving her a fat smile. But he said nothing more.

•   •   •

"I told Mother not to let Sabine near you."

She turned around slowly. All her things had been moved into the baron's master suite, and he had just walked through the connecting door into her new room, wearing a blue dressing gown that looked old and comfortable, his feet bare, and she knew he was quite naked beneath it. But he seemed so easy, his voice so light, so unthreatening.

"Why wouldn't I want Sabine here?"

She was still wearing her lovely gown, the one Charlotte had given her.

"Turn around," he said, "and I'll get you out of this thing."

"Why?"

"What? Oh, Sabine." He was staring at the back of her white neck, at the several lazy curls that lay against her flesh. His fingers were tanned, looking so very dark and alien next to that white skin of hers. "Sabine would have given you advice—that, or she would have told you that you wouldn't be able to pleasure me properly."

"*What?*"

"Well," he said slowly, pausing but a moment, to lean down and kiss her neck, "Sabine likes me. She wants to have her way with me. In short, she would like to bed me."

She turned stiffer than the oak sapling he'd planted just last year in the place of a dead maple at the foot of the gardens.

He kissed the new patch of white flesh he'd just uncovered as he unfastened another one of those tiny buttons. If he wasn't mistaken—and he wasn't—she shivered, just a bit, but enough to make him kiss her again and smile.

"Naturally, I would never sleep with one of our people. It is not done."

"Naturally. Even if that person was quite lovely and French?"

"Oh, being French has little to do with anything. It is English ladies who delight in calling French ladies sluts. It isn't true and English ladies know it. It's just this game they enjoy playing.''

Three more buttons opened. He was down to her chemise—actually it had to belong to his mother. It was all lace and satin and slick and soft and a very pale yellow. Goodness, this was a feast for the senses.

He parted the gown, gently easing it off her shoulders. But he didn't pull her free of the sleeves. No, he just let the gown hang low at her elbows, holding her prisoner. Then he lightly shoved the thin straps of the chemise, one and then the other, off her shoulders. He kissed every inch of flesh each of those soft straps had covered.

''Rohan?''

''Hmmm?''

''If you would unfasten a few more buttons then I could see to the rest myself.''

''No.''

''I can't move. It's disconcerting, what with you kissing me everywhere.''

He wanted to tell her he hadn't even begun to kiss her, but he didn't. Not yet. ''Don't you like me to kiss you?''

There was pained silence, then, ''It's not too bad. Actually, it's not bad at all, but it makes me nervous. It's a prelude to other things that I know are horrid.''

''Hmmm,'' he said, and the chemise straps joined the gown at her elbows. He pulled down the chemise. Unfortunately he couldn't get it past her waist, but that was just fine. For now. He eased his hands around her, and without touching her breasts, he slipped the chemise down to her waist.

The breath whooshed out of her and she jerked away from him.

She whirled to face him, struggling desperately to pull the chemise and gown back up, but she couldn't manage it. She could only cross her arms over her breasts.

''You look delicious.''

She was shaking her head. She took one step away from him, then another.

"I'm not going to rape you, Susannah."

Her back was nearly against the wall now. He just smiled at her and walked toward her, saying nothing. When he reached her, he said, "I just want to put my arms around you. Lower your hands. I'm not even looking at your breasts. I'm not embarrassing you. Come closer, Susannah, and let me hold you. That's all I want to do." That was a lie of great tonnage, but who cared?

She didn't move. He took hold of her wrists and lightly tugged until her arms were again at her sides. He didn't look down. It was important that he keep looking her right in the eye. Then he drew her slowly against him. His arms were around her back. The feel of her was incredible. There was only his dressing gown between them, but it didn't matter. He could feel the softness of her, the giving of her flesh. He wished he could rip off his dressing gown this minute. To feel her breasts against his chest—he shuddered, but held on.

"Kiss me, Susannah. Just a small kiss, just a kiss to tell me that you're not too worried about all this, just a kiss to tell me that you like being my wife."

She closed her eyes and pursed her lips.

He stared at those pursed lips. Hadn't George even kissed her properly? He felt an odd moment of utter contempt, then even greater relief. He touched his fingertip to her mouth.

"Open your mouth just a little bit and bite the end of my finger. Not hard, just a little nip."

Her eyes flew open. "Why?"

"No, that's too wide. Just enough so you can get the end of my finger with your teeth. Why, you ask? Well, I doubt you'll find it disgusting, and I would enjoy it." His fingertip was soothing her bottom lip, light, easy, when she closed her eyes again, opened her mouth just a crack, and bit him.

It wasn't a nip. On the other hand, he didn't bleed. He laughed. "That was a start. Now, just a bit easier. Don't try to draw blood, all right?"

He laid his finger on her mouth, waiting. Finally, she parted her lips, not far enough, but it was a start.

"Just a little bit more, Susannah."

She nipped it just like he'd told her to. He felt a nice bolt of pleasure and wondered if perhaps she had as well. Then to his astonishment, she sucked on the end of his finger. He thought he would die right in that very instant, simply sprawl in a heap to the floor. He looked at his own finger in her mouth and thought he would go into convulsions.

She must have noticed how he stiffened, how his eyes had glazed over, because she immediately released him.

"Is that what you wanted?"

Her mouth was wet. It was very hard not to stare at her mouth. "It was a beginning," he said. "Now I want to kiss you—nothing profane, Susannah, nothing threatening—just a light little kiss, but I want you to open your mouth a bit, just like you did to bite my fingertip."

He didn't give her time to protest, merely leaned down and found her mouth. "Part your lips," he said against her mouth. She did, just a bit. Very slowly, he slid his tongue along her lower lip, then entered her mouth, just a very little bit.

She jumped, pressing her hands against his chest. But she couldn't pull back because she was naked to the waist. He saw her dilemma in her eyes—such very expressive, beautiful eyes she had.

He slid his hands up her back, until he could reach his fingers around and lightly touch her earlobe. He pushed her hair away from her ear, always touching her warm flesh, and now he looked at her ear, then leaned down and kissed her, then slowly tugged on her earlobe. When he let his tongue trace the outline of her ear, she jumped again, only this time it was from surprise and, perhaps, from a bit of interest.

"Why are you doing that?" Her voice was soft and warm and thin as a plume of smoke against his neck.

"Don't you like it?"

"I don't know. It's very strange. Your tongue—I never knew that a tongue could be so very warm and, well, perhaps it's also a bit stimulating. I remember feeling a bit stimulated when you kissed me right after the ceremony."

"Stimulating, such a big word for what I'm doing and what I did in all innocence." But this wasn't at all innocent. This was seduction. His breath whispered into her ear. She actually clutched him, her fingers moving on his upper arms.

He was in a sorry state. Seduction was a trying business, and success was measured in such small steps. He left her ear, tangling his hands now in her hair, pulling the pins out and strewing them on the floor. He massaged her scalp, enjoying the feel of her, feeling her slowly ease. He began to wrap her hair around his hands, enjoying the softness of it, the thickness. He went back to her mouth, and to his utter pleasure, she opened her mouth for him.

He moaned into her mouth. He hadn't meant to, but he did. The warmth of her, the sudden yielding and giving, it had done him in.

It had done her in as well. She leapt back, her hands over her breasts again, and she was as pale as a cleric's collar. Then when she saw that he was looking at her breasts, she flushed, that lovely flush of hers that sent color to her hairline.

He'd scared her. He'd embarrassed her.

Well, hell.

He gave her a crooked grin, praying she wouldn't look down his body because if she did she would see that he was quite ready to throw her on the bed and come into her. But she didn't. She just stared at him, still scared witless, saying nothing, not moving, nothing.

"I'm sorry I startled you," he managed to get out of his mouth at last. "You opened your mouth to me freely and naturally, and it delighted me so much I couldn't help myself. A moan was the natural sequence of things after you did that. I didn't tell myself to moan. It just happened. Surely a simple moan isn't all that bad?"

She swallowed, shaking her head.

"If you turn around I will help you out of that gown."

At her gasp, he added quickly, "I meant to say that I will free you so that you can put on your nightgown. I won't leap on you, Susannah."

18

SHE TURNED HER BACK TO HIM. HE STARED DOWN AT ALL that white flesh, trembling slightly when his fingers touched her. He unfastened the remainder of the buttons, then helped her free her arms. She was able then to pull the gown over her breasts. Too bad.

"You know, Susannah, you gave me fifty years."

"No, I never agreed to any length of time, did I? Actually I really don't remember what we agreed to. Was it an heir?"

"The heir's a beginning. That could take ten years."

"How could that be true? I became pregnant with Marianne almost immediately." She turned to face him, her face no longer hectic with color, more calm now that her gown covered her. She was more certain of herself.

"Well, there is absolutely no way I will have you pregnant every year, Susannah. I don't want my wife to become ill or worn out from too many childbirths. I don't want you old by the time you're thirty. That happens far too often. It will not happen to you. No, when you become pregnant it will be when it is appropriate. I am not a pig, nor am I going to put your health at risk with too many pregnancies."

"But you said you wanted a dozen children."

He smiled at her, lightly touched his fingertips to the tip of her nose. "We will see."

"Then you're thinking you will just keep me around without using me?"

"What a very strange thing to say. I will keep you around because I want you to be around. I hope that soon you will want me around you as well. By 'using' you, you mean having sex with you? Of course that's what you mean. But you and I will make love until we're exhausted and sweaty and grinning like fools at each other. There are ways to prevent conception, Susannah, and I will use them.

"We will see about children. Both of us will discuss what we want. But I will not have you pregnant every year."

"My mother died in childbirth. It was a little girl. She died as well."

"You won't die. I won't allow it. Now, you have done quite well. I will leave you so that you can change into your nightgown. When you are ready, you will come to me."

"I don't know if I want to, Rohan."

"I won't force you. I've told you that. I would be pleased if you would bring yourself to believe me. No, what I'm saying is that since you're my wife, you will sleep beside me until we both cock up our toes and pass to the hereafter."

She was quiet a moment, staring down at her slippers. Then her head whipped up and she nearly yelled at him, "You're being nice to draw me in! You want me to let down my guard. When I'm asleep you will do whatever you want and I won't be able to stop you."

He realized he was pulsing with anger at her, proper raging anger, for the very first time. He wanted to shake her until she begged his forgiveness, but he didn't. He remained standing where he was, his hands relaxed at his sides. Then he merely shrugged, turned on his heel, and went back into his own bedchamber. He said calmly over his shoulder, not looking at her, "I will expect you in ten minutes, no longer."

He waited exactly ten minutes. There was no sign of Susannah. Truth be told, he had expected her to come to him. He was surprised. He had expected that level of obedience from her, because she was a woman of her word. But she hadn't given her word, had she? Well, no. However, she had promised to obey him. Maybe she hadn't heard Mr. Byam dictate that in the ceremony.

Yes, he'd believed she would slither through the adjoining door at exactly the ten-minute mark, her head down, afraid of him, her breath shallow, so wary that she would jump if he even snapped his fingers.

But she hadn't come.

She'd surprised him. He had to grin at that. No woman had surprised him in a very long time. The question was: Now what was he to do?

There wasn't really a choice. He walked through her door and saw that the room was plunged into darkness.

"Susannah?"

No answer.

He walked to the bed. It was empty.

He was flummoxed. It was his wedding night. He had decided not to try to make love to his wife. He'd been more than reasonable about the whole thing. He'd taken her a bit of the way, and he knew that she'd been surprised at some of the things he'd done. Surprised and pleased. But then he'd moaned—made the sound of a man deeply in the throes of lust, a man who just might be on the edge of being crazed and out of control. Didn't she know he never lost control? Who the hell cared about a moan? He had given her her way. He had left her. Surely she hadn't expected him to attack her when she came to him, had she? Evidently so. Perhaps he hadn't been clear with her. But it didn't matter— she should have understood, should have trusted him.

Curse it. It had been that moan of his that had sent her scurrying for safety.

He'd given her ten minutes to compose herself. And she'd had the absolute gall to disappear.

He was furious.

This would have been unacceptable in a wife. In a bride of only one day it was a stunning rejection.

"Susannah? Where are you? Perhaps you are behind the

wainscoting, and you've painted yourself as brown as the boards?''

No answer. Curse her. Strangling her was becoming a pleasant expectation.

He was not going to search through Mountvale House to find his bride. A man had to have some dignity. He had to nurture and maintain his pride. Pride was an excellent friend in situations like this. Surely that was true, since there was not much else.

He went back to his own bedchamber, slamming the adjoining door behind him. That felt good. He rather hoped she would take a chill wherever she was hiding. He didn't care. He shrugged off his dressing gown and climbed into bed.

The sheets were cold, but not for long. His anger warmed them up very quickly. She was a dolt. He would decide in the morning how he would deal with her.

He turned on his side and began to count cats. Ozzy Harker had taught him to count cats when he'd been only a young boy. Ozzy had claimed that sheep were the very devil to count, they were all so fluffy, all the same color, thus all fading into each other, all of them *baa*ing in exactly the same tone. Could he imagine sheep racing? No, certainly not. Silly bleaters would just stand around looking stupid.

Now, cats, that was quite different. There were tabbies and brindles and calico cats. So many sorts of cats. Some of the dear little buggers were blacker than a sinner's pleasures— no reference to Rohan's father, naturally—nor was Rohan to forget the glorious long-haired white cats that wouldn't race even if the Regent offered to take his clothes off for them. On the other hand, who would move a single toe for such a treat as that? And then . . .

Rohan counted five more cats—tabbies all—then fell asleep, but his dreams weren't pleasant.

Susannah was on her knees, her bottom in the air, that bottom facing him, playing with her new racing kitten. Ozzy Harker was sitting on the floor opposite her, telling her, "Ye may name the littil bite, milady."

The kitten in question didn't look like an enthusiastic racer. He or she was lying in Susannah's cupped hands, sound asleep. Slowly, careful not to disturb the kitten, Susannah rose, turned—and nearly dropped the animal.

"Rohan," she said, her voice blanker than a schoolboy's tablet. "Oh, goodness, it's you, isn't it?"

"I believe that is true. Good morning, Susannah, Ozzy. This is our new future champion?"

"Aye, milord. Ain't he a beaut? Come on, ye littil divil, wake up, and show 'is lordship wot yer made of." A big rough finger scratched beneath the kitten's chin. The kitten opened its eyes and stretched, sending its arms and legs flopping off Susannah's palms.

She laughed and raised the kitten to her face. "You're a darling." She kissed the kitten, rubbing her cheek against his soft black fur.

Rohan rather wished she would do that to him.

"What's his name, Susannah?"

"I haven't decided yet. Do you have any suggestions, Rohan? Ozzy tells me that as a boy you spent a good amount of time with the cats. That you would have made a very good racing master, if only you weren't the heir and thus had to follow in your father's and mother's footsteps."

"Well, I did spend a bit of time with the racing cats. As for this little fellow—" Rohan lightly stroked his fingertip over the kitten's white belly. There was a bit of gray mixed with the black on his back. "How about Gillyflower?"

"Goodness, that is so romantic." Susannah stared at him. Had she attempted a guess at what he would have called the kitten, it doubtless would have been a more manly name, like Brutus or Satan or perhaps even Caesar. "Why Gillyflower?"

"Did you know that 'gilly' is the Old English for 'July'?"

"No, I didn't know."

"Yes. I assume that's because the gillyflower makes its

appearance in July. The flowers are large, and very fragrant, especially at night. My favorite is colored rose-purple. It will soon be July, and this little fellow does smell sweet.''

"How would a man of your reputation know all that about a gillyflower?''

"I am a Renaissance man, a man of many fine parts. Ah, just look at that face. I don't think he'll be a flat-out racer, Ozzy, or a mean one to chew up his opponents, but he'll fly, light and high. Yes, let's name him Gillyflower.''

" 'Gilly' for short, sir?'' Toby said, coming into the estate room.

"Yes, that has a nice sound to it.''

"Not bad, milord,'' Ozzy said, nodding. He rose to his feet. "Well, milady, I'll be off to the gardens now. Tom is in the roses this morning. 'E's not all that nifty wif roses.'' He saluted Rohan and took himself out of the estate room.

"Thank you, Ozzy,'' Susannah called after him. "I will see you tomorrow morning for Gilly's lessons.''

Her eyes remained on the kitten, who was now curled up in her lap. "He is adorable, isn't he?''

"Yes, quite adorable,'' Rohan said.

"What kind of lessons can you give a kitten?'' Toby asked. "All he'll want to do is play and eat and sleep.''

"Not too many, since he's so young,'' Rohan said. "It's just what you'd call an introduction to racing. You'll see, Toby. Now, you two, would you care for breakfast?''

Rohan picked up the sleeping kitten out of Susannah's lap, lightly rubbed his fingertip under its chin, and laid it on his shoulder. It was all so very natural. Only for an instant did Susannah wonder if the kitten would fall off, but he didn't. No, Rohan knew exactly what he was doing.

She followed him to the breakfast room. Toby left them to ride to the village for his lessons with Mr. Byam.

They were alone. Rohan left the kitten on his shoulder.

When the silver dome on the platter of bacon was raised, however, the kitten's nose started twitching. "No, you won't eat on the table,'' he said, and set the kitten on the rug beside his chair. He crumbled a small portion of bacon on a plate and set it in front of him. Alongside it, he placed a small saucer of milk. He said absently to Susannah, "Just a tiny bit of bacon. It's too strong for a kitten's stomach, but just a taste won't hurt him."

"Are we going to Oxford today?"

Rohan straightened in his chair. The kitten was lapping up the milk. He'd snaffled down the bacon in two frantic bites.

"Why would you ask?"

"You said yesterday that we would go."

"I can't imagine your wanting to come with me now, Susannah. You would have to share a room with me at the inns we will stop at. There would be no place for you to hide."

"Oh, that."

Her eyes were on her place. The slice of buttered toast was limp in her hand.

"Yes, that. Doubtless I would wait until you were asleep, and then I would attack your fair person."

"That is a possibility, but I'm willing to chance it." She raised her head and looked at him intently. "I want to get this mess solved, Rohan. I want to find out about this map and why these men are so desperate to get it." She paused just a moment, then drew a deep breath. "But most important, I want to find out who George really was."

She was serious and he'd been goading her about sex. He sighed. He still wanted to take a strip off her, but now wasn't the time. "I'm not certain it's safe to take you with me," he said finally. "Our Mr. Lambert, God give him grace on the high seas, wasn't a nice man. I don't expect that the others—there are always others, I've found, when it comes to sin—will exceed his level of civility. They will be dangerous."

She leaned toward him, her elbows on the table. "I was thinking about that. I understand your concern, but remember, George was my husband—"

"Do keep your voice down, my lady."

"You're right. I'm sorry."

"It's critical that you wipe all of it from your mind. I caution you, anything known by the master and mistress is usually known by the staff. We must be very careful. Fitz has ears that extend to the stables and beyond to the east pasture."

"I understand. I will be very careful. Now, regardless, I have given this a good deal of thought. You must have friends at Oxford, a family we could visit for a week? Marianne and I would have the protection of the family, would we not? Wouldn't it be safer than if we were all staying at an inn?"

"You didn't spend your entire night finding ways to thwart me, Susannah? Damn you, don't draw back in fright. Very well, I will think about it. As to a place we can visit, I had planned on that already. I have a longtime friend whose country home is very near Oxford. His name is Phillip Mercerault, Viscount Derencourt. We went to school together. It's more than likely that he is in London. I wrote him last week, telling him of our proposed visit to Oxford. I have no idea if he received it or if he is even now at his country estate, Dinwitty Manor. No, don't giggle. Dinwitty Manor was named after a wife brought into the family way back in the seventeenth century."

"She must have been an heiress."

"No doubt. But to force the house to carry her name is asking a lot, isn't it? We'll leave for Oxford tomorrow, if that pleases you."

"Ow!"

Rohan laughed. The kitten had just climbed up Susannah's skirt, digging his claws into her leg along his journey.

She was laughing then, grabbing the kitten and shaking him lightly, all the while giving his little nipping kisses.

Just like he'd wanted her to nip his tongue.

19

"Ro-han!"

It was Marianne, in high good humor, balanced on Lottie's hip. She immediately scrambled down and ran to him, reaching up her skinny arms until he picked her up and set her on his leg. "You hungry, pumpkin? I see, you don't care a whit about food. This little fellow is named Gilly and you're to be very gentle with him. He's just a little fellow, not a big girl like you are."

Within five minutes Marianne was chasing the kitten throughout the breakfast room, shouting, laughing, the kitten having a fine time himself.

"I will have to tell Ozzy that the kitten had his first lesson today," Rohan said. "It's called survival. A racing cat can never learn about survival too soon. Just look at them. Look at him fly. I'm hopeful that we just might have a champion, Susannah."

She was staring at him. This man—her new husband—was a libertine? A womanizer? A lecher? And yet here he was laughing and quite enjoying himself watching a kitten and a little girl. He knew all about gillyflowers? She said slowly, not looking at him, "Did you know you can use gillyflowers for flavoring? In jams and in sauces?"

"Certainly. It's an excellent flavoring since it has the smell of cloves." He suddenly stilled at the expression on her face. "Tell me what you're thinking, Susannah."

"I was thinking that you're a puzzle, my lord. I was thinking that many of the pieces appear to be unrelated, as if the puzzle the world sees isn't the puzzle you really are."

He laughed. "Does this mean that from now on you won't preface every comment with 'a man of your reputation'?"

"Reputation," she repeated slowly, frowning now at him. "Those three old biddies believed I was a slut before you jumped in with both feet and your wits to save me in your own peculiar way. It would have become my reputation. But I am not a slut. All this is curious, don't you think?"

He looked at her and wanted her desperately. He couldn't think of a thing to say and thus simply nodded.

His wife wasn't a virgin, and that, strangely enough, made things worse. He had never before encountered a problem of this sort. It would require a lot of thought, a lot of planning and strategy.

He posted another letter to Phillip Mercerault, this one to Dinwitty Manor, informing him again of his imminent pleasure if he chanced to be there. Then he brooded. That bored him quickly. He got Marianne from Lottie and took her for a ride on Gulliver. She screamed with pleasure and Gulliver snorted over his shoulder at her. He had just wheeled about on the country road when Lady Dauntry came by in her landau, a tall bonnet on her head, sporting four ostrich feathers dyed purple. It was difficult not to simply stare at those purple feathers.

He smiled at her, bidding her good day.

"Baron," she nodded. "Is this the little girl?"

"This is *my* little girl, Marianne. Pumpkin, say hello to Lady Dauntry."

"Hello. May I have a purple feather?"

To Rohan's astonishment, Lady Dauntry pulled one of the feathers from the bonnet and handed it to her. Marianne enjoyed instant bliss.

"Thank you, ma'am," Rohan said. "That is very kind of you. Isn't she a darling?"

"Yes, she's adorable, the very image of you, baron. You were wrong not to bring the little girl and her mother to Mountvale House for so very long, but I suppose that they're here now and that's what is important. You have faced your responsibilities. I dare say that Charlotte is bewildered by all this?"

Marianne was waving the feather over the top of Gulliver's head. He was snorting, his head going up and down, trying to get that feather out of Marianne's hands and into his mouth.

"That's enough, pumpkin," Rohan said. "Gulliver just might knock both of us into a ditch." Without thinking, he kissed the little girl's temple.

Lady Dauntry tsked. "Your father used to kiss you just so when you were just a little nit, baron. Now, about poor Charlotte?"

"My mother adores both Susannah and Marianne, ma'am. She is dealing well with my early marriage."

"Ro-han!" Marianne waved the feather in his face.

"I see she is getting bored. We'd best be off before she does something outrageous. A pleasure to see you, ma'am."

"She doesn't call you Papa. But not surprising, I suppose, given that you didn't see her all that often. I trust you will rectify that soon. Tell dear Charlotte I shall visit her." Lady Dauntry poked her coachman in the back with her cane. The man jumped, then the horse.

That was a good point, Rohan thought, hugging Marianne, who wasn't having any of it. She was bouncing up and down on his leg. Gulliver was snorting.

He decided it was time to return home. When they neared the stables, he heard Jamie singing at the top of his lungs, in a rich, broad West Country accent:

"There was a young lady of Lynn.
Who was so uncommonly thin

That when she essayed
To drink lemonade,
She slipped through the straw and fell in."

Marianne roared with laughter, then turned to Rohan. "What does 'essayed' mean?"

He kissed her nose. "It means she tried to drink her lemonade through a straw. Let's go find your mama. Jamie, all goes well with you?" He realized in that moment that he'd forgotten to speak to him about the marital situation.

Before Rohan could say a thing, Jamie said, nodding, "I quite understand, milord. Mum's the word. Don't ye worry none about me trap flapping."

"Thank you. I won't. Forgive me for not speaking to you about this situation sooner."

"Tan't nuthin' t'worry ye or me. Now, Marianne, come down to Jamie."

"How can you recite limericks in Etonian English and then in the next breath decapitate the language?"

"Talent, milord. Sheer talent."

The later it became, the quieter Susannah became. When the clock struck ten deep strokes, she was mute, staring down at her toes.

"Whatever is wrong with you?" Charlotte asked, leaning over to place her palm on Susannah's forehead.

She gave her mother-in-law the most pathetic look Rohan had ever seen. "Oh, nothing, Charlotte. I'm just tired."

"I know," Rohan said, yawning behind his hand. "I am tired as well."

Charlotte beamed at both of them. "Then you should certainly excuse yourselves. Ah, marital bliss." She sighed. "I do miss your father, dearest. He continued to improve upon his skills, if you can believe that, Susannah. Yes, indeed, he was much sought after. Even by his wife." She sighed again, then she smiled, a quite beautiful bittersweet smile. "Your father and I always enjoyed being next door to each other.

We simply opened the door between us and then opened our arms. I do miss him very much.

"You are very lucky, Susannah, for Rohan's father gave him excellent training in the art of lovemaking. Speaking of training, I saw Marie Claire when I was in London, dearest. She sends her love to you, naturally."

"Who is Marie Claire?" Susannah asked.

"She is the charming woman who gave dear Rohan his early training. What were you, dearest—fourteen? It was past time, your father believed. But I discussed it with Marie Claire, and we both agreed that fourteen was just the right age."

Susannah couldn't believe she was sitting in a nobleman's drawing room listening to her mother-in-law talk of affairs, speaking affectionately of the woman who had sexually trained her son and was her husband's mistress.

"I never had any training," Susannah said, forcing her chin up. She would not act like a shocked ninny.

"Women don't need training as much as men do," Charlotte said, patting Susannah's knee. "Well, they do, but they learn more quickly how to give pleasure. And, well, gentlemen are so very obvious and predictable in that area, don't you agree, dearest?"

"Yes, Mother, certainly," Rohan said, his voice as serious as a judge's. "Ladies must be treated very carefully, very gently. That's what Marie Claire always told me. It's a matter of trust."

Charlotte gave him a proud look. "How right you are. Now, why don't the two of you retire to enjoy yourselves. Susannah, if Rohan is like his father, then you must be blissfully happy."

Susannah looked as if she would scream.

Rohan grabbed her hand and pulled her up. Without a word, he lifted her in his arms, laughingly called good night to his mama, and carried his wife up the stairs.

"I have given this a lot of thought."

"Hmmm?"

"I mean it, Rohan. You may begin impregnating me tonight."

"Now there's a jolly thought." He tightened his arms around her.

"What I mean is that I won't run off again. That was unworthy. I was a coward and I apologize. I know this is important. We will do it."

"My heart begins to race."

"There is no reason to be snide and sarcastic."

"Perhaps, but allow me the latitude, Susannah. Otherwise I might be tempted to pin your ears back for that stunt you pulled last night. Where did you sleep?"

"With Marianne, in the nursery."

"Oh? And what did Lottie think about that?"

"I left very early, before she came in."

"So you do have a care for appearances. That is a small forward step."

"I don't think your mother has ever been disappointed in her life."

"I assume we're speaking of that loathsome male demand? Of course we are. If a man had disappointed my mother, she would have told him so. She would have instructed him in proper lovemaking technique."

She reared back in his arms and stuck her nose in his face. "But I didn't know anything! I still don't. I couldn't instruct anybody!"

"After tonight you will be able to instruct the pope, if the need were ever to arise."

She sank back down. "I can walk."

"I trust so, but I enjoy the feel of you. Where's our racing kitten, Gilly?"

"With Toby. After he survived his first lesson this morning with Marianne, he slept most of the day in any patch of sunlight he could find."

"When I was a boy, there would be up to half a dozen cats sleeping with me at any one time. There are none now, since I spend so much time in London. Ozzy said it wasn't fair to the cats, expecting to find me in my bed and the bed being empty and all. He said it put them off their feed.''

She laughed, a sweet, mellow sound. She was easing. Good. Finally.

''Shall I import some cats to sleep with us?''

The laugh fell off the cliff.

''There are occasionally fleas—mainly in the summer months. But that's another thing a married couple can do together.''

''You mean pick fleas off each other?'' She laughed again, only to stop abruptly when he opened the bedchamber door. It was to his room, not hers. He kicked the door closed behind him. He eased her down slowly, letting her feel every inch of him on the way.

''Now, my dear, we are going to think of you as a racing kitten. You are going to have your first lesson right now.''

''Is it an introduction to survival?''

He laughed, hugged her hard, and said, ''The trainer's survival, madam, not yours.''

20

SHE MOISTENED HER LIPS. "SHALL I FETCH MARIANNE?"

"Oh, no, it won't be Marianne chasing you about the bed-chamber. No one will be chasing anyone, actually. It will be just me, teaching you to laugh and kick up your heels and groan when a wave of pleasure washes over you."

She stared up at him as though he'd grown three heads.

"Let's get you out of your clothes." He didn't bestow any kisses on her neck, her ears, her shoulders—no, he got that gown off her within a minute flat. He allowed her to keep her chemise on, but nothing else. He'd made a big mistake the night before, leaving her. He'd scared her, what with all his fine technique and overlong warm-up.

"Don't move." He was naked in under thirty seconds.

She gasped and backed away from him. He felt a stab of impatience. He wasn't a vain man, but he knew that his body was well formed, with not a patch of fat on it, and since he spent two days a week at Gentleman Jackson's he knew he showed strength, but surely not enough muscle to scare her or disgust her. Nor was he overly hairy, like one of his friends who had hair curling on his back. "Come on now, Susannah, you've certainly seen a naked man before."

"Well, no, actually," she said, staring fixedly at his belly.

"I haven't. George always snuffed out the candles. I just felt him."

"You're jesting with me," he said slowly, looking so utterly appalled that she was forced to laugh. But it was difficult, because he was naked, standing right in front of her, and he was eyeing her chemise like a hunter eyeing a pheasant.

"No, he never took off his clothes when the candles were lit. I didn't realize, I hadn't imagined—"

"It doesn't matter. You are not to worry about it. Trust me on this, Susannah."

Again, he didn't hesitate. He got the chemise off her in a trice. Then he simply pulled her up tight against him. "Now," he said. "Now. Forget everything that happened to you before right this instant. You're my wife now. From now on, it's just you and me."

This way he had of feeling her, this way of letting her feel him—it was very intimate, yet all he was doing was simply holding her against him. It wasn't bad, except for his sex pressing against her belly. George had hurt her. And surely he hadn't been made like this. On the other hand, she really didn't know.

"I don't know if this is a good idea," she said in an air-thin voice while he was busy nuzzling her neck.

"Don't be a ninny," he said, raising his head. "It's a wonderful idea." He picked her up in his arms, carried her to the bed, and dropped her in the middle. She landed sprawled on her back, her arms and legs wide.

"I like that. Don't move." He came down beside her, not touching her, just looking at her, starting with the top of her head, down to her toes. Then he turned to move the branch of candles closer.

She tried to draw away, but he grasped her arm, holding her still. "No, Susannah, no." He didn't turn into a wild man. He knew she expected that, curse George.

He looked down at her face, no other part of her, and she knew it. He kissed her then, a long, slow, deep kiss that lasted until she opened her mouth to him. "Well done," he said in her mouth at the same moment that his hand cupped her breast. The weight of her breast, the heat of her flesh, it made his fingers tremble, made his hand jerk, very nearly made his teeth chatter and his jaw lock.

As for his bride, she nearly leapt off the bed.

He didn't move his hand, just settled her breast in his palm. "I am not hurting you. Not a bit of it. Don't you like that? It's my hand, Susannah, touching you. Just me. I'll do this every night for the next fifty years. Get used to it. That's right, draw a deep breath, pretend you're suffering me. That's a beginning. That's all a man of my reputation needs for encouragement."

"I'm embarrassed. You promised that you wouldn't embarrass me."

"I lied." He began kissing her again. She opened her mouth this time, without his instruction. He smiled to himself. "But it's just a little lie, at least in terms of time. In a maximum of three minutes from now you won't be embarrassed at all. Actually, it might be just one minute. You want to know why, Susannah?"

"Well, yes."

"You're going to run that soft hand of yours that's right now clutched against my underarm down my chest to my belly. When you reach my belly, you're going to flatten your palm against me, feel me, and then move lower. You're going to tease me, Susannah."

Susannah hadn't the foggiest notion of what was happening to her. Rohan was talking, incessantly talking, his hand still cupping her breast, and he was going on and on about how she was going to tease him. It made no sense. She wanted to very calmly rise from this bed of iniquity and go to her own room and put on a nightgown that made her look twelve years old.

Then his thumb lightly caressed her breast.

She jumped.

"Nice, huh?"

"No, it's horrid."

"So I will be the parent to teach our Marianne about always telling the truth. For shame, Susannah. In just another moment, you're going to groan. What do you think?"

His fingers were on her stomach. Surely a man's fingers weren't meant to sit on a woman's stomach, just lying there doing nothing at all. Well, now they were moving slowly, so very slowly downward, and she knew that wasn't right. This was what he'd wanted her to do to him? No, certainly no sane woman would do something as mortifying as that. On the other hand, he seemed at the moment not to have a lustful bone in his body. He wasn't heaving or breathing fast or trying to crush her beneath him. He wasn't groaning. She would try reason. "Rohan, perhaps you could consider—"

His fingers were suddenly touching her. His fingers were on her flesh, private flesh, her own flesh that hadn't ever had anyone's hand near it. George had never touched her there. She should say something. She should shriek. She should, at the very least, lodge a formal protest.

She moaned when his fingers pressed gently inward and down on her.

"Yes," he said, and began kissing her again, deep, long, drugging kisses that made her brain go blank. Her brain had never gone blank in her life, except when she fancied herself in love with George, more fool she, and said yes she'd marry him. And then he'd ravaged her in the dark. She had found it very difficult to tell him she loved him after he was through with her.

His fingers began a rhythm that was surely a heathen rhythm, a rhythm that surely no proper lady even knew about, a rhythm that made her want to press her hips upward, a rhythm that made her want to dance and yell both at the same time. Instead, she moaned again.

"It's horrid!" she yelled, appalled at herself, then moaned yet again, jerking upward.

Rohan watched her face, the absolute astonishment that widened her eyes just the instant before her release shook her to her very nice toes. She was wild, arching madly, her hands in his hair, pulling him down so she could kiss him, and still he worked her, gently, then harder, his movements deep, then slick and shallow. He held her there, beyond herself, experiencing something every human being should experience, something he planned for her to experience every night of their lives. When he felt the spasms easing, he lessened the pressure, just stroking now, soothing her until her eyes had nearly lost their wild look. Then he reared over her and came into her in one long, deep stroke.

She yelled, heaving upward, bringing him so deep he touched her womb. She was tight, her flesh pulsing around him, making him insane with lust, but he knew he wasn't hurting her.

He wanted it to last, surely he had the wherewithal to make this business last for just a moment longer, but it somehow seemed beyond him. It was her own release, he thought, his teeth gritted, that was bringing him low, but surely that wasn't right. But it didn't seem to matter. She moved, holding him tightly, her mouth on his throat, and the waves of intense pleasure crested, sending him into oblivion.

In that instant he wondered if he were going to die. His heart was pounding like a madman's, he couldn't seem to catch his breath. He managed to keep his weight off her, balancing himself on his elbows above her. When at last he could speak, he said, "You're not embarrassed now, are you?"

She stared up at him, feeling him deep inside her, feeling the small shocks of pleasure, like memories of a precious moment, making her breath hitch. If she had been standing, she knew she would have collapsed. He moved slightly, and she could feel him inside her, actually feel him. He was a man, alien to her, and yet he was within her.

"It's horrible."

"Hmmm."

Reason reasserted itself. She couldn't believe what she'd done, what she'd felt. It was more than she could deal with.

Shame and tears choked in her throat. She couldn't bear herself. "I was an animal."

"You expected maybe a bird?"

She gave him this lost, shuttered look that made him feel like a brute. He dipped down and kissed her mouth. "A very beautiful, very responsive animal. I don't think I've ever felt like this before, Susannah."

He sounded bewildered to her sensitive ears. Surely that couldn't be right. He was a libertine, a satyr, his very being was lascivious, it was bred into his bones. Why, he had enjoyed more women than there were folk in Mountvale Village. She was just one more woman in a very long line, nothing special. After all, she hadn't even let her palm flatten on his belly. She hadn't sent her palm lower to do this teasing of his.

He was kissing her mouth, the tip of her nose.

"You know you don't have to tell me any lies. I'm your wife."

It was gone in just a flash, but she would have sworn she saw anger in him, would have sworn even that she'd felt that anger course through that lean body of his. His body. He was still inside her. He hadn't fallen off her and rolled onto his back. No, he was with her, and now, he was moving again, very slowly, gently. Then, suddenly, he stopped.

"I can't. I would be a selfish beast. It's been a very long time for you," he said, a wealth of disappointment in his voice. "I don't want you sore. However, I might wake you early in the morning. You will like that, Susannah."

He raised up between her legs and watched himself come out of her body. Then he closed his eyes, his hands fisted on her thighs. She felt him move into her again, but then he drew a very deep breath and pulled himself out of her.

He cursed. He rested on his knees between her legs, his head down, his breathing deep and rapid. Then he looked at her and lightly touched her. "You are beautiful, Susannah." She actually felt her flesh begin to pulse. It was mortifying. She wanted him to keep touching her, she wanted . . .

His fingers were gone. "Just maybe next time you'll caress me. A man enjoys that as much as a woman does." He eased down beside her, then cursed again. He got up, soon to return with a basin of water and a cloth. "Hold still."

He bathed his seed from her. She was so shocked that she doubted she could have moved in any case. She closed her eyes. The water was cool against her. It felt wonderful. "Maybe now you won't be so sore," he said, and gently eased the wet cloth, wrapped around the end of his finger, inside her. He held his finger perfectly still.

She felt drugged, outside herself, as if she were standing apart from the woman on the bed who was lying there like a strumpet. Surely a strumpet was what she was, just lying there, with his finger inside her, and she was enjoying how his finger made her feel. She wanted his finger to push deeper inside her. She wanted to press against his finger, she wanted . . . Then he was gone.

He lifted her and eased her beneath the covers. He snuffed out the candles. When he pulled her against him, she began to weep.

He said nothing, merely stroked her hair, impossibly tangled now because she'd been such a wild thing, and that blessed memory made him smile, made him feel like a god all the way to his toes. Then he frowned. He hadn't lied to her. He had never before in his life felt that way with any other woman. Naturally she didn't believe him.

Of course he had never been married before. Perhaps it was those words spoken by Mr. Byam that sanctioned this mysterious, even frightening reaction he'd had. There had simply been too much pleasure and too little control. He'd lost himself and he didn't like that one bit. He wondered if she'd felt that way. He saw that lost look in her beautiful eyes and imagined that she had. He rather hoped so. A woman shouldn't be afraid of her husband. She should want him and use him and enjoy him.

She'd used him very well. Finally, her sobs became hiccups. Still, he said nothing, for what could he say to her? He knew the moment she was gone from him into sleep.

He'd known her for one day less than a fortnight.

He didn't wake her the following morning, for the simple reason that he didn't awaken until there was a soft knock at the bedchamber door. She was warm, wrapped all over him, her hair tickling his nose, her knee over his belly.

The knock came again.

Why hadn't he awakened before?

He sighed, gently eased himself away from her, covered her well, then shrugged into his dressing gown.

"Good God," he said upon opening the door, "it's you, Tinker. About time you got here."

"Yes, my lord, and Mr. Pulver is with me. He had a putrid throat, my lord, and I could not very well leave him. Thus he was ill and I was his nurse. But we are here now, my lord, to take care of you."

"I've already been well taken care of, thank you, Tinker. But perhaps my cravats have suffered injury in your absence."

"Mr. Fitz told us that you have *married,* my lord. *Married!* Not just newly *married,* but *married* for many years, even a few years before your dear father died, and you have a child, a *little girl.* You are a father. And you kept it a secret. You didn't even tell *me.* Not a hint. Nothing at all. This is all unusual, my lord. You kept it from Mr. Pulver as well. If his throat were not still sore, he would tell you of his torment that you had no trust of him. I cannot credit this, my lord, surely not, for a man of your appetites wouldn't—"

"Perhaps you could find a less-bramble-filled verbal path to trod upon, Tinker. Yes, I'm married, thank you. If you look beyond me, you'll see my wife in my bed. Yes, I kept it secret from everyone, including my mother. Does that make you feel less slighted? Now, what do you want?"

Pulver suddenly appeared behind Tinker. His voice was low and raw. "We do not mean to intrude, my lord"—he coughed vilely— "but surely you must realize that we are stunned. We are nearly without speech."

"I would say the only thing you are missing is a modicum of wits. I'm pleased you didn't croak from your putrid throat, Pulver, but you still sound like the very devil. Go see Mrs. Beete. She knows every remedy for every malady. Then get yourself to bed, at least until noon. Now, again, what do the two of you want?"

Suddenly there was a look of utter surprise on Tinker's pinched face. "My God, I've been bitten!"

He whirled about to see a little girl grinning up at him. Once he'd moved, she was past him in a flash, grabbing Rohan's leg.

He immediately reached down and picked her up. "Good morning, pumpkin. Did you sleep well? Did you draw blood when you bit Mr. Tinker's leg?"

"He was in my way," Marianne said and surveyed the two dumbfounded gentlemen from her new height in Rohan's arms.

"Tinker, Pulver, this is my daughter, Marianne."

"She looks greatly like you, my lord."

Rohan didn't hesitate. "Yes, she does."

"Mayhap she will have her grandmother's glorious character," Tinker said. "Oh, dear," he quickly added, his brows beetling, "her exquisite ladyship is now a grandmother. What an appalling notion. It's quite unthinkable, preposterous really. She must be prostrate. Oh, dear."

"Don't worry. My mother is quite pleased with Marianne and with my wife. Also you will meet Toby, my wife's younger brother. He's a good lad, studying with Mr. Byam until he's off to Eton. Now, once more, what do you want?"

Marianne pulled away. "Mama," she said, and pulled some more.

It wasn't to be. All his tender visions about waking Susannah, watching her beautiful eyes all vague from sleep go wild when he came deep inside her, faded into the wainscoting. "Go," he said, and set Marianne on her feet. He watched her run to the bed and set about climbing up. She managed to pull most the covers off Susannah as hand over hand she shimmied to the top of the bed.

He heard a groan from Susannah, then a laugh. "Lovey, good morning to you. How pretty you look this morning. Come and hug me."

Soon Rohan heard the sucking of fingers and smiled. He looked back at Tinker and Pulver. They were staring at him as if he'd grown fangs and would soon froth at the mouth.

The smile disappeared. "Now, what is it? Surely it's still morning, surely there's no fire in the west wing? Mrs. Beete didn't put either of you in the attic?"

"Well, my lord," Pulver said, "the fact is, Miss Lily came to your house in London because she was very worried about you. We didn't know what had happened, since you had not communicated with us until the letter requesting our presence here. We could tell Miss Lily nothing. She is upset, my lord. Not distraught, because she isn't that way, but definitely upset."

"Well, damn," Rohan said. He'd forgotten Lily existed, which wasn't well done of him.

"We thought you would like to know immediately," Tinker said, sounding portentous. He lowered his voice, saying behind his hand, "Your father, my lord, never forgot to keep all the ladies informed of his whereabouts."

Rohan rolled his eyes. "Thank you for informing me. Pulver, since you are here, I will put you to work. No, wait— you'll rest in bed until after luncheon. Then you will wade into those piles of accounts for the estate farms. I will join you later, maybe, if I decide to flagellate myself. But to be honest, it's unlikely."

He shut the bedchamber door in their faces.

21

R OHAN TURNED TO SEE SUSANNAH SITTING UP IN BED, THE covers pulled to her throat because she was quite without a stitch on beneath. Marianne was on her lap, singing a song that sounded suspiciously like one of Jamie's limericks.

He walked to the bed and eased under the covers. "Well, pumpkin, will you sing to me now?"

"I must speak to Jamie," Susannah said, sighing.

"I thought I recognized that tune." He leaned over and kissed his wife's cheek. He splayed his fingers and began to smooth the tangles from her hair. She just stared at him.

"You feeling like an animal again?" He rubbed her scalp, then resumed easing the tangles out.

"Marianne is here."

"Why are you playing with Mama's hair, Rohan?"

He told her the truth without thinking. "She has the most beautiful hair in the world, soft as a mink's fur, and I love to touch it. But she slept restlessly last night. I'm just brushing out the tangles with my fingers."

Susannah snorted.

"What's a mink?"

"It's a kind of fur. I will get you a mink muff for your birthday." Marianne stared at him, tilting her head to one side, just the same way George did. She lifted her hand to touch her mother's hair. "Soft," she said, then her fingers went back into her mouth. She settled sprawled out on her mother's chest. The sucking eventually became quieter. Rohan said, very low, "I have worried about erasing George, you know, rearranging the past so that he never existed. I will even take his daughter. Will we tell her the truth someday? I don't know. But this bothers me, Susannah."

She was lying naked in his bed, her daughter asleep on top of her. All of it felt so very strange. But not as strange as last night had felt. Beneath the seriousness in his voice she heard pain. She cleared her throat. "George doesn't deserve to be erased. Nor, on the other hand, does he deserve to have Marianne as his daughter."

"He was very young."

"So was I. Even younger. Does that excuse him?"

"No, certainly not, but ladies appear to be more aware of the needs of life than do men. He was still a boy."

"He was not a boy if he was in on a scheme with that Mr. Lambert. He was not a boy since he hired this man to pretend to marry us."

"Yes, you're right, of course. Still, to be honest, Susannah, I'm praying we will find something in Oxford to mitigate George's apparent thoughtlessness, his selfishness."

"Mitigate his illegal activities, perhaps?"

"Yes."

"Rohan, we will find the truth. Then we will deal with it, with whatever we discover. I hope that George isn't a villain, but what I have learned about him isn't encouraging. May we leave today?"

"Tomorrow morning, I promise. I keep putting it off, don't I? But there's much to do today. The two men you saw in the doorway—Tinker, the short, plump one, is my valet, my father's valet before me. The skinny one who looks ready to fit into a coffin is Pulver, my secretary. I must get them settled, get Pulver immersed in the estate work. If he's not working, he won't eat anything at all. I don't want to be responsible for his starvation."

"They came just to tell you about your mistress?"

"You heard that, did you?"

"She was so worried about you that she went to your house in London? That's done? A mistress visiting her protector's house?"

"No, but, you see, Lily doesn't write well. Actually, she has a very difficult time with it. I have taught her quite a bit, but when she's upset, she forgets how to write even her own name."

"You have taught your mistress how to write?"

"Why not?"

"As in man cannot live by sex alone?"

"That's about the size of it. Even a man of my reputation occasionally has other things than just sex on his mind. You would like Lily." He paused a moment, looking at a long-dead Carrington on the far wall, then added, "I have known her for a long time. She isn't a girl of twenty. She's a mature woman."

"Isn't that odd?"

He raised an eyebrow. His hair was rumpled. Since he was blond, there was little beard stubble on his cheeks and chin. There were, however, tufts of blondish hair on his chest. Susannah had stroked that chest, feeling that hair sift between her fingers. She had quite enjoyed doing it.

"Oh, I see. Does she train the new females who come to your harem?"

"Now, what do you know about harems, Lady Mountvale?"

She looked suddenly very bereft. "Not much. Just that I appear now to be part of one."

He raised his hand and resumed stroking his fingers through her hair. "Soon I'm going to have to get on the other side of you. This side's nearly smooth as silk, all the tangles long gone."

She sighed and leaned against him, her cheek against his shoulder. Marianne obligingly shifted until she was half-sprawled on each of them.

The door opened and Toby's head appeared.

"Toby, before you come in, go see Fitz and tell him we would like breakfast served here. You may join us. As you can see, Marianne has already staked her claim." He waited only until Toby skipped down the corridor. Without pause, he said to Susannah, "What if I were to tell you that I don't have a harem?"

"Come now, a man of your reputation? You have dozens of women. I should not have been at all surprised when you made me lose my head last night. Aren't you renowned for your prowess?"

"Actually," he said, his voice very thoughtful, "last night came as quite a surprise to me. When I caressed you with my fingers, you exploded. It was well done of you, Susannah."

"I didn't mean to do it. I had no idea that a man could do such things to a woman."

"Oh, yes, and there's so much more. Passion is like that—sometimes you have no control at all. That's what it was like for me last night. I'd rather hoped to have a repeat performance this morning, but what can one do?"

Marianne sucked louder on her fingers.

"Did he please you last night, my dear?"

She shouldn't be shocked, Susannah knew she shouldn't, but still, this was her mother-in-law asking her about being naked in bed with a man and having him do all sorts of things to her with the result that she had enjoyed herself. Susannah gulped, then squared her shoulders. What was one to do in Rome? "Yes, ma'am, he did."

"My sweet boy," Charlotte said. "He has never disappointed me." Charlotte looked dreamy, and a dreamy-looking Charlotte was an incredibly beautiful creature. "I shall never forget when his father discovered that Rohan was reading a book on planning a garden. *Planning a garden,* Susannah! Well, my dear boy quickly saw the error of his ways. He quickly realized that a man of his father's reputation would be drawn and quartered before he would read a book on planning a garden. It was just a small lapse. Here one day and gone the next.

"No, my beautiful boy has never failed me. Indeed, he has been an inspiration, except for his lapse in marrying you when he was so very young, but that is forgivable, I suppose, when a young man is experiencing incredible throes of lust and the young lady isn't mistress material, which, naturally, you weren't." Charlotte sighed. "Yes, a dear boy."

She stopped speaking, at last. Susannah was staring at her. She was profoundly grateful that Rohan wasn't in the room. What would he say to all his mama's outpourings? She was certain that his mother, at this particular juncture, would have patted him on the head.

Susannah cleared her throat. "We are leaving tomorrow for Oxford. I wanted to ask if you would oversee Marianne's care."

"Really, my dear girl, I should be delighted. But Susannah, you must be gowned properly. Just look at you. Rohan told me you will be visiting Phillip Mercerault—if he is at Dinwitty Manor, of course, which he might not be, but his servants all know Rohan, so you will stay there regardless. Now, Phillip—there's another boy with a maestro's eye and a flawless technique, or so I've been told. Not as flawless a technique as Rohan's, no doubt, but quite acceptable nonetheless."

Susannah had been the recipient of a flawless technique, nothing more. Was Rohan, in his own way, like the great Edmund Kean performing *Macbeth*? Evidently so. It was a pity she didn't realize she should have applauded him, after she'd managed to restore her wits. That such a thing was even possible still staggered her. She was still having great difficulty coming to grips with it. She had truly lost her head.

"Susannah?"

"Yes, ma'am? Oh, my gowns. Do you truly believe I look needy?"

"You look like a poor relation. You don't want to shame

Rohan. You are the Baroness Mountvale. You now have a responsibility. After all, a wife must always be dressed better than her husband's mistresses. If she is not, then it redounds to the husband. Surely you do not want dear Rohan to be thought begrudging with his groats?''

"No, of course not," Susannah said. "Oh, Charlotte, speaking of mistresses, Tinker said that Lily came to Rohan's London house. She was worried because he hadn't communicated with her."

"Rightfully so," Charlotte said, nodding. "Poor woman, she must have been frantic. Usually Rohan is excellent about telling his women when he will be gone and when he will return. I know his father told him that was a gentleman's responsibility, and Rohan has never shirked his responsibilities. I assume he is even now sending a messenger to London to relieve her mind. And, naturally, others' minds as well."

"Naturally. You sound as if you know this Lily."

"Certainly. She and Rohan have been together for nearly six years, which, I admit, is rather odd of him. I do believe Lily was the first mistress he mounted when he came to London. I also recall that he was still studying something—I have no idea what—at Oxford. That was odd as well, both his father and I agreed that it was. Why, in heaven's name, would our dear boy want to forgo even a moment's pleasures by continuing to study at Oxford?

"Yes, Lily and Rohan are fond of each other, as is appropriate. No one wants a mistress or a lover who is rapacious and uncaring."

"No, I guess not," Susannah said, wanting to cry. "Do you think she has interviewed all the mistresses that Rohan has collected since that time?"

"Now that is an interesting question," Charlotte said thoughtfully as she poured herself a cup of tea with incredible grace. "I shouldn't be surprised. Lily is a very intelligent woman. If a girl weren't proper for Rohan, then Lily could steer him away from her. Yes, I shall have to ask him."

Suddenly, Charlotte paused her teacup's ascent to her mouth. She said, her voice incredulous, her blond eyebrows raised a good inch, "Susannah, you aren't jealous, are you?"

"Jealous about what, Mama?"

Charlotte looked up to see her beautiful boy standing in the doorway, looking very interested, his eyes on his wife. "Oh, dearest, Susannah and I were just speaking of Lily. Do you have Lily look over a girl before you take her under your protection?"

His eyes nearly crossed. He couldn't believe what his mother had just said. Well, actually, yes, he could. He shot a quick look at Susannah. She looked cold and withdrawn, yet at the same time there was something else. He did believe it was anger radiating from her. Now this was interesting. It pleased him inordinately. He managed not to smile. "No," he said, in all seriousness. "Lily has never done that."

"Perhaps it is an idea you should consider," Susannah said, her chin up, those beautiful eyes of hers so cold they could have frozen the tea in her cup. "Surely a man doesn't want a mistress who is rapacious and uncaring."

"No, that's true," Rohan said, stroking his chin with thoughtful fingers. "I believe that you, Mama, have used those exact words. Interesting. Perhaps I should give it some thought." He turned to his mother. "What's this about jealousy?"

"Oh, nothing, dearest," she said with great disinterest, obviously protecting Susannah, which pleased him excessively. "Now, Rohan, attend me. Susannah must have some new gowns before you go to Dinwitty Manor. Actually, are you committed to leaving on the morrow?"

"I would like to," he said, walking to the fireplace and leaning against the mantel, his arms crossed over his chest. "So would Susannah. It's time we learned the truth about everything."

"Very well," Charlotte said, rising to shake out her skirts. "There is only one thing to do. I shall visit my closet. I will have Sabine alter at least four gowns for you. Goodness, you don't have a maid, Susannah.''

"She can have one in the future, Mama. I'll play her maid at Dinwitty Manor as well as on our trip there.''

A wistful look came into his mama's eyes. She sighed softly, saying, "I'll never forget how your dear father enjoyed unfastening the buttons down the back of my gowns. The smaller the buttons, the more he enjoyed himself. Your father was a darling wicked man, dearest.''

Rohan flushed red.

She shook herself. "Enough of that. I must get Sabine busy. Where is Marianne? I wish to see her before I begin my labors." Charlotte wafted out of the drawing room, leaving the light scent of jasmine in the air and the echo of rustling silk.

Susannah said very low, "This is difficult to bear.''

He didn't pretend to misunderstand her. "I imagine that it would be. Actually, it's difficult for me as well. But my mother, as well meaning as you know she is, is not one to remain in any one place and grow roots. No, she'll be off before very long, probably to Venice." He looked down at his shining Hessians. "There is no one else like her, you know.''

She felt helpless, beaten down—all by a woman who was really quite nice and seemed to care about her. "She treats all of this so matter-of-factly.''

"Yes. It is the way she is, the way she will always be. I assume she accused you of being jealous?''

"She mistook my reaction to all her mistress talk as jealousy, which it wasn't. I told you, Rohan, I am not a milksop female, nor am I like your mother.''

"I have told her that you would be an interfering wife.''

"Goodness, and she still wanted you to marry me?''

"Oh, yes, she thinks you'll change, under her tutelage, and under the sheer glut of other women trekking in and out of my bedroom.''

"I would prefer it if you wouldn't do that.''

"I have no intention of parading women under your nose, Susannah. I have told you that."

"Yes, but—"

"No buts. Contrive to trust me, Susannah. Now, I don't think we should take Toby with us to Oxford. Indeed, I have arranged for Mr. Byam to take him to the seashore for some botany studies. I think he'll find that of much more interest than wandering about Oxford with us."

"Yes, he already mentioned it to me. He's very excited. In fact, he—"

They heard a howl from the entrance hall.

Rohan burst through the door so fast he nearly tripped on the suit of armor that stood too close to the room. He cursed, then saw Toby flat on his stomach, his arms and legs sprawled. Ozzy Harker stood behind him, nodding placidly.

"My God, what's happened?"

Susannah skittered to a stop beside her brother and fell to her knees. She shook his shoulder very gently. "Toby, are you all right? Are you hurt?"

Toby gave his sister a disgusted look, pulled himself to a sitting position, and said, "I'm fine. It's Gilly. He leapt out of my arms and Ozzy told me I was to chase him, even yell at him if I wanted to. I did and went sprawling over one of Marianne's toys." He raised himself and pulled a small wooden block with painted faces on each side of it from beneath his bottom.

Toby looked back and grinned at Ozzy. "Gilly's fast, really fast. Did you see him fly across the tiles? I don't think I had a chance of catching him."

"'E's got th' champeen's blood," Ozzy said and nodded again, so pleased that Rohan thought he would yell with his fervor. But he didn't, just nodded again and took himself off. "Tom'll be pleased, 'e will. Lordie, 'e's a fast littil sprat, our Gilly cat."

"Where is the bloody cat?" Rohan said, looking around. Then they heard a scream of laughter at the top of the staircase. There was Marianne, racing around in circles, with the kitten trying to climb up her dress. Charlotte stood over her, smiling down at her, doing nothing.

Susannah collapsed against the wall in laughter.

22

THEY ARRIVED AT DINWITTY MANOR TO FIND PHILLIP MERcerault, Viscount Derencourt, in residence. No, he hadn't received Rohan's first letter, since, obviously, he wasn't in London. He had, however, received the second letter, which Rohan had sent to Dinwitty Manor. He greeted Susannah with pleasure, hiding well his astonishment. A lady described in a letter was one thing; a lady greeting him in person was quite another.

"You're here to visit me, you say, Rohan?" he said after all the greetings were passed about.

"Yes."

"Don't tell me that this is your bridal visit? Surely you would have more imagination than this."

"No, it's not our honeymoon, but sort of. Susannah and I have only been wed for five days, as I wrote to you."

"Ah."

Susannah sent him a stricken look, to which her husband said smoothly, "As I told you, Susannah, Phillip and I have been friends for so many years we can't even remember when it started. Probably with me pounding him into the dirt. In any case, I wrote him the truth. He won't tell anyone, will you, Phillip?"

"Not even a racing cat, if I owned one, which I don't,

since the Harker brothers never believed my commitment profound enough.''

She looked from one to the other. Men such as these left her wits scrambled. Phillip Mercerault was a fine-looking man—not as handsome as Rohan—perhaps a year or two older, nearly as tall, his features strong and blunt. He had the look of a man who was rarely disconcerted. He looked as if he would accept a racing cat with a boy chasing it across the entrance hall of his home with great equanimity. He also looked as if he enjoyed laughter.

''Forgive me,'' Phillip Mercerault was saying now. ''Ma'am, you must be weary. If I know the baron here, he rushed you from London to my refuge in a day.''

''We came from Mountvale House,'' Rohan said. ''We took three days.''

''And three nights, I assume. But here I am making comments that make me deserve to have my teeth slammed down my throat. Please come into the drawing room, and doubtless tea will come sailing into port in a very short time.'' He turned to Susannah. ''My housekeeper and cook are both sweethearts who spoil me endlessly. The only problem is that they are on a quest to make me fat, just as they tried to do to my father. They failed with him too. Cook's cakes are beyond delicious.''

''This is a strange house, sir,'' Susannah said, then blinked, for surely that was on the rude side.

Phillip Mercerault just grinned at her. ''It has, hopefully, become even stranger under my reign. I have plans, ma'am, to fashion myself a crenellated tower onto the end of the west wing. Just one tower. I strive for imbalance and eccentricity. Dinwitty Manor has a reputation, you know. Perfect strangers come to visit and to stare. If I am ever at low ebb, my pockets to let, I shall simply charge admission. Yes, with a suitable admission, and Dinwitty's inclusion in a tour book, we shall spread our eccentricity throughout the whole of England. Did you not, Lady Mountvale, drop your jaw when you saw the Moorish arches just to the side of the Tudor manor wing?''

''As I recall, she laughed her head off,'' Rohan said. ''Then she punched me because I hadn't told her about the treat in store for her. You've a grand pile here, Phillip. Fashion away. The Medieval touch—I like it.''

''I was also considering a Medieval herbal garden. Perhaps you will be able to help me with that?''

Susannah was eating a lemon tart, having lifted it within a second of the time the butler had placed the shining silver tray on the table in front of her.

''Certainly. We will speak of it later.'' He looked briefly at Susannah, but her eyes were closed as she chewed that lemon tart.

''That was delicious,'' she said, wiping her fingers on the whitest, softest napkin she'd ever felt or seen. ''As to your house, sir, I believe you will succeed admirably.'' She was eyeing that tray of goodies again, and Rohan laughed. ''When you marry, Phillip, you must be sure not to let your wife live here more than a week at a time or you will find yourself married to a very fat lady.''

Rohan then turned to his bride, who had just pushed the remainder of a scone into her mouth. ''As for you, you're too thin. Eat, but we won't be here more than four days. You should be in quite perfect form by Friday.''

''I pray you will tell me the purpose of your visit, Rohan. You told me nothing at all in your letter. I trust I will be of use to you.''

Rohan and Susannah had discussed this on their trip to Dinwitty Manor, located only five miles east of Oxford. Phillip was aware of just about everything that went on in that town and in each of the various colleges. He knew everyone. They'd been friends forever. Yes, he'd immediately made up his mind to confide everything to Phillip. Actually, truth be told, Rohan hadn't really thought all that much about anything, since all he could think about was getting Susannah out of her clothes and onto her back.

He had caressed her for an hour before their arrival at the inn in Mosely. She'd been so beside herself that he had barely gotten the bedchamber door locked before she hurled herself at him. Ah, that was glorious. He gave her a perfectly fatuous grin now.

She swallowed her scone, staring at him. She knew exactly what he was thinking. About that low-ceilinged inn in Mosely that smelled of delicious ale and sweat and the two of them. She had been perfectly frantic, utterly beyond herself; she'd become an animal again. It wasn't to be borne. She leaned close to him and bit his earlobe hard.

He yelped, drawing away from her.

"Don't you dare look at me like that again, Rohan Carrington!"

"The marvels of married life," Phillip Mercerault said, leaning forward, and snagging an apple tart. He grinned at his guests. "I allow myself two a day, no more. I refuse to let her make me fat."

Susannah wanted to make a jest about that, but she was too busy chewing a tiny apricot pie with fluted pastry edges.

Rohan and Phillip Mercerault visited the Reverend Bligh McNally the next afternoon in his small apartment on the second floor of an eighteenth-century townhouse just off High Street.

Phillip said, "How subtle do you want to be with this fellow?"

"I was thinking about breaking both his arms."

"A beginning. It will gain his attention. Then subtle?"

"Something like that. It's the entire truth I want, Phillip." Rohan banged his fist against the door. No answer. He banged again, longer and louder this time.

Still no answer.

Rohan pressed his ear to the door. He heard nothing at all.

"He could be out marrying another innocent girl off to some worthless little sot. Sorry, Rohan."

"No, don't apologize. George was what he was. What he

did to Susannah, well, I'm sorry he's dead, but if he were alive and I found out about this, I'd probably kill him myself. Actually, so would my mother."

"Ah, glorious Charlotte. Knock again, Rohan."

He did. Then he turned the knob. Both expected it to be locked. It wasn't. Rohan looked over his shoulder at his friend, a blond brow raised.

The men entered a long, narrow hallway. On the right was a small drawing room. No one was in it. At the back of the apartment was the bedchamber. The door was shut.

It was then that they heard a woman's giggle.

"I was getting worried," Rohan said quietly. "At least now we know the bastard isn't dead."

"You were thinking that as well?"

"As I told you, that villain Lambert had no scruples. Where there's one villain, there are usually more waiting in the wings." Slowly, Rohan turned the doorknob. The door was well oiled and eased open soundlessly. The two men stood just inside the room, their eyes on the big bed opposite them. A red-haired woman was astride a man, both of them naked, the man obviously inside the woman.

"Hello, Reverend McNally," Rohan said, jovially.

The woman twisted about, stared at the two strange men, and shrieked. She jerked off the man and scrambled to grab a blanket to cover herself. As for the man, he was obviously dazed, but he was quickly getting his wits back together. He shook his head as he sat up.

He looked at them, heedless of the fact that he was naked. He said to the woman, not looking at her, "Do go make us all some tea, Lynnie. Ah, and dress yourself, for I fear there is nothing much else for us today."

His voice was deep and mellifluous, its timber soothing and confident. He then said, "Baron Mountvale, I believe. And you as well, Lord Derencourt?"

"You are not a particularly pleasant specimen," Rohan said as he strode to the bed. He threw the man his dressing gown. "Cover yourself. Come to your drawing room. We will await you there."

"I suppose there's no choice," McNally said, looking thoughtfully from the baron to the viscount. "No, I didn't think so. It's a pity that the only way out of here is through the front door. You would spot me for sure, wouldn't you?"

"Spot you and then shoot you," Rohan said. "With a good deal of pleasure, I might add."

Not ten minutes later the Reverend Bligh McNally sauntered into the drawing room, Lynnie at his heels carrying a tea tray that badly needed polishing.

"Please be seated, gentlemen."

"Set the tea down and leave," Rohan said to the woman.

"Yes, Lynnie, you may leave now. Ah, you will also keep a still tongue in your head, won't you? No need to raise any eyebrows."

"Aye, milor'."

Phillip Mercerault raised a brow at that. "Milord? She thinks you're a milord? Good God, don't tell me that actually works?"

McNally shrugged. "Sometimes. Money isn't always necessary. Lynnie isn't very shrewd, poor little love. It's a pity, but she will require money from me as soon as she becomes wiser in her business. Now, what may I do for you gentlemen? I don't suppose either of you wishes to wed in that very special sort of way I have? I have had new licenses designed. They would fool even you for a good minute or two."

Rohan just smiled at the man, who was about the age Rohan's father had been when he'd died in that wretched carriage accident. He was thin as a stick, and wore a thick beard. He looked like a Methodist. That was probably why young girls trusted that he was indeed a man of the cloth. Rohan walked to him, took his wrist in a fast, smooth move and wrenched it up high behind his back.

McNally moaned, tried to free himself but couldn't manage it. "Wha— what is this, my lord?"

"This is to gain your attention, McNally. Now what I want is for you to cast back your marvelous memory to five years ago. You performed one of your sham marriages for my brother George Carrington to a young lady named Susannah Hawlworth."

"That is a very long time, my lord. I am not a young man. You must understand that it is difficult—"

Rohan twisted the arm higher and McNally groaned in pain. He whispered in his ear, "I will break it if your memory doesn't make a brilliant recovery. Immediately."

"All right. Please, release me. I'll tell you all I know."

McNally rubbed his arm as he spoke, "What happened, my lord? After your brother died, the young woman came to you? You, naturally, knew that there had been no marriage? She wanted money? Did she still believe herself wedded to your brother, or had he left her long before?"

"It is none of your concern, McNally. Tell me what you know, now." Rohan made a move to take McNally's arm again.

McNally backed up quickly, his hands spread in front of him. "All right, all right. I remember now. It was in the spring. May, I think. A lovely time, really. Young Carrington came to me and asked me to perform one of my special marriage ceremonies. I agreed, since that is my business, and he paid me sixty pounds, my going rate when the young man in question has very rich and celebrated relatives.

"I did not meet the young lady until the day of the wedding. She was quite young, very fresh and very scared, but young George diddled her as well as any of the other young scoundrels I've ever dealt with. He soothed her and kissed her nose and told her that it was the best thing for them to do, the only thing for them to do. Did she not love him? Did she not want to be with him? Truly, my lord, young Carrington was quite good at it." McNally paused a moment and poured himself a hefty brandy. "Gentlemen?"

Both nodded. Rohan said, "Continue." He thought his heart would both break and be torn asunder. His youngest brother George, so serious, such a scholar—such a damnable rotter.

"Well, as I was saying," McNally went on after he'd given each of them a glass of brandy, "the young lady was scared, but she was excited too. What never ceases to amaze me is the ignorance, the stupidity of these young women. But this one had at least the beginnings of some wit. She couldn't have been more than seventeen years old, scarce out of the schoolroom. And she was indeed a lady, not some flight o' fancy a young man could pay for. No, this one was a lady, no coy protestations from her, and that is why I remember the whole thing so well. Because of her. She had no notion of what was really entailed in getting married, but still, she asked me about having bans read. Wasn't that required? I gave her all sorts of nonsense answers that I'd developed over the years, quite fluent arguments, actually. She appeared satisfied. But then, just before the brief ceremony, she asked if it was legal, since neither she nor young Carrington had parental consent. Neither was of age.

"This is a more difficult question, as you can imagine. But between us, young Carrington and I soothed her fears. I remember that he lied extremely well. I do believe, upon reflection, that I might have felt a brief stab of remorse for that young lovely."

Then he shrugged and poured himself more brandy. "Actually, I lost remorse many years ago. A man has to live, perhaps with just a bit of pleasure occasionally. I am not greedy. Ah, but she was a sweet young creature. Perhaps, my lord, you will tell me what happened to her? I know that your younger brother—her supposed husband—drowned nearly a year ago. A very unfortunate accident that. I proffer my condolences. What became of her? Or did he simply leave her once he'd had his fill of her? Many young men do that, you know. She did come to you, did she not? She did want something, didn't she?"

"I have already told you that is none of your affair. Now, what I want to know is about the men who accompanied my

brother that day.'' It was a stab in the dark, but he was right.
McNally was nodding.

''Men,'' McNally repeated, then tossed down the rest of
his brandy. ''I remember that they weren't as youthful as
young Carrington. No, they were perhaps five or so years
older. They were dressed properly enough, but young George
dismissed them before the young lady appeared. I remember
I wondered about them at the time, who they were, and all
that. Obviously they were friends of his.''

''What were their names?''

''Surely, my lord, you can't expect me to—''

McNally moaned when Rohan twisted his arm behind his
back again. ''Their names,'' Rohan said softly into Mc-
Nally's ear. ''I really don't want to have to ask you again.''

''Oh, my God, how am I to remember their names?'' He
groaned, sweat breaking out on his forehead. He looked toward Viscount Derencourt, but that damned gentleman was
sitting back on the settee, sipping his brandy, swinging his
leg, as indolent as a snake sleeping in the sun. ''All right.''
His voice was breathless. He hated it, but he knew when a
man was serious. ''I would prefer not to tell you anything
about them because they are dangerous men. They would
kill without hesitation if it gained them what they wanted. I
swear that I had no idea why they were with young Carrington.''

''Their names.''

''They were Lambie Lambert and Theodore Micah,
strange names, both of them. Into all sorts of foul activities,
they were. One saw them wherever there was wickedness
afoot. They seemed on the best of terms with your brother.
I will tell you this, though—if your brother had dealings with
them, then it wasn't good. They are scoundrels, as I said.
Young George didn't have their years of wickedness under
his belt. No, he wouldn't have had a chance with those
men.''

''And you're not a scoundrel?''

''No, not in the same way. Either of them could slip a

stiletto into a man's heart before he could draw a breath. A man who could do that is not a man I ever wish to deal with.''

"Yes, you're a regular saint, aren't you, McNally? You ruin young ladies.''

"She did write you, didn't she? But that's odd. It's been nearly a year. Why did she wait so long?''

"She didn't write to me.'' Rohan released the man's arm. McNally took a step back, rubbed his shoulder, shook his arms, slugged down the rest of his brandy. Finally, his wits more gathered together than not, he said, "Then why are you here? How do you know of all this? Why do you care about these men?''

"That,'' Phillip Mercerault said, as he rose, stretching lazily and slowly, like a man who's just made love to a woman, "is none of your business. Rohan, are you satisfied?''

"Not just yet. Were there any other men you ever saw with my brother? Not fellow students—men.'' As he spoke, he looked lovingly at McNally's arm.

"No. Well, perhaps there was one other. I swear to you, my lord, at first I did not know this one. He was standing in the shadows.''

"You said you didn't at first recognize him. But you did at some point. Well, who was he?''

McNally frowned, appearing to be deep in thought. He poured more brandy, but he didn't drink it. "It was some time after I'd married young Carrington to the girl. I was in one of the bookstores on High Street—you know the sort, my lords—all the students frequent them. The sort that carries very old manuscripts, some even original editions from the sixteenth century. I remember seeing young Carrington saunter into one of those old bookstores. I was meeting a friend at the same store and followed him in, without guile, you understand. Well, he met this man, this shadowy man I couldn't begin to describe to you. He was in a recess of the shop, well hidden. They spoke quietly together, at least ten minutes.

"I was finished with my business, but something about the two of them, well, it quite held my attention. There was a whiff of no good in the air. Then this man buffeted young Carrington on the shoulder, then he left, head down, hat pulled low, but I recognized him."

"Come," Rohan said, his patience shredded now. "Stop this game of yours. Who was this man? What did he look like, this shadow man you saw clearly?"

"Very well, my lord. He looked very much like young Carrington," McNally said finally, and there was sadness in his voice and a great weariness. "You have another brother, don't you, my lord?"

Rohan didn't move. Everything in him froze. He had no ready words, no thought, nothing, save this vast emptiness that held nothing alive, just this voice and darkness.

"Yes, he does, as you very well know, McNally," Phillip Mercerault said, rising. He strode quickly to them. "Who was he, dammit?"

"He was Tibolt Carrington," McNally said. "But who cares, my lord? Two brothers meet each other. What mystery is this? There is surely no mystery. They are brothers. They meet. They talk together, then one of them leaves."

"Now you dissemble. I dislike your attempts at irony. You heard nothing they said?"

"No, my lord. More brandy? It was smuggled in from Calais just last Tuesday."

Rohan said very slowly, "You know that my other brother is a vicar? A man of God? A devout young man whose future just might include becoming the Archbishop of Canterbury? A brilliant young man who is Bishop Roundtree's acolyte, his protégé? Of course their meeting was just that, a meeting between two brothers. They were always close as boys. Why are you intimating that it was something else?"

"It's very possible it wasn't anything at all. But I ask you—why would a man meet his own brother in the shadowy recesses of an old bookshop? There was something going on between them, I would swear to it. They didn't want to be seen. By Lambert or Micah? I don't know, but it quite set me to wondering for several days. I never saw young Carrington with his brother again. I am sorry, my lord.''

''No, Rohan, there's no reason to kill the villain.'' Phillip Mercerault was holding Rohan's arm, tugging him back, away from McNally. ''We've heard enough, at least for now. McNally can't leave Oxford without either of us knowing of it.'' He turned to the man then, saying, ''If you remember more, you will send a message to Dinwitty Manor.''

McNally was many things, Rohan knew, but he wasn't stupid. He had never in his life been stupid. Besides, all of them knew that it couldn't harm his health to have aided two noblemen. ''Yes, my lord. I do my best thinking in the twilight hours.''

''See that you stretch your brain,'' Phillip said. ''Come, Rohan, we will leave him be until tomorrow. If we think of more questions, I'm certain the dear man will be here and willing to assist us.''

''Certainly, my lord,'' McNally said, rubbing his sore arm.

''Yes,'' Rohan said slowly, ''until tomorrow.''

23

"I SHALL KILL YOU! CURSE YOUR BEAUTIFUL EYES, YOU left me here to do nothing but eat Cook's biscuits, tarts, scones, and those incredible apricot cakes. I nearly collapsed from all that wonderful food. I will begin to waddle. I will have to wear a corset. It's all your fault for leaving me to wallow in this den of food iniquity. And what did you do? Whom did you see? Ah, it was unfair of you, Rohan, to leave me whilst I still slept. I will get you for this."

He lightly laid his hand across her mouth, then pulled her against him. He kissed her hair. "You really think I have beautiful eyes?"

Phillip Mercerault was shaking his head. "All that, Susannah, and he heard only your compliment, which was surely unintentional in the first place. Hmmm. Or was it?"

She pulled back in the circle of his arms. "It was completely accidental. Phillip is right. Why did you batten onto that? I am angry, Rohan, outraged, really maddened. Your eyes are beautiful, but that's nothing to the point. Now, what did you do?"

"I will tell you if you will kiss me first."

"Sir, this is a gentleman's residence. You are a gentleman visitor. I am a gentleman's wife visitor. That isn't proper, it isn't—"

He kissed her very lightly, then tapped the end of her nose with his fingertip.

"I suggest, Rohan, that you fill her ears with our adventures. They weren't adventures you would have enjoyed, Susannah. I promise you. Now, I beg of you, walk through my gardens and discuss Rohan's eyes, what we did today. You know, Susannah, that Rohan—"

"Enough, Phillip. Enough. I will take Susannah for a nice long walk. We will see you at dinner."

Phillip Mercerault gave them a mock bow. "As your host, I am gratified for any meager attention whatsoever that you choose to toss in my path."

"Pay him no heed, Susannah. He will spend his time most happily making drawings of his crenellated tower."

"Exactly." Phillip Mercerault gave them a salute and took himself off.

"He is an interesting man," she said, staring after him. "He is handsome, I thought that yesterday—not as handsome as you are, of course, but he is also fascinating. Why is he not yet married?"

"Phillip is a rake, a lascivious satyr, a . . . help me, I seem to have run out of the words that describe a man of his reputation."

"Stop laughing at me. I want to hear everything. You want to walk in the gardens? Very well, I have already walked extensively in them and met Phillip's three gardeners, but I will do it again. His gardens are quite lovely. Not as lovely as those at Mountvale House, but quite acceptable. None of the gardeners has a racing cat, though. Come along, my lord."

He would have preferred to take her to bed, but it was not to be. She was being womanly, had been for the past three days, and it was killing him.

"Do you, uh, like the garden?"

"I just told you it is quite lovely—the way it is designed, there is so much color, so many gradations of color, and all the small paths are delightful. Why do you care? To a man of your reputation, a garden is just a garden, a place to walk, a place perhaps where you sniff now and again.''

"You don't know everything, Susannah.''

She looked at him a moment, a tiny frown furrowing her forehead. "No, I never really expected that I did. Only a bit of you is on the surface, Rohan, and sometimes I wonder if that little bit is even you at all.''

He kissed her mouth again, then smiled. "Let's go for a walk. I do have some rather startling news that has shaken me to the core. I hope you will have some ideas about all this. You see, my brother Tibolt is now involved.''

"The vicar?''

"Yes, the vicar.''

Two mornings later, Baron and Baroness Mountvale left Dinwitty Manor, their host waving to them as they disappeared around the final curve of the graveled drive.

"When will Phillip's crenellated tower be finished, do you think?''

"The only reason Phillip was here this time of year was that he wanted to get it started. We will visit him again in the fall. It will be done by then. Phillip never lets moss grow when he wants to move a rock.''

"That was a very strange metaphor.''

He nodded, distracted. The morning was foggy, the air chill and heavy, with rain threatening soon.

"It's a pity we didn't discover anything more yesterday,'' she said. He nodded, taking her gloved hand in his and flattening it palm down on his thigh. He covered her hand with his own.

"The inn we visited yesterday where I was with George and those two men—it brought back so many memories. It was nearly five years ago, Rohan. I was so young and naive. So stupid, really.''

"No, you weren't stupid. You were just taken in by a young man who knew quite well what he was about and how to get what he wanted. You were seventeen years old, for

God's sake. You did very well, Susannah, given your circumstances.''

"Thank you. I'm sorry no one could tell us about Lambert or Theodore Micah. Is his name really Lambie Lambert?"

"Evidently so. I think that Micah went into hiding when Lambert didn't come back. If he has a scintilla of a brain he buried himself deep in a cave somewhere. Maybe that cave near the cliffs at Beachy Head that George could have told him about, the one the three of us played in as boys.''

She was thoughtful a moment, then said, "You know what, Rohan? We must think of a way to make him come to us. If we put our brains together, I wager we'll come up with a good plan.''

He stared at her. She was wearing a delightful bonnet of cream-colored straw trimmed with small silk daisies, a pale yellow ribbon tied in a bow beneath her chin. She looked elegant and intensely feminine, and yet this had just come out of her soft mouth. Surely a female wasn't to come up with such strategies—strategies that belonged only to the male mind, or at least should.

"You will think of nothing at all. I don't want the bastard to come anywhere near you."

She turned her hand up and squeezed his. "There will be a difference this time. We will be ready for him. We will play him like a fish on a line. We will reel him in. We will then cosh him—after, naturally, we find out what is going on here." She paused a moment, looking at the window when the rain began coming down, a miserable cold, gray drizzle. She shivered, and he pulled her a bit closer to him. He spread the soft wool carriage blanket over her legs.

"There will be no reeling unless I am the reeler and you are safely stashed away to keep you safe. I cannot undergo another crisis like the last one you placed me in."

She gave him a siren's smile, and he knew he was in trouble. But, dammit, she was his wife. It was her duty to obey him. What sort of woman had he married? "I would very much like to make love to you," he said, and sighed, knowing that he couldn't, not just yet. "Tomorrow? Please tell me tomorrow is the day. I'm in dire straits, Susannah."

"Are you certain a husband should discuss such things with his wife? Aren't there rules about such things? It's awfully personal, Rohan. It embarrasses me. Don't you remember? You promised you wouldn't embarrass me, but you've done it again."

"As I recall, I was quite right about your first bout of embarrassment. It lasted only a minute, no more."

"But this is different. I won't moan this time."

It was Rohan who made a deep moan in his throat, leaning his head back against the squabs. He closed his eyes. "I won't look at you. That should help. That mouth of yours drives me to distraction. And then there are your ears—thank God your bonnet is covering those ears of yours."

Her fingers tightened around his. "Perhaps tomorrow is just fine," she said. He turned his head slightly away from her so she wouldn't see the satisfied grin on his mouth. The smile fell away quickly enough.

Tibolt. He remembered how proud his parents had been of their second son until he had locked himself in Mr. Byam's vicarage and shouted that he wouldn't come out until his father promised he wouldn't make him trod the path of sinful pleasure. No, his father must allow him to become a man of the cloth. His parents were flabbergasted, baffled. They told him that he would follow in their footsteps, then in those of his wonderful older brother—namely, Rohan. Finally they agreed, still hoping, doubtless, that Tibolt would change his mind, for he was young yet and hadn't really experienced the lust of youth. But the years had passed and he hadn't changed his mind.

At least, they'd said to each other, and in the hearing of their eldest son, namely, Rohan, at least they had him, and he would follow in their footsteps, he would be all things to them, he would carry on after they were gone, they counted on him. Did he not already swagger just like his papa? Did the girls not already look soulfully at him whenever he passed?

Rohan shook all those memories away. It was Tibolt who was important now. What had happened? Had Tibolt really been somehow involved in something nefarious with George before George had drowned? It seemed mad. Perhaps McNally had been lying. Perhaps Tibolt knew nothing about anything. Perhaps even if McNally had seen Tibolt, their meeting was innocent. But he knew he had to find out. Rohan had merely said to both Phillip and Susannah the previous evening at the dinner table, "Tomorrow we will travel to Branholly Cottage to see Tibolt. I want to know the truth. I *must* know the truth. If there is nothing, then I will come back to Oxford and break both of McNally's arms."

Phillip had nodded and said, after he swallowed a particularly tasty bite of baked lobster smothered in lemon sauce, "I will keep an eye on our Mr. Bligh McNally. If Theodore Micah shows his face, I'll hear about it. I will put it about in the proper quarters that I want him. You and Susannah will return to Mountvale House? Or will you go to London?"

"I'm not certain yet," Rohan had said slowly. "There is much to resolve here. We will see."

And now they were riding in a carriage bound to the south of England to Branholly Cottage, situated not more than fifteen miles east of Mountvale House.

Rohan was afraid of what he was going to discover. On the other hand, McNally was a scoundrel. He had lied all his wretched life. Why should he not have lied about Tibolt?

Susannah, as if sensing his thoughts, squeezed his hand.

Tibolt Carrington, a very popular young man in the small market town of Edgeton-on-Hough, was renowned for his piety, his wisdom, surprising in one so young, and his quiet yet devout tending of his flock. He always had time for even the most dissolute of his fold, even Jasper the blacksmith, who drank so much he was known to have shoed his horses backward on the morning after a particularly debauched night. He looked up from his half-written sermon when his man, Nelson, cleared his throat from the doorway of his study.

"Your brother is here, sir."

"My brother? Goodness, Nelson, the baron is here?"

Tibolt Carrington was on his feet in an instant, a wide smile lighting his face when his brother strode into the room.

"Rohan! Welcome. What are you doing here? Oh, is Mother all right? Has anything happened? You are well?"

"Oh, yes, I am quite well, Tibolt, as is everyone else. I have brought you a visitor. Susannah, do come in."

Susannah came into the room and found herself face-to-face with a man she had never seen before, a handsome man who had much the look of Rohan and George, but yet there was something different about him. Perhaps it was the fierce intensity in his eyes or the hard set of his mouth. She wasn't sure. He had the male Carrington cleft in his chin and the green eyes. His smile toward her was meaningless, vague and blank. She stood very still beside Rohan, waiting.

Rohan was watching his brother's face very closely. Unlike Susannah, he thought he'd seen a flicker of surprise, of recognition, but it was so quickly veiled that he couldn't be sure. He wondered if he would discover that he didn't know this brother any better than he had known George.

Tibolt gave Rohan an inquiring look, raising his eyebrow in the identical way Rohan did.

"I see you recognize Susannah," Rohan said quietly, without preamble, going with his instinct. "You saw her how long ago? Five years ago at Oxford? Did George want you to come to his mock wedding?"

Rohan saw clearly now that his brother wanted to lie to him. He quickly raised his hand. "No, don't, Tibolt. Tell me the truth. I imagine that if you, a vicar, lied, your punishment would be much harsher than mine in hell. I am your brother. I deserve the truth from you. Come, spill it out."

"Yes, my punishment would be harsher than yours would be. Oh what a tangled web we weave—"

Rohan's voice fell in hard and cold, with a goodly lacing of contempt. "Spare me the literary platitude. All I want from you is the bloody truth."

"Very well, Rohan. George made me promise I wouldn't tell anyone, particularly you. I found out by accident, I swear it to you. I was visiting Bishop Roundtree and stopped to see George. He was preparing for his, er, wedding. It was then that he told me. As for you,—" he was staring at Susannah, the hard set of his mouth now fashioning itself into an ugly sneer, "since you are with the baron, you obviously went to him and told him what had happened. You have obviously blackmailed him. He has taken care of things, hasn't he?"

He turned back to his brother. "Rohan, will you give her money and send her to the Continent? She would enjoy Paris, no doubt—a woman of her sort. Yes, Rohan, it was no tragedy. George wanted her, but she pretended to be a lady, so he had to resort to McNally, something not at all uncommon at Oxford. So what is a bit of money to you? You are rich. She will gain a new protector quickly, I would just ask that you send her from England. It would harm my reputation— all our reputations—were she to parade herself about in front of everyone and announce what a Carrington had done to her. Even if no one believed her, there would be talk. My own precious flock wouldn't understand. They would stand by me, don't get me wrong, but it would be a blow."

Rohan looked mildly interested, no more. Susannah realized, however, that he was furious. Odd how she knew him so well after less than three weeks. As for herself, she was so shocked by his brother's words that she hadn't moved from Rohan's side.

"Tell me, Tibolt," Rohan said now slowly, easily, his fists smoothed out at his sides, "what do you mean, it would be a blow? You mean that your flock would perhaps question your character were they to find out that your younger brother was such a perfidious little bastard?"

"They wouldn't question me at all, for I would tell them

the truth—well, perhaps not the entire truth. That wouldn't be necessary. Listen, Rohan, George was just weak, I told you that. He wanted her, but she was coy and wouldn't let him bed her. He told me she even lived with this old man who pretended to be her father and this small child, a little boy she claimed was her brother. George told me the little boy was probably her son, that she had begun in her sinful ways very early.''

''Ah, when she was twelve or thirteen?''

Tibolt just shrugged. ''It doesn't matter. Listen, George wanted her. No, my congregation would revile her, not George—for is it not the woman who is the sinful creature in our world? Does she not lead men astray?—but still it would cast a blot on our family name. Don't you see, Rohan? She must go, she must leave on the first packet to France. Oh, dear God, you haven't become her protector, have you?''

''Her protector? Susannah, do you consider me your protector?''

''You are the best of protectors,'' she said in a loud, clear voice. ''But, you know, just perhaps I would prefer Tibolt. He reminds me of George, and I was fond of George. You are too knowing, too experienced, my lord. I would be unable to manipulate you as I did George. But then, George got the last laugh, didn't he? I wasn't really married at all. Tell me, Tibolt—''

''I am Mr. Carrington to the likes of you!''

She gently tugged on Rohan's coat so he wouldn't dive across the small study and throttle his brother. She heard him draw a deep breath.

''All right, *Mr.* Carrington. Tell me, is there hope for me? Surely you have more money salted away than what you gain from this living? I have had protectors who had very little and others were quite rich. I am not particularly greedy. Did I not let George keep me for only ten pounds a quarter? Nor am I uncaring. What do you say, *Mr.* Carrington? It would save the baron many difficulties and you would have me.''

''You are a strumpet, madam,'' Tibolt said, drawing himself up as stiff as a lightning rod. "I do not bed strumpets."

"Oh?" Rohan said, taking a step forward. He felt Susannah's hand on the back of his coat, and slowly stepped back again. "Whom do you bed, Tibolt? The wife of the local wine merchant? The draper's wife?"

"I am discreet, Rohan, unlike you, unlike our wretched mother. I do not flaunt myself or my liaisons. Unlike you, I do not bask in the reflected infamy of our parents." Tibolt walked quickly to his brother, clutching at his arm. He glanced briefly at Susannah, his mouth twisting with revulsion. "Listen, Rohan, just send her away. Isn't that for the best? You are the head of the family. You owe us all protection. We are your responsibility."

"And what if one of the family is involved in villainy, Tibolt? Am I not also responsible for righting any wrongs committed by one of the family?"

"What villainy? What wrongs? What George did was a boy's prank, no more. It wasn't as if he hurt a young lady. Just look at her, Rohan, you can tell by her eyes that she is wicked, that she knows exactly what she is doing. Look at her clothing—a strumpet's gown, a strumpet's bonnet. I'm only surprised that she hasn't weighted her face down with cosmetics. Ah, just look at her. She is now gloating that we are disagreeing."

"Is she? I hadn't realized that you saw so very much, Tibolt. Her eyes look wicked? Really?" He turned to Susannah and gently cupped her face in his hands. "No weight there with cosmetics. Are you a strumpet in an innocent's clothing?"

She shook her head, her eyes never leaving his face.

"Are you gloating?"

"Actually I cannot bear this any longer. It is too much. Please."

"You're right, I'm sorry. I will bring this awful business to a close." He looked back at his brother, the young man he'd thought he knew so very well. Had he been right about the character of anyone in his family? Perhaps his aunt Mir-

anda—that maiden lady of so many good works—was really
the jade of Brighton? He turned back to his brother.

"Did you know, Tibolt, that you are an uncle?"

"My God, Rohan, you have sired an illegitimate child?"

"No, George did. He and Susannah had a baby girl—
Marianne. She's three and a half years old. Did not George
tell you?"

"No. He probably didn't think it mattered. Why would he
care? Doubtless the child wasn't his."

"That would be difficult to swallow, since Marianne is the
very image of George. One could easily take you or me for
the father as well."

Tibolt drew a deep breath, a calming breath. He moved
away from his brother to the narrow windows that gave out
onto the small vicarage garden. It was a paltry garden, Susannah could see that from her vantage—overgrown, too
much ivy that was choking out the poor rosebushes.

"You speak of all my responsibilities as the head of this
family, Tibolt. Tell me, then, why didn't you or George inform me of this sham marriage? If he wanted out of it, why
didn't he simply come to me and tell me?"

Tibolt said very simply, "He knew you would kill him. I
agreed with him."

Did his brothers see him as both a satyr and an avenging
saint? How could that be possible? On the other hand,
George had been right—he would have killed him. Rohan
sighed. "George wasn't so stupid after all. Yes, I would have
been very tempted to kill him. But he died all by himself,
leaving a wife and a daughter."

"She is not his damned wife!"

"She believed she was. Let's cut to the chase. I would
like you to meet *my* wife, Susannah Carrington, Lady Mountvale. Ah, and Tibolt, I recommend that you monitor the
words you wish to speak before they come out of your
mouth. I am feeling particularly violent at the moment. As
a matter of fact, I cannot recall when I have felt more violent
than I do at this exact instant. Heed me well."

24

TIBOLT WASN'T CAPABLE OF SAYING ANYTHING AT ALL. He stared with perfect horror from his brother to Susannah and back again. He swallowed, opened his mouth, then closed it again. "No," he said finally, his voice hoarse, barely above a whisper. "It can't be true. Why are you torturing me like this, Rohan? It's true that I knew what George was doing, but he was my brother. He has our parents' blood. He had this vile streak. I had to protect him."

"How many other girls were there, Tibolt?"

"But I didn't—"

Rohan moved so quickly, Susannah had only an instant to suck in her breath. He had his brother by his collar and he was shaking him. "Listen to me, you pious little sod. How many girls did George lead through that sham marriage routine with McNally?"

"Three. Tarts, all of them. Who cares?"

Rohan took a step back and struck him clean in the jaw. Tibolt collapsed where he stood. Rohan stood looking down at him, rubbing his knuckles.

Susannah was shaking her head back and forth. "Three? He did this to two other girls? But how did you know?"

He saw that she was trembling with shock, with humiliation, then with pure rage. He gathered her to him and kissed her temple. "It wasn't much of a guess really, Susannah. I'm so very sorry about all this." He held her more firmly to him. She embraced him tightly. His pain was palpable, as was hers. Susannah spoke first, her voice low and quiet. "It will be all right," she said against his neck. "I swear it will be all right. We will see all this through together."

"All the deception, it is difficult, Susannah."

"I know. But we will see it through together."

"My lord!" It was Nelson, standing horrified in the doorway. "What happened to my master?"

"He had some sort of attack, Nelson. Why don't you leave him be? I'm told that a man shouldn't be moved right after an attack. Oh, and Nelson, do tell your master, once he recovers from this attack, that I will return this evening for another brotherly chat. Ah, I would like you to meet my wife, Nelson. This is Lady Mountvale."

"My lady, it's a pleasure," Nelson said, not looking at her, just staring helplessly down at Tibolt, who was now twitching a bit and groaning.

Susannah nodded to the manservant, pulled away from Rohan and walked to where Tibolt lay on the floor. His eyes fluttered open. She looked down at him and smiled, the coldest smile Rohan had ever seen. He saw the rage in her and it pleased him.

"That you would dare call yourself a man of God must surely astound Him. It astounds me. You are a very bad man, sir. You are a fraud, a pious hypocrite. Are you more than that? We will find out if you are. You do not deserve to have Charlotte as your mother. She is good. You, sir, are a toad." Susannah kicked him hard in the ribs.

Nelson rushed to his master's side, falling to his knees beside him. "Why, my lady?" he said, twisting his neck to look up at her. "Surely you shouldn't have kicked him. His lordship just said one wasn't to move a man who had just had an attack."

"I didn't move him at all," Susannah said. She turned on her heel and with her husband left the vicarage.

• • •

When Rohan left her at the inn that evening, Susannah didn't argue. She felt sick, truth be told, sick to her very soul. Her belly roiled, nausea struck her, low in her throat. And she was worried about Rohan, but he just shook his head impatiently when she tried to keep him from going back to the vicarage. "It must be done," was all he would say. "I must know the full of it." He kissed her, and she felt the raging emptiness in him, the pain, the dread of the further knowledge he might discover.

He had managed to quash his fierce anger and his equally deadening pain. He prayed that Tibolt would face him tonight, not run away like he half feared his brother would. But no, he hadn't run away. Light shone from every window in the vicarage.

His brother awaited him in his study, probably the only room where he felt at all confident. Rohan nodded to Nelson, then strode into the study, closing the door behind him.

"Well, Tibolt, I am glad you are here."

His brother shrugged. "Where would I have gone? This is my home. The people of this town are my responsibility. Of course I would be here. You are not so frightening, Rohan, although you still have a nasty right hook." He rubbed his hand over his jaw. There was a faint bruise. Then he shrugged, looking directly at his brother. "So you have married a strumpet. I trust you knew what you were doing. Given your reputation, such a mating would probably suit you. However, it is none of my affair."

He was making it easier for him, Rohan thought, walking to the desk and seating himself in one of the old cracked leather chairs. He steepled his fingers, drumming them thoughtfully together. "No one knows that Susannah was married to George. I have told everyone that she married me nearly five years ago and I kept her hidden. Why did I do this? all of Society will ask. I will tell everyone I did it because I was too young to admit I'd fallen in love and married. I was foolish, but I love my wife and daughter dearly. You will maintain this fiction. Marianne is my child. Mother is the only other person who knows this, and Toby, Susannah's brother, naturally. It is a question of family honor, of salvaging George's reputation. Do you have any questions?''

''No, if that is what you want done about it. Everyone will be shocked when they find out, naturally. You, the Carrington satyr, married for the past five years, keeping your wife all tucked away while you continued to bed every female in London? That smacks of real wickedness. My flock will be suitably shocked.''

''Possibly, but I have already gone a long way toward redeeming myself. Rest assured that I will go the full mile. There will be tears in many eyes by the time I am through with my touching explanations. However, brother, if you do discover shock among your parishioners, you will remember what you owe to your family. Now, when we return to Mountvale House, we will have another party. I will announce my marriage—although with Lady Dauntry's assistance I imagine that every sentient creature in England already knows about it. I will contrive to look properly contrite. I will be chagrined and charmingly sorry, with downcast eyes. Then Susannah and I will go to London and repeat the performance. Do you have any questions?''

Tibolt slowly shook his head. He was giving his brother an odd look, as if he were a stranger, a man he'd never really seen before. ''I had not expected this of you. I do not understand why you have done this. She is nothing to you, nothing. And this child—''

Rohan couldn't bear it. He interrupted his brother before he betrayed himself further. ''Oh? What if you had discovered that you had a niece, that your brother had gone through a sham marriage because he wanted to bed your niece's mother?''

''I told you what she was.''

''Yes, you did. But it is so utterly absurd, so completely far from the truth, it makes me wonder about your motives, Tibolt. She is indeed a lady. Did you proclaim her a strumpet because you had to justify to yourself what George had done? Yes, that is it, isn't it? I can see it in your eyes.''

"No, I saw her, just as I saw the others. Even though she was young, dreadfully young, I still saw no reason to change my opinion of her. She seemed just like the others.''

"Then I begin to imagine that George did this to three very innocent young ladies. If, however, you simply saw what you wanted to see, then you made a grave mistake. You did not live up to your high calling, Tibolt. You should have sought her out and told her the truth. You have some serious praying to do about this. She has been used badly by our family. But no more. Now she belongs to me, as does Marianne.''

Again, Tibolt shrugged. "But what of the others? What if I was wrong and they weren't strumpets? Will you try to wed one of the others to me?''

"You say that George did this to two other young girls. Do you know who they are?''

Tibolt shook his head. "But if this one came to you, then why not the others?''

"She didn't come to me. Now, you will contrive to forget all the nasty little things George told you. Are you so ignorant, Tibolt, that you actually believed George? After he did this three times? Tell me, was Susannah the third?''

"No, she was the second.''

"She was seventeen when George talked her into marriage. She was born and bred a lady.''

"She kicked me in the ribs. No lady would kick a man of God in the ribs.''

"Tibolt, you are trying me sorely. Would you say that I'm a gentleman?''

"Naturally.''

"Very well. I hit you as hard as I could in your face.''

"That is different.''

Rohan rolled his eyes. "You amaze me. Now, if it would please you, I would be delighted to escort you to that miserable little plot out back that you call a garden and pound you until your brain begins to function again.''

Tibolt raised his hands. ''No, I will do as you say. It is nothing to me, really.''

Then Rohan sat forward and said softly, ''Now you will tell me about the map.''

He saw only confusion on Tibolt's face. ''Map? What map?''

''You know very well what I'm talking about. Tell me about the damned map. I know that George told you about it.'' It was then that he saw the knowledge, but Tibolt held himself silent.

''Tell me, damn you!''

''George did mention a map to me right before he died,'' Tibolt said slowly. ''But George always had some map or another. They fascinated him. I thought little to nothing about it at the time. It had nothing to do with me.''

''You know Theodore Micah and Lambie Lambert, don't you?''

''Yes, certainly. Mainly they were cronies of George, but I knew them as well. I was only two years older than George, remember. Why? What is all this about, Rohan? What map?''

''It was really only half a map. I have no idea what the full map leads to, but it's something that these men want very badly.''

''Whatever do you mean?''

Rohan studied his fingernails, then the quill atop Tibolt's desk, not looking at his brother as he said, ''Either Lambert or Micah—or both—broke into Susannah's house three times trying to find George's half of the map. Then Lambert broke into Mountvale House once, failed again, and kidnapped Susannah.''

''My God, you aren't serious?''

''Oh, yes.''

''Did you kill him?''

''No, actually, he was induced to join His Majesty's Navy.

Unfortunately, he wouldn't tell us a thing. But he was committed to finding that map, Tibolt.''

Tibolt looked honestly shaken. The bruise on his jaw stood out starkly in the candlelight. ''I had no idea,'' he said, shaking his head, looking straight into his brother's face. ''No idea at all. I will tell you that Theodore Micah came to me just a week ago and asked me if I had any idea where George's half of the map was. He had to remind me about it. That's all I know, Rohan.''

''Where is he, Tibolt?''

''He told me if I remembered anything I could find him in Eastbourne. He said that there were certain men he had to avoid and thus he was disguising himself. He said he had moved in with a widow on the waterfront. As I said, that was a week ago. He wanted me to go to Mountvale House and search for the half of the map. I told him that even if I found it, it surely wasn't enough, was it? He told me I wasn't to worry about that. He also told me there was a tiny golden key. I remember saying that I felt uncomfortable about going to Mountvale House and asking about some map that had been in George's possession. I told him what good would half a map do him? I asked him what it was to. I asked him who had the other half of the map. He just smiled at me— a very evil smile, Rohan.

''There's nothing more, I swear it. Except, of course, that he would kill me if he knew I had told you where he was.''

''I want to know where he is staying. I want to know what he looks like. I will not have any more danger hanging over any of our heads.''

Tibolt sighed. ''I beg you to be careful of him. He is an actor. He is quite good. What he looks like . . . he must be near thirty now. He is not at all tall, he is rather slender, and he usually dresses like a dandy—a big watch fob, high and stiff shirt points, loud waistcoats, and the like. His hair is black as midnight and his eyes are just as dark. They're empty eyes, Rohan, flat and cold. I never liked looking him in the face. Even if he smiles, you know it isn't really a smile, that he doesn't mean it. He is detached from his fellow man, very probably dead inside. I don't think you should go after him. But knowing you, you will try to find him. You've always managed to get whatever you wanted, haven't you? I caution you again—if you find him, watch out for yourself.''

Rohan nodded, then rose. ''If, Tibolt, I discover that there is more to this, and that you are involved, I will take measures to see that you are punished, even though I know it will hurt Mother. She is upset by what George did. Were she to know that you were aware of his perfidy, she would likely come here and kick you in the ribs herself.''

''Just like your wife, our mother is no lady either. She was never an appropriate helpmeet for our father.''

Rohan could only stare at his brother. He said not another word. He wondered if Tibolt was lying. Probably, but he still had no idea why or how Tibolt could be involved in this mess. He still couldn't bring himself to believe that Tibolt was the man who had broken into Mountvale that first night. No, that wasn't possible. But he knew there had to be more, much more. Damnation, he hated this.

Susannah's head was on his shoulder, her breathing light and shallow against his flesh. He knew she wasn't asleep. He knew she was thinking about what he had told her. She hadn't questioned him closely. He wondered if she suspected he'd omitted facts, which he had. He'd said nothing about Theodore Micah, nothing about his being in Eastbourne. She was probably hatching plots. It pleased him, this forthright nature of hers, this fearless deviousness of hers. It also pleased him that he was coming to know her well enough to realize what she was thinking. But he would not tell her about Micah. He didn't want to frighten her. He didn't want to take the chance she would scurry to Eastbourne and try to find him by herself.

He kissed the top of her head. He doubted he would ever regret his marriage to this woman—not Susannah, a woman with grit and pride and ruthlessness. He tightened his arm around her. "Susannah, we're nearly home."

He wanted to tell her as well that when he got her home, when he got her to their bedchamber, when he finally got her into his bed, he would kiss every luscious inch of her, particularly the soft flesh behind her knees. His breathing hitched.

"I know. Thank you for letting us leave the inn, Rohan. I didn't think I could bear staying there another night."

When he'd walked into their bedchamber after his meeting with Tibolt, she'd been standing in the middle of the room, fully dressed, their valises at her feet.

She'd taken one look at his face and walked to him, pressing herself against him, her arms around his back.

She'd said nothing, just held him.

"Not more than fifteen minutes now." It was nearing one o'clock in the morning. There was a light drizzle falling from a black sky. It was cold; the fog was rising, a thick swirling gray, now nearly to the level of the carriage windows.

"You won't tell me more, will you?"

"There is little enough more, really."

She sighed. "I don't believe you. You're trying to be chivalrous. Do you believe that George is the one involved with the map?"

"I don't know, and that's the truth. Tibolt isn't telling me the entire truth, and I just can't seem to separate fact from falsehood."

Suddenly the quiet of the night was rent by the explosion of a gun. There were two shots. Rohan heard Elsay, his coachman, scream. Oh, Jesus, he'd been shot!

He shoved Susannah onto the floor of the carriage and grabbed his gun from the leather side pocket of the door.

The horses came to a plunging, rearing halt. Then Rohan heard a man yell, "All of you out of there now. No foolishness, my lord, else this wounded little man will get another bullet through his gullet. Come out now, bring that little tart as well."

The first thought in Rohan's head was Thank God it wasn't Tibolt. Just who the man was, he had no idea.

Despite his wound, Elsay wasn't about to have his master face the villain. He cracked the whip and yelled at the horses. Rohan was hurled on top of Susannah as the carriage abruptly started up.

There was another loud shot. A man's loud curses, the sound of a horse galloping after them.

"Stay down, Susannah."

Rohan eased his head out the carriage window. The man was some twenty yards back, galloping hard. He wasn't firing. He could have only one or two bullets left. The horses were racing wildly now, out of control. Elsay must be hurt badly.

Rohan slipped the gun into his waistcoat pocket, turned on his back and pulled himself out of the carriage window. He grabbed the brass railing that circled the top of the carriage. It was sturdy. He managed to pull himself up. Then the coach lurched to the left, the horses now galloping madly toward a dangerous curve that gave to the cliffs at Beachy Head.

The wind made his eyes tear, whipped his hair across his face, blinding him, but he managed to climb to the top of the carriage.

"Elsay? Hold on, I'm coming."

There was no answer from the coachman. Rohan saw the man on horseback drawing closer. The rain thickened. If one of the horses slipped, they would die.

He saw Susannah leaning out the window.

He crawled to the front of the carriage, letting himself down slowly onto the driver's bench. Elsay was gripping the wooden brake with all his might.

"Hold on," Rohan said again, as he eased into position. Then he saw that the reins were loose and hanging down between the two horses. "Damn," he said. "Well, there's no hope for it."

"Mi'lord, be careful."

The horses veered left, nearly overturning the carriage.

Rohan simply dove onto Ramble's back, managing to catch his harness to keep himself from falling beneath their hooves. He began talking to the horses, trying his damnedest to soothe them. He only wished he could sing like Jamie.

He grabbed the reins from between Ramble and Oscar. Both horses were blowing hard, frightened, out of control. Slowly, very slowly, he began to pull up on the reins. He kept talking to his horses, hopefully soothing nonsense, and pulling on those reins. Back further, then a bit further. The horses lurched off the narrow road, causing the carriage to spin out behind them, and now they were headed straight for the cliffs over Beachy Head.

He was inching back on Ramble's rump to gain more leverage. He pulled and pulled, harder now, because if they didn't stop soon, they would go crashing over the cliffs and fall some hundred feet to the beach below.

An eternity passed with the rain blinding him, the wind howling like witches from hell.

Finally, he yelled, "Ramble, Oscar, you damned bleaters, pull up! That's an order!"

To his astonishment and utter relief, Ramble reared up on his hind legs and ripped sideways. Oscar yelled and went with him. They slowed, stumbling. Finally, after another eternity had passed, they came to a wrenching stop.

They were parallel to the cliffs. If Ramble hadn't thrown himself sideways, they would have gone over.

Rohan was so relieved he couldn't move. He just sat there on Ramble's rump and breathed in huge gulps of air.

"Rohan!"

The carriage door flew open and Susannah stumbled out. She fell to her knees, then was up and running to him. She stopped suddenly, realizing that she might scare the horses. "It's all right, Oscar. You just wait, you brave lad. Jamie will sing to you and feed you carrots."

"Actually, it was Ramble who saved the day."

She smiled up at her husband, then said to the horse, "You were wonderful, Ramble. I will personally feed you the best oats and barley in the whole county. My lord, are you all right?''

"Yes,'' he said. Slowly he eased down between the two horses, patting them, soothing them. They were lathered, still blowing hard.

The man. Rohan whipped about, but no one was there. The man hadn't followed them.

"Elsay, how badly are you hit?''

"Me right arm, mi'lord. Not too bad, jest bleeding like I were a . . . well, niver ye mind that. I'll live, no thanks to that sot wot shot me.''

"And thanks to old Ramble here,'' Rohan said, feeling oddly detached from himself. He knew it was shock, but he also knew he couldn't succumb to it. "We'll wait here just a while until the horses have rested. Susannah, tear off some of your petticoat. We'll need to bind Elsay's arm.''

"That man wot shot me, mi'lord. Who the devil be 'e?''

"I think it was a very bad man that I will find and kill. Don't you worry, Elsay. You just hold on. We'll get you all fixed up.''

"Ye'll not fetch the young dapper doctor, will ye, mi'lord? 'E fair scares me to me liver.''

"Yes, I will, but I'll stand at his elbow and if he dares to cause you pain, I will pound him. All right?''

"Aye, that's jest fine,'' Elsay said and fainted dead away.

25

"I'M GLAD THAT ELSAY IS ALL RIGHT. I'M RELIEVED THAT both Ramble and Oscar aren't lame. Your father was very fond of Ramble. He always said that Ramble had guts. Obviously I'm relieved that you and Susannah are without injury. Neither I nor Susannah, however, knows who was shooting at you. Nor do I understand why. Do you, Susannah?"

"No, ma'am." But she had a very good idea, he could see it in those clear eyes of hers. He'd again refused to tell her anything about Theodore Micah, merely repeated to her that Tibolt had denied everything. He'd lied to her because he was trying to keep her safe. To him, that meant keeping her ignorant.

Rohan looked at his mother over a forkful of scrambled eggs. She was regarding first Susannah and then him with deep suspicion. It was ten o'clock on the morning after their harrowing ordeal. He'd been up at dawn, leaving Susannah sleeping soundly. He had hired men from the village to patrol Mountvale House. Hopefully neither his mother nor his wife would find out about them. He'd told the half dozen men that they were to detain any stranger they discovered.

He knew in his gut that Theodore Micah must have been watching Tibolt's house. He must have followed them in order to stop them. Rohan couldn't bring himself to consider that Tibolt may have sent Micah after them. His brother was a scoundrel, but could he be that evil? Rohan guessed Micah would have threatened Susannah if he'd gotten to them, perhaps even taken her. He must have ridden away quickly when he saw that the horses were out of control. If they had gone over the cliff, then all would have been for naught. Damnation! He hated the mystery of all this, the secrets, the uncertainty about his brother. He hated the danger to Susannah. He hoped she wouldn't realize that there would always be someone guarding her, and Toby as well.

He heard his mother say again, "Dearest? Didn't you hear me? Susannah claims not to know a thing, but you do. Come now and cough it up."

But he couldn't cough up anything. He wasn't about to tell his mother that her other son very possibly was involved in this mess, whatever mess it really was. Macbeth and Pope Leo IX. What could those two possibly have had to do with each other? He merely shook his head. "It was a robber, nothing more, Mama."

"Yes," Susannah said. "It must have been, Charlotte. Just a thief trying to steal my jewels and Rohan's watch fob." She glanced briefly at her husband before looking down at the rasher of bacon on her plate. She wouldn't mention Tibolt. She'd spare Charlotte that.

"You know, dearest, I'm not at all certain that it was a thief. There is this business of the map and King Macbeth and Pope Leo IX. Couldn't there be someone else other than that dreadful Lambert man involved?"

Without thinking, Rohan said, "Actually, I plan to ride to Eastbourne this afternoon to do a bit of checking. I think it likely that Lambert was staying there. If there is someone else, perhaps I'll be able to locate him."

"I will, of course, accompany you," Charlotte said, giving him a sweet smile.

"No, I will accompany you," Susannah said, suddenly leaning forward in her chair.

Curse his loose mouth, Rohan thought. "No. Actually, neither of you is coming with me," he said, every ounce of firmness in his entire brain coming out with that one sentence.

"Dearest, I'm sorry, but if you aren't reasonable about this, then Susannah and I will simply ride to Eastbourne and make inquiries."

"Both of us, Charlotte?"

"Naturally. I am willing to let you share the excitement. Ah, the art of detection. I find it fascinating. I am quite good at it. I was the one who found Lady Perchant's ruby ring, you know. Perhaps there will be young men to question. I am very good at getting just about anything out of young men. They haven't a chance."

Rohan threw his napkin into the air. It fluttered down over his plate, still filled with delicious scrambled eggs and bacon and a rather tasty scone heaped with clotted cream.

"Me! Me!" Marianne shouted, pulling free of Lottie's arms and running full tilt toward Rohan. "Me go too!"

Rohan groaned. "It is too much. Am I not the master in my own house?" He wasn't about to put any of his family in danger. Surely Susannah realized that it had probably been Theodore Micah who fired at them the previous evening. Surely she realized he was more dangerous than Cleopatra's asp. He appreciated her keeping her suspicions to herself.

"I will see to Marianne, sir," Toby said.

"Yes, but first give me a go at her." Rohan held out his arms. "Ro-han!" He picked her up and sat her on his lap. He lifted his napkin from his plate and the two of them ate his scrambled eggs.

Susannah stared at the man whose wife she had been for more than two weeks now. He was holding her daughter, playing with her, quite at ease with her. Nothing new really, but this time she felt something powerful move deep inside her. This something powerful—it was like a flower, she thought, a lily: it was radiant and white and pure and was coming into full bloom. It was very frightening. She'd never had much luck growing lilies.

There was no way she would let Rohan ride into danger alone. She knew that Theodore Micah had probably been the one to ambush them the previous night. Perhaps he had been following them, perhaps he had been hiding near Tibolt's vicarage. No, she wouldn't allow Rohan to go alone. She had to protect him.

What the baron did an hour later was underhanded, but it worked. Lady Dauntry and her two companions, Mrs. Goodgame and Mrs. Hackles, came by for a visit. It was too early for a proper visit, Charlotte said to Susannah, but she couldn't very well tell them to leave.

Susannah didn't trust Rohan an inch. She hoped he wouldn't take advantage of this visit to run off to Eastbourne without her. She knew he thought he had her best interests at heart, but he would soon smother her with such protectiveness. She watched Rohan go to his estate room and close the door. He looked as if he would wait until the ladies left. Still, she didn't trust him. But she also knew it would be intolerably rude of her not to play hostess to the "three battleships," as Toby called them. So, Rohan had a chance to leave.

The old biddies had come by for a good gossip, Charlotte explained in a whisper. It was the family's responsibility to feed the women appropriate tidbits. It was even their duty, and an excellent opportunity as well. "After all," Charlotte said, "if we tell what we want everyone to know and believe, then they won't be encouraged to make up their own little tales, which, trust me, would bear only incidental resemblance to the truth. I will, naturally, tell them all these little bits in strictest confidence. Also, Susannah, Rohan has gone into the estate room. He is hopefully doing correspondence with dear Pulver, not planning to go by himself to Eastbourne."

Rohan waited until both ladies were well occupied. He put Pulver to work and told him to stay in the estate room until he returned to let him out. He went to the stable and told Jamie to take all the horses to the east pasture for at least three hours and not come home until the time was up. He said he was to pull two wheels off the two carriages as well. He himself saddled up Gulliver, even as Jamie and the other stable lads made a chain of the horses and led them away.

He was whistling when he rode Gulliver away from Mountvale House down the splendid graveled drive lined with lime and oak trees. A man did what a man had to do, he thought, and he'd bested them. He wished he could have smiled at his duplicity, but he was too worried. He waved at Jamie, who was well beyond the brightly painted white fence, too far away now for either his mother or his wife to bring him back. He stopped briefly and spoke to two of the patrolling men. They'd seen no one suspicious.

He was so relieved with his stratagem that he belted out a limerick he'd heard Jamie sing several times. He yelled it out at the lovely blue sky overhead, at the top of his lungs.

> "There was an old lady of Kent
> Whose nose was remarkably bent
> One day, they suppose
> She followed her nose,
> For no one knows which way she went."

Gulliver's head snapped around. He snorted at his master, then tried to bite his boot.

When Rohan reached Eastbourne an hour later, he rode directly to the waterfront. It didn't take him long to find out the name of the woman who rented rooms. Indeed, she had rented a room to an actor fellow who had the sweetest smile and the deadest eyes that Alice, the incredibly buxom barmaid, had ever seen in all her born days.

The actor fellow was gone. A man who had Rohan's reputation would have been easily seduced by the buxom barmaid Alice, but instead he rode home. He didn't relish returning home, but there was no hope for it.

He thought ahead to the ball for all their neighbors, at which he would confess his sins and seek redemption. He needed to practice. He wanted his performance to be perfect.

"I think," his fond mama said, "that we should forgive him for this, Susannah. After all, he said he didn't discover anything. My son obviously did not get his gift of detection from me. He failed in his mission. He failed because he treated us like sheep and slipped away. Stupid sheep that are good only for making wool."

"Now that's an innovative idea, Mama," he said, suddenly wishing he were in London, where no one would look at him as if he were a sod. Mothers, he supposed, were to keep one humble.

"I agree with your mother, Rohan. You will not do such a thing in the future or else I shall have to take a hand, or something."

He raised an eyebrow at that. "Oh, Susannah? And just what might that hand be? Or that something? Is it interesting?" He rather wished she could have taken a hand or something the night before, but she'd been exhausted. He'd kissed her nose, her left ear, and by that time, she was fast asleep.

Charlotte, on the point of further berating her son, chanced to look at her daughter-in-law and saw that she had flushed scarlet to her hairline. "Goodness, Susannah, whatever are you thinking? Ah, you must be thinking of Rohan. Is that the reason for your embarrassment? But Rohan said nothing untoward, nothing that could have made you think about intimate things or luminous fancies." She smiled fondly at her son. "Your father, dearest, loved to call me luminous. He rather loved to see me wear luminous nightgowns. Ah, such a pity." She sighed deeply, then blinked, bringing herself firmly back into the room with them.

"She's thinking of my hands, Mama. Just my hands—and look at her face."

"You are splendid, dearest. Just the mention of your hands

and you render her speechless. I am impressed with you, and
here you've only been married such a short time. Not that
I'm all that surprised, naturally.''

Susannah, routed, picked up her skirts and fled the room.

A seamstress came to Mountvale House from Eastbourne and
remained for four very happy days, for Baron Mountvale was
paying her more than she could earn in six months, all for
sewing new clothing for his new wife, who was, indeed, in
dire need of her excellent services.

The only problem Mrs. Cumber suffered was with the new
baroness. She was twitchety. She didn't enjoy being on the
receiving end of such largesse from her husband. Largesse?
Goodness, Mrs. Cumber thought, it was only four gowns and
two riding habits, not to mention a good half dozen chemises
made of the most wicked French silk, which the baron's
mama had brought back from Paris.

Mrs. Cumber was there to assist her ladyship on the evening of the party welcoming the new baroness—or rather the
newly revealed baroness—to the area as the now emerged
Baroness Mountvale. Mrs. Cumber gently smoothed down
an errant pleat. Then she stood back to behold her magnificent creation. The young baroness looked so lovely, Mrs.
Cumber was impressed at the depths of her own genius.

It was then that the adjoining door opened and the baron
strolled into the room. Ah, what a splendid-looking gentleman he was, tall and well formed, a merry sparkle in those
lovely green eyes of his and a very nice smile on his mouth,
a mouth that made Mrs. Cumber wish she was twenty years
younger and not a seamstress. Why, a man of his reputation
would never look at a seamstress and think of frolic. She
wondered if it was true that he kept at least three mistresses
at any one time.

''Ah,'' Rohan said, stopping and stroking his chin as he
looked Susannah over thoroughly. ''The cream. It is amazing
what you do to that color, Susannah, along with that delicate
Valenciennes lace around your neck, just hinting at all the

lovely flesh . . . well, never mind that much detail. It's all that
sinful mink hair of yours that enhances the gown. Sabine did
an excellent job. I like all those lazy curls floating over your
shoulders and down your back. Mrs. Cumber, you are to be
congratulated. You have managed to flatter an already quite
perfect figure.''

''Thank you, my lord,'' she said in a very demure voice,
though she wanted him powerfully. This little wife of his
likely didn't know a bloody thing, not that Mrs. Cumber
knew much more, but she knew some.

''I do have a token to further enhance your beauty,'' he
said to Susannah, and opened his hand. Diamonds and sapphires flowed over his palm, sparkling, glimmering in the
rich candlelight, snatching her breath away.

Susannah stuck out her hand, then quickly withdrew it.
''Oh, goodness, I've never seen anything so exquisite. You
cannot mean you want me to wear this incredible jewelry?
No, I cannot. What if I lost some of it? What if I—''

He merely smiled at her, shook his head, and clasped that
incredible necklace around her neck, then lifted her wrist,
kissed the inside, and fastened the bracelet on. He handed
her the earrings and watched her secure them in her ears.
She took a step back and looked at him helplessly.

He stared at her, he couldn't help it. To him, she was the
most beautiful woman in the world. And that was all that
mattered. From the look on his handsome face, Mrs. Cumber
determined that he wanted his wife more powerfully than
she, Mrs. Cumber, wanted him. No, she thought just a moment later, that wasn't possible.

He kissed his wife's hand. She was looking at him now,
not at the luscious jewels. ''Look in your mirror and tell me
what you think.''

She looked down at her wrist. The brilliance of the diamonds and sapphires nearly blinded her. She made an un-
dignified dash to her dressing table with its wide mirror, sat
down, and stared at her reflection. She lightly touched her
fingertips to the necklace, then to her earlobes.

She turned around. She seemed oddly vulnerable, sitting there, looking like a princess. There were tears shimmering in her eyes. "I have made you cry, Susannah?"

She could only shake her head and swallow furiously.

He said to Mrs. Cumber, who was looking at Susannah more avidly than Lady Dauntry had that evening when Rohan had announced that he was Susannah's husband, "Thank you. My wife is glorious. You may leave us now."

She left the bedchamber with a lagging step. At her age one had to enjoy such splendid animals as the delicious baron vicariously.

"Now, why the tears?"

She shook her head, her face down. He came down on his haunches in front of her. He took her hands in his, smooth hands now, for she hadn't scrubbed any floors at Mountvale. "Susannah. Look at me. What is wrong?"

She scrubbed her fist over her cheeks. It made him smile. He should tell her that no female wishful of a man's regard would do such a thing. How ridiculous. He found it endearing.

She blurted out, "Why are you being so generous to me? I have brought you nothing but pain and heartache and responsibility, even danger. A lot of danger. Because of me you have discovered that George was a rotter. Because of me it's possible that Tibolt is a rotter as well. It is likely that you would never have known about them were it not for me. That man could have killed us, he could have shot Elsay again. It was all my fault. Truly, I am a trunk filled with rocks, a clinging ivy to choke you, a wasp to bring you incalculable pain, a—"

"A leech to suck my blood? A ringworm to ruin the innards of our racing kitten? A lead-filled pillow to smother me?"

She was laughing now, despite herself, despite her gloom, hiccuping, trying to shove him with her fists, but he grabbed her wrists and held her firm.

"What you are," he said slowly, "is the woman who is

my wife. As for the other, there will be answers. Because I am a superior man I will find the answers we need."

She was utterly distracted. It had been well done of him, and he knew it. Then she flung her arms tightly around him, sending them both backward onto the carpet, an unexpected bonus to his brilliance.

"I would like to stay here with you for a fortnight and do everything that it is possible to do to your lovely self." He leaned up and kissed her mouth. "Unfortunately, you will make all your fine curtsies tonight and charm all our neighbors. I will be contrite and by the end of the evening everyone will be on the road to forgiving me my perfidy because it is obvious that you have."

Curse him and bless him, Susannah was thinking sometime after midnight as she stood fanning herself behind a palm tree, he'd been right. Of course, it was his own lazy, self-deprecating charm that gained him forgiveness from all and sundry.

Her feet hurt, and she stood on one leg to wiggle her toes. On top of everything else, her husband was an excellent dancer. When she'd told him that, laughing up at him when they came together, he'd said simply, "Isn't that what you would expect from a man of my reputation?"

She'd frowned at him. She frowned now, thinking about it. He was charming, vigorous, and wickedly handsome, she'd heard one of the ladies say behind her hand. But he was also something more, something a lot more.

She heard his laugh and came out from behind the potted palm. He was dancing with his mother, and the two of them were so beautiful, so graceful together, that several of the couples had moved back to watch them.

She heard a voice say softly behind her, "Well, well, just look at them. Makes you wonder, doesn't it?"

Susannah turned around slowly to look up at Tibolt.

"You were not invited," she said slowly, not moving. He

was dressed immaculately in black evening clothes, his shirt as white as the chalk cliffs.

"No, but then again, I'm a Carrington and thus can come and go as I please. Just look at them," he said again, staring at Rohan and his mother. "You can see where Rohan gleaned all his carnal knowledge. From her. Do you know that she seduced my tutor? Yes—he was young, filled with the Lord's fervor, cloaked in grace, until he saw her and was lost.

"I preach that women are the snare of the devil. My folk believe me because when I say the words—oh yes, I say them often—they know I believe them utterly. Yes, just look at her. Have you ever seen a mother look like she does?"

"Why are you here, Tibolt?" Susannah wasn't about to speak about Charlotte to him. That he could speak of his own mother in such a way only lowered him more in her eyes.

"Did you know that she scarcely paid me any attention at all once I was determined upon my course to become a man of God? Even when I told both her and Father that I would eventually become the Archbishop of Canterbury, they paid me no heed. I would crown kings, I told them, but they didn't care. I disappointed her, you see. She and my father had hoped that I would become like Rohan. They wanted two sons like themselves. Then, of course, she birthed George. They believed they'd gotten another priggish puritan like me, but now at least Mother knows differently. George was a budding rotter. I have wondered whether if he hadn't drowned he would have become a complete rotter with the years."

Susannah wished the music would end. She wished Rohan would magically appear beside her. She felt uncomfortable with Tibolt, no, more than uncomfortable, she was beginning to feel a bit alarmed. "Why are you here, Tibolt?" she said again.

"Why, I came to see my little niece, the little bastard you foisted off on Rohan." Suddenly she felt a pistol pressed hard against her stomach. "Actually, Susannah, you will give me your half of the map and that little golden key. You and I will simply walk out the glass doors here and onto the balcony for a bit of fresh air. Then we will go around the gardens to the side door into the estate room and from there upstairs. If you make a sound, trust that you will regret it."

"Why are you doing this? Why?"

"Shut up. I haven't much time. Let's forget my little niece on this visit, hmmm?"

She wondered if she should simply pretend to faint from sheer fright and collapse at his feet. Would he shoot her? No, surely he would not. She sucked in her breath, but he grabbed her arm, whispering with ferocious calm in her ear, "You try to deceive me in any way and I will take that little bastard of yours and no one will ever see her again. I will put her in a workhouse, where worthless little bastards belong. Do you understand me, Susannah?"

Oh, yes, she understood. She nodded.

"Hurry, then."

26

TIBOLT CARRINGTON EASED INTO HER BEDCHAMBER AFTER her, then very quietly closed the door. Only one branch of candles was lit. The air was redolent of some sweet spice, coming from the candles.

Tibolt sniffed. "It is my mother's doing, isn't it? Imagine a candle smelling like a brothel. I expect that you fit right in. It sickens me that you and Rohan will breed another generation of degenerates. I must congratulate you on the matchless job you did of trapping my brother. Rohan has always believed himself so superior to the rest of us, but just look at what he has saddled himself with for life.

"And Rohan's bedchamber is just through that adjoining door," he said, waving the gun toward the door. "I wonder if that door ever closes. I also wonder how you tricked him. All his experience with whores and sluts, and yet you netted him. You're not even beautiful. You're quite ordinary really, except for those breasts of yours. He appears to admire you. I don't understand it. It seems he wants to protect you. Oh, yes, I saw all those men he'd set about guarding the house and patrolling the grounds."

What men? Then she realized that Rohan was indeed trying to protect her, to protect all of them. He'd been worried after they were attacked, she'd known that. She'd been worried too. Why hadn't he told her what he'd done?

"Yes," she said simply. "How did you get past them?"

"I know my way in here," he said. "If Rohan were really as smart as he believes he is, he would have suspected me enough to set a guard against that small gate nearly hidden now by all the shrubbery just behind the apple orchard. My superior brother must have forgotten about it and the entrance into Mountvale from there that lets into the chamber just off the library. How do you think I got in here that very first night he brought all of you here?"

She stared at him, her memory righting itself. Marianne had said the man looked like Rohan, but none of them had taken her seriously. She could only shake her head. "It was you, not Lambie Lambert."

"Oh, yes. Lambie saw the lot of you in Oxford and rode immediately to tell me. I sent him to kidnap you. But he couldn't even manage to do that properly, the half-wit. What did you do, try to seduce him? Always weak of the flesh, was Lambie."

"No, I tried to kill him, but failed. Rohan saved me."

"Then you simpered and fainted and you trapped him. My proud, licentious brother, shackled to the likes of you. Now, enough of this. Give me the map and key."

She had to know, she just had to. "There were small letters etched onto the golden key. We couldn't make out what they were. Do you know?"

That startled him. He stared at her, then shoved her into a chair so hard that the chair nearly fell over backward. She managed to steady herself and right the chair, even as he said, "Don't move, damn you. I won't tell you anything."

So Rohan had been right. Tibolt did know; he just wasn't talking. She had to do something, but what? He was standing away from her now, not more than three feet between them, his gun pointed directly at her chest.

"You're not worthy to know. No one is but I. All those old fools protecting the secret . . . but that isn't your affair. Hurry and tell me. I suspect my brother will look for you soon, then he will worry. He will probably imagine that you are making love in one of the antechambers with a neighbor. Do it, damn you, or I will take Marianne.''

Susannah stared at that gun, at Tibolt, the vicar, her husband's brother, who was aiming it at her. He was looking alternately at her and all around her bedchamber. Did he expect to see the map propped up on the mantel?

But she couldn't tell him where they were, not yet. She swallowed her fear and said, ''You told Rohan that George had only mentioned the map to you, that was all. You told Rohan that you knew nothing else. But George wasn't involved, was he? It was you all along, you and those two dreadful men.''

Tibolt raised his hand slowly, so very slowly. She knew what was coming, but she wasn't fast enough. His fist struck her cheek. She felt a sharp, digging pain, then the sting of blood. He stepped back from her, panting. ''I cut you, but it isn't deep. I doubt it will scar, more's the pity.'' He looked down at his hand, and she saw the heavy ring he was wearing. He hadn't worn that when she and Rohan visited the vicarage. She would have remembered it. It looked to be solid silver, cut flat across the top. Tibolt was rubbing his fingers where the ring had cut him when he'd hit her. There was something on the ring, a figure etched into the silver. Susannah strained forward to see. At that moment, he happened to turn the ring toward her. It looked like a churchman wearing a bishop's mitre. Were there words beneath the figure? She couldn't tell. What did it mean?

He said slowly, rubbing his finger, ''George wouldn't tell me where he'd put the map. Before I had a chance to get it out of him, the little sod had the gall to get himself drowned.'' He added, more to himself than to her, ''A pity, but there was nothing any of us could do about it. Enough now, Susannah. Give me the map and the key.''

''Why won't you tell me what the map is for?''

''You don't deserve to know. I will tell you only that the prize is mine by moral right. I will be the future Archbishop of Canterbury, if that is what I choose to be. Actually, I will be the most powerful man in the world, if that is what I choose to be. I will rule wherever I wish to rule. No one will be able to go against me. I will have ultimate domination. Do you understand me? I will be as a god." He was almost shouting now, his eyes wild and nearly black in the dim candlelight. He drew a deep breath, steadying himself. "Now, shut up and get it, Susannah, or I will strike you down and take Marianne. Everyone is in the ballroom; even Marianne's nurse is sitting at the head of the stairs, singing with the musicians. I saw her there myself. Do as I bid you."

Susannah knew she had to do something. Think. No, she couldn't take the chance that he would hurt Marianne. There was no hope for it. She reached up to unfasten the necklace with its locket, only to realize that she was wearing the exquisite diamond and sapphire necklace Rohan had given her.

"Well?"

"I don't know what Rohan did with it. He didn't tell either Charlotte or me."

"Very well. I shall fetch Marianne." He strode toward her, and she knew he would strike her again.

She raised her hand to stop him. "The map and the key are behind two miniatures in a locket that George gave me. I always wear it, which is why that man Lambie Lambert could never find it. After we discovered the map and key in the locket, we decided to keep them there. It seemed safest.

"This evening Rohan gave me these jewels. He took off my locket and slipped it into his pocket. I swear to you, Tibolt, that is the truth. Just look at the necklace. You know I would only wear this for a very special occasion."

Tibolt rolled his eyes, his anger building. His mouth tightened, his lips a thin line. Damnation, he believed her.

Susannah could picture that austere, vicious look when he exhorted his congregation. She held her breath as he said finally, "You're too afraid to lie to me." He cursed long and fluently. He was silent for a long time, that gun of his never wavering from her chest. Finally, he waved the gun at her and said, "Rip off a strip of your petticoat. No, I'm not going to kill you. It would gain me nothing. When I have the power I desire, perhaps I will then." She ripped off a long strip.

He pulled her arms behind the chair and tied her wrists together, tight. Then he tied her ankles to the chair legs. For an instant his hand rested on her ankle and his fingers stroked over her stocking. She felt such fear that she knew she'd choke on it. Then he rose. He was breathing hard. He stuffed the rest of her petticoat in her mouth, ripped off more, and tied it firmly behind her head.

"There, that should hold you for a goodly time. You're still bleeding a bit. It's a pity that George had you first. And now you've had Rohan as well. Wouldn't you like to try all three brothers? It could be a competition of sorts. Of course, you'd have to be the judge."

If her mouth had been free, she would have spat on him. As it was, there was nothing she could do except gaze at him as if he were nothing more than dirt beneath her feet.

He was on the point of leaving when he turned very suddenly toward her dressing table. "My God, you little liar! I should have known, a woman always lies, always . . ."

He picked up the locket on its gold chain and swung it from his fingers. "So Rohan put it in his pocket, did he?"

He walked back to her, all the while swinging that gold chain. He struck her hard across her cheek, with the flat of his hand this time. She felt a narrow rivulet of blood course down her face. He ripped the sapphire and diamond necklace from her throat and stuffed it into his pocket.

Then he was gone, closing the door very quietly behind him. Susannah looked toward the two candles. They were burning low.

Rohan looked across the vast Mountvale ballroom, built in the mid-eighteenth century by his grandfather, Alfred Montley Carrington. It was a splendid room—much too large, he'd always believed, but it had admirably suited his purpose this evening. There were seventy-five guests, every local family of any note within a twenty-mile radius. Even the ancient Mr. Loomis, a relic from the Colonial war who had actually stood at Cornwallis's right hand when he'd surrendered at Yorktown, was grinning with toothless glee at Mrs. Pratt, who was young enough to be his daughter and Rohan's grandmother. All the guests had appeared to enjoy themselves. He'd made his announcement midway through the evening, Susannah on one side of him, his mother on the other. He'd presented his wife to them with all the pride he felt, remembering only belatedly that he'd supposedly been a bounder and kept her in hiding. He'd been contrite. He'd pleaded youth and confusion. Of course, everyone had already known. Probably all their servants and pets had known as well. When their guests had congratulated him afterward, Susannah had pinched his hand, for he had been shameless in his manipulations.

And his mother had said, "Dearest, I vow never to aggravate you to the point that you will strangle me. I am convinced that your peers would congratulate you on how well you had killed me. Naturally, this group wasn't much of a challenge, but still, you did well. I'm proud of you."

Talk about proud, his mother and Susannah had done *him* proud. The long line of glass doors stood open onto the balcony. Fresh flowers from the Mountvale gardens and potted plants of many varieties were scattered around the room. There were even three palm trees he'd managed to obtain from a captain who had just come from the southern coast of Cornwall. The orchestra sat on a small dais at one end. At the other end were three long tables laden with food and drink.

It was one o'clock in the morning. To the best of his reckoning and Fitz's, no one had as yet left. He wanted his wife, but he saw that she wasn't on the dance floor. He hoped none of the local ladies had gotten hold of her and were hurling sweet-barbed questions at her upstairs in the lady's withdrawing room. No, there was Lady Dauntry, and she was actually smiling at something her husband had said. That must surely be a miracle, he thought, although the champagne punch *was* strong enough to make a nun dance.

His mother was dancing with Colonel Nemesis Jones, a man of middle years and apparently the only man in the whole south of England who might be immune to Charlotte's array of quite tangible charms. He heard her laugh—a real laugh, not one of her flirtatious laughs. It was the way she laughed with him. The way she had laughed with his father. He could tell the difference from the age of ten. Colonel Jones did not change expression, as far as Rohan could tell from his distance.

Where was Susannah?

He went on a mission of rescue. He was certain the old biddies were at her again. But who? Every old biddy he was concerned about was present in the ballroom.

There were several ladies in the withdrawing room, and they were suitably shocked to see him stick his head in the door. He was charming; he was chastened and apologetic. All three of the ladies encouraged him to remain. What he had to suffer because of his reputation, he thought, as he hurriedly removed himself.

He frowned as he walked down the long corridor to the nursery. He looked in. Lottie was asleep in her narrow bed in the small adjoining room, Marianne in her bed beside her.

No Susannah.

It was at that instant that he felt a sudden tremor of alarm as sharp as if someone had just grabbed him and shaken him. Something was wrong, he knew it. Dear God, what had happened? He'd checked with the men patrolling the grounds. He was told that no strangers had attempted to come into the house. He hurried to his bedchamber, flinging open the door. The branch of two candles was nearly burned down.

No Susannah.

He opened the adjoining door and strode into her bedchamber. At first he couldn't credit what he was seeing. She was tied to a chair, staring helplessly at him from above a gag, making slurred noises in her throat.

At that point one of the candles flickered, wavered, and burned out.

"My God!" he yelled and ran to her. He pulled off the strip of petticoat and jerked the wadded cotton from her mouth.

"What happened? Are you all right? Who did this?"

Susannah was working her mouth to get the feeling back, rubbing her fingers over her lips. "It was Tibolt. I'm sorry, Rohan, but he forced me up here. He said you should have posted a guard near that little gate behind the apple orchard. He said it led to a small door into a chamber next to the library. He was indeed the man who put Marianne out on the ledge that first night, the man she said looked like you. He took the locket. It is a pity, but he saw it lying on the dressing table. He ripped off my beautiful necklace and took that as well."

Who cared about the bloody locket or the necklace? He could only stare down at her, wanting desperately to believe that she'd made a mistake. He reached out his hand and cupped her chin. "He struck you. By God, that bastard struck you." There was utter rage in his voice.

The other candle burned out.

27

THE GUESTS WERE FINALLY GONE. IT WAS JUST AFTER three o'clock in the morning. Charlotte, Susannah, and Rohan were in the library, sipping brandy. Fitz and Mrs. Beete stood side by side in the doorway. Susannah's cheek was bandaged. Rohan would have preferred to tell them nothing, but they were his family and so he'd told them most of it. Only George's role in this had to be kept quiet.

"Lordie," Mrs. Beete said, clutching a bowl of ice between her large hands as if it were a man's neck. It was intended for Susannah's cheek, to reduce the swelling. "Mr. Tibolt. I'm sorry to say this, milady, but he was such a little sneak as a boy. Always spying on the housemaids, hiding behind the stairs to see them straightening their stockings. I always hoped he would outgrow it."

"True enough," Charlotte said, staring down at her swinging foot. "He was a sneak," she continued, not looking up from her slipper. "I didn't know he spied on the maids. That was not well done of him. His father would have been appalled." She had danced so much there was very nearly a hole in the sole of her shoe.

"Apparently he did outgrow it," Fitz said. "He went on to more wickedness. I wish now that he would have remained a sneak. That would have been tolerable, but this? He actually struck her ladyship. My lord, what are we to do now?''

"First things first, Fitz. Her ladyship had to give him the locket. He threatened to take Miss Marianne, you see. He also told her that it belonged to him, to no one else, and that he had a moral right to have it, which is an interesting and perhaps telling thing to say." Of course Susannah had told him and Charlotte everything Tibolt had said—strange, all of it. Neither Fitz nor Mrs. Beete had asked where Susannah had gotten the locket, thank God. Perhaps someday they would wonder.

"He will be the future Archbishop of Canterbury, if he chooses to be so," Rohan said slowly, thoughtfully, his fingers still curled around his brandy snifter. "He could be the most powerful man in the world, if he chooses to be so. He would have ultimate domination." He looked up. "This makes no sense at all. It sounds like some sort of magic potion, but what the devil could he mean by all his claims?"

"He was in such a rage that his eyes were nearly black," Susannah said now. "I remember thinking that he seemed to be beyond himself. He was nearly screaming at me when he said all that."

Charlotte rose and shook out her skirts. "Well, tonight was a success in terms of our neighbors. That is something. As for this, it is confounding. There was nothing else, Susannah?"

She raised her hand to the bandage on her cheek. "Yes. The reason my cheek was cut is that he hit me with his ring. He cut himself with the ring as well. It was big, heavy."

"What ring?" Rohan asked. "I've never seen Tibolt wear a ring."

"Neither have I," Charlotte said.

"It was silver, flat on top. I remember thinking it was very odd-looking, so I tried to get a good look at it. I think there was a carving of a bishop in his mitre on the top of it."

"Can you draw it?"

"Yes, certainly." She started to rise, but he stopped her. "No, wait here, I will fetch foolscap and a quill."

When he returned, it took Susannah only a minute to render the ring's likeness. "There, this is as close as I remember. Also, there were words beneath the etching. I couldn't make them out."

"It is a bishop wearing a mitre," Rohan said slowly. He was silent, staring at the shadowed painting of a long ago Carrington on the far wall. He said slowly, "Someone had to give George that half map." He looked quickly up at Fitz and Mrs. Beete. Thank God they were speaking between themselves and hadn't heard him. He would have to be more careful in the future. He said aloud to Susannah and his mother, "Why? For safekeeping, perhaps? In any case it must be someone in Oxford."

Susannah said slowly, "Tibolt said something about 'all those old fools protecting the secret.' I just remembered George told me about a churchman he'd assisted, 'a grand old man,' was how he'd described him. Could there be a connection there?"

"Do you remember the churchman's name?" Charlotte asked.

"Yes," Susannah said. "It was Bishop Roundtree. Could he have given George the half map and the golden key?"

"I have never believed in coincidences," Rohan said as he rose and stretched. "Tibolt is wearing a ring with a bishop in a mitre carved on it." He kept his voice low. "George assists a bishop—the same bishop—and that in itself is quite a coincidence. George shows up with half a map and a golden key." He reached out his hand to his wife. "Come, my dear, it's time for you to rest. We will go to Oxford tomorrow. I very much want to meet Bishop Roundtree."

"Dearest, what you are thinking is very disturbing," Charlotte said, still staring at her slippers. "Tibolt and a bishop both involved in this mystery."

"Yes, it is, but I can see no other course open to us. You may be certain that my brother is no longer at Branholly Cottage."

"My lord."

"Yes, Fitz?"

"Mrs. Beete and I have discussed it. We recommend sending Augustus to Branholly Cottage, to spy out the lay of the land. He's a good lad and if there's anything to discover, Augustus will sniff it out. He's got that Welsh nose."

"Very well. I trust that neither you nor Mrs. Beete will mention any of this to anyone?"

"Not a word, my lord!"

"Never, my lord. None of it, not even those bits about Master George we've heard you mention. You can trust us."

"Thank you both. As for George, well, he's dead. Bringing him into this would solve nothing." The two old servants nodded. Rohan turned. "Mother, are you ready for your bed?"

She didn't respond.

"Mother?" Alarmed, Rohan went to her. She was crying, not making a sound, the tears simply streaming down her face. "I'm sorry, Mother, so very sorry." He pulled her to her feet and enveloped her in his arms. "It's all right. Everything will come about, you will see. I'm so sorry." He kept speaking, low and quiet, rocking her against him.

Mrs. Beete sniffed back her own tears. Fitz looked fit to kill, his arthritic hands fisting and unfisting at his sides.

As for Susannah, she felt as if she'd been pounded into the ground. She leaned her head back against the lovely blue brocade settee and closed her eyes. She heard Rohan's soft voice as he spoke quietly to his mother. Poor Charlotte. What a blow for a parent. Two of her three sons—rotters. She just prayed that Tibolt wasn't more than a rotter. But of course he was. She lightly touched her fingertips to her cheek. It still throbbed.

"How will I ever get my crenellated tower built if you two keep kidnapping me for your treasure hunt?"

"No treasure hunt just yet. We've lost both our half of the map and that bloody little key. And you know Oxford so very well, Phillip. You are the perfect confederate. Come, don't whine. It doesn't become you. You are pale. You need to be outdoors. We will entertain you.''

"You know Oxford as well as I do, Rohan. What is it you really want from me?''

Susannah laid her hand on Phillip Mercerault's sleeve. "We wish to visit Bishop Roundtree. We believe he is somehow involved in all this.''

"Bishop Roundtree? He's a thundering old curmudgeon who hates everyone—particularly the fairer sex—and thinks everyone—particularly the fairer sex—is destined for Hades. He tries his best to exhort all the students to forgo the pleasures of the flesh and adhere to their books. I've always thought he was rather mad, but harmless. You honestly believe he could be in the thick of these shenanigans? With your vicar brother? You say Tibolt broke into your house and struck down Susannah? Astounding.''

Rohan nodded. "Yes. As for this bishop, it seems to be our only path to follow right now. God knows where Tibolt has gone to ground.''

Susannah said, "If this bishop is involved, if he does have the other half of the map, then Tibolt must be close. He will have to have both halves to gain this prize of his.''

"Yes,'' Rohan said, looking briefly at the healing cut on her cheek, at the bruise around it, which was now yellowish green. He felt anger flow through him each time he saw the evidence of his brother's cruelty, his lack of control. "We must keep a lookout for him. Since Pope Leo IX did give Macbeth something, it seems likely that it's of a religious nature.''

"You mean like Saint Peter's thighbone hidden away somewhere in a cave?''

"Something like that,'' Rohan said. "An artifact of some sort. But we have no idea really. Tibolt spoke to Susannah about it giving him ultimate power.'' He suddenly looked defeated as he said, "It doesn't look good, does it?''

"No,'' she said honestly, "it doesn't. But we will find out the truth. I pray it will not be too awful to bear.''

Phillip Mercerault stroked his chin. He whistled a moment under his breath. It was not a tune either Rohan or Susannah recognized, though it was catchy. When Phillip visited Mountvale, he would have to teach it to Jamie. Surely Jamie could set a limerick to it. The viscount said finally, "I will join you gladly. To be truthful, life has been too bland of late. Even the design of my tower doesn't amuse me much anymore."

Phillip turned to Susannah. "Rohan and I were boys together at Eton. We protected each other's back. If a bully wanted to smash one of us, then there were suddenly two for the bully to take on. I've always trusted Rohan, as he has me. Yes, let's have an adventure. My spirit soars at the thought of it. I will immediately shove my drawings for my tower back into the desk drawer. Let's have a spot of luncheon and then we're off to see Bishop Roundtree."

"I can't wait to see the look on that old sod's face when he sees Susannah," Rohan said, and chuckled. "Also, we have more to tell you about this mess."

"Must we eat luncheon here, Phillip?" Susannah said. "It will be so delicious that I will stuff everything into my mouth then fall into a gluttonous stupor."

The afternoon was pleasant, only a light breeze to stir the oak leaves. They rode toward Oxford from the west, past Nuffield College. They turned from Queen Street onto St. Aldate's Street, passing by Pembroke College to the left and the magnificent Christ Church quadrangle on their right. Rohan said to Susannah, "Both Phillip and I were here at Christ Church, as was Tibolt. We called it The House—"

"Don't forget to show off your Latin, Rohan."

"Very well. 'The House' is from *aedes Christi,* meaning 'House of Christ.' And that is nearly the extent of my scholarship."

"That doesn't say much for your brain, since every student knows that."

Susannah laughed, but she was clearly distracted by the

Great Quadrangle, also known as Tom Quad, Rohan told her behind his hand as Phillip kept up his monologue. She half-listened to Phillip telling her that the library, a superb example of Italian Renaissance architecture, was built in the early eighteenth century.

"Bishop Roundtree is frequently in his vast offices in the cathedral," Rohan said. "It is likely we will find him there."

"Yes, he should be there. If we have time, Rohan, let's take Susannah to Trinity College. I want her to see Blackwell's Bookshop."

They didn't find Bishop Roundtree in his offices or in the cathedral itself. One of the black-garbed curates told them the bishop's address. "I expected him this morning, but he did not come," the man said. He was quite bald, his head shining with sweat beneath the afternoon sun.

Bishop Roundtree lived on Brewer Street, not far from Christ Church, in a tall Georgian house of deep-red brick. It was a busy thoroughfare, with houses on both sides, carriages, drays, and horses fighting for the middle of the narrow street. The bishop's house was set back a bit, with a narrow graveled drive.

The knocker was answered by a very pretty young man wearing black and white livery and a snow-white periwig of the last century. He couldn't have been more than twenty years old. He frowned at Susannah, then ignored her. He addressed Rohan: "Yes, sir?"

"I am Lord Mountvale. This is Lord Derencourt. We wish to see Bishop Roundtree."

"I am afraid that the bishop has given me orders that he is not to be disturbed. He is preparing a sermon." Then he actually turned his back to Susannah and directly faced Rohan.

"This is extremely important. We wish to see him now."

The young man bit his lower lip. He looked uncertain.

"Now," Phillip said. "As in this very minute, not a minute from now."

"I will see if the bishop can see you gentlemen. Please step inside."

He obviously wanted to shut the door in Susannah's face, but knew he couldn't. He left them all standing in a dimly lit entryway. There were several dark portraits of past bishops, all of them fat-jowled and thick-lipped, looking more stern than hanging judges.

Susannah shivered. "I don't like this place."

"Well," her husband said, leaning down to kiss the tip of her nose, "that precious boy playing at being a butler doesn't like you."

"I know, but it makes no sense. I said nothing rude to him. I smiled. And he is so pretty. Why is he dressed like a butler of twenty years ago?"

"You don't want to know," Phillip said, patting her sleeve. "Really, you don't. Trust me on this."

"I fear he will never like you, Susannah. However, please don't let it worry you. I like you immensely. Phillip, because he isn't married to you, likes you less immensely than I do."

"Ah," Phillip said, "but there is still some liking involved. After all, you have put my friend out of his misery. That reputation you've so carefully nurtured has ground you down for too long, Rohan. Now it's over, thank God."

"But—" Susannah began.

They heard a high-pitched scream.

In a flash the men were running toward that scream, Susannah on their heels. They dashed up the stairs, even as three more piercing screams rent the air.

At the head of the stairs, they saw the young man who had greeted them lurching out of a doorway at the end of the corridor.

"My master . . . oh, my God, my master! Hurry!"

At the doorway, Rohan grabbed Susannah by her upper arms. "You will stay here."

"Bosh," she said, dogging his heels again. But just in a few moments she was wishing profoundly that she had reconsidered. She didn't want to look, but she did.

Bishop Roundtree was sprawled in the center of a magnificent carpet in the middle of the room. His arms and legs were spread. He'd been struck very hard on the forehead, several times. There was blood everywhere and not much left of the bishop's head. Susannah felt dizzy and leaned against the wall of the bishop's study. A dark wall, she noticed. Thankfully, no blood had splattered this far. She heard a gagging noise. It was the butler, that pretty young man in his old-fashioned periwig, vomiting in the corridor. She managed to make herself look at the bishop. There was a bloody brass andiron beside the body. Oh, God, the thought of another human being bringing that andiron down on someone's head—she couldn't bring herself to accept it. It was a man in a rage. Or a woman. No, a woman couldn't do such a thing. The force of the blow bespoke a man, surely. Besides, surely that pretty butler wouldn't allow a woman in this house, much less in the bishop's study.

She watched Rohan drop to his knees and gently search for a pulse in the bishop's neck. Finally he shook his head. "He's been dead for a while. He's stiffening up," he said over his shoulder to Phillip. Then he saw his wife leaning against the wall, heard the butler vomiting. "Dammit, Susannah, you have less color than that creamy satin chemise you're wearing beneath your gown. Don't you remember how I nearly drooled all over myself before you managed to pull your gown up and cover that wicked confection? Yes, now I see that you well remember. I won't tell you again—get yourself downstairs and wait for the magistrate." Rohan rose. He said to Phillip, who was staring blankly down at the body, "Shall you go or shall I?"

"My God, this is unexpected. All I wanted to do was build my tower, and look what you've got me into. Hell, I even volunteered. More than hell, I was even enthusiastic. That will teach me. I'll go. Lord Balantyne became a magistrate just about a year ago. He lives over on Blue Boar Street. I know him. He's not stupid, he cares, thus he does try to do a decent job. Of course, the proctors will shriek that he shouldn't be involved in this, since in their eyes it will be a university matter. But Lord Balantyne is just powerful enough to do as he pleases.''

"This is a murder, Phillip, a very vicious murder. I hope the poor man is up to it.''

"We will soon see, won't we?''

"Tibolt can't be a part of this. None of us could bear it if he is. No, he can't.'' But Rohan was afraid, more afraid than he'd been since Lambie Lambert had kidnapped Susannah.

28

THE PARLOR IN BISHOP ROUNDTREE'S HOME WAS AS DULL
and dim and depressing as the entry hall. Roundtree antecedents hung on the walls, a grim lot, an undoubtedly pious
lot as well, all looking so self-righteous that it made Susannah shudder. She and the pretty young butler sat there as
silent as statues, waiting for Jubilee Balantyne, Rohan, and
Phillip to come down from examining the body of Bishop
Roundtree.

"He was my master," said the pretty butler. "I loved
him."

"What is your name?"

"Roland. I was named after Roland, Charlemagne's fore-
most warrior from the *Song of Roland*." Roland sighed
deeply. "My father disowned me when he realized that I
would never even make a decent wild young man, much less
a warrior, if there is any such thing about in these modern
days. Well, I was a wild young man, but not in the way he
wished me to be."

Whatever that meant. "How long did you work for Bishop
Roundtree, Roland?"

"Two years now. He took me in when I was a pathetic
scrap living with a woman who was about to kick me out
because I wouldn't bed her. My master gave me grand

clothes from the last century to wear and this magnificent wig. He gave me three wigs, actually, each of them in a different style, depending on the occasion. The one I am wearing is designed for everyday use, but today isn't every day, is it? It began as an every day, but look what happened.'' He stared down at his clasped hands. Susannah didn't say anything.

He raised his head finally and looked at her. A spasm of distaste crossed his pretty face. ''I don't expect you to understand. You're only a woman. But I loved my master. He gave me everything. I would have done anything for him.''

Why, she wondered, wouldn't she understand? She said as nicely as she could, knowing he was profoundly distressed, ''You said he was writing a sermon in his study. Lord Mountvale told me he thought Bishop Roundtree had been dead for several hours—his limbs were stiffening, you see.''

Roland gulped, then nodded.

''But if he was closeted in his study, with you guarding the front door, then who could have gotten in to kill him?''

Roland gave a start. Then he leapt to his feet. ''Dear God, you're only a female, a creature offensive to my eyes, a creature the bishop castigated as a useless appendage to man save for her womb, yet it is a question that has merit. Who killed my master when he was alone? And I was always here, at my post. Two men came, but I turned them away. They were tradesmen. I merely sent them about their business. They were worth nothing.''

''But Roland, someone had to have gotten in. Someone went to the bishop's study on the second floor. Someone struck him with the andiron. It had to be someone he knew— because he was struck in the forehead. That means he was facing the person. If he had been afraid, surely he would have called out to you, wouldn't he?''

''Oh, yes,'' Roland. ''Oh, yes.'' Then he buried his face in his hands. His periwig listed to the left. He straightened it without moving. He raised his head finally, tears streaming

down his face. "Oh, my God," he moaned, rocking back
and forth in his chair. "Oh, my God. I did leave my post. I
remember now. A boy came—from the cathedral, he said,
and I was to go to the corner and meet one of the young
curates. He would give me some papers for the bishop. Oh,
God. I went to the corner, I didn't even think it an odd
request, but I should have. Why didn't the young curate simply come here? He was nothing, and the bishop was the
master of the cathedral. It is all my fault."

"No, it wasn't, Roland. You did what was proper. Tell
me about this young curate."

"He was there at the corner. He was dressed like a curate.
He looked ascetic, if you know what I mean—which is odd,
since his cheeks weren't sunken and he wasn't thin like as-
cetics are supposed to be. I never questioned that he was
who he said. He handed me a packet. I brought it back, but
I didn't disturb the bishop. He had told me he wasn't to be
bothered unless Oxford was falling into the sea. Well a simple packet wasn't a dire matter, so I didn't take it up. Oh,
my poor master. I let him die. It's all my fault."

"No," Rohan said from the doorway. "No, it isn't, unless
you struck him with that andiron."

"His name is Roland," Susannah said. "Roland, do you
still have that packet of papers the young curate gave you?"

"Why, yes, I do. I put them next to the salver on the table
in the entryway."

"Perhaps we should look at them," Rohan said.

Roland leapt from his chair, as if thankful for something
useful to do that would lessen his guilt. When he returned,
he handed the packet to Rohan, never looking at Susannah.

"Look at this," Rohan said finally. "Blank pages, the entire lot of them, all blank."

"Oh, God, if only I'd looked, I would have known that
something was very wrong. But I didn't look. I just whistled
after I'd set the packet on the table, made myself some tea
in the kitchen, and didn't think a single odd thought."

"Don't blame yourself, Roland," Jubilee Balantyne said

in a voice smoother than a rock in a creek bed. "Obviously the man who killed your master came in when he saw you leave. However, it isn't your fault. You did what you were supposed to do. You performed a service requested of you. Now, tell me about this young curate. He had to be in on the scheme, you see. It was his job to get you away from the house."

Roland rose slowly to his feet. He really was lovely. Had he been wearing a gown, Susannah would have believed him a beautiful young woman.

"My lord, I don't know," Roland whimpered and burst into tears, covering his face in his hands. Rohan shot Susannah a harassed look.

She frowned at him.

"I'm sorry, Roland, take your time," Rohan said. His voice, if not gentle, was at least a bit more restrained. "This is naturally quite a shock to you. But surely you want us to find who did this to your master. Please think. That's it. Focus your memory on meeting that man who was dressed as a curate."

Roland was obviously thinking. He began to pace. He looked, Susannah thought, like a very beautiful actor from a play of the last century.

Susannah said nothing, merely waited. Phillip was standing beside the open door, his arms crossed over his chest. As for the magistrate, he was saying not a word, just sitting next to Rohan, watching the young man and his perambulations.

"He was young," Roland said suddenly, "not much older than I am. He had a lot of hair, black hair, and it was too long for a curate. I remember thinking he should get it cut. He was taller than I, but not much. He was very fit, not lean but muscular. I've never seen a curate built like he was. Oh, God, I killed my master."

"Roland, you're doing fine," Susannah said, "but you must continue to hold yourself together. What you tell us will help find the man who did this awful thing."

Jubilee Balantyne cleared his throat, winked at Susannah, and said, "Did he tell you his name?"

Roland shook his head. "No, my lord. He was pleasant, spoke a moment about the weather, asked me how long I'd lived in Oxford. What did I think of Bishop Roundtree? Oh, God! I see it all now. He was keeping me away from the bishop while his accomplice was murdering him. Oh, God!"

"That is true," said Jubilee Balantyne. "But you had no way of knowing it was a ruse. Come now, do pull yourself together, as Lady Mountvale told you to do. Did you notice anything at all unusual about the young man, anything distinctive?"

Roland was shaking his head, wringing his hands, his periwig crooked, but it didn't matter to him, for he was too upset to speak.

"Think, man!"

"Yes, yes, I remember now. He was wearing this ring on his left hand. Bishop Roundtree has one identical to it. I started to ask him where he got it, then he gave me the packet and there was no time."

"Tell us about this ring."

"Better than that," Balantyne said. "Let me go fetch the bishop's. You're certain it was identical?" Roland nodded. Susannah didn't envy him his task. He was back very soon, standing in the doorway, frowning.

"He isn't wearing a ring."

Roland jumped to his feet. "No, my lord, the bishop always wore that ring, always. I asked him once about it, and he became so angry at my impertinence I thought he would strike me. Of course he didn't. He never struck me. Well, he did just one time, but that was because it pleased him to do it."

"Then the man who killed him took it. None of us noticed this before. One of the bishop's fingers was cut off, likely the one upon which he wore that ring. Evidently his killer couldn't simply pull it off, thus the mutilation."

Roland fell into a dead faint.

Susannah wished she could join him. Instead she left the drawing room and found her way to the kitchen, a small, dim room at the rear of the house. She dampened a cloth and returned to Roland, who was still on the floor, now moaning like a child. She came down to her knees and gently wiped his face. "It will be all right," she said, then said it again, but she doubted it sincerely. She looked at her husband. His eyes were closed.

She knew what he was thinking. He was thinking that it was the same identical ring. Both of them wearing the same sort of ring? Was it some sort of club? Then she remembered Tibolt's words: "All those old fools protecting the secret . . ."

The ring, Roland finally told them, after drinking a snifter of rich smuggled French brandy, was heavy silver, an etching of a bishop in a mitre atop it. Yes, there were words beneath it, but he didn't know what they were.

"Interesting," Balantyne said.

"It was very big, very heavy," Roland said. "Does that help somehow?"

"It could," Rohan said.

Balantyne dismissed poor Roland, telling him with a bit of disgust in his voice that he should have a liedown after he brought Balantyne the names of all Bishop Roundtree's relatives. He himself would see to the acquaintances.

Jubilee Balantyne looked thoughtfully at Phillip Mercerault. "I do believe it's time you tell me what this is all about, Phillip."

Phillip, after a quick glance at Rohan, shrugged, saying, "I'm sorry, Jubilee, but there's little I can tell you. Lord Mountvale and I have been friends for many years. The only reason I am along is because I know Oxford so well. Rohan wished to visit the bishop. Didn't you tell me, Rohan, that he was a friend of your father's?"

Rohan nodded. "That's right. Unfortunately, we were unlucky in the timing of our visit."

"I see. I don't suppose you know anything about this ring?"

"The ring? Not a thing."

Jubilee Balantyne said nothing as he rose to his feet. "This is a bloody mess. Everyone in Oxford is going to want to nail my hide to the wall if I don't quickly discover who did this. The proctors will want to take over. I should probably let them and wash my hands of it. Ah, but I won't. Now, why don't you three discuss what's happened and then come and talk to me. I really need your help. If you go off on your own, I cannot be responsible."

"A perceptive gentleman," Susannah said after the magistrate had left the bishop's house. "What are we going to do?"

"Not tell him the truth, that's for sure," Rohan said.

"I told you he wasn't stupid," Phillip said. "I want to leave this place, all right?"

Phillip gave them what he called the best bed in Dinwitty Manor. The bedchamber was low-ceilinged and somewhat damp, but the bed was indeed magnificent. It was after midnight, after an evening spent discussing everything and coming up with not a single answer. Susannah was pressed against Rohan's side, her cheek on his shoulder, her palm wide over his chest.

"I bloody well don't know what to do," he said to the dark ceiling. "I've thought and thought. My God, Susannah, what if Tibolt murdered the bishop?"

She kissed his shoulder. "We have no notion if that could be true. It seems more likely that it was Tibolt who diverted poor Roland. He was wearing the ring, after all. He must also have been wearing a disguise. I do have an idea, however."

She kissed him again on his shoulder while her palm stroked down his chest, her fingers threading through his hair down to his belly. His muscles contracted. His breathing shifted from steady and slow to a leaping roar.

Her fingers went lower until she touched him.

He nearly bounded off the bed. All thoughts of the day were swamped by lust so great that he was shaking with it. Her fingers wrapped around him.

"Susannah, do you know what you're doing?"

"I'm not certain, but I think you would tell me if I don't do something correctly, wouldn't you?"

"Oh, yes. What you're doing is quite acceptable." He moaned.

She kissed his mouth, saying as he parted his lips, "We have been distracted for far too long. There have been too many questions, too many bad things that have happened. You told me that we would share, Rohan. I need a different kind of sharing now. I need you."

They hadn't made love for several days. It had occurred to Rohan upon occasion that Susannah was his bride, yet he'd kept his hands to himself, and his mouth and every other part of him as well. Both of them had been distracted. She was right. It was time to bring the two of them together again, like their first night, like that incredible night at the inn.

He slowly turned on his side to face her. Thank God she didn't release him.

He began kissing her, his hands on her breasts, roving to her belly, around to her buttocks. "Damned nightgown," he said in her mouth, then raised her to pull it over her head.

Unfortunately she released him to help him get the garment off.

He fell back, bringing her on top of him. "It's just as well. I would be in a sorry state were you to continue holding me like that. Perhaps sometime you could put your mouth on me, Susannah."

She blinked down at him. It was dark and she could see only the vague outline of his face. She said, surprise clear in her voice, "You want me to kiss you there?"

"Oh, yes, and more."

She fell silent. She'd never imagined such a thing. She'd

believed her hand on him was beyond bold, something a lady shouldn't ever do, yet she'd enjoyed thoroughly the feel of him, the warmth and hardness of him.

He pulled her completely on top of him. "Kiss me," he said, and when her mouth touched his, he splayed his fingers over her hips and began to knead her soft flesh. Soon his fingers were pulling her thighs apart. Then his fingers were touching her flesh and she reared back, staring down at him.

"Don't you like that?"

"Oh yes, but it's shocking." He eased his finger into her, and she gasped.

"Rohan, you touched me like you did our first night together, like that evening in the inn, well, other nights as well, but I'd forgotten how it felt. It's been a long time. It's been three whole days." Then she moved against him. He squeezed his eyes closed. It was going to be close.

When he came into her, her legs wrapped around his flanks, his hands cupping her face between his palms, he whispered against her mouth, "Shall we make a babe, Susannah?"

She thrust her hips up against him, whispering on his neck, "I don't care, I don't care. I just want you, just you. Rohan . . ."

He took her pleasure into himself. It was deep and raw and he moaned his own release into her mouth.

The three of them were seated at the breakfast table the following morning. There was little conversation until Rohan dropped a piece of crisp bacon and said, "What if the bishop's half of the map is still at his house? Still in his study? What if the killer failed to find it? He didn't have all that much time. And the way he killed the bishop, he appeared to be in a rage, as if the bishop had refused to tell him what he wanted to know."

Susannah tossed down her napkin and rose. "That's what I was thinking as well. The bishop must have the other half of the map hidden somewhere. Let's go see."

Phillip said to Rohan, "I've never met a woman like her before."

"Perhaps when you do find a woman like my Susannah, you'll marry her before she can get away from you."

Phillip stared hard at her and said finally, "Perhaps. Perhaps."

29

"I'LL BE DAMNED," PHILLIP MERCERAULT, COMING TO HIS feet. He'd been lying on his back under Bishop Roundtree's desk. "Look at this. It was fastened to the underside of the desk."

It was a narrow cloth book. It looked very old.

Rohan and Susannah gathered around him. They had nearly given up searching the bishop's study.

"It's very fragile," Phillip said as he slowly opened it. "There are only three pages here, all written in Latin. And this." His smile was dazzling as he gently pulled a single half of a small map from a pocket on the back cover.

"You've taken first prize, Phillip. This looks like the other half of the map."

"The first thing I suggest we do, gentlemen," Susannah said very quietly, "is to contain our excitement and leave this place immediately. I don't want Roland talking to Lord Balantyne, telling him about our find. Or telling anyone else, for that matter. We will act like we finally gave up."

"She's right," Rohan said. He kissed her, then whispered in her ear, "We found it!"

"None of that," Phillip said. "It makes me jealous. I dislike being jealous. It is too petty, too common. Rohan, no more nibbling her ear. Now, once outside, we must be certain that no one is watching the house. Everyone keep a long face.''

Once downstairs, they found Roland in the kitchen, sitting at the table, his head on his folded arms, fast asleep.

"What will become of him?" Susannah asked as Rohan helped her into the carriage.

"If the bishop had relatives, and they move in here, then I'm afraid he won't be long welcome," Phillip said.

"Why ever not? He is so very pretty and even though he doesn't care for ladies, he does seem efficient. You certainly cannot fault his admiration and affection for the bishop.''

"Well, it's not quite that simple," Rohan said, took her hand in his and kissed her knuckles.

"Why don't you offer him a position, Phillip?" Susannah said after she managed to look away from her husband's beautiful eyes and his even more beautiful mouth, a mouth she seemed to be staring at more and more often of late. She'd never imagined that she could feel about a man the way she was coming to feel about him. And the way he made her feel when he touched her, when he came inside her. A window had been opened and she had flown through it. She never wanted that window to close. She didn't ever want to leave her husband. Despite his reputation, she knew he was hers, that he would always be hers. As for herself, Susannah had no choice in the matter. She brought her thoughts away from her husband's mouth that she wanted to kiss until they were both breathless.

"Well, Susannah, it's like this," Phillip began, looked for a long, very helpless moment into her lovely, innocent face, and groaned. "I can't."

"Susannah," Rohan said. "I am your husband. You will trust me that Roland, as loyal and affectionate as he is, would not fit in well in the Dinwitty household.''

"All right," she said slowly, her head cocked to one side in question. "I will get this mystery solved when I have you alone, Rohan." She leaned against him, kissed his ear, and whispered, "You will tell me anything once I have you at my mercy."

It was her husband's turn to moan.

"I feel another bout of jealousy coming on," Phillip said. "To distract myself, I will look out the window to be certain no one is following us."

They were back at Dinwitty Manor within the hour. It was raining hard by the time the carriage rolled into the long drive, the sky a dirty gray by three o'clock in the afternoon. But it didn't matter. Their excitement would have carried them through a flood.

"Damn," Phillip said as they went into his study. "I wish we had the other half of the map."

"Well, we do, sort of," Susannah said. She grinned at her husband. "I had planned to surprise you. Now is the perfect time, don't you think? I copied the other half of the map. Unfortunately I couldn't very well copy the gold key. I have the half I drew upstairs. I'll be back in a trice."

"I'm going to throttle you, Susannah," Rohan shouted after her. "She copied it. I should have known." He added to Phillip, "She's an excellent artist."

"You married a very smart lady, Rohan," Phillip said as he handed his friend a snifter of brandy. "I wonder when you will tell her the truth?"

"In my own good time. A man of my reputation never rushes things. That's one thing I have learned well over my profligate years on this earth."

Phillip was laughing when Susannah came dashing back into the room, out of breath. "Here it is! Look at what I've done. See here, I wanted to make certain that the proportions were as close as possible to the original and that's why it's so small."

Because she had the most delicate touch, Susannah carefully fitted the two halves together, smoothing them down so they wouldn't bend. They weren't an exact fit, but they were close enough. "Look," she said, stepping back. "It's Scotland, all right. Here's a town called Dunkeld—the 'DU' is on one side of the map and the rest is on the other, so you couldn't tell what it was without the entire map. And look at this tiny drawing of a church spire. Half of it is on one side of the map and the other half is on the other part of the map. Again, without both parts put together, it was impossible to tell that it was a church. Do you think the treasure, or whatever it is, is inside this church?''

"It seems likely," Phillip said as Rohan began to read from the flimsy cloth book. "This seems to be a rambling diatribe on the quest for power and immortality—nothing specific, just how good is lost to mankind, but evil flourishes and is real and dangerous. It speaks of the *Devil's Vessel,* and here's a reference to something like *Pure Flame,* whatever that means. Ah, here we are. 'Pure Flame' refers to Hildebrand. He is called here the cardinal subdeacon, the administrator of the Papal States under many popes, the one guarding the vessel from thieves and greedy men." Rohan fell silent, reading the following lines to himself. Then he said, "Hildebrand was evidently the pillar of sanity in the chaotic years of the different popes' reigns, the power behind the throne. It was he who urged Pope Leo IX to give it into the keeping of Macbeth of Scotland—a man of worth and honor, a man to be trusted. The writer says that danger was too close and Hildebrand did not believe he could keep the vessel safe. He feared for the pope's life. He feared for the safety of mankind if the vessel fell into the wrong hands. Thus, the pope placed it in a reliquary and gave it to Macbeth, adjuring him to keep it hidden for *it can be neither destroyed nor freed.*" Rohan looked up. "Those final words were set off—'*for it can be neither destroyed nor freed.*'" He shook his head. "This is all very strange. Those words make it sound like it's alive."

"What is a reliquary?" Susannah asked, wishing she could read Latin, for there were several more faded lines in that cloth book.

Phillip said without looking up from the map, "A reliquary is a small chest or box that holds relics. They're usually carried from one holy place to another so worshipers can be impressed.''

Rohan turned the fragile last page. "Look, here's a drawing of a reliquary, evidently the one Pope Leo IX gave to Macbeth.'' The lines were crude, wavering, but the outline of the cask was clear. It was impossible to tell if it was wood or silver or gold. It was a rectangular cask whose sides sloped up, like the sloping roof of a house. The sides appeared to be smooth. There was a long bar across the top of the box that had small circular handles at each end.

Phillip said. "This reliquary—it must hold the Devil's Vessel. Macbeth must have seen that it was hidden somewhere in this cathedral in Dunkeld. Those final words—'it can be neither destroyed nor freed'—that sounds apocryphal.''

"It sounds evil,'' Susannah said, shivering. "I wonder what could have frightened the pope and this Hildebrand so much that they gave this Devil's Vessel in trust to Macbeth? I suppose that someone must have discovered its existence. Perhaps like Tibolt, this person believed he could control the world if he had this—whatever it is.''

Rohan was nodding. "Yes, that seems likely. Tibolt said he would rule wherever he wished to rule. He would have ultimate domination. He would be as a god.''

"What the devil is this thing?'' Phillip said, smacking his fist down on the mantelpiece. A Dresden shepherdess teetered for a moment until he righted it.

Susannah said, "Don't forget that Tibolt also mentioned 'those old fools protecting the secret.' The ring Tibolt was wearing, the ring that obviously Bishop Roundtree was wearing before his death—it has to be some sort of secret society, one founded a very long time ago to keep the Devil's Vessel hidden.''

Rohan sighed. "And Tibolt is a member of this society. Bishop Roundtree was the leader. He suspected danger. He couldn't have suspected Tibolt or he would hardly have given George half the map. He kept the other half. He must have been murdered for the other half, but the murderer didn't find his hiding place."

"Tibolt," Susannah said and shuddered. "I hope it wasn't Tibolt who killed the bishop."

"I agree," Rohan said, "but it doesn't look good."

"Who else is a member, if there are more members?" Phillip asked.

"Bishops," Susannah said. "The society must be primarily bishops. Since Tibolt is a member, not all of them are, but evidently those who aren't bishops when they're made members are destined to become bishops or to go even higher in the church."

"To become Archbishop of Canterbury," Rohan said, "has always been Tibolt's goal."

"And they wear the ring to identify each other."

"I wonder if they ever meet," Rohan said. He turned to watch his wife pacing back and forth from the fireplace to the windows. He said slowly, "We have a problem here that we must face. We must make a decision. Do we destroy this small book and this half of the map?"

Susannah stopped dead in her tracks. "Destroy? Oh, no."

"Rohan has a point," Phillip said. "The Devil's Vessel, whatever it is, poses a threat to mankind—at least that's what many people evidently believed for many hundred years. What these men still believe. If Bishop Roundtree hadn't believed it, surely he wouldn't have given George half of the map to protect its hiding place. He could just as easily have destroyed the gold key, the map, and the book himself."

"But he didn't," Susannah said. "There must have been a very good reason why."

Rohan said, "Who's to say that Bishop Roundtree was the only member of this bishops' society to have a copy of the map? Surely there must be at least one other copy of both the map and the book. What if Tibolt becomes the leader of this society? What if it is the leader who is one of the protectors of the map and the book?"

Phillip was shaking his head. "Listen to me. You actually

believe that this vessel—whatever that means—actually can confer power to the one who has it in his possession? It can actually make a man as a god? Give him ultimate domination? Surely that is taking this supposed magic to ludicrous heights.''

"I agree with Rohan," Susannah said. "I don't think we should take the chance of Tibolt's finding this Devil's Vessel." She drew a deep breath. "Perhaps in the future there will be another greedy person who breaks faith and wants the vessel. No, I think we should find it and hide it in a new place. Then we will be certain that whatever danger is inherent in this vessel will be lost for eternity."

"So you believe that it is magic? That it is a threat to mankind?"

"Don't raise that supercilious eyebrow, Phillip," Rohan said. "It was Hamlet who said, 'There are more things in heaven and earth, Horatio / Than are dreamt of in your philosophy.' I cannot discount it. There is too much in life that simply occurs—" He broke off, somewhat embarrassed.

"Things," Phillip said quietly, "for which there is no logical explanation, no framework to assuage the intellect."

Susannah turned the last page of the book. "Ah, here it is. I wondered where this vessel was hidden in the Dunkeld cathedral. It isn't written in Latin, so it must have been added later. She stared hard at the faded spidery words. She read slowly,

> "Beneath the abbot's resting stone
> Down the rotted stairs.
> Reach inside the wall that screams
> The *Devil's Vessel* lies in-between."

Rohan whistled. "It won't win any prizes for poetic merit, but I fancy that once we find the church in Dunkeld, we'll find the reliquary and this mysterious vessel inside it."

He looked first at his wife, then at his friend. He smiled faintly. "I imagine that we are going to Scotland?"

They said not a word, merely nodded.

Phillip walked to a bookshelf and pulled out a book of maps. It didn't take him long to find Dunkeld. "It's only about fourteen miles north of Perth." Then he walked to the far wall and perused his books. Finally, he selected one and thumbed through it. "Ah, here it is. Dunkeld has a cathedral, a very big, important cathedral. This is where we'll find this bishop buried. This is where we'll find the reliquary. If we can find that screaming wall."

"Look, Rohan," Susannah said suddenly, tugging on his sleeve in her excitement. "Look at what's written in these spidery black letters underneath the inside back cover. The paper came up and I could see there was some writing."

"The Bishops' Society," Rohan repeated. "Exactly as we suspected. Just imagine, a society of men who have devoted themselves to protecting this Devil's Vessel and keeping it hidden. It bespeaks a great respect, perhaps even fear, for the power of this thing."

"I would have liked to have been a member," Susannah said. "Just imagine them meeting in a private room somewhere, with curtains drawn. Do you think they still meet upon occasion?"

"Doubtless," Rohan said. "And we'll never discover who they are."

"Except Tibolt."

"Yes, except Tibolt," Rohan agreed. "Our reason for finding this ancient magic."

"A club," said Phillip. "A secret organization that's lasted probably a goodly number of years. But I do wonder how it could have lasted from the eleventh century until now. The map is old, but not eight hundred years old, nor is the book. Not more than a hundred years, if that."

"You're right," Rohan said, running his fingers lightly over the binding. "It must have been lost, then rediscovered."

Phillip said, "I believe before we travel to Scotland to fetch this reliquary and this Devil's Vessel, we should visit

an old teacher of mine—Mr. Leonine Budsman. If he isn't
a member of this club, he will know all about it. He knows
about everything. I think the more information we can glean
about this, the better. Perhaps,'' he added, frowning, ''perhaps we'll even be safer.''

They all stared at each other. Susannah knew that each
was thinking about a magic that was older than any of them
could accept, a magic that was perhaps evil, magic that, if
Tibolt found it first, could give him limitless power.

Phillip's old teacher wasn't just old, he was archaic. Rohan
was afraid to shake his hand for fear he would crush his
fragile bones. He doddered to his chair and threw back his
head—a gesture of obvious long standing—sending his thick
white hair to flow down his collar. His show of vanity, Rohan thought, charmed by the old bird. Phillip inquired po-
litely after Mr. Budsman's health. The old man just looked
at him with his rheumy eyes and remarked to the ceiling that
if he wasn't dead by the morning, it would be no fault of
his.

That sent a temporary pall of silence over everyone.

''Sir, Lord Derencourt says you know everything that's
worth knowing,'' Rohan asked, waving away the tea that a
very old butler served. ''We must know about the Bishops'
Society. Do you know anything of this?''

Without warning, Lord Balantyne walked into the small,
musty parlor. He bowed to Susannah, nodded to Rohan and
Phillip. ''This is an interesting gathering, to be sure. Good
day to you, sir. You are looking fit. You have more hair than
I do. I have always wondered about the justice of that.''

To Susannah's surprise, the ancient old man preened, actually preened, and tossed his head again. ''It's old, very
warm, close-held air that preserves hair, Balantyne. No secret
to that. All you young men stroll about in the open air and
leave the windows open at night when you sleep. No surprise
that all sorts of miserable things befall you.''

''You are doubtless right, sir,'' Phillip said. He overcame

his chagrin at seeing Balantyne so suddenly upon them and said, "As you see, we have need of you. I have told my friends that you know just about everything. Will you tell us about the Bishops' Society?"

The old man settled back into his chair, like an insect in a cocoon. He wrapped his frail, age-spotted hands around a cup of tea. "It was begun about the time I was born by a Bishop Jackspar, now long dead. I don't know how it happened, but he stumbled across documentation of this strange legend, lost for centuries. The theory went that long ago Pope Leo IX gave King Macbeth of Scotland a reliquary that held an ancient magic known as the Devil's Vessel. What exactly this vessel was I have never learned. If its essence, its physicality, is actually known by some of the members, then it has been a close-held secret. Devil's Vessel. It conjures up curious images, doesn't it? It makes one think of sorcerers and potions, wild hermits with long white hair and magic wands. On the other hand, perhaps it is indeed some sort of vessel, a cup, something that holds liquid. That sounds odd, doesn't it? What could such a cup be? Who knows?

"The only other information I have is that it is believed to be dangerous, this Devil's Vessel. Perhaps it is evil. It certainly bears an ominous name. Naturally, all of this is speculation."

Lord Balantyne said when the ancient old man remained quiet, sipping his tea, "I imagine that all this has to do with Bishop Roundtree. I don't suppose any of you will tell me what exactly this is all about?"

"You must surely know as much as we do," Rohan said.

Lord Balantyne grunted.

Susannah said thoughtfully, "Do you know any of the members of this Bishops' Society, sir?"

"Poor old Roundtree was a member. Who else? I don't think anyone knows, even many of the members themselves. They meet, I've heard, in very small groups. That was a good question, young lady," Mr. Budsman added, nodding approval in her general direction. "I, er, suppose you are young?"

"Yes, sir. Do you believe this Devil's Vessel really exists?"

"Oh, yes. Why not? Now, if you will excuse me, it is time for me to rest."

From one moment to the next, Mr. Budsman was speaking clearly and cogently, then softly snoring, his head back, his lovely white hair falling to his shoulders, his mouth open and showing three remaining teeth.

Lord Balantyne quietly led the way out of the parlor. They were met by another very old gentleman, the one who had tried to serve them tea. He managed a creaking bow. "My master helped you?"

"He did," Rohan said. "He is now reposing himself."

The old man nodded. "He does that at least twenty times a day. I believe I shall join him." The old man nodded toward the door, then tottered toward the parlor where Mr. Budsman was resting.

"A fascinating pair," Susannah said, laughing. "I wonder how long they have been together?"

"Longer than anyone can remember," Phillip said. "They were together when my grandfather was here."

On the street outside Mr. Budsman's small house, Jubilee Balantyne said, "The three of you will now tell me what's going on. Young Roland came to me, telling me that you were searching Bishop Roundtree's study. I am willing to wager that you were looking for the Devil's Vessel."

"Unfortunately we didn't find a thing," Phillip said. "We doubt it has anything to do with the bishop's murder. Sorry, Jubilee, but that's how it is."

"I don't suppose you have any new theories about who killed the bishop?"

"Not a one," Rohan said.

30

ROHAN WAS BREATHING HARD AND FAST. HE THOUGHT HE was bound to meet his Maker very shortly. He hoped it would be the right Maker. It should be, since he'd not committed any foul deeds. He thought his heart would burst from his chest. He managed to keep himself balanced on his elbows and looked down at his wife. She looked to be near the end herself, all sprawled out, so much beautiful white flesh, most of it beneath his body. Her hair was damp from her exertions, her lips slightly parted, her breathing coming in short gasps.

"A close thing," he said.

She managed to open one eye and look up at him. She looked suddenly very thoughtful. "You're still inside me."

"You really didn't have to say that, Susannah." He moaned, unable to prevent himself from jerking forward, deep and high, touching her womb again.

To his delight, her hips rose just a bit, but then she seemed to collapse in on herself. "It is too much. I am willing, but my body is beyond my control. My body is wafting away like an autumn leaf in a crisp breeze."

"That's a terrible analogy."

"It was at least an effort to describe the state of my female corporeal self. Surely it wasn't all that bad. I can't believe your powers of judgment are worth much at the moment. But I am willing to admit something, Rohan. Men are stronger. Just look at you, above me, holding up your own weight so you won't crush me. If I were the one on top, I would be plastered flat against you.''

He thought it took a lot of energy to talk. She was doing a lot of it. He pressed inward again. She moaned, then raised herself slightly to tighten her arms around his back, bringing him down on her.

''I don't want to hurt you,'' he said against her mouth, feeling all of her. Oh, God, it was wonderful.

''You're not hurting me, at least not yet. The mattress is very giving.''

''That's probably why Phillip gave us this bedchamber. He saw that I was looking at you like a hungry wolf and he thought of how we would fit quite nicely together in this lovely bed. Kiss me again. I can take no more. I know it's over for me. I want to cock up my toes with your mouth against mine.''

''How can you string all those words together?'' But he kissed her, deeply. He didn't believe it, but energy was flowing back into his body—all of his body. Was he a pig? Was she really on the edge of oblivion? She certainly seemed boneless beneath him. Then he began pushing more deeply inside her.

''Rohan?''

''Hmmm?''

''I didn't realize it until just this moment.''

''Realize what?'' He had a rhythm now, and it was slow and deep and easy, not too difficult for him to sustain.

''That I love you.''

''*You what?*''

''I know we haven't known each other for much longer than a month. Do you think it's possible I could come to love you so quickly or do you think it's lust and I am deceiving myself?''

She loved him? By God, he could now sustain the earth

on his shoulders, just like Atlas. She loved him? He slowed, shaking his head even as he stared down into her face. Her eyes were closed. No, it was lust, plain delicious lust. This sort of deception wasn't at all a bad thing. But say it wasn't just lust, but more. To be loved by Susannah, that was something else . . . he found a burst of new energy.

"Come to me again, Susannah," he said against her mouth, taking in her small cry of surprise and pleasure as he moved over her, easing his hand between their bodies to find her.

This time he knew it was all over for him. In just a moment from now he would be no longer of this earth. He would be spiritual matter. He would have to hover over her in the blankness of air and admire her as would a phantom.

If he had to become a spirit, it had been worth it. It meant he would have given his all to his wife.

He was so sweaty he knew he would slip off her. Bless her delicious female self, she was just as sweaty as he was.

"Susannah?"

No answer, just a feeble movement of two fingers of her left hand that was still resting on his shoulder.

"Aren't you ready to recite me a Shakespeare play? You were doing so well after our first time. You spoke fluently, with verve. What's the matter?"

No answer, just a small pinch of two fingers of her left hand that was still resting on his shoulder.

"Lust is a very nice thing," he said, "a very nice thing. Do you really think it's possible that you love me, that you're not deceiving yourself because I am such an extraordinary lover? I remember you did tell me I had beautiful eyes. Did you mean it?" He thought his heart would certainly explode if he kept using all his energy to form words and get them out of his mouth. Did she really love him?

She leaned up on her elbows, her eyes still closed, and bit his shoulder.

He dipped his head down and kissed her nose.

"I will think about this, Susannah. Surely a man of my

reputation is quite used to having ladies telling him every hour of at least every other day that they love him, adore him, even worship him. What do you think?''

To her own astonishment, she heaved him off her and onto his side. "You're a baboon," she said, and pressed herself close, giving him nipping bites and kisses on his neck, his shoulders, his chest. Then she reared up to look down at him. "I'm married to a baboon with a reputation. I'm sorry, Rohan, but I've thought a good deal about it. I've decided that you must rid yourself of all those other women. I don't wish to disappoint Charlotte, but I don't believe I can let you keep them about. You will be with me every night or else it won't go well for you. I can be mean if it is required of me. Very mean.''

"All right.''

"All right what?''

"No more other women.'' He yawned deeply, caressed her breast, then scratched his belly. "How could I go to another woman? You have laid me flat. I am barely breathing. I am barely still of earthly matter. You have nearly brought my heart to a standstill.''

"Good,'' she said and kissed his throat. "Goodness, I'm wet from you.''

He actually shuddered, thinking of his seed inside her body. "Don't forget that you were an active part of this delightful amusement. Not all is from me.''

He fell onto his back, bringing her with him. She snuggled against his side, her hand flat on his belly, her head on his shoulder. She loved the scent of him. She realized, of course, that he had not told her he loved her as well. It had only been a month. He had quite a number of bad habits to break before he realized how fine it would be to have her as his wife, to have just one woman—namely her—who would be with him all her life.

No, a man of his reputation couldn't be expected to so easily forget all the delightful female variety available to him on every front. She just wanted to be his only front from now on. She wanted very much for him to be content with just her in his life.

He kissed her forehead, her ear, and mumbled something about how lovely she was and how satisfied she made him feel. She fell asleep smiling, filled with hope. She dreamed of a Scottish king who was wearing not only a kilt but also blue war paint all over his face. He was yelling at soldiers, not his own soldiers, of which there were multitudes, but a huge number of soldiers facing him from a goodly distance away. His huge claymore was swinging rhythmically over his head. He was very strong. Then she saw his face a final time when suddenly he turned to face her. There was no war paint this time. It wasn't a Scottish king she saw, it wasn't Macbeth. It was Tibolt.

She prayed that Tibolt hadn't killed Bishop Roundtree, but she knew even if he hadn't been the one to strike the bishop down, he had known about it, he had approved the act.

It was odd that life could be so exciting yet so filled with tragedy, all at the same time.

She couldn't wait to see what the Devil's Vessel was.

They left Dinwitty Manor the following morning, in the dull light of dawn. Thank God it wasn't raining. It looked to be a brilliant, warm day. It would take them five days to reach Dunkeld, a town whose cathedral was founded in the year 815, Phillip had read to them the previous evening.

Rohan sighed, pulled Susannah tightly against him, and felt her soft breast against his arm. She recited quietly:

> "Beneath the abbot's resting stone
> Down the rotted stairs.
> Reach inside the wall that screams
> The *Devil's Vessel* lies in-between."

"I can't get it out of my mind," she said. "I've said it over and over to myself. I just hope that when we find something, I'll know what to do and where to go."

"I've memorized it as well," Rohan said. "We are a lot alike, Susannah. That pleases me."

Phillip rolled his eyes. "Well, I'm not like either one of you and I've also memorized the damned thing. Now, I've asked Railey, our coachman, to keep his eyes open for anyone appearing to be following us. He told me at our last stop that he hasn't seen anyone."

"Thank God for that," Susannah said. Then she added, "But I don't trust Tibolt. I really don't."

"Unfortunately," Rohan said, "I agree with you. We'll keep watching."

The Cathedral of Dunkeld, converted from a church to a cathedral in 1127 by David I, Phillip had told them, stood on Cathedral Street in the midst of thick oak and sycamore trees, gardens and walkways along the River Tay. Rising beyond the river's shores were mountains covered with huge tracts of forest. The cathedral was badly in need of restoration, a project, the local innkeeper told them, that would happen in its own good time, as did everything of a civic nature. But Rohan's eye found the ancient parts of the cathedral from the twelfth century. Certainly their abbot must lie there.

The innkeeper was master of one of the Little Houses that were lined up on Cathedral Street. They had been rebuilt, the innkeeper told them, after the devastation caused by the battle of 1689. In the inn there were only six small rooms, a tiny dining room, and a taproom.

Susannah was so excited that she could barely pay attention as the innkeeper, truly a kindly old man, continued in his thick brogue: "Ye probably wonder aboot this battle in 1689—'twere between the Highlanders—Jacobites the lot of 'em—and the extremist Covananters. Aye, the Highlanders fought their way into the town, but the Covananters fired everything. The town were gutted, ye ken. Burnt to the ground and below. The Jacobites withdrew and the cause of James II was lost fer good. William and Mary were assured of the English throne."

"And the cathedral," Phillip said as the innkeeper opened the door to a tiny, quite charming little room with beamed ceilings, a narrow bed, and a long, skinny window that gave onto the River Tay. "What happened to the cathedral?"

" 'Och, it survived well enough, as ye can see, but there's much work to be done."

"And the original twelfth-century portions, which are they?" Rohan asked as the innkeeper opened another door onto a larger bedchamber, the bed at least large enough for Susannah pressed against her husband. There wasn't enough room for an armoire, so the innkeeper had put a row of pegs on the walls. There was a lovely silk screen in the corner of the room. It was charming, but Susannah didn't believe she wanted to spend the rest of her life here.

"The nave piers are from the whole way back, for surely they're older than the graves sunk around the cathedral. Most of the cathedral dates from the fourteenth century. Ye'll see that the nave and aisles had no roof since the savage Reformation desecration of 1560."

This was one too many desecrations for Susannah. She walked to the narrow window, pulled back the soft white lacy curtain and stared out onto the beautiful river, surrounded with gardens and so many trees.

Rohan had thought he was tired to his very bones when they had finally arrived in the small town of Dunkeld. But now, looking at that beautiful old cathedral, with piles of rubble lying about, parts of the roof caved in, yet still looking glorious and proud, he wondered what it had looked like before the desecration of 1560—or was it the desecration of 1689?

Phillip was standing in the doorway of their bedchamber, rubbing his hands together, his eyes sparkling. "Anyone ready for a stroll?"

The cathedral rose elegant and ruined from the tree-shaded lawns beside the Tay. The townfolk eyed the two gentlemen and the young lady. There was suspicion on some faces and smiles on others. The town was very small but busy, with drays, one carriage, and at least a dozen horses. Housewives moved through the streets carrying baskets, wearing old-fashioned gowns with shawls that crossed over their bosoms and tied at their waists in the back.

"I hadn't thought of this," Rohan said. "We're drawing attention. Damnation, I don't see any way around it now. Even if we adopt the local garb, there will still be attention."

"Then let's act like newlyweds and visit the cathedral."

Rohan laughed down at her, took her hand to rest it on his forearm, and the three of them strolled to the cathedral. "You, Phillip, can be her brother."

They walked through the ruins, ever watchful. " 'Beneath the abbot's resting stone,' " Rohan said. "There's a tomb with the remains of Wolf of Badenoch, whoever that was."

They walked gingerly through the twelfth-century nave, careful where they stepped because many varieties of birds had made their nests here and the floor stones were splotched white with their droppings.

It was Susannah who saw it, a tomb so flat into the stones that the years had very nearly erased the face of the man buried there and his name.

Rohan went down on his knees, took out his handkerchief and carefully wiped the filth away from the inscription.

"This is the tomb of the abbot of Dunkeld, Crinan by name. He died in 1050, at least seventy-five years before the cathedral was built. So his body was transferred here then, out of respect. One of his followers who shared the secret must have placed the Devil's Vessel beneath the stone. There must be a passageway or catacombs beneath the tomb."

"Yes," Rohan said, "and there must also be some way to get the tomb stone up."

They were all on their knees feeling carefully along the edges of the tomb. It was Rohan who whistled. "I think I've found something."

"Not yet," Phillip said, rising quickly. "We have company."

A group of holiday visitors was coming into the church, a curate leading them. He was telling them the history of the cathedral and about each separate devastation. They could do nothing until the group left, which took another half hour.

Then there were some boys who came in to chase birds.

Finally they were alone again. "Now," Rohan said, "now." He was on his knees, feeling again at the particular spot at the upper left-hand corner of the tomb. "It's a latch of some sort, well hidden, not meant for common use. Do you see anyone else about?"

"Not a soul," Phillip said, coming down to his haunches beside Rohan. Susannah hovered over him.

He lifted the latch ring. At first nothing happened. He gripped it more firmly and tugged hard. There was a faint groaning sound.

Phillip added his strength, and together the two men pulled straight up on the latch ring. Slowly, the entire stone lifted upward. "Ah," Susannah said. "The rotted stairs there were in the clue. Would you look at them? Oh dear, we didn't bring candles and it's pitch-black down there."

They rose and dusted off their hands. "It's better that we come back when it's dark," Rohan said. "I don't want to chance someone walking in on us. Also, we have no idea what awaits us at the bottom of those steps."

"A wall that screams," Susannah said and shuddered. "My imagination won't let go of that one."

"That's a mystery that I can't wait to solve," Phillip said, rubbing his hands together. They returned to the Jacobite Inn in the third Little House on Cathedral Street. Although their dinner was tasty, none of them was particularly interested in food. Finally it was late enough.

The men dressed in dark clothes. Susannah fidgeted with her gown, a pale silver that seemed to her to be as bright as a beacon. "No, it's fine," Rohan told her, pulled her against him, and kissed her mouth. "You are so sweet," he whispered against her lips. He was pleased to feel the telltale tremor go through her. Phillip just grinned at them.

"You truly shock me. I am an unmarried man. I am all alone in the world, innocent of the ways of married people. This enthusiasm of yours is daunting." He sighed deeply. "I wonder if I will ever find a lady who will wish to indulge me the way you do Rohan, Susannah."

"I will speak to her when you find her, Phillip. I will explain things to her. I will tell her how to keep her husband blissfully happy and content."

"Thank you." He gave her a flourishing bow. "Now, let's fetch the ladder from the stables."

"Good idea," Rohan said.

31

IT WAS AFTER MIDNIGHT. THERE WASN'T A SOUL ON THE street. There wasn't a soul in the cathedral. A full moon overhead cast eerie shadows throughout the roofless parts of the cathedral, sending shafts of light through shorn beams, deflecting them into strange shapes. Birds, disturbed, fluttered overhead. Shadows seemed to move without reason. Susannah pressed close to her husband.

"This is a place of worship," she whispered, "yet I'm scared to death."

"Me too," he said and gave her a quick hug. "I'm glad to see it's only we and the birds who are here. Ah, here is our abbot's tomb. Do you think he knew about the Devil's Vessel?"

"According to history, Abbot Crinan was one of Macbeth's enemies," Phillip said, carefully setting down his ladder. "Macbeth killed his son, you see, and after Macbeth was elected to the throne, the abbot tried and failed to overthrow him. I think rather that his tomb is just a convenience to cover whatever is beneath."

"We will soon know."

A pigeon flapped directly overhead. Phillip grunted when a glob of white landed on his coat.

Rohan and Phillip tugged on the latch ring until, creaking,

groaning from hundreds upon hundreds of years of disuse, the stone sealing the tomb inched upward. "Careful now," Rohan said. "We'll have to pull it entirely back."

Beneath them was a well of darkness. Susannah brought the branch of candles closer. Shadows cut across rotted steps that led into the pit.

"I hope it's not too deep for my ladder," Phillip said and swung it down into the hole. It hit the wooden stairs and they fell away, crumbling. "Thank God. It's not that deep. There, solid ground."

Rohan and Phillip turned as one to look at Susannah.

"Don't either of you even consider it," she said, hands on her hips.

"You're wearing a bloody gown. You'll trip all over yourself and break your neck."

"No, I will tie my skirts up." She pulled a long strip of fabric from her cloak pocket. "I came prepared. No more arguments. This involves me as much as it does you. More than Phillip. You will not keep me out of the adventure."

"But we need someone to keep watch, to warn us if someone comes, to make certain the stone doesn't climb back up and fall down upon us."

"Leave her be, Phillip. Will you at least let us go down first, Susannah?"

"If you swear not to leave me up here."

"I swear." Rohan took off his coat and laid it down upon the stones. He climbed down a good half-dozen steps of the ladder, then said, "All right, give me the candles."

Before Susannah handed the branch down to him, she looked about the cathedral one last time. She saw no one.

The black well lit up, but still there was nothing to see. Just more black beyond the candlelight.

"What do you see?"

"Nothing yet, Susannah. I'm on solid ground now. It's sandy. I'm looking as far as the light allows me. Still nothing. It seems more like it's a cavern than a catacomb. I'd say that we're about eight or nine feet down."

"Hold, Rohan. I'm coming."

Soon Phillip was also on the ground. "God, it's dark down here."

"I'm coming!"

Rohan nearly dropped to the ground when he realized that she'd tied her skirt up about her waist. He put out his hands to clasp her waist, but she said, not even looking at him, "I am all right. I will not be a burden. Stand aside."

When she reached the ground, Susannah calmly untied her skirt and let it fall to the ground. "I hope there are no rats or insects."

"I will shout for them to crawl up my leg if I see them," Phillip said. "Now, which way? This passage seems to go in both directions."

Rohan was silent a moment. "We are beneath the nave, approximately where the railing for the choir would have been. I think we should go toward the altar." He took the candle branch from Phillip and turned left. "I hope there is no draft. I would hate to be entombed down here in the dark."

The passageway was no more than six feet wide, and eight feet high. It became wider in some spots, then narrowed again. The walls were smooth. There were as yet no turns. The ground remained sandy. They were walking away from the river. The air was heavy with age, with dust that hadn't stirred for many hundreds of years. Each breath was difficult.

"Now we're looking for the wall that screams," Phillip said.

A spiderweb looked like a delicate spray in the candlelight. Rohan ducked away from it, Susannah following him.

Suddenly the passageway twisted sharply to the right and came to a dead end. In front of them was a wall. It was filled with skulls, dozens and dozens of skulls.

Susannah sucked in her breath, refusing to scream. Rohan raised the candle branch high. "This is either a catacomb or was used as one during one of this town's eternal devastations. I wonder if the bodies are piled behind the skulls."

"The wall that screams," Phillip said, taking a step closer. "Impossible to tell how old these things are. They might even be before the devastations."

"The clue said to reach inside the wall that screams," Susannah said. "Oh, dear."

"Well, hell," Rohan said. He handed Susannah the candle branch and began to roll up his sleeve. Phillip followed suit. "I will do this as well," Susannah said firmly and set the candle branch on the ground.

"There isn't enough room," Rohan said. "Stay back, Susannah, and hold the candles high. That's it. Don't complain. You don't have to do every dirty thing to be part of the adventure. Allow the men to wallow in some of the filth."

The feel of crumbling skulls was probably the most repulsive sensation either Rohan or Phillip had ever experienced. "Oh my God, there are so many teeth, Rohan. I keep shoving them out of the mouths."

There was no hope for it. Skull fragments fell to the sandy floor. "It goes way back," Rohan said, trying not to think so much about what he was doing. "My arm's all the way in now, at least as far as I can reach. The rest of the bodies are here. Doubtless the designer of this place believed that having all the skulls face outward would protect it from violation."

Susannah said from just behind Rohan, "Remember the last line of the clue says, 'the *Devil's Vessel* lies in-between.' "

"In between what, I wonder?" Phillip said, reaching so far in with his arm that a skull was not an inch from his face.

"I've been thinking about it," Rohan said, still digging as gently as he could, but it didn't matter, bones crumbled or fell forward and onto the floor. "This in-between business, it's got to mean in between the bones and the back wall, doesn't it? Could it possibly mean something else?"

"Well, well, I think I've found something that isn't a bone or a skull." Slowly, Phillip drew out a cask—a reliquary. It was identical to the drawing in the cloth book.

It was so very old, Phillip was afraid it would crumble in his hands. Very gingerly he set it on the ground.

Rohan and Susannah were on their knees beside Phillip, staring at the beautiful, impossibly ancient wooden cask with its inlays of gold and silver along its sides.

Rohan was gently pulling at the thick bar that held the cask together at the top. "It won't come free," he said. "Damn, it would be immoral to break into it. I wish we had the bloody key."

"Wish no longer, Rohan. I've got the key. Here it is."

It was Tibolt Carrington. Susannah was so surprised that she whirled around and fell onto her bottom. She felt a skull crush beneath her. She stared incredulously at Tibolt, who was standing not four feet away from them, a very large and ugly gun in his hand. In his other hand he was waving the tiny gold key on a golden watch chain and holding a single candle. Only one candle. That was why they hadn't noticed any light other than their own branch of candles.

Rohan rose very slowly. "Tibolt. We didn't believe you were following us. We looked."

"Hello, brother. And I suppose this is the equally infamous Phillip Mercerault?"

Phillip also rose, moving slowly a bit further away from Rohan. "Yes. You, I imagine, are the faithful, devout clergyman who is so beloved by his flock?"

"More devout than either of you philandering bastards. Rohan, has Mercerault slept yet with our mother? No, I doubt it. He must be all of twenty-six or twenty-seven—too old for dear Charlotte."

"You will have to ask her," Rohan said.

"Perhaps I will. I knew you would realize it was more than likely that I would follow you here. Both Teddy and I were very careful. We knew you were coming to Scotland. It was just specifically where in Scotland that we didn't know. We kept well back.

"Now, I would like for Susannah to hand me the cask. I have many times wondered if it really existed, if such a miracle could have survived, buried away, rotting. It's so very old. And now it is mine."

"And the Devil's Vessel is inside," Rohan said, his eyes on his brother's gun.

"I pray that it is. I saw the three of you pay a visit to old Mr. Budsman. I suppose he told you all he knew about the Bishops' Society, all about Bishop Jackspar. What you can't know is that Jackspar evidently eased the last days of an old Knight Templar. The man told him of the vessel and gave him the ancient writings, the key, and a crumbling map, begging him to keep it safe, saying that the future of humanity would now lie in his hands. He said that the Templars had guarded the secret for many centuries, but there were none left to trust. Then he died—that or Jackspar murdered him. Who knows? It was Jackspar who made up the cloth book and wrote into it all that had been in the crumbling original parchment. You found the book, didn't you?"

"You know that we did. It provided the clue to find the cask."

"I knew when I saw the three of you coming out of Bishop Roundtree's house, trying to look as if you'd found nothing at all. It amused me because none of you could prevent the excitement from bubbling out of you. You found the other half of the map as well?"

"Yes, it was in the book," Rohan said.

"But I had the other half. How did you manage?"

"I drew it on another piece of paper," Susannah said.

"So you have uses other than the obvious ones. Hand me the cask now, Susannah."

"Wait," Rohan said. "Just a moment, Tibolt. Tell us now, just what is this Devil's Vessel? How does it come by its power? What is the bloody thing?"

"I told Susannah about its power. With it, I will rule the world. I will live forever. I will be as a god. There is nothing more to tell you."

"Yes," Phillip said, "there is. What is it?"

Tibolt laughed. "You will see soon enough if the vessel is indeed what I believe it to be."

"Where is Theodore Micah?"

"He is waiting for me in the cathedral. He is keeping a watch."

"Once I give you the cask, what will you do?"

He looked down at Susannah. "I won't kill you, though you're worth little enough. As for you, my brother, no matter that you're as lecherous, as filthy and perverted as our parents. But no, I am a man of God. I won't kill any of you."

Phillip took another very small step. Now he and Rohan were in a half circle around Tibolt.

"Enough, dammit. Give me the cask, Susannah. Be very careful with it. It's older than anything one can begin to imagine."

Very slowly, Susannah picked up the cask. She was terrified that it would crumble in her hands, but it didn't. It was heavy. She took the two steps to Tibolt.

"You can't take it. You don't have a free hand."

He realized she was right. She would have sworn that he flushed. "Take it beyond me and set it on the ground. Soon you will see the Devil's Vessel."

Tibolt handed Susannah the watch chain. "Here is the key. Open it, Susannah. Don't try to be a heroine or I will shoot your husband."

"He is also your brother."

"I won't kill him, but I will shoot him in the knee. He will never walk again. Perhaps some of his dozens of women will even remove themselves. Who knows?"

She took the chain from him. The tiny gold key felt very warm in her fingers. She was pleased that her hand wasn't shaking. She was scared to death. How to stop him? What to do? She saw that Rohan and Phillip were well separated now. But still, if one of them managed to get to him, he would be able to shoot the other.

"I need more light," she said after a moment of running

her fingers over the thick bar of wood that held the cask together. "I can't find the hole for the key."

Tibolt moved beside her. He leaned down and placed his single candle on the ground. She watched his fingers move slowly over the thick wooden bar. He didn't find the hole either. He sighed. "Everything is difficult in life. I am only twenty-four, and yet I have already learned that."

"Wait until I find you," Rohan said easily, "and then you will truly come to comprehend how difficult life can be."

"The philanderer speaks. A threat. Ah, yes, I know that you are a noted member of Gentleman Jackson's salon, that few want to take you on in the ring for fear of having their jaws broken or their teeth knocked out. I wouldn't be surprised to learn that you've shot some husbands after you've seduced their wives."

"Is this truly what you think of me, Tibolt?"

Tibolt shrugged. "You are like our parents. They are immoral, wicked. The old man died, but she lives on. Ah, I have found it. The bar is simply a decoration. The keyhole is right here, at the juncture where the cask slopes up." He looked away just for a moment.

Susannah lunged upward, throwing herself at him, knocking him onto his back, both her hands grasping at the hand that held the gun.

"You little bitch!" He struck her hard in the jaw with his fist. She cried out, then sprawled unconscious on top of him. "No, brother, don't you move or I will kill you. Stay back, both of you."

"No, Rohan, no." Phillip's voice was quiet, calm.

"Now, let me roll her off me and we'll see what we've got here. Stay back, Rohan, she is all right."

He was soon on his knees in front of the cask. "Both of you, back up another two steps. That's right, against all those lovely skulls."

Tibolt fit the tiny key into the lock. Nothing happened. He cursed, gently working the tiny key back and forth. Finally, the key turned.

It was now or never, Rohan thought, ready to lunge. At that moment, Tibolt raised his head, smiled and pointed the gun at Susannah's chest. "Yes, Rohan, just try it."

Rohan held up his hands, not moving. He watched Tibolt push up on the lid of the cask. He saw that Susannah had raised herself up and was staring at that cask.

"Are you all right, Susannah?"

"Yes, but a bit blurry."

Tibolt wasn't looking at any of them now, but he held the pistol close to Susannah's breast.

He stared down into the cask. His eyes widened, overwhelming joy broke over his face. "The Devil's Vessel," he said, his voice exultant. "Yes, yes, it is exactly as I had imagined it to be." He was caressing it with his hands. "So old, so blackened, just as it should be. I never believed it had anything to do with the devil, but we will soon see."

"What is it?" Rohan took a step forward.

32

"DON'T MOVE, BROTHER." SLOWLY, TIBOLT LIFTED A very old goblet from the reliquary. It was gold, but so old that it was seamed in black. It was plain, no ornament, no jewel to decorate it. It stood about eight inches high. It was tarnished, but somehow it seemed to shine in the dim light.

"So this is the Devil's Vessel," Phillip said. "It is indeed a vessel, a goblet, a very old cup. But what is its significance? What *is* it?"

"We will soon see. Take the goblet, Susannah. Yes, be very careful. As Derencourt says, it is so very old." Tibolt reached into his pocket and drew out a flask. "Hold the cup steady." He poured only a few drops into the goblet.

"And now, we will see," Tibolt said. "You will drink from the goblet, Susannah."

Rohan was frantic. "No, Susannah, don't drink!"

Tibolt cocked the gun and aimed it at her head. "Actually, Rohan, it's holy water, not poison. Now, Susannah, you will drink or I will shoot Rohan."

"Susannah, you will not give yourself in my place. You will not be the sacrifice. Throw the goblet down."

"If you care so very much for him, Susannah, you will drink now or he will die."

She looked at Rohan. He was pale, ready to leap upon

Tibolt, but for Phillip's hand on his arm. "It will be all right," she said, "I promise you it will be all right." Then she smiled at him and raised the goblet to her mouth. She let the cool water touch her lips. It tasted strangely sweet.

"Drink it all," Tibolt said. "Now, damn you."

She tilted the goblet and drank down the few drops, then she swallowed.

Tibolt said nothing, he only stared at her. "Put the goblet back into the cask."

She did as he instructed.

"Now stand up, Susannah."

"It was poison, wasn't it, you damned little sod?" Phillip grabbed Rohan's arm, jerking him back.

"Wise of you, Derencourt. I hesitate to make my brother a cripple." He turned to Susannah. "You look quite fit."

Susannah was looking only at her husband. "I will be all right. Don't worry, Rohan."

Tibolt was right, Rohan thought. She looked quite fit. Her eyes were sparkling with light and determination. Then he prayed. Who the hell knew what that liquid was?

Tibolt said nothing more, merely backed away from the three of them and leaned against the passage wall. He kept the gun pointed at Susannah.

Suddenly, he shouted, "I was right! By God, those old fools had it all wrong. For centuries they had it wrong! I've won!"

They stared at him in confusion. Rohan yelled at him, "What do you mean, you're right and the old fools were wrong? What are you talking about?"

"This," Tibolt said, scooping the reliquary up under his arm, "isn't the Devil's Vessel. Oh, no."

"What is it?" Susannah said. "What is that goblet? Why did you make me drink holy water out of it?"

"I made you drink the holy water to ensure that it wasn't a tool of the devil, fashioned to destroy anyone who drank from it. That's been the legend passed down—that anyone who drinks from the goblet dies a vile death. But it was a lie, passed down by all those old fools so no one would search for it. Just look at you—you didn't die, you didn't even sicken. You survived. You look healthier than you did before you drank from it. There is this light in your eyes that you didn't have before.''

"This is nonsense, Tibolt," Rohan said.

Tibolt only laughed. He paused a moment, looking at each of them in turn. "This divine magic isn't dangerous at all. This will give me immortality. This will make me the most powerful man on this earth.''

He laughed even as he grabbed Susannah's arm and jerked her toward him. "You want to know, don't you? You want to know what it is, what it represents. The lot of you are too stupid to figure it out. None of you has the vision to grasp what you were really dealing with, much less understand it.

"All the clues were there, all of them, but you saw nothing. Now it doesn't matter. It's mine, all mine!''

"What is it, damn you?'' Phillip shouted at him.

Tibolt ignored him, saying, "Now, Susannah, you and I are leaving here. Don't move, Rohan. She's coming with me. Any of you think to attack me, think again."

She didn't move.

"Get up and walk or I'll shoot your damned husband! I will kill him, you know.''

"Susannah, love, are you all right?''

He'd called her love. She raised her head and gave him a blinding smile. "Yes,'' she said. "I'm all right. Don't worry about me.''

"He had better worry about you, Susannah. If you don't do exactly as I tell you, I will hurt you badly. To kill a little whore like you wouldn't bother me at all. You do know that now, don't you, brother?''

Rohan nodded. "Yes, but it's difficult to accept. When did you change, Tibolt?'' He wondered if Tibolt would answer him. He desperately wanted time, just moments of time in which Tibolt might look away or trip or be distracted enough so that he could leap upon him. To his surprise, his brother laughed, then shook his head. "You fool. I didn't change. I simply went underground and waited. I knew there must be something for me, and there was." He whispered, "I have it now, no one else. It's mine." He shook his head, his eyes clearing. "Now my every wish will come true."

"You will not tell us what it is?"

They knew Tibolt was playing with them, taunting them. He just smiled at them, clearly enjoying himself.

"Did you kill Bishop Roundtree?"

Tibolt flicked a glance toward Phillip. He laughed again and shook his head. "No, you'll not want to believe it, but it was his little butler, Roland, who killed him. I came in on them after the little sod had struck the bishop in the center of the forehead. He was whimpering like a lost little boy, the pitiful sod, was rocking back and forth over the bishop's body while he sobbed in his hands. I told him to keep his mouth shut and he just might get away with it. Then I searched and searched the bishop's study. I found nothing, as you well know, since you did. I left but moments before you arrived. I assume that Roland had cooked up an excellent tale for you and the magistrate?"

"I don't believe you," Susannah said. "No, Roland was much affected by his master's death. He found his body and vomited. He cried and cried. He was distraught. No, it wasn't Roland, it couldn't have been."

"The bishop," Tibolt said, contempt deep in his voice, "was a damned pederast. Roland suited his fancy for a while, and so he took him in. But then he found Teddy, through our careful planning, naturally, and was preparing to send pretty little Roland on his way. It still amazes me how Teddy managed to flirt with the old bastard without vomiting, but he did. The bishop wanted him powerfully bad. And when the bishop told Roland, the miserable little bastard killed him in a jealous rage. Enough of this," Tibolt said. "The two of you stay right where you are. Susannah, carry the branch of candles. I'll be right behind you." Then he blew out the single candle. Soon Rohan and Phillip were plunged into darkness.

"Stay by the skulls, gentlemen, or I'll shoot the little whore."

Rohan immediately took off his boots. He held them in one hand and began walking soundlessly after Tibolt. Phillip quickly followed suit.

The walk back to the ladder seemed to take only a moment. Suddenly he heard a shriek, and Susannah came hurtling into him, knocking them both back against Phillip.

They heard Tibolt talking to the man above him—it had to be Theodore Micah. They heard the ladder being hauled up, the scraping of the wooden rungs against the edge of the open tomb.

"What is the damned cup?" Phillip shouted up at him.

Tibolt laughed, an eerie sound, for he was now above them. "Good-bye, Rohan." Then, louder than a clap of thunder, the stone crashed down.

They were plunged into the blackest pit of hell.

"I really don't like the dark," Phillip said. "Even as a boy I hated the dark. Really."

"Susannah, are you all right?"

"Yes, but I agree with Phillip. I've never seen black this black. It's very frightening."

"That's my hand, Rohan, not your wife's."

"Oh, sorry. At least we're all here and alive."

Susannah said slowly, "He toyed with us. He isn't sane, Rohan. We must get out of here and find him. We must. We must save the cup."

He couldn't see her, but her voice was intense, filled with purpose. "Yes, you're right. He's proved that he's quite mad. Do you feel all right, Susannah?"

She felt his fingertips tracing over her face. She kissed his palm. "Oh, yes, I feel wonderful."

"Now let's get out of this place. We've been in one direction, and it ended in a wall of skulls. We must go the other way."

"I don't suppose I could hoist you up on my shoulders, Rohan, and you could push open the stone?"

"We could try, but I doubt it."

"If we don't find another way out," Susannah said, her fingers still clutching his sleeve, "we can try it. I'm very strong. You'll see."

They all held hands, Susannah in the middle. They stayed against one wall. Rohan felt ahead with his free hand. "Damn," he said after feeling a spider run over his knuckles. "I wish I had my gloves on."

They walked for what seemed to be forever.

The ground sloped upward. Suddenly Rohan ran straight into a wall of dirt and rock. They searched the surface of that rock with frantic hands. "Nothing," Phillip said finally. "I fear we are trapped."

"No," Susannah said very clearly, "we're not."

"I know you're trying to keep our spirits up, love, but—"

"No," she said again, her voice as radiant as a blinding light. "Come, we must go back to the wall that screams."

"But we've already been there," Phillip said. "I think we should position ourselves beneath the abbot's tomb. Rohan can lift me and I can try to shove it open."

"No, it is too heavy. Come with me." She left them. They heard her light footfalls fading down the passageway.

"She's running?" Phillip said. "But it's dark."

"She'll hurt herself," Rohan said and hurried after her, stumbling, cursing, but now slowing.

"Susannah! Wait for me!"

But she didn't. They found her at the other end of the passage. She was leaning against the wall looking toward the skulls.

It was odd, but it wasn't completely black now.

"Our eyes must have adjusted," Rohan said slowly. "I can begin to make things out."

"Yes," Susannah said. "It's really quite clear now. Oh dear, I can't reach the latch."

Rohan grabbed her and pulled her against him. "It's all right, love. We'll get out of here. Don't worry."

"I'm not worried." She pulled away and smiled up at him. "You've got dirt all over your face."

"You can see me that clearly?"

"Oh, yes, and Phillip, your hair looks gray from all the dirt. Now, Rohan, go stand directly in front of the wall of skulls. Then reach in your arm as far as you can and press it to the wall. You will find a small latch. Pull it toward you."

He stared down at her. He could barely make out the outline of her head. "What are you talking about? You're ill, aren't you?"

"No, do it, please. I want to leave this horrible place."

"But I don't understand—" Phillip began.

It was then that Rohan realized there was something different about her. There was a soft nimbus around her. He shook his head. No, that couldn't be right. But why could they see? She was smiling at him, utterly calm, her expression serene. He had never seen her look more beautiful.

He said very slowly, so scared it shook him to his very being, "You can see everything clearly, can't you?"

"Yes. Don't worry. Go pull the latch toward you, Rohan. It's been used only once, many hundred years ago, but it still works. It's very smooth, so you won't cut yourself."

She knew, he thought. She saw the latch. He walked toward the wall of skulls. Slowly he felt his way to the edge and forced his arm through. He felt nothing but the powdery dryness of the wall, dusting his probing hand. He felt nothing more. Yet he knew she wasn't wrong. He pressed deeper, a skull against his face now.

Suddenly he felt a small knob. His fingers closed around it. He slowly pulled it toward him.

"You have something, Rohan? You found it?" Phillip was crowding behind him. There was utter disbelief in his voice. "No, you couldn't have found anything. There isn't any way that Susannah could know anything, is there?"

"Quickly," Susannah shouted, "jump back!"

Neither man questioned her. Just as they stumbled backward, there was a loud creaking sound, then a massive crash, bones slamming and grinding into each other, smashing against the floor below.

"My God, what is happening?" Phillip said, lurching back toward the wall of skulls. He reached out his hand. "The skulls are gone. My God, there seems to have been some sort of trapdoor beneath all those skeletons. When you pulled the knob, Rohan, it opened the door and all the skeletons fell through. But to where?"

Susannah said calmly from behind them, "Just to the floor beneath, not more than five feet down. Now, push the knob back, Rohan, quickly, quickly."

He did. The open doors pulled back up. They stared into a black hole. "What is this?" he asked slowly. "What has happened?"

"There's an escape door at the back of the opening. All of us will fit, don't worry. Quickly, we must leave this place."

Rohan turned around to face her. He saw her clearly, as if she were standing in a pool of light. He felt something calm fill him, felt the panic of the unknown recede. He knew in that moment that all of them would survive this. He knew that whatever had happened to Susannah would probably fade, but the part of it that had shown the strength in her, the inherent goodness, would never be gone. He accepted it, and was immensely grateful. He grinned at her. "Come, madam, let's get out of this place." He lifted her up into the opening. He and Phillip were right behind her. The space was nearly high enough so that they didn't have to bend. Rohan looked back into the passageway. There was a dim, eerie light, but it was blacker than a pit deep within the opening where all the skeletons had lain for so very long.

"Ah, here it is," she said. "Stand back just a bit, Rohan. Yes, that's good." In the next instant, a narrow, low door swung inward. Beyond was another passageway. "Don't worry," Susannah called over her shoulder. "This one opens onto the edge of the river. Everyone believes it to be a simple cave that goes in only about fifteen feet."

Suddenly there was clear, fresh air on their faces. They all breathed in deeply.

"Here," Susannah said. "Help me move these rocks and branches. They're only partially hiding the opening."

It was still dark, the moon high in the sky, when the three of them stood by the river, winded, filthy, and very relieved.

Rohan pulled Susannah down beside him. Phillip sat cross-legged next to her. He cleared his throat after a moment, cleared it again, then said slowly, his voice a croak, "I do not understand what happened, Susannah. You knew what to do; you saw everything. I don't understand."

Rohan had pulled her against his chest, folding her in his arms. She said, "I don't either, not really. It's just that everything was suddenly so very clear." She shrugged. "It's difficult to explain. But I simply *saw* everything and I knew that we would survive. There was simply no doubt in my mind."

Rohan said, "I know what Phillip is feeling. It bothers anyone when he can't logically explain something. If he can't feel it or touch it or understand it."

She merely leaned over and kissed his dirty cheek. "I know, but we can't sit here much longer. We must find Tibolt. I don't really want to, but I know that we must. We must get the vessel from him. He can't keep it."

Phillip said, "He left us to die in that passage, Rohan. I'm very sorry."

"So am I."

Rohan looked down at his dirty wife, at her right sleeve that was torn off her shoulder, drew her against him again, and kissed her once, then again, more thoroughly this time.

"It was the goblet, wasn't it?" Phillip said, his voice stark, layered with fear, fear of the unknown, fear of what none of them understood.

"Yes," she said, her voice jubilant. She was nearly dancing, laughing now. "It was the goblet. But now I know what it is—at least I think I do."

Both men spun around to stare at her.

She said simply, her voice calm and sure, "It's the Holy Grail."

The only sound breaking the stunned silence was the croaking of a frog in the water reeds close to Phillip's boots.

"But that's a myth, a legend," Rohan said slowly, trying to grasp the truth of it, trying to make it fit with what he knew. "Surely that can't be true."

"Yes, it is. That's why Tibolt let me drink only a few drops from it. He feared that if he gave me more that I would gain the power, not he." She pulled away from Rohan and jumped to her feet. "We must hurry. We must get the Grail from him. You know he would abuse it endlessly."

Rohan rose slowly, dusting the dirt off his britches, more to give himself time to think, time to come to grips with this business that he couldn't understand, much less accept. "Yes," he said finally, "we must find him."

"We've got to go back to the inn and clean ourselves."

Susannah was shaking her head, nearly jumping in her anxiety. "No, who cares if we're on the dirty side? I want to find Tibolt. We must find him. He might escape. We can't allow him to escape with the Grail."

"I'm sorry about Tibolt, Rohan. He did leave us to die and then, well, somehow Susannah saw things we didn't, and that hidden door saved us. But there is no reason for him to leave Dunkeld until morning. Let's go get ourselves clean. Then we'll find him."

They met again at the front of the inn twenty minutes later, the three of them as clean as one basin of tepid water could make them.

Where were Tibolt and Theodore Micah?

33

IT WAS JUST AFTER THREE O'CLOCK IN THE MORNING WHEN they walked to the Dunkeld stable.

It was a moldering old building of wattle and daub with a thatch roof. It smelled of decades-old sweat, cracked leather, linseed oil, and horse manure. A horse neighed when they eased inside. They could see very little even with the stable doors wide open.

"I hope the owner doesn't come down with a gun," Phillip said quietly. He gave Susannah a brooding look. "I suppose if the owner does come, then she can simply wave her hand at him and he'll forget we're there. That or he'll offer us his services with a smile. I don't like this, Susannah. It makes me feel cold inside."

"I as well, Phillip," Susannah said.

"We will get through this," Rohan said. "Come along, you two, and keep quiet." Even as Rohan turned away from them, he heard his mother telling him about her vision of him and a young lady in a cave and they'd been frightened, only Susannah hadn't been frightened at all.

They stepped into the stable. "There are no empty stalls," Phillip said after exploring. "One of the old mares actually bit my arm, then she smiled at me. I wonder if there are some oats about for that old girl over there. I think I'm in love.''

Rohan sighed. "No clue here. If one of these horses is Tibolt's, I don't recognize him. There must be other inns in the town. There is only this one main street. We will simply walk the length of it. If he's still here, he must be in another inn.''

They did wait the one minute it took Phillip to feed some oats from a half-hidden bag, which was probably meant to be wholly hidden, to the sweet old mare who had bitten and smiled at him. They heard him say, "I will send for you, my pet. You are meant to be mine. Rohan says I must have a wife. I believe that to accustom myself to the concept, I will begin with a mare. I wonder if a wife will bite, then smile.'' He turned to face them. "Damnation, for those few moments I forgot. The Holy Grail,'' he added on a near whisper, "it exists, it has powers a man can't accept, and yet it is real. All right, let's get to it.''

"Yes. Now,'' Rohan said to Phillip once he'd rejoined them, wiping his hands on his breeches.

Ten minutes later they stood in front of the Abbot's Inn, the very last building on Cathedral Street. It was set back a bit from the street, very old, three stories high, and completely dark, except—

"Oh, goodness, look,'' Susannah whispered, "a light. In that third-floor window, there on the corner.''

Phillip looked down at the gun he'd just pulled out of his pocket.

Rohan cursed, and said in a low voice, "It's got to be them. Damn, there's no hope for it. My brother is a rotter, more than a rotter. He would have left Dunkeld faster than a snake if he'd thought we could have escaped. This is too much to bear. But we must bear it. We must have the goblet.'' He realized he had great difficulty calling the goblet what it was: the Holy Grail. It was too wondrous, too fantastic, too otherworldly. He agreed with Phillip: it wasn't easy to accept even though they'd seen it with their own eyes.

The front door of the inn was securely locked, just as the front door of their inn had been. They found an unlatched window in the Abbot's Inn just off the big old kitchen that had soot and stains older than the three of their ages piled on top of each other.

"We need a candle," Susannah whispered, once they stood in the middle of the kitchen, which smelled of old grease, fresh carrots, and sour ale. "We can't take the chance of bumping into things and perhaps waking the owner."

Rohan grunted and began to root about for a candle. "Aha, here we are." He raised the candle for them to see. Once they got it lit and the flame protected with Rohan's cupped hand, they made their way toward the inn stairs. They were narrow, very old, and creaked louder than a shrieking maiden aunt with each landing footfall.

No one came out yelling at them, thank the good Lord. Rohan was beginning to wonder if anyone at all was staying in this inn. It even smelled empty, except for that fresh carrot smell in the kitchen.

They walked to the chamber at the very end of the dark hallway. A thin line of light showed beneath the old door.

Rohan drew a very deep breath. He pulled Susannah against him and whispered against her ear, "You will stay out here. There is no way you will come into that room. If you even try it, I will become irate. I will seethe. My belly will cramp and bow me to my knees. Swear to me you will remain out here."

It was difficult. He could see that she wanted to argue, since she wanted very much to be in that room, to face down Tibolt and Theodore Micah. She'd been in on everything since the beginning, and he hadn't, at least not the three robberies at Mulberry House. His look never wavered. Finally, giving in to that look, she nodded. "All right, I will stay here, but only because the room is probably small and there would be too many of us and it could be chaotic."

''That's exactly what I was thinking,'' Rohan said. ''Stay pressed against the wall.'' He looked at Philip, who was smiling very grimly.

He handed Susannah the candle. He nodded. Phillip very gently turned the doorknob. The fools hadn't even locked the door. They'd been that sure of themselves and their safety. That made Rohan so furious he could have howled with it. The door wouldn't have been unlocked if they expected any trouble. It was difficult to accept, but he had to. Tibolt had left him to die—had left all three of them—without a backward glance.

Very carefully, he eased the door open, then paused at the sound of arguing.

''You expected brilliant gems, but that doesn't matter. It's the Holy Grail, you bloody fool! You will have as many gems as you desire.''

Theodore Micah was silent for a moment, then he said thoughtfully, ''I think, Tibolt, that I don't wish to be your lieutenant, your flunkey. I want to be the one to hold the Grail, the one to drink holy water from it. I want the power, the immortality. You said that George's slut came to no harm after drinking from it. You have proved that this Devil's Vessel was all a sham carried through the ages to keep robbers away from it. You proved that it is indeed the magical Grail.''

''I can't let you do that,'' Tibolt said slowly. ''It is mine, only mine.''

''It belongs to neither of you. Don't move, either of you, or I will blow your brains out of your heads.''

Tibolt and Theodore Micah were standing in the middle of the floor, the cask lying on a tabletop between them. They didn't seem to be doing anything except staring into that cask.

''Rohan,'' Tibolt said, stumbling back. ''It can't be. There was no way out of the catacomb. I checked. Theodore looked and looked. There was no way out!''

''It appears you were quite wrong, both of you. There was a way out and we found it.''

Theodore Micah made a dash for his gun, which lay on top of the bed. Phillip kicked his arm away. He didn't care if he'd broken the bone. Micah yelled in pain. Rohan called out, ''Susannah, come in and close the door. Yes, everything's all right now. Now, stand against the door. You were right, there's very little room in here.''

As for Tibolt, he didn't move, except for shifting his gaze back and forth from his brother to Susannah, who was now standing with her back flat against the closed door. As for Teddy, his face was drawn in pain. Mercerault had broken his arm with that kick. It had sounded like a very solid kick.

He turned to Rohan. ''There was no way out. I left you in total blackness. How did you do it?''

Rohan wasn't about to tell him that Susannah had seen through the darkness, had seen the small knob against the wall with all the skeletons and skulls pressed against it, that she had seen the ancient door that led to freedom. No, first he wanted to have the Grail.

Theodore Micah was whimpering in pain. Tibolt turned on him. ''You stupid puking little sod. Shut up!''

''I'm not a stupid puking little sod. What I am is unlucky to believe such a coddy bastard as you. So they couldn't escape, could they? What about your blessed Grail? It probably has no more power than a paper knife.''

''Phillip, why don't you quickly search these two?''

Phillip leaned down to Theodore Micah. He found a knife strapped to his ankle. ''Nasty little thing,'' he said, pulled it out of its strap, and shoved it into his belt after he'd straightened. ''Tibolt,'' he said quietly, ''don't move. It would give me too great a pleasure to batter you to a pulp.''

Even though he was wounded, Theodore Micah had other plans. In a flash, he grabbed the reliquary and threw it with all his strength at Rohan's arm, sending the gun flying. He lunged at Susannah, pulling her back against him in an instant. He pressed a small blade against Susannah's throat.

"Damn you, where did that second knife come from? How can you move your damned arm? Phillip broke it."

Theodore Micah laughed. "You did know that I am an actor, did you not? An actor learns many things, my lord. No," he said quickly, turning to face Phillip, "don't move or I will cut her throat." He continued in a meditative voice, "The first woman whose throat I sliced lived in Honfleur. I had taken a packet over to meet a smuggler friend of mine. She listened to a private conversation. I will never forget the gurgling sound she made and all that bright red blood. Heed me, gentlemen, for I am serious here. You may take your damned brother, my lord, but I will have the Grail. It's there on the floor. The key is right beside it. Now hand it to me."

Rohan was breathing hard, nearly beside himself. He should have tied Susannah up and left her with Phillip's mare in the stable. Damnation! How could he have allowed this to happen twice? He was a damnable protector. He saw no hope for it. "Don't hurt her."

"Then you'd best hurry, my lord. Give me the cask."

Rohan didn't even open the lid, just picked it up and rose slowly.

"Give it to me and be careful."

Susannah gave a small gasp. Rohan and Phillip saw the bright red blood from the nick in her throat.

Rohan said, "If I give it to you, what will you do?"

"I must take her with me, but I swear to you that I won't kill her if you stay back."

"You swear?" Phillip said. "You wretched little bastard. How can we believe you? You're a damned criminal. You're lower than a bloody slug."

"I swear I will not kill her. Give me the cask or you will have a dead wife, my lord."

Rohan handed him the cask. It was heavy. How could it be so heavy with just that old beaten-up gold goblet that held more power than any man could imagine?

"No!" Tibolt shouted. "He can't have the Grail!"

It was Tibolt, holding a gun, taking a step toward Theodore Micah. "You can't have it, you bastard!"

Suddenly Susannah crumpled to the floor. Micah was so startled that he let her fall. The next instant, Tibolt fired and the bullet ripped through Micah's throat. There was a hideous gurgling sound, then Theodore Micah whispered, "I was a fool to trust a man of God. Look at you, more the devil you are." Suddenly, his shirt was wet with blood, and he fell heavily to the floor.

"Good, the little bastard's dead. Back into the bedchamber, all of you. I couldn't kill you before now even though I wanted to. I imagine that any second now we will have company. Get back, damn you!"

Tibolt shoved his brother back into the room and quickly pulled the bedchamber door closed behind him. He heard a man yelling, then another. A door was yanked open.

"What's going on here?"

Tibolt stuffed the gun in his coat pocket. "I locked the thieves in my bedchamber. They shot my friend here. Quickly, where is a magistrate?"

"Aye," a little man with a huge sleeping cap said, his thin legs bare beneath a voluminous white sleeping gown. "I'll fetch the feller, but chances are, he's on his butt, his head pickled with the brandy he pours into his mouth, ye ken?"

"No, no, I'll fetch him. Just keep those thieves in my bedchamber. Don't take any chances!"

In the next moment, Rohan threw open the door. The four men, all in their nightshirts, two of them with caps on their heads, gawked at the man who held a gun and looked more furious than a man just cheated at cards. "Damnation," Rohan shouted. "He's gone! Quickly, we've got to get him. He's got the Grail!"

A man and a woman came dashing out of the bedchamber after the first man. They paid no attention to the men in their nightshirts. The guests at the inn were left standing over a man obviously very dead, all his blood flowed onto the floor.

• • •

"He's not got but ten minutes on us," Phillip shouted, as Rohan tossed Susannah into her saddle.

"Thank God the stable owner saw he was traveling the road east," Susannah said, stuffing her skirts around her legs.

They were off, the bright moonlight illuminating the narrow road in front of them.

They said nothing, merely pushed and pushed the horses until Rohan pulled his horse to a halt and said, "We must let them rest for a moment. Susannah, are you all right?"

"Yes, but we must find him. We must get the Grail from him."

"What if he's already drunk from the Grail?" Phillip said. "If he has, then we're lost. And why wouldn't he? He could have drunk from it the moment he was out of the inn. He could be waiting just up ahead, waiting to smite us."

"No," Susannah said very quietly. "No, I just realized that he hasn't yet drunk from the Grail. He can't, you see."

Both men whirled about to face her. "Why the devil not?" Phillip nearly shouted at her.

"Because," she said very simply, "he left the holy water. I just remembered seeing the flask on the bed."

"She's right," Rohan said. "My God, she's right. And that means that he's got to find holy water before he can drink from the goblet."

"And that means a church," Phillip said. "There was a church in Dunkeld. Why didn't he simply get some holy water there?"

"Because he knew we'd be right behind him," Rohan said. "He didn't want to take the chance. Let me think. All right, we're nearly to the coast. Just up ahead is the small town of Monfieth. He'll think it's safe for him to stop there and steal some holy water."

"We haven't much time," Susannah said, kicking her mare in the sides. "Hurry! We can't let him drink from the Grail."

There wasn't a church within Monfieth. There was an ancient abbey just away from the town lying on the cliffs overlooking Buddon Ness. The sky was lighting, the moon faded away now. It was nearing dawn.

As they came around the bend of the narrow, rutted road, the air was strong with the smell of water. Then suddenly they saw the old abbey, standing tall, most of it in ruins atop a small promontory, backing to the very edge of the cliffs. They saw Tibolt's horse, its reins loose, feeding from the brothers' garden.

There were no lights in any of the abbey windows.

Then, Susannah saw Tibolt, carrying the cask under one arm and a beaker filled with water in the other hand. He was racing toward the ruins that held the highest ground. He turned then and saw them.

They heard him laugh. "Come," he shouted to them. "Come!"

Their horses joined Tibolt's in the brothers' garden. Rohan and Phillip pulled out their guns as they ran after him.

He was standing atop a fallen beam. They watched him pour the holy water into the goblet.

"No!" Susannah shouted. *"No!"*

Tibolt raised the filled goblet, laughed in triumph, and drank it down.

34

THEY SLOWLY WALKED TOWARD HIM, KNOWING THERE was no hope now. He'd won. The world had lost.

"Oh, God," Phillip said, staring at Tibolt, who was standing tall and silent, waiting, just as they were waiting. "What will he do?"

Then suddenly Tibolt began to tremble. He quickly set the Grail on the stone. He was shaking so hard that the glass beaker fell to the rock-strewn ground. He cried out, clutching his chest, then slammed his palms against his ears. Susannah took a quick step toward him, but Rohan grabbed her arm, pulling her back. "No," he said. "Don't move. Oh, God, what has he done? What is happening?"

Tibolt raised his trembling arms wide, staring up into the sky. "God, I have drunk from the holy chalice. Grant me power. Grant me immortality."

He stopped trembling suddenly. Now he shuddered, his body heaved. He seemed to draw in on himself. He yelled into the silent heavens, "Grant me my rightful power!"

They moved closer, slowly, very slowly, not taking their eyes off Tibolt.

The horizon was a vivid pink with slashes of blue and gray in the sky above. The sun was just beginning to rise behind him, beams of light coming through the ancient ruins of the abbey.

Suddenly he became utterly still, as if he were a stone, as if he were frozen in place. Slowly, slowly, he began to change. He began to shudder again until his whole body was dancing with the power of the convulsions.

Then Tibolt was no more. Shadows and light played over him, seeming to erase him. It was as if a giant hand were molding him, then remolding, pressing here, pushing out there. He was changing.

Suddenly they were staring at Susannah. Tibolt had turned into Susannah. It made no sense. It was terrifying. "No," Rohan whispered at the ghastly image of his wife, weaving back and forth on the beam in front of them. "No."

The false Susannah said from where she stood on that rock, "Now I know how you got out of the catacombs. All that power you had with just a few drops of holy water from the Grail. Now I see it clearly."

The false Susannah suddenly began to choke, her hands clutched at her throat, but she began to change again, now slowly becoming a very old man dressed in one-hundred-year-old garb. His voice sounded as ancient as the rock upon which he stood. "I must give the Holy Grail over to you. Guard it well, bishop. Guard it well. Tell no one what it really is. Call it the Devil's Vessel. Tell everyone that whoever drinks holy water from it will die a horrible death."

"The old Knight Templar," Phillip whispered between frozen lips.

Then the old knight was gone and in his place was a vigorous man in his prime, dressed oddly, and there was a crown on his head. His head was thrown back, his voice rang out proudly. "Aye, I accept the Grail. I will guard it with my life. I will take it home to Scotland. No one will ever find it there."

"Macbeth," Susannah whispered. "It is surely Macbeth accepting the Grail from Pope Leo IX."

"He is becoming everyone who touched the Grail," Rohan said, not wanting to believe it, but even as he stared at the ancient king of Scotland, he was changing, changing yet again. He was an old man now, dressed like figures in a drawing Rohan had seen of the ancient disciples. He was garbed all in white. Sandals were on his feet. He wore a long beard.

"Who is he?" Susannah whispered.

"I don't know. Perhaps someone close to Jesus after the Last Supper?"

"I am Joseph of Arimathea," the man screamed at them, his voice thin from age. "Jesus gave me the holy vessel after he'd drunk from it. He told me to collect his blood and pour it into the vessel. I buried him and I took the vessel."

Then Joseph of Arimathea was no more. Flashes of other men, all biblical in their dress, passed in front of them, the vision quickly moving from one to another.

There were twelve of them.

Finally, there was utter stillness. Tibolt had no human form now. All features that had made him human were gone from his face, smoothed out as if he were now stone. His arms and legs froze against him, losing definition. He had the look of a pillar, frozen, lifeless. Then in the next instant, the pillar simply disappeared. There was nothing.

The Holy Grail still sat atop the rock. Suddenly, from behind it slithered a serpent, green and scaled, its head huge, its mouth open, hissing toward them. It slowly began to wind itself about the Grail, its thick body overlapping on itself as it circled once, then again and again. Finally its huge head was resting on top of the cup. The mouth opened. What came out was Tibolt's voice.

"It spared you. I know now why it spared you. I know all now, but it makes no difference, for I am no more."

The sky, which had just an instant before been glistening in the dawn sun, blackened. Thunder boomed. Lightning split the darkness, great streaks of it that sent the lake below foaming. Suddenly a crater of light appeared over the serpent—

wide, fathomless. Then there was blackness again, as if it were midnight.

They could see nothing.

Susannah turned her face against Rohan's chest. She felt the stiffness of him, the shock of what they had seen. There came a soft rumbling noise. The rumbling continued until the rocks began to shake. One ancient arch crumbled and fell over the cliff into the lake below. The massive rock upon which Tibolt had stood, upon which the hideous serpent had wound its body around the Holy Grail, was empty.

There was no serpent, no Holy Grail.

They jumped when the rock stood upright. The white became brighter, blinding them, then it seemed to spread, opening itself.

The rock disappeared into the blinding white.

The rumbling stopped abruptly.

There was nothing.

The sun appeared, the day continued its dawning. A sparrow sounded in the silence.

They walked as one to where the rock had stood. It looked as if nothing had happened here for more than a hundred years. Even the reliquary was gone.

Susannah cocked her head to one side and pointed. She leaned down and picked something up. She turned wordlessly to Rohan and held out her hand. In the center of her palm lay the tiny golden key.

"The key to the reliquary. It was left for us."

"No, Susannah, the key was left for you," Rohan said.

Phillip stared at that key, then at where the rock had stood. The broken glass beaker lay in shards on the ground.

Susannah was looking off into the distance, through the abbey ruins, over the water. She swallowed, clutching the golden key in her hand. "The Holy Grail had known only good until Tibolt took it."

"All the forms Tibolt took," Rohan said slowly, "they were the people who had held the Grail, who had held the Grail or drunk from it. The reason you weren't harmed, Susannah, is because you are good. And that is what Tibolt saw so clearly at the end.''

Phillip shook himself. ''I want to leave this place. There's nothing more for us here.''

''You're right,'' Susannah said. ''Both the good and the evil are gone.''

''That's not quite true,'' Rohan said, pulling his wife against him. ''The three of us are here. We survived.''

He closed his hands over hers. He thought he felt the warmth of the tiny golden key she still clutched in her palm.

He knew in the deepest part of him that they would never speak of this again. He also knew that the tiny golden key would bind the three of them together for the rest of their lives.

''Let me deal with my little angel here first,'' Susannah said, lifting a squealing Marianne into her arms. As for Marianne, after spending no more than fifteen minutes with her mother's undivided attention, being rocked and praised and told an exciting story of nothing that actually happened, Marianne was ready to be set down and see to Rohan.

Rohan bounced her on his knee until she tired and leaned back against his chest, still certain that she had his full attention. Her fingers were in her mouth.

Toby said, ''I have tried to train her not to put her fingers in her mouth, Susannah. But whenever I pull them out, she howls, and I finally gave up. Charlotte said her ears couldn't take the punishment. I'll try again, Susannah, but we have to be alone. She doesn't howl when we're alone, isn't that odd?''

''Not at all,'' Susannah said. ''Why would she howl if she didn't have an audience?''

''Ro-han!''

''Yes, my perfect little princess?''

''Lunnon. I want to go to Lunnon.''

''We will,'' Rohan said slowly. ''We will go there very soon now.''

"I don't suppose that fine tale you just spun for your daughter has any resemblance to the truth," Charlotte said.

"No, Mother," Rohan said. "Actually, I am sorry, but Tibolt is dead. It was an accident. He tried to save me, but fell over a cliff himself. There was no treasure. It was all a legend, a myth, if you will. There was nothing, just betrayal. But never forget, Mother, that Tibolt died as he lived. I would that you and Toby not speak of it more."

Susannah merely nodded.

"I don't like this," Charlotte said, then broke off when they saw that neither her dear son nor her daughter-in-law was going to say another word. Tears welled up, but she managed, for the moment at least, to sniff them back. She knew there was more, but the result was Tibolt's death. He'd died trying to save his brother. As Rohan had said, Tibolt had died as he had lived. She swallowed again and said, "I am relieved that Tibolt didn't turn out to be like George. That would have broken my heart, I think."

A month later, Lord and Lady Mountvale left for London, taking their daughter with them. It had taken nearly that long for Marianne to learn to call Rohan Papa.

Colonel Nemesis Jones proposed to Charlotte on a bright, warm day that even held a rainbow after a light rain shower. All thought she would accept him, but she didn't. She left for Venice instead, taking Augustus, the Welsh footman, with her, to act as her bodyguard, among other things.

Mountvale Townhouse in London had been stunned to hear of the baron's nearly five-year-old marriage, even more stunned to learn of his little daughter.

But that response was nothing to the reaction of Society. There had been endless foment, endless speculation, endless dire predictions on what would come of this obviously doomed marriage, made when the baron was naught but a wild young man. Well, truth be told, he was still a wild young man, but now he was more a discreet wild young man. Wasn't he? Then—five years before—he'd just been wild, headstrong and impulsive.

However, Lady Sally Jersey, an unchallenged leader of Society, just chanced to speculate that perhaps the baron was done sowing his wild oats. Perhaps that was why he had brought his wife and little daughter out of exile. He was a reformed philanderer.

No one agreed with that—there was no joy in it, no promise of wickedness. No one, however, disagreed with that assessment either—at least not to Lady Sally Jersey's face. No one had the nerve.

All waited avidly to see the new baroness. All waited to see how long it would be before the baron would tuck his wife away again and resume his dissipations. Surely all his mistresses—numbered in the legions—were pining for him.

Pulver, the baron's gaunt-faced secretary, said to his friend David Plummy, "They've been here for four days now. I don't understand any of it. The baron hasn't left the house at all in the evenings unless it is to accompany his wife somewhere. He's given no hint when he plans to resume his former life. When we were at Mountvale House, he was a model of husbandly rectitude. It depressed my spirits."

To which David Plummy said, "Buck up, Pulver. He'll be going to that other little house of his any night now. He's a man who loves women, isn't he? Isn't he the firstborn of his parents? Isn't he a satyr and thus must have infinite variety? With a man of his reputation, it shouldn't be much longer now. There simply wasn't a woman in the country that he wanted."

That was hard to believe, surely.

But Pulver wasn't so very certain about that assessment. He had seen the baron and baroness together. She wasn't as beautiful as many of the women the baron had been seen with. She was pretty enough, but not dazzling, like, for instance, the baron's mother. But there was a kindness in her, a quickness about her, a way of speaking, that had the baron laughing more than anyone had ever heard him laugh. The two of them also appeared to spend quite a bit of time in the baron's bedchamber during the middle of the day.

It was a mystery to everyone.

As for the little girl, Marianne had decided that she fancied Pulver. It quite convulsed the poor man, sending him into the kitchen to hide.

"She's a child," he said to Tinker, his lordship's valet, "a *child,* and yet he lets her sit on his lap, he lets her touch his face with those little fingers of hers that are always in her mouth. She shrieks—*shrieks*—with laughter and he appears to enjoy it. Sometimes she shrieks with a tantrum. The baron just kisses her and tells her to be quiet, and she does. It is amazing, Tinker. And now she fancies me. I cannot bear it, Tinker. It is not in my nature to abide a little child."

But within a week, Pulver was quite delighted whenever Marianne touched her wet little fingers to his cheek. The first time she kissed him, he nearly swooned with delight. But whenever she stomped her foot and yowled, he was out of the room, calling for the baron. It was Toby, however, whom Pulver came to admire greatly, even though he was only a little boy. They read together and went to the British Museum together. Rohan remarked to Susannah that he had never before seen his cadaverous secretary so animated.

As for Susannah, she was scared to her toes every time they stepped into the house of another member of London Society for some sort of ball or soiree or card party. She knew that everyone believed the poor baron had made a grave error. She knew that everyone believed the poor baron had gravely compounded his error by suddenly producing this wife and little girl. She knew that everyone believed he would soon have her and Marianne gone again so he could resume his dissolute ways. It depressed her profoundly.

"Chin up," Rohan always told her before he helped her out of the carriage. On this Wednesday night, at Almack's on King Street, her chin was already so high he feared she would hit the top of her head on the carriage door frame.

Rohan grinned at her as he clasped his hands around her waist and very slowly lifted her down, watching her eyes darken at the feel of him. He wanted to tell her that it made him feel like a bloody king when she looked at him like that, but he said instead aware that his voice sounded low and raw, "Did I tell you that you looked rather lovely this evening? I like your hair in that coronet with all the blue ribbons threaded through the braids."

"Yes, but you didn't really mean it. The ribbons match the blue in the gown. Ah, Rohan, you're trying to build me up so I don't run and hide in the ladies withdrawing room."

"Found out," he said and kissed her. "Who made you so cynical?"

"I am just a realist."

"What you are is a ninny," he said and kissed the tip of her nose.

This was observed from a short distance by Sinjun Kinross, Countess of Ashburnham, who showed no reticence at all. She yelled out, "Rohan! Is this your wife?"

"This, my love," Rohan said to Susannah, who was staring at the beautiful young lady who was bearing quickly down on them, "is Sinjun Kinross. She is a favorite acquaintance of mine. That gentleman striding after her is Colin Kinross, her husband. I doubt he ever catches her unless she wants him to." He grinned at Sinjun and released his wife. "Well, little one," he called out to the very tall young lady, "you're looking fit as ever. Colin, you still seem to be breathing evenly."

"I shouldn't let Sinjun near you," Colin Kinross said, eyeing Susannah with interest. "But she said that since you're married, she's safe from all your amorous advances, not that she can ever recall you even attempting to advance, which disappointed her. She imagined herself ugly and uninteresting. It took me nearly a week to dissolve that silly notion."

"Susannah," Sinjun said after a moment, "this can't be all that easy for you, particularly given Rohan's reputation.

I think that we should march right in this dismal place and take the dragons head on. What do you think of that?''

To Rohan's delight, Sinjun Kinross took Susannah under her wing and led her about, as if she were a proud mother presenting her little chick.

Lady Sally Jersey, when presented to Susannah, said, ''Tell me, my dear, have you yet met your incomparable mother-in-law?''

''Yes, ma'am. I am blessed. Charlotte is the sweetest, kindest, most beautiful woman I have ever known. She has been wonderful to both me and Marianne, our daughter.''

Lady Jersey obviously wasn't expecting such an enthusiastic review. It somewhat curdled her smile. Charlotte wonderful? Sweet? Well, Charlotte was many things. Perhaps this was simply another side of the incredible woman. ''Hmmm. Ah, but what does dear Charlotte think about being a grandmother?''

''She and Marianne—our daughter—are great friends.''

''Just imagine,'' Lady Jersey said, ''our dear boy a father. And he was just a very young boy when he married you and sired the child.''

''I was a younger girl than he was a young boy, ma'am,'' Susannah said, her chin well up. ''But I ask you,'' Susannah continued, wearing a fat smile now, ''who could turn down Rohan? He has a charming, wicked smile. I much enjoy being his wife and always have.''

Lady Drummond Burrell, another patroness at Almack's, said, ''Surely dear Charlotte wouldn't allow herself to be dubbed a grandmother. She is far too beautiful, too accomplished, too—ah, there are so many things that Charlotte is. But a grandmother? That is difficult to comprehend. Surely she can't accept it with equanimity.''

''Perhaps it is difficult for any lady to accept yet another generation. It means that we are all growing old, surely a disagreeable thought. Actually, ma'am, Marianne calls her Charlotte. It seems to suit both of them.'' Susannah smiled with just a bit of effort at Lady Burrell, a very plain lady who had the tongue of an adder and all the warmth of a lizard and who, for some reason unknown to anyone, had managed to become one of the most powerful Society ladies in London.

"Your story is so very romantic," Lady Jersey said, sitting forward, her eyes avidly fixed on Susannah's face. "Here our dear baron was riding *ventre a terre* to visit you whenever he wasn't visiting one of his many ladies here in London."

Lady Burrell said in a clipped voice, "I imagine the dear baron would only ride *ventre a terre* for a month or so. This marriage has lasted close to five years. Surely his visits weren't all that regular, particularly after the child was born. Gentlemen do not care for pregnant ladies or for infants."

Rohan, bless him, seemed to know whenever Susannah was close to falling into a social abyss. He came to stand beside his wife now, saying easily, his charm so palpable that Susannah felt herself glowing, "With Susannah, it was always *ventre a terre*. It's odd, but my horse Gulliver loves her as much as I do. I could have slept in the saddle, and he still would have run his hooves off to get to her."

He smiled that wonderful smile of his at Mrs. Burrell. "Actually, when you meet my daughter, you will want to do nothing more than have her lay her wet little fingers— she sucks her fingers, you know—on your cheek. It is endearing."

Even Mrs. Burrell smiled, an event, Roland later told Susannah, that should be recorded for posterity, since no one would believe it.

35

THE FOLLOWING MORNING TOBY CAME INTO THE BREAK-
fast room, carrying Susannah's racing kitten, Gilly.

"Cook was feeding him little bites of roast pork," Toby
said. "I have told her that Gilly is a racing kitten and must
be kept lean and tough, but she just laughs and says the little
mite would race only if he could see food as a prize."

"That isn't a bad idea," Rohan said, taking the kitten,
who wasn't so much of a kitten anymore. He held the cat up
and looked him right in the eye. "Is this true? Will you run
only for food?"

Gilly batted Rohan's nose.

Toby said, "Gilly really should be in training, Susannah.
He really should be taking classes with the Harker brothers.
They both believe he has potential as a first-rate racer."

"What do you think, Rohan?"

"I would just as soon return to Mountvale House. We've
been in London a good two weeks. It grows wearing. We
can return to the country for a month or so, give our Gilly
all the racing instruction he needs, visit a few cat races, perhaps do some sailing, go on some picnics."

"What about me, Rohan? I just got a letter from Mr. Byam
yesterday. He says I need to resume my instruction as well
if I'm to go to Eton soon."

"I believe the decision is made. We will leave on Friday."

The future champion of racing-cat history meowed loudly and dug his claws into Rohan's britched leg.

The baron had finally left without his wife. Pulver was relieved that things were returning to normal, yet at the same time, he was disappointed. Very disappointed.

The baron was a married man. He had a child. He had a brother-in-law who was a brilliant little chap. The baron shouldn't be visiting one of his many women. But he was gone, just after dining with the baroness and his brother-in-law, playing for half an hour with his daughter.

Pulver went to the baron's study and pulled out some accounts, but his study of the figures was cursory. He was distracted. He wondered what the poor baroness was doing, what she was thinking. Finally, he couldn't bear it.

He walked out of the estate room, bound for the drawing room to console the poor wife, when he heard a sweet laugh. He turned to see the baroness skipping down the stairs, wearing a cloak, obviously preparing to leave herself.

Had his lordship indeed married himself to a lady like his own dear mother? Could she be leaving to meet a lover? He felt himself swell with pride. No, not yet. She had not yet borne The Heir. Surely she knew that.

"Ah, Pulver. Marianne is sound asleep. Toby is reading. I am going out, as you can see. But I will return, as I'm sure the baron will as well."

With those few words, she was gone.

The coachman pulled up in front of the charming Georgian house on Grace Street, not more than four streets from Cavendish Square. Susannah's eyes glittered. She looked down at the slip of foolscap in her hand. The coachman obviously knew this house.

She had no idea what she would find. Her husband had left the note for her on her dressing table, telling her to come to this address. Surely he wouldn't have a mistress here, would he? Yet it was a charming house—a second house—

and what man needed another house unless it was to keep a mistress in? Still, she was smiling when she lightly tapped on the brass knocker on the front door.

He himself opened the door. "Good evening, my dear. I'm delighted you found my note and hied yourself here."

"Hello, my lord. Is there a naked woman in the bedchamber? Or is she in the drawing room, posed seductively on a settee? Or perhaps in the kitchen sprawled out on a table?"

He struck a pose, looking very disappointed. "There wasn't even a single woman anywhere the last time I looked." He kissed her lightly, then removed her cloak and tossed it over the back of a chair in the small entrance hall.

"Come, Susannah."

He held her hand, drawing her into the cozy drawing room that was lit by myriad branches of candles. The room was dominated by a large desk that was piled with papers. There were also papers on the floor all around the desk.

There was no naked mistress displayed on the settee.

There wasn't even a portrait of a naked woman over the Italian marble fireplace. The wallpaper was a pale blue, not a vulgar scarlet.

"I decided to show you rather than tell you."

"Show me what? Tell me what?"

Rohan looked strangely embarrassed. "Actually," he said slowly, "it's time I told you the truth. Phillip was berating me, told me it was time, but I wanted to wait until the moment was right."

What was going on here with her utterly perfect husband? "Well, you know, I have found that the truth is usually exactly the right thing, at least most of the time."

He drew a deep breath. He was having difficulty continuing.

She said nothing, merely smiled up at him, waiting. Finally, she said, "Do you know that you are more handsome right this moment than you were just two hours ago at dinner?"

"You won't make this easy, will you, Susannah?"

"Certainly. I wouldn't want you to think me a difficult, uncooperative wife. Now, husband, why the devil do you have this charming little house? You have no need of a second house only four blocks from your town house. Why do you have that big desk in the drawing room? What are all those papers?"

He drew that deep breath again. "I hope you will not be disappointed, Susannah, but the truth of it is that I'm not a womanizer. I'm not a philanderer. I haven't a single rake's bone in my body. I haven't bedded every lady in London. My wild oats could fit into my coffee cup."

Now this was a kicker. She just stared up at him. "But a man of your reputation—"

"Exactly," Rohan said. "It's my reputation, not me."

"But why? Why this pretense? Why make everyone believe you're a satyr, a rake, a—, a—"

"Run out of words? There are more, but perhaps you can forget even those you've already spoken." Rohan leaned down, kissed her quickly, then took her hand.

"It's very simple, really. I didn't want to disappoint my parents. They desperately wanted me to be just like them. And believe me, there was no deception involved in their respective reputations. I knew soon enough that Tibolt and George weren't going to follow in their footsteps. That left me. But you see, it just wasn't me—not the real me."

"But you make love to me like you've done it more times than a man should be entitled to make . . . oh, dear." She stared up at him, chagrined at what had spilled out of her mouth.

"Well, yes, but that's different. I told you the truth about that. My father did turn me over to one of his mistresses when I was fourteen. I girded my loins and did my best. Actually, truth be told, I quite enjoyed myself. But I have never had the compulsion to bed every woman I laid eyes on. Just you. Every time I look at you I want to throw you over my shoulder and haul you off to my bed. But only you, Susannah, only you."

To his worried eye, she looked unhappy, as if she'd expected mutton for dinner and gotten trout instead.

"Oh, damn, I'm sorry if I've disappointed you. I'm sorry if you wanted to satyr, Susannah. I'm sorry if you regarded me as a challenge."

She gave him a radiant smile. "Oh no, Rohan, you have made me the happiest woman in Britain. But you know, I'm not surprised. You have simply never behaved as a man of your reputation should. I love you, all of you, no matter who or what exactly you are."

"Show her your bloody drawings, Rohan. Then in the morning if there is no blasted rain, take her about and show her all the gardens you've designed."

Susannah turned to see a plump, very pretty woman standing in the doorway. The woman gave her a smile and a curtsey, "I'm Lily, his lordship's housekeeper. I keep his little house here all neat and tidy."

Susannah decided at that moment that nothing more would surprise her. "Hello, Lily. I'm Susannah Carrington."

"Yes, I know well enough who you are. Well, at last, Rohan, you're confessing all your lack of sin. Not one sinning bone in his entire body, my dear. Now, would the two of you care for some tea?"

While Lily was fetching the tea, Rohan showed Susannah the drawings on the big desk. "This garden will be for Lord Dackery, for his house in Somerset. You see that it won't be terraced like our garden at Mountvale House. It will be sprawled out, with high hedges separating the various different aspects of the garden. There will be a pond here, a rather large one, I'm planning, with all sorts of lily pads and water reeds around it, to make it look natural. Lord Dackery is a lover of roses, so I've planned many rose bowers—see here, one just here, one some twenty feet away from it, a bit larger, with a lovely bench and several chairs beneath it. It would get the benefit of the afternoon sun. It's also on a slight incline facing west. There is also a delightful breeze many spring and summer days from this vantage point. What do you think?''

She was just staring at him. ''You have visited Lord Dackery's estate?''

''Certainly. We will begin work in a couple of weeks.''

She threw her arms around him. She nuzzled his neck. ''Oh, I love you. You were made for me, just me. I should love to be involved. You know that I am very good with plants and flowers, that they grow wildly for me because I have my mother's affinity for plants. Oh, please let me—''

He was laughing, then hugging her tightly against him. ''What if I hadn't found you?'' He kissed her ear, the line of her smooth jaw, then her mouth. ''Do you know that you were made for me as well?''

Lily cleared her throat from the door.

''A man of your reputation, my lord, shouldn't be showing so much affection to his wife. It would give your poor mother a spasm.''

''My mother, as you well know, Lily, is made of stern stuff. She turned only a bit pale when she first found out she had a granddaughter.''

Lily laughed. ''I will let the both of you alone, then. Welcome, Susannah. Enjoy your husband. He is really quite an excellent man. The good Lord knows, there aren't all that many of them running about loose.''

''He's not loose,'' said Susannah.

Rohan laughed again and hugged her tighter.

Susannah said against his neck once Lily had quit the drawing room, ''How long have you known Lily?''

''Hmmm, let's see. About seven years, I think. She was my mistress, and then we simply became quite used to each other. She's a very good friend and helps me maintain my satyr's reputation.''

''Rohan, will you ever tell Charlotte that you're not a philanderer?''

''I've thought about it, but I decided not to. Why make

her miserable? There's too much misery already with her other two sons. You won't mind, will you, Susannah?''

Susannah gave a deep sigh. "I will maintain your fiction. Charlotte will perhaps come to admire my tenacity since she will see that I'm obviously keeping you happy. But you know she will console you because you don't have a dozen mistresses. You must not laugh, Rohan.''

"Never," he said. "Now, let me show you where I'm putting my bearded irises, my spiderwort, and my Canterbury bells. Ah, would you like some candytuft? It's a lovely flower—''

"Candytuft is what I was admiring in my own garden when you first came to Mulberry House! Oh, goodness, Rohan, this will be such fun. I hope my candytuft is still flourishing.''

"Possibly not. It requires a lot of care. If you like, you can oversee its planting yourself. Do you think our children will take after my parents or after us?''

"Maybe, my lord," she said, kissing his chin, "if we are very lucky, they will be a little of both. Oh, Rohan, shall we try some running myrtle? I never had a bit of luck with it, but perhaps at Lord Dackery's estate—''

"If not, we will try to see if the myrtle will run at Mountvale House. If not, we'll try devil's guts—now there's a dandy flower.''

She hugged him close and said against his chin, "I wonder how Charlotte is faring with Augustus.''

"With any luck at all, he's not dead of exhaustion yet.''

36

GILLY STRAINED TO BREAK FREE OF SUSANNAH'S ARMS. SHE kissed the top of his head, whispering, "No, no, not just yet, not just yet. Be patient. Soon you can run your paws off."

Squire Bittle, next to her, had his cat, Ornery, on a leash. The calico looked bored. Squire Bittle looked worried. "He's been a mite off his feed," the squire said to Susannah, who looked properly saddened, but was, in fact, quite pleased with this news.

Mrs. Lovelace, owner of the Pride of the Valley Inn, as broad as she was tall, had tucked her gray tom, Louis, between her immense breasts. Susannah wondered how the poor cat could breathe. Mrs. Lovelace was humming to her cat.

Horatio Blummer, the local butcher, his huge middle straining against his waistcoat, held Glenda, muscled, black, and spitting, close to his leg, his hand around her neck.

Mr. Goodgame, who traced his ancestors back directly to William the Conqueror, was whistling as loud as he could to Horace, to distract him, Susannah supposed. Horace was a long, skinny white cat that looked more like a cannon than a cat. Horace was ready to run.

The Harker brothers were more worried about Horace than any of the others.

"A lot of experience 'as old 'orace," Ozzy said, shaking his head. "Fast littil bugger."

"Aye, but 'e's got this funny nose. Always smelling things, and can't stand not to find out wot's causing the smell. Always sends 'im off track. Leastwise it usually does."

"At least Blinker won't be racing today," Ozzy said. "Ole boy's got a sprained back leg. Too much training Grimsby gave 'im, the ass. I told 'im long time ago no more than ten laps a day with Blinker. 'Is legs be too short."

"Gilly will take all of them," Toby said. "Just wait. We have a *Secret Weapon*."

Both Harker brothers raised bushy eyebrows. *Secret Weapon*? What was this? They had overseen Gilly's training. What was this about a *Secret Weapon*? Toby just grinned at them, saying nothing.

The track was a third of a mile in length and very wide—a good ten feet—because the cats tended to rove back and forth a bit when they ran. There was a larger than usual crowd today since this was Gilly's first race, representing the Mountvale mews, and there was heavy betting. The Harker brothers, it got out, had personally trained the cat. The ladies held parasols over their heads to protect themselves from the sun; the gentlemen laid wagers, smoked cheroots, and discussed the finer points of each racing cat. Everyone was looking forward to the first race.

It was said that occasionally there were corruption and cheating at the racetrack. The Harker brothers kept even a keener eye on the proceedings when this nasty rumor got out, ready to rout out any malefactors. To date the only miscreant they had caught cheating was old Mr. Babble, who'd tried to feed one of the racing cats fresh bass, so he would be too bloated to run fast. This was six months previous.

Lady Dauntry presided up on a narrow dais. She had been the Lady of Ceremonies for five years now, never missing a cat race, even in inclement weather. The cat racing season ran from April to October.

Lady Dauntry bellowed at the top of her lungs—which was not at all difficult for her—"Everyone ready!"

Every trainer or owner readied his cat.

"Everyone set!"

Cats pulled and heaved. Trainers and owners were tensed, ready for action.

"Free the cats!"

The race was on.

Ornery jumped three feet into the air at Mr. Bittle's loud hand clapping right next to his ears. He jumped forward, running a good twenty feet, then stopped to look around at all the shouting people. Mr. Bittle, heaving, gasping for breath, finally reached Ornery. He clapped his hands again right next to Ornery's ears. Ornery obliging raced as fast as the wind another twenty yards.

Mrs. Lovelace's Louis raced after small Charles Lovelace, who was running as fast as he could, dangling a dead fish off a line. Since Louis could outrun Charles, the little boy, finding himself caught by the cat, had to go onto his tiptoes so Louis wouldn't tear the dead fish off his line.

Mr. Goodgame's long, sleek Horace pranced along the track, his green eyes ever forward, ignoring all the other cats around him, ignoring the crowd and the noise. He kept a steady pace. Mr. Goodgame simply stood at the finish line grinning and rubbing his hands.

Horatio Blummer's Glenda ran for half the track, just behind Horace and well ahead of all the others. Then, suddenly, she pulled up and looked at a large woman who was cheering and jumping up and down. In a flash, Glenda ran beneath her wide skirts.

As for Gilly, he immediately bounded free of Susannah's arms. But he stopped almost immediately, looking back to her, to see her hopping up and down, shouting, "Run, Gilly, run!'' Then he looked over at Rohan, who was holding Marianne, shouting, "No dinner if you don't run your legs off!''

Marianne shouted, "No dinner!''

But he didn't move. If a cat could frown, Gilly frowned. He licked his right paw.

Then, quite suddenly, there came a loud, very sweet baritone singing from halfway along the track:

"There was a young man who was bitten
By twenty-two cats and a kitten.
Cried he, 'It is clear
My end is quite near.
No matter! I'll die like a Briton!' ''

It was Jamie. Gilly reared up, his fur stiffening, his ears cocking forward. Then he was off, racing toward that voice, which was singing the limerick again, louder this time, the voice going higher into a falsetto, an angel's voice.

Since Jamie had started a goodly distance away, he could keep trotting further along the track, his voice clear and loud.

But it was Mr. Goodgame's long, sleek white Horace who was the clear leader. Jamie sang louder. Gilly ran. He was gaining on Horace.

Susannah was yelling her head off. She screamed at Toby, "That wretched Horace, he's faster than Marianne is at snagging a tart off Rohan's plate.''

"He'll do it," Toby said.

"No dinner!'' Marianne shouted.

"The Secret Weapon," Ozzie Harker said in an awed voice, yanking on Tom's sleeve. "A new racing device.''

"That 'orace is in fine fettle," said Tom, shaking his head. "Jest look at 'ow 'e stretches out that long body o' 'is. I don't know if Gilly's got enuf time to catch 'im.''

Gilly was nearly at Horace's flying white tail. Jamie was singing so loud the entire crowd was now clapping to the beat.

Horace and Gilly were neck and neck. Then, with no

warning, Horace whipped to the side, bit Gilly on the neck, and turned in his tracks. He was running the other way. He was running right at that dead fish at the end of little Charles Lovelace's line. He cannoned into Louis, knocking him off his paws, leaped up and caught the fish, now a bit worse for wear. He broke the line free, sending Charles backward on his bottom, and ran faster than the wind through the crowd, carrying his prize between his teeth, Mrs. Lovelace and Mr. Goodgame screaming behind him.

Louis was running as fast as he could after Horace and *his* fish.

"I've ain't niver seen Louis run so fast," Ozzie said, shading his eyes against the glare of the sun. " 'E might even catch ole 'orace. It's 'is fish, after all."

"Naw," Tom said. "Mrs. Lovelace will get 'orace first. Then the fur will fly."

Gilly didn't slow. No, if anything, he ran faster.

Jamie was waiting at the finish line. When Gilly crossed it, the clear winner, beating Glenda by at least six lengths, Jamie was belting out, "No matter! I'll die like a Briton!"

There was loud applause.

Marianne shouted, "Dinner for Gilly!"

Rohan shouted, "Dinner for Jamie!" Susannah swore she could hear Gulliver neighing loudly.

The Harker brothers shook their heads. They had seen many training methods over the years, but this was a first. A limerick.

Jamie was still singing, but very softly now. Gilly was sitting proudly on his shoulder while Jamie walked slowly and carefully to the winner's circle.

Gulliver managed to nudge his way through the crowd to reach Jamie. He butted his great head into Jamie's shoulder. Gilly yowled and jumped onto Gulliver's back. Gulliver's eyes narrowed. Jamie, desperate, broke into another limerick.

Marianne, so excited she was bouncing up and down, wet herself and her father's shoulder, where she was perched.

This was the first time in southern England racing cat history that all the losing cats, their owners, and their trainers, were laughing and applauding and meowing to see the winning racer preen and bathe himself atop a huge horse that was neighing to the rhythm of a limerick.

Epilogue

CHARLOTTE CARRINGTON READ OVER THE FINAL WORDS she'd written. How to end the missive with subtlety, she wondered. That was surely necessary, wasn't it? She would have to try. She chewed on the end of her quill. "... my dearest, it has reached me through several sources that you and Susannah are devoted to each other. This I applaud. It bespeaks a respect and fondness that your father and I shared. But, dearest, there is also word that you haven't resumed your proper ways, that Susannah is with you constantly, both she and Marianne, who is, naturally adorable, but still ..."

"My beauty."

She turned in her chair toward the bed. Augustus had just awakened. He was sitting up, the sheet only to his waist, looking tousled and utterly delicious. She loved a man with black hair on his chest, loved that black, silky line of hair that ran down his belly.

"My beauty," he said again, his voice low and scratchy from sleep. "What are you writing?"

She rose and came to him. "A letter to Rohan."

"You are not preaching at him again, are you?"

She laughed, easing herself down on top of him, smoothing down his dark eyebrows, kissing his beautiful mouth. "Well, I try not to, but he has changed utterly. He is a *family man.* Not that his father wasn't everything a child could desire in a father, but there was more, so much more.'' She paused and sighed. She kissed him again, then frowned at the bedpost. ''Could it be that there is another way to live?''

''What do you mean?''

''I have begun to wonder if Rohan and Susannah may not have stumbled onto something that could be rather appealing.''

''And what is that?'' He was combing his fingers through her hair. God, it was so smooth and silky. He never tired of the smell of her hair, the sweet smell of her body.

''That perhaps a man could really be happy with just one woman.'' She paused, eyeing him to see if he would laugh.

Augustus wasn't laughing. His large hand stilled on her hair. She leaned her head against his palm.

''That perhaps a woman could be happy with just one man.''

Augustus still didn't laugh. One large hand was stroking the satin of her peignoir.

''Why would such a thing not be natural?'' he asked, kissing her nose.

''I don't know. Such a thing is just so utterly different from how I've lived my life, how I've thought of myself and others.''

Augustus pulled her down into his arms. He didn't kiss her passionately. Instead, he pulled her against him as he would a child to be comforted. ''Life,'' he said against her hair, ''life has given you to me, my beautiful Charlotte. I cannot imagine that I could be more greatly blessed than to have you with me forever. Perhaps you could consider that.''

''Perhaps,'' she said, then raised her face for a kiss. As they kissed she heard the call of one gondolier to another, just outside the open windows that gave onto the Grand Canal. Venice was waking up. She thought the sound of the waves splashing gently against the pilings was like soft music. She found his kiss delicious. It felt like coming home.

Author's Note

I have always believed in the Holy Grail. Not just in the myth of it, the flamboyant romance of it, but that there was an actual physical cup that Christ drank from at the Last Supper. Was it really given into the safekeeping of Joseph of Arimathea after Christ's death? I choose to think that it was.

As for the meaning of the Grail, I chose to make its core the sharp differentiation between good and evil. Because of its history, it was impossible for evil to gain power from it.

Many people believe the Holy Grail still exists. Perhaps there is another Bishops' Society guarding the secret of its hiding place. Perhaps this Bishops' Society, like its predecessor, calls the Holy Grail by another name to keep it safe.

The real Macbeth ruled Scotland wisely and well for seventeen years, from 1040 to 1057. He did travel to Rome, where he did meet with the pope. There was turmoil and rampant corruption surrounding the pope at that time. The real power behind the popes, during this period was Hildebrand or 'Pure Flame,' as he was known.

In my story, it is Hildebrand who convinces Pope Leo IX to give the Holy Grail to Macbeth for safekeeping, because he fears that evil men discovered that it is in the pope's hands. Macbeth was a man of honor, a man of his word. He would naturally take the Grail and guard it to the best of his ability. A Knight Templar might have been his best choice for an accomplice in this mission.

Shakespeare immortalized Macbeth in his great play, and as a result, Macbeth is the best known of all the Scottish kings. It's just a pity that Shakespeare's Macbeth is nothing like the real Macbeth of history.

Can you begin to imagine drinking from the Holy Grail? I hope that, having read *The Wild Baron*, you can. But only, of course, if you are good.

FBI Academy
Quantico, Virginia

She was in Hogan's Alley, the highest crime rate city in the United States. She knew just about every inch of every building in this town, certainly better than the actors who were paid eight dollars an hour to play bad guys, and better than many of the bureau employees who were witnesses, robbers and cops every day in Hogan's Alley.

Today she and three other trainees were going to catch a bank robber. She hoped. They were told to keep their eyes open, nothing else. It was a parade day in Hogan's Alley. There was a crowd of people around, drinking sodas and eating hot dogs. It wasn't going to be easy. Chances were that the suspect was going to be one of the people trying to blend in with the crowd, trying to look as innocent as an everyday guy, she'd stake a claim on that. She would have given anything if they'd gotten just a brief glance at the robber, but they hadn't. It was a critical situation, lots of innocent civilians milling about and a bank robber who would probably run out of the bank, a bank robber who was possibly dangerous.

She saw Buzz Alport, an all-night waiter at a truck stop off I-95. He was whistling, looking as if he didn't have a care in the world. No, Buzz wasn't the bad guy today. She knew him too well. She tried to memorize every face, so she'd be able to spot the robber if he suddenly appeared. She slowly worked the crowd, trying to look calm and unhurried.

She saw some visitors from the Hill, standing on the sidelines, watching the agents role-play crimes and catch criminals. She couldn't kill a visiting congressman. It wouldn't look good for the Bureau.

It began. She and Porter Forge, a Southerner from Birmingham who spoke beautiful French without a hint of a drawl, saw a man dash from behind a side door of the bank, followed by a bank employee frantically waving and yelling at the top of his lungs at the fleeing man. She and Forge got no more than a brief glimpse. They went after the robber. He dove into the crowd of people and disappeared. Because there were civilians around, they kept their guns holstered. If any of them hurt a civilian, there'd be hell to pay. It didn't matter. Three minutes later they'd lost him.

It was then that she saw Dillon Savich, an FBI agent and computer genius who taught occasional classes here at Quantico, standing next to a man she'd never seen before. Both were wearing sunglasses, blue suits and blue-gray ties.

She'd know Savich anywhere. She wondered what he was doing here at this particular time. Had he just taught a class? She'd never heard of him being at Hogan's Alley. She stared at him. Was it possible that he was the suspect to whom the bank employee had been waving? Maybe. Only thing was that he didn't look at all out of breath and the bank robber had run out of the bank like a bat out of hell. Savich looked cool and disinterested.

Nah, it couldn't be Savich. Savich wouldn't join in the exercise, would he? Suddenly, she saw a man some distance away from her slowly slip his hand into his jacket. Dear God, he was going for a gun. She yelled to Porter.

While the other trainees were distracted, Savich suddenly moved away from the man he'd been talking to and ducked behind three civilians. Three other civilians who were close to the other guy were yelling and shoving, trying to get out of the way.

What was going on here?

"Sherlock! Where'd he go?"

She began to smile even as agents were pushing and shoving, trying desperately to sort out who was who. She never lost sight of Savich. She slipped into the crowd. It took her under a minute to come around him from behind.

There was a woman next to him. It was a very possible hostage situation. She saw him slowly reach out his hand toward the woman. She couldn't take the chance. She drew her gun, came right up behind him and whispered in his ear as she pressed the nose of the 9mm SIG pistol into the small of his back, "Freeze. FBI."

"Ms. Sherlock, I presume?"

She felt a moment of uncertainty, then quashed it. She had the robber. He was just trying to rattle her. "Listen to me, that's not part of the script. You're not supposed to know me. Now, get your hands behind your back, buddy, or you're going to be in big trouble."

"I don't think so," he said, and began to turn.

The woman next to them saw the gun and screamed at the top of her lungs. "Oh my God, the robber's a woman! Here she is! She's going to kill a man! She's got a gun! Help!"

"Damn you, get your hands behind your back!" But how was she going to get cuffs on him? The woman was still yelling. Other people were looking now, not knowing what to do. She didn't have much time.

"Do it or I'll shoot you."

Savich moved so quickly she didn't have a chance. He knocked the pistol out of her hand with a chop of his right hand, numbing her entire arm, bulled his head into her stomach and sent her flying, wheezing for breath into a mass of petunias in the flower bed beside the Hogan's Alley Post Office.

He was laughing. The bastard was laughing at her. She was sucking in air as hard and fast as she could. Her stomach was on fire. He stuck out his hand to pull her up.

"You're under arrest," she said, and slipped a small Lady

Colt .38 from her ankle holster. She gave him a big grin. "Don't move or I'll do something mean to you."

His laughter died. He looked at that gun, then at her, up on her elbows in the petunia bed. There were a half dozen men and women standing there, watching, their breaths held. She yelled out, "Stay back, all of you. This man's dangerous. He just robbed the bank. I didn't do it, he did. I'm FBI. Stay back!"

"That Colt isn't bureau issue."

"Shut up. No, don't twitch or I'll shoot you."

He'd made a very small movement toward her, but she wasn't going to let him get her this time. Into martial arts, was he? She knew she was smashing the petunias, but she didn't see any hope for it. Mrs. Shaw would come after her because the flower beds were her pride and joy, but she was only doing her job. She couldn't let him get the better of her again.

She kept inching away from him, that Colt steady on his chest. She came up slowly, keeping her distance. "Turn around and put your hands behind you."

"I don't think so," he said again. She didn't even see his leg, but she did hear the rip of his pants. The Colt went flying onto the sidewalk.

"How'd you do that?"

Where were her partners?

Where was Mrs. Shaw, the postmistress? She'd once caught an alleged bank robber by hitting him over the head with a frying pan.

"Damn," she heard him say, then he was on her. This time, she moved as quickly as he did. She knew he wouldn't hurt her, just disable her, jerk her onto her face and humiliate her in front of everyone. She rolled to the side, came up, saw Porter Forge from the corner of her eye, caught the SIG from him, turned and fired. She got him in mid-leap.

The red paint spread all over the front of his white shirt, his conservative tie, and his dark blue suit.

He flailed about, managing to keep his balance. He

straightened, stared down at her, stared down at his shirt, grunted, and fell onto his back into the flower bed, his arms flung out.

"Sherlock, you idiot, you just shot the new coach of Hogan's Alley High School's football team!" It was the mayor of Hogan's Alley and he wasn't happy. He stood over her, yelling. "Didn't you read the paper? Didn't you see his picture? You live here and you don't know what's going on? Coach Savich was hired just last week. My God, you killed an innocent man."

"She also made me rip my pants," Savich said, coming up on a graceful motion. He shook himself, wiping dirt off his hands onto his filthy pants.

"He tried to kill me," she said, still pointing the SIG at Savich.

"I'm already dead, remember? Although you might as well shoot me again; the clothes are ruined."

"He was only defending himself," said the woman who'd yelled her head off. "He's the new coach and you killed him."

She knew she wasn't wrong.

"I don't know about that," Porter Forge said, that drawl of his so slow she could have said the same thing at least three times before he got it out. "Suh," he continued to the mayor who was standing at his elbow, "I believe I saw a wanted poster on this big fella. He's gone and robbed banks all over the South. Yep, that's where I saw his picture, on one of the Atlanta PD posters, suh. Sherlock here did good. She brought down a real bad guy."

It was an excellent lie, one to give her time to do something, anything, to save her hide.

Then she realized what had bothered her about him. His clothes. They didn't fit him quite right. She reached her hands into Savich's pockets and pulled out wads of fake one hundred dollar bills.

"I believe ya'll find the bank's serial numbers on the bills, suh. Don't you think so, Sherlock?"

"Oh yes, I surely do, Agent Forge."

"Take me away, Ms. Sherlock," Dillon Savich said and stuck out his hands.

She handed Porter back his SIG. She faced Savich with her hands on her hips, a grin on her face. "Why would I handcuff you now, sir? You're dead. I'll get a body bag."

Savich was still laughing when she walked away to the waiting paramedic ambulance. He said to the mayor of Hogan's Alley, "That was well done. She has a nose for crooks. She sniffed me out and came after me."

Savich walked away, unaware that his royal blue boxer shorts were on display to a crowd of a good fifty people.

Then there was rolling laughter. Even a crook who was holding a hostage around the throat, a gun to his ear, at the other end of town looked over at the sudden noise to see what was going on. It was his downfall. Agent Wallace conked him over the head and laid him flat.

It was a good day for taking a bite out of crime in Hogan's Alley.